GHOST STATION

GHOST STATION

DAN WELLS

Trade Paperback ISBN: 978-1-952825-64-4
Ebook ISBN: 978-1-952825-65-1
Cover Art copyright © Kristy S. Gilbert of Looseleaf Editorial & Production

Interior layout and design by Kind Composition

Prince of Cats Trade Paperback Edition 2022
Published by Fearful Symmetry in Association with
Prince of Cats Literary Productions
New Jersey, USA 2022

CONTENTS

West Berlin

———

Two months after the Wall

THE TRAIN SEEMED to hold its breath.

The crowd hadn't been particularly boisterous to begin with. It was the morning commute, and most of the passengers had still been half-asleep as they stood in the underground station, clutching the newspapers they hadn't dared to read. They filed into the D train in a somnambulant haze, finding their seats or standing and clutching the bars. But then the train had lurched into motion, creeping forward into the darkness, and the feel of the silence had changed abruptly.

It wasn't sleepy anymore, but solemn. Tense.

Frightened.

It was time for the ghost stations.

The D train started its journey in the French sector of

Berlin, in Gesundbrunnen, and then moved to Voltastrasse where Wallace Reed and several others shambled aboard to join them. Now it moved into the Soviet sector, where two months ago the East German police had started building a wall through the heart of the city. For the first few days Reed and the others had been able to delude themselves that it was only temporary, that the Wall was just a show of force, and that the East German government—the GDR—would bring it down again after they'd gotten whatever it was that they'd wanted. Those delusions had evaporated just a few days later when the East German police had started bricking up the windows in the buildings along the border.

The first of the ghost stations was Bernauer Strasse, and the GDR had filled its doors with bricks as well. It was inside of East Berlin, but it served only a West Berlin train, so it existed now only as a passing ruin; an abandoned platform barely visible in the darkness. Reed looked out the window as the train moved through it, seeing nothing but vague impressions of walls and columns. The next two stations were the same: closed and empty, like forgotten mausoleums. Reed wasn't the only passenger who peered out as they rumbled through, hoping to catch a glimpse of … something. People, maybe, or light. Some riders didn't look at all, but simply slumped in their seats, sleeping or pretending to, pushing the ghosts away and thinking of anything else.

And then the train passed through Alexanderplatz, and they couldn't ignore the ghosts anymore because they could hear them: Alexanderplatz, and Jannowitzbrücke after it, were still in use by East German trains, clattering through in the levels above. Somehow, Reed thought, that made it worse. The western train passed through the eastern stations like a phantom, never pausing, never interacting, just two parallel worlds that overlapped without touching. Shapes and sounds and memories, here and gone in an instant.

Two months, thought Reed. Ten weeks. Forty-nine work days, there and back, which meant ninety-eight train rides in total. Ninety-eight chances for the GDR to say, "No, we're not letting you through this time."

Or, worse yet: "No, we're not letting you back out."

The last ghost station was Heinrich-Heine-Strasse, and that one always made Reed the most nervous of all. Would something happen? Would they make it through this time? If there was a problem on the tracks, would the West German maintenance workers even be able to reach them? The empty station passed by in the shadows, barely more than a wide space in the tunnel, and soon they were back in the light again, back in the West, pulling to a stop at the bright, bustling station of Moritzplatz. *Well,* thought Reed, *maybe not exactly bustling, but after the ghost stations anything felt like a riot of color and life.*

He always had to stop himself from just leaving the train right here and walking the rest of the way to work, but it was only nerves. They were safe now. He breathed again, feeling as if he'd held his breath through all six stations, and rode three more stops to Hermannplatz. Then he transferred to the C1 train for one more stop, got out at the Neukölln Rathaus, and walked the last few blocks to, ironically, the Wall again. It twisted through the city like a snake, swinging one way and then doubling back on itself.

Reed's office was right on the edge, so close that on a sudden impulse he walked ten steps past the building door and right up to the Wall itself. Chest-high cinder blocks, with three more feet of razor wire rising from the top. On the other side was a building that was an exact twin of his own, facing it like a reflection: six stories tall, with rows of windows so close you could wave from one side to the other. In the small park next to it, people strolled or talked or sat on benches. Life seemed much the same as ever.

Almost.

Reed rested his hands on the Wall—almost disconcerting in its normalcy—while an East German policeman watched him from a few meters away. The border police were called Grenztruppen, or Grenzers if you weren't feeling especially respectful, and they were everywhere. Even before the Wall, Heidelbergerstrasse had been a border between the American and Soviet sectors of the city; now the border was more visible, and more ominous.

Half a block down from him two women chatted, one on either side—lifelong neighbors, perhaps—now locked in separate nations. If either of them tried to cross, or even to hand something to the other, the Grenzers would leap into action.

They'd shot someone just a few days ago, trying to cross one of the canals.

It made Reed nervous to work this close to the Wall, but there would be little point in putting his office anywhere else; he was a cryptographer, and the office was a listening station designed to spy on the Soviets and the GDR. He tapped the Wall a final time, then turned and went into the building.

It was an apartment, like most in this area, but an entire floor had been fully converted to their office space. It was a joint intelligence office, staffed by both the American CIA and the German BND. Someone before Reed's time had scrambled the two acronyms and nicknamed the place CABIN D. Reed thought it was corny, but it had stuck, so there it was.

He took the elevator to the fourth floor—*technically the fifth,* he thought, *but Europeans numbered them differently*—and showed his ID to the guard. The man waved him through, and Reed stepped into the main office.

"And look who's here," said Frank Schwartz, looking up from his desk with a smile. "Nice of you to drop by."

"Cut him some slack," said Chuck DeMille. "He's two minutes late. What is this, East Germany?"

"Not funny," said Harald Wagner. He was the new guy in

the office, and Reed didn't know what to make of him yet. It was hard enough for Reed to interact with people as it was, and Wagner made it even more difficult by living up to every stereotype of the humorless German pragmatist.

"He was looking at the Wall," said another voice, and Reed looked over to see Johannes Ostertag, his cryptography counterpart from the BND, sitting in an open window blowing cigarette smoke into the morning air. Ostertag smiled, and pointed out the window. "I saw you."

Reed sat at his desk, and picked up the stack of papers the secretary had left for him. "I should have expected that." He was no good at small talk, or any talk, really, but he was trying to teach himself to be better. Should he say something else? There was only one reason Ostertag sat in the window, and he ventured to ask about it. "Is she there?"

"Every morning," said Ostertag, and flashed a wolfish smile. "My East German Aphrodite."

"I think it is obscene," said Jannick Wohlreich. He was the asset handler on the team, which always struck Reed as an odd match for someone so prudish. "All of those poses, and in a public park? It is pornographic."

"It's called yoga," said Frank. "It's the big new thing back in New York."

"Then it should stay in New York," said Wohlreich.

"I am happy with her right where she is," said Ostertag, looking out the window. His mouth curled into a smile. "Doing exactly what she's doing."

Wohlreich grumbled, and Reed laughed, and then a woman's voice rang through the room, and the mood changed abruptly from lechery to embarrassment.

"She is on the other side of the Wall," said Lise Kohler. She'd just come in from a hallway; Reed wouldn't have laughed at Ostertag's joking if she'd been in the main room. She crossed to her desk and sat down. "You may as well give up."

"The Wall does not stop me from looking," said Ostertag with a leer.

Lise raised her eyebrow. "What is the point of looking if you never get to talk to her?"

Ostertag smiled again. "Why spoil a good relationship with talking?"

"That," said Wohlreich, "is the worst comment yet."

"Is this an office," asked the stoic Wagner, "or a locker room? Some of us are trying to work."

Ostertag took another drag on his cigarette, then flicked it out the window and slid the pane closed. "Not much to look at these days anyway," he said. "It is too cold; she wears sweatpants."

"Widerlich," Wohlreich muttered.

Ostertag grinned, and sank down at the desk across from Reed's.

The main room in the Cabin held eight desks, grouped into pairs: two analysts, DeMille and Lise; two surveillance men, Wagner and Schwartz; two cryptographers, Reed and Ostertag; and a fourth pair of officers that included Wohlreich the asset handler and Gisela Breuer the researcher. Both Wohlreich and Gisela were BND, but every other pair was split: one BND and one CIA. Similar listening stations dotted West Berlin, each organized slightly differently but all focused on one main goal: to know everything the other side did before they did it. The Wall had caught the West by surprise. They had sworn that nothing else would.

Gisela swept into the room from the back hall and started handing out a new report for the top of each officer's pile. "New information on Werner Probst. It looks like he was a criminal."

"Was it an execution?" asked Ostertag.

"No," said Gisela, moving to her seat. "Definitely an escape attempt. But he had a criminal record."

Reed scanned the report quickly. Werner Probst had tried to flee the GDR five days ago by swimming the Spree river. He slipped into the water by the Schillingsbrücke, probably hoping to hide in the bridge's shadow, but the Grenzers had seen him, warned him, and then fired on him when he refused to turn back. He died on the western shore, but the GDR had picked him up in a boat and taken him back before anyone in the West had time to respond. The BND hadn't even figured out his name until recently. Now Gisela had turned up new information: Probst was a high school dropout, twenty-five years old, who had been arrested for stealing. Before he died he'd been living with his parents.

"This does not fit the profile," said Ostertag. "The ones who try to cross the Wall are idealists, or at least ideologists. This man seems like he would be happy to live in a state determined to take care of him."

"Maybe he loves freedom for its own sake," said Frank. "He didn't want teachers bossing him around in school, and he didn't want communists bossing him around outside of it."

"His parents' home was only a few blocks from the bridge," said Lise, tapping the paper. "That suggests this might have been impulsive, rather than planned."

"And it *does* fit a profile," said DeMille. "Not for a runner, though; for an agent."

Ostertag frowned. "One of ours?"

"One of theirs," said DeMille. "Werner Probst is exactly the kind of man the Stasi like to use: checkered past, unsettled present. Someone morally flexible enough to do their work, and poor enough to need it." The Stasi were East Germany's spies and secret police. Chuck pursed his lips, staring at the paper, and then nodded. "Five bucks says he was Stasi."

"Only five?" asked Ostertag.

"Ten," said Chuck. Reed watched the exchange quietly, wishing he had something to add.

"So," said Frank, "why'd the Russians shoot him?"

"The East Germans," Wohlreich corrected.

"We all know it's the Russians calling the plays," said Frank.

"If he was a Stasi agent," said Lise, "the Grenzers who shot him probably didn't know it. Which means either he was tired of being an agent and wanted to defect, or he had been ordered to join the refugees on our side, as a double agent who could report back on our activities. So the Grenzers are either heroes for stopping him, or someone is going to lose their job."

"Find out which," said Wohlreich. He wasn't their boss, but he usually acted like it.

The conversation was interrupted by Bettina Schaal, the Chief's secretary. "Wallace," she said from the doorway to her office. "We have another Longshore message."

Reed grabbed a pad of paper and a pencil, and stood up. "Maybe he knows about Probst." Longshore was their own agent, working undercover on the other side of the Wall. He'd been with the Stasi for years now, and still managed to send a coded message almost every day. He was easily the most valuable asset the Cabin had.

"Good luck," said Ostertag, and followed it up with a wink at Bettina. Reed frowned; the man would wink at anything in a skirt.

Reed followed Bettina through her office and into the Chief's beyond. Gordon Davis sat at his desk, skimming through a copy of Gisela's report.

"Chief," said Reed, and Davis looked up. "We have a Longshore message."

"It just came in," said Bettina. "It is on the recorder."

"Good," said Davis, and gestured at Gisela's report. "Maybe he can shed some light on this."

"That's what we were hoping as well, sir," said Reed. "Do you have today's confirmation code?"

Every coded message included a confirmation somewhere in it, a secret code-within-a-code that let the receivers know that the sender hadn't been compromised. In a case like Longshore, where the messages came in simply as Morse code blips on a radio broadcast, the confirmation appeared as the first and final letters of every message. It was their only way of knowing that the message came from the right person.

"Today's confirmation code is V," said Davis. "Bring it to me as soon as you're done."

"Of course, sir." Reed nodded to the Chief, then to Bettina, then walked into a side room where the radio equipment sat heavily on a desk. Longshore's messages usually came in the early mornings, but they could arrive at any time of day or night, so a triggered recorder had been set up to automatically tape anything that appeared on the frequency. Reed pulled the reel of tape from the recorder, threaded in a new one, and then took the tape into yet another room, completely bare except for a table, a chair, a tape player, and a steel safe welded firmly to both the floor and the wall. He locked the door behind him—much sturdier than the rest of the building's doors—and carefully latched all of the extra bolts. This was the most secure room in the Cabin, and with good reason. If an enemy agent got their hands on the contents of the safe, they could figure out not just Longshore's codes but maybe even his identity.

Reed set his pad and pencil on the table and the tape reel beside it. Last of all he pulled his sidearm from the holster under his jacket, and checked the chamber to make sure it was loaded and ready to fire. It was a High Standard .22LR with an integrated suppressor, which was standard issue for a CIA operative. If someone tried to breach the room while he was in it, he was ready to defend it.

Reed knelt, twisted the combination lock on the safe, and dialed it carefully through the sequence of numbers. It opened with a click, and he pulled out the code key. It was a hardback book, maybe an inch thick, the dust jacket missing and the blue fabric stained from water damage: *Player Piano* by Kurt Vonnegut, Jr.

Reed threaded the tape through the player, hit play, and listened to the scratchy, empty static. After several seconds the first part of the message appeared: a burst of noise so fast he could barely interpret it as Morse code, lasting about eight seconds. He kept listening, and almost sixty seconds later another burst came through. Four more followed, each about eight seconds long, each about a minute apart. He waited for five more minutes, listening to the staticky silence, before confirming that this was the whole message: six bursts.

He rewound the tape, slowed it to a crawl, and started transcribing the Morse code as it played through again; where before each burst had taken eight seconds, it was now nearly forty. The dots and dashes were more discernible, and he wrote them down quickly, rewinding and relistening several times to be sure he'd gotten it right. Then he started decoding the message.

The first letter was not a V.

This was the forty-first message Longshore had sent using the *Player Piano* code system. Reed had personally decoded every one of them. He knew what he was doing, and the first letter was supposed to be the confirmation code: V. And yet it was an X.

Longshore hadn't used the proper confirmation.

Reed let out a long breath. This could mean any number of things. Perhaps the Stasi had cracked their encryption system—always a danger since they'd started using *Player Piano*—and this was Longshore's way of telling the Cabin that someone was listening, and all of the information in the message was actually fake. Or perhaps it was the much worse, and far more likely, scenario—that Longshore had been captured or compromised, and the Stasi was forcing him to send misinformation. Either way, nothing in the rest of the message could be trusted.

But the Chief would still want to know what it said. Reed decoded the second letter, and found—another X. Only a handful of English words started with X, and none of them seemed likely to show up in a coded message from a Stasi double agent. Was he using an abbreviation?

Reed tried the third letter, and got a C.

Then an E.

Then an O, P, J, N, and A.

This wasn't an abbreviation or an acronym or any other explanation Reed could think of. It was gibberish. A botched confirmation code would be bad news, but this appeared to be an entire botched message. Reed checked his work again, and then went back to the tapes and started over from the beginning, slowing the reel even more to make sure he'd transcribed it correctly. He had. His methods were sound, and his figures added up.

And yet every bit of it was meaningless nonsense.

At least with a bad confirmation code they would know what to do. They had procedures and contingency plans.

When the entire message was bad ...

This was so much worse.

11:30 AM

West Berlin

WALLACE REED and Section Chief Gordon Davis walked briskly through the city, sidearms loaded and ready under their jackets. An armored briefcase was handcuffed to Reed's wrist, and tightly locked. They were headed west, toward a US military office near the Tempelhof Airport. The mysterious Longshore message was no longer an issue for just one listening station; the government wanted a full report.

"Stop looking over your shoulder," said Davis. "You look like a spy."

"I'm sorry," said Reed, and shook his head to clear it. He forced himself to calm down. "I'm just worried that somebody's following us."

"Of course somebody's following us," said Davis. "It's Wohlreich; he's about a block behind, watching our backs."

Reed swallowed. "Who's watching his?"

"He was the BND's best field agent before he came to us." Davis was silent a moment before continuing. "And the best in the Wehrmacht before that. He's fine."

Reed kept his eyes forward, matching pace with Davis.

"Are you comfortable with that, Chief? Working with Nazis, I mean."

"*Former* Nazis."

"Does that make it better?"

"It's inarguably better," said Davis. "Whether that moves it all the way to good is up for debate."

"I don't like it," said Reed.

"The BND are our best allies against the GDR and the Soviet Union," said Davis. "And the BND gets much of its strength from former Nazis; it's run by one, for goodness' sake. I'm not any happier about that than you are, but the communists are a bigger threat right now, and intelligence work requires a flexible morality. You know that."

"I know," said Reed.

"And you're in the thick of it now," said Davis. "The US and the USSR are global superpowers, and that gives them something far more dangerous than nuclear weapons."

"Surveillance?" asked Reed.

"Momentum," said Davis. "They're like windup toys, and we've wound them tight, and they're never going to stop until they've reached the end."

"What's at the end?"

"The dissolution of the Soviet Union, and the triumph of American democracy." Davis cast Reed a sidelong glance. "Didn't you read the brochure?"

Reed tried to laugh at the joke, but jingoism hadn't been nearly as funny since the Wall had gone up. Too many people took it seriously now. Even so, he tried gamely to play along.

"Of course, I've read it," he said, and smiled. "Twice."

"Never admit that out loud," said Davis. "True patriots believe it the first time through."

They walked on, and when they reached the Tempelhof building they showed their identification at the door, and a US Army soldier escorted them to an elevator. They stood in an upstairs waiting room for barely a moment before an older man with a gray, military haircut ushered them into his office.

"Thank you for coming," he said, and locked the door behind them. "I'm Mike Hogan, US State Department."

"Gordon Davis. Section Chief in Listening Station 7." He shook Hogan's hand. "This is my lead cryptographer, Wallace Reed."

Hogan held out his hand, and Reed tried to shake it only to realize that his right hand still held the handle of the briefcase. "Sorry," he mumbled. He transferred the briefcase to his left hand, and stuck out his right as far as the chain would let him. "Sorry," he said again. "Wallace Reed, sir. It's a pleasure to meet you."

Hogan shook his hand, saying nothing about the awkward fumble, and moved around toward the large, black chair behind his desk. "Have a seat. I understand you've lost a field agent?"

"Nothing's certain yet," said Davis, "though it doesn't look good." He pulled a small key from a hidden compartment in his waistband and unlocked the chain on Reed's wrist, then used a separate key to unlock the case. All three men sat down, and Davis continued. "A BND operative codenamed Longshore has been working as a double agent inside of the Stasi for almost three years now. He runs one of our numbers stations, and when the Wall went up he stayed in his position to continue sending us intel. He's sent us forty-one messages in total, but today's—Message 41—is ... suspect, to say the least."

"I'm not a spy," said Hogan, "so you'll have to forgive my ignorance. What's a numbers station?"

"Sorry," said Davis. "A numbers station is simply a person with a radio, who broadcasts coded messages as strings of numbers; it's a good way of sending messages, especially in a city like this, because the enemy can't trace who is listening, and has no idea what the agent is saying. We have five or six numbers stations working for us, both on our side of the Wall and on the other. The Stasi have several of their own, and the CIA is constantly trying to root them out. Our job at the listening station is to receive and interpret some of our messages, and to eavesdrop on their messages and figure out what they mean."

"During the war my unit worked behind German lines," said Hogan. "Not spycraft, like you, but special ops, that sort of thing. The Nazis could never find our radio when we were receiving a signal—you can't trace a signal to a receiver—but they came after us every time we tried to transmit. How has Longshore managed to survive three years over there without getting caught?"

Davis looked at Reed. "Wally?"

"Yes," said Reed, and pulled the briefcase up onto his knees. He clicked it open, raised the lid, and pulled out a small metal box with four black dials. He tried to speak clearly, without *umm*-ing or mumbling. "This is an FS-7 transmitter, which is standard issue for covert operations. It fits in the palm of your hand, as you can see, so it's portable and easy to conceal. But it can generate a signal strong enough to send a message anywhere in the city, and well out into the countryside if it needs to."

"The danger's not the size of the radio," said Hogan, "it's the length of the transmission. The Nazi army used detection rigs in the backs of trucks—they'd just drive them around the countryside, looking for signals, and the longer we stayed on the air the more time they had to narrow in on us. I assume the Stasi have the same thing."

"Technology's advanced," said Davis. "Today they have portable detection rigs that can be hidden under a trench coat— we have the same thing. They pick up a signal, and then buzz a little when you get closer to the source."

"But Longshore is never transmitting long enough to trace, sir," said Reed. He set the transmitter on the desk, and pulled from the briefcase another box, thicker than the first, but with a smaller footprint. "This is an RT-3 Burst Encoder. Inside it are two cylinders—well, let me show you." He pulled off the lid, revealing the machinery inside, and Hogan leaned over his desk to see.

"It looks like my daughter's music box," said Hogan.

"A programmable music box, yes," said Reed, and pointed at a row of metal tabs. "You set these switches to the letters you want to broadcast, and then turn this crank. Er—" A small handle rested inside the open box; Reed took it out, plugged it into a hole in the side, and started turning. "—*this* crank. As one cylinder moves across the other, it translates your message into Morse code, and sends it through the FS-7. It takes thirteen turns of the crank to broadcast a full cylinder—that's twenty-five characters. A trained operator can do that in about eight seconds—though if you're really pressed for time you can put the crank in this other hole instead and do it in three." He moved the handle to a second hole and demonstrated the faster speed. "It's not as easy to interpret on our end, because even when we slow down the recording the Morse dots and dashes start to blend together. Sometimes it's worth it, though, if you're really worried about being found. The recording this morning was done at normal speed, so we got a very clear transcription."

Reed started moving the switches, clicking through them one at a time to show how easy it was to set them.

"A practiced operator—with the message already encoded on a separate piece of paper—can set a full twenty-five characters in about a minute, turn the crank to send it, and then set another twenty-five characters, and so on. The message this morning took six cycles to complete, which is almost seven minutes in total, but only forty-eight seconds of that was active transmission time, and that was broken down into eight-second bursts. It's virtually impossible for a directional signal finder to track a transmitter in such a short amount of time. So, yes, we're fairly certain the Stasi know about Longshore's transmissions, but there's ... virtually no way they can ever find him."

"Virtually," said Hogan. He stared at the Burst Encoder for a moment, then put a finger on one of the cylinder switches and clicked it back and forth. "Are you sure you didn't miss a letter?" he asked, looking up. "Even one dropped dot in the Morse could throw off the entire sequence."

Reed smiled nervously. "I promise that that's not the issue with this message, sir; I've gone over it nearly twenty times—"

"I'm not doubting you," said Hogan, "I'm just making sure. If you weren't good at your job you wouldn't be here." He looked at him for a moment, then back at Davis. "Let's talk about the encryption itself. How are the messages coded?"

"We used to use a one-time pad," said Davis. "That's a sheet of random numbers that helps scramble the message. He had one copy, we had the other."

"Scramble?" asked Hogan. "How?"

"By adding them together," said Reed. "The first step is a simple Caesar Cipher: A equals 1, B equals 2, and so on, so if I were going to say 'hello' it would be—"

"A equals 1?" asked Hogan. "Surely the CIA could come up with something a little more sophisticated than that?"

"This is only the first step," said Reed. "It doesn't matter what A equals, because of the way they get scrambled in the second step, so we use something easy. But—back to the example: if I were to say 'hello,' like I was saying, we would start with the numbers 8-5-12-12-15."

Hogan raised his eyebrow. "You know that off the top of your head?"

"He thinks in codes," said Davis.

Reed felt himself blush a little, but pressed forward; it was easier to talk about encryption than about himself. "So I take those numbers: the first is 8. Then I look at my one-time pad, and let's say the first number there is a 2. I add them together, get 10, and *that's* what I transmit. And anyone with an identical pad will see the 10, subtract the 2, and say 'oh, he means 8, so this letter is an H.' And anybody who doesn't have that exact pad will be completely lost. It's impossible to break."

"Virtually," said Hogan.

"No," said Davis. "Literally. With a properly randomized number sequence, a one-time pad is one hundred percent secure. The number 10 in Mr. Reed's example could represent any letter in the alphabet; it's like a mathematical singularity. All of the things cryptographers use to break codes—all the patterns in the data—completely disappear."

"Impressive," said Hogan, though he spotted the downside barely a second later. "So your only weak points are physical— getting and keeping a copy of the pad, without the Stasi finding it."

"That's exactly right," said Davis. "It's called a one-time pad because you can only use it once; use it twice and you've put patterns back into the data, and that makes it crackable. Before the Wall, we used a dead drop to deliver a week's worth of number pads in one go. Longshore could pick it up hours later, so none of us ever had personal contact with him. His position inside the Stasi is too precarious to risk. But then the Wall went up and we couldn't reach our dead drop locations anymore, and there was no way to establish any new ones—the only thing both he and we can reach is the Wall itself, and it's watched far too closely."

"Official government personnel can move through the city at will," said Hogan. "Even beyond the Wall. One of us could drop it for you."

"We have an entire branch of the joint CIA and BND dedicated to watching every move the GDR's officers take when they come on our side," said Davis. "I assure you, you're all being watched at least that closely when you travel over there."

Hogan scowled. "I suppose that's true."

Reed reached into the briefcase and grabbed something, but didn't pull it out. "We're about to show you something incredibly secret."

Hogan's look darkened, but Davis jumped in quickly to assuage any insult. "This is secret even within our own office, even among people who are technically cleared for it. Reed isn't here because he's higher ranking than the others; he's here because he and I are the only people in the world who hold this secret. Us and Longshore, of course. Even a casual reference to the *nature* of this secret, overheard by the wrong ears, could get our man killed."

"Understood," said Hogan. "Proceed."

Reed swallowed. "Longshore's last message on the old pads established a new system: a new pad that he and we both had access to, with enough numbers to keep him going for as long as possible." Reed pulled his hands from the briefcase, and set the copy of *Player Piano* on the desk.

"A novel?" asked Hogan.

"Longshore had a copy with him when the Wall went up," said Reed. "His final message on his last pad was to lay out this new system: he started at the beginning of chapter one, and translates each letter of the book into the same A-1 cipher we use on the messages. Each subsequent message picks up right where the previous one left off. We went out and bought the same edition of the same book, and use that to decode what he's written, so in practice it's just like having a one-time pad."

"Except the numbers the book generates aren't random," said Hogan, catching on immediately. "Your mathematical singularity breaks down."

"It's not as secure as a truly random pad," said Reed, nodding. "If the Stasi figure out that he's using a book, they can start to look for patterns they wouldn't have otherwise noticed."

"Not to mention," said Davis, "that if they can figure out

which book they can just read the messages straight out. We understand the risks. But it's the best we could do under the circumstances."

"The Wall caught us all by surprise," Reed added.

"If you'd done your jobs right it wouldn't have," said Hogan. Reed reeled at the verbal attack; Hogan seemed done playing nice. "If you've got a man inside of the Stasi, and you still didn't know about the Wall going up, maybe he's not really *your* man inside of the Stasi."

"We have considered that possibility," said Davis.

"And?"

"And Longshore's information is too consistently accurate to be a disinformation campaign by a suborned agent. He's helped us too much. Plus I'll remind you that he's only one of several dozen double agents the CIA has placed in the GDR—he's the only one *we* work with directly, and goodness knows how the other listening stations are staying in touch with their operatives—but the point stands. None of them warned us about the Wall. Either every single one of our undercover agents has turned on us, or the GDR is very, very good at keeping secrets."

Hogan thought about this for a moment, then shook his head. "I still don't like it. You're using a questionable agent with a crackable code system; you're lucky he lasted as long as he did. At this point, we have to consider him broken."

"I think you're wrong, sir," said Reed. Hogan looked at him, and Reed felt a sudden stab of nerves. "There are ..." He swallowed, and started again. "There are two main scenarios for a compromised agent: first, that the enemy knows he's a mole, and feeds him false information to confuse us. We've always been able to verify Longshore's reports through other sources, so we're fairly certain that this hasn't happened with him."

"But you won't *be* certain until the current messages are also verified," said Hogan.

"How can you verify gibberish?" asked Davis. "The scenario Reed is talking about is always a concern, but it doesn't explain *this* particular message."

"Fair enough," said Hogan. "What's the second scenario?"

"That he knows they're feeding him false intel," said Reed, "but he remains loyal to us. In this scenario the compromised agent has two options: first, ignore the false stuff and keep sending us good stuff, at the risk of being caught and killed. The Stasi have no use for a spy they can't manipulate, after all, so if they can't use him to confuse us they'll simply remove him altogether."

"Death isn't a very good option," said Hogan.

"Certainly not," said Davis. "But it might still be useful if there's something of dire importance to tell us, something worth giving his life for."

"The rise of the Wall, for example," said Hogan.

"If he'd known about it, yes," said Davis. Reed could tell he was getting angry at the constant insinuations of distrust.

"A compromised agent's second option is very clever," said Reed. "He can pass us whatever false information the enemy wants him to pass us, but he can *mark* it as false with a confirmation code, so we know not to trust it."

"For Longshore that's a single letter," said Davis. "Assigned daily. If the message is 'real' he puts that day's letter at the front of each message, and pads it out with more of the same letter at the end. If the information in the message is false, he uses a different letter, and we know that the information is not to be trusted."

"Wait," said Hogan, leaning forward. "You said earlier that you couldn't contact him. Now you say you're sending him a daily code?"

"The delivery system for the confirmation codes is a secret not even Mr. Reed knows," said Davis. "Suffice it to say that it's only one letter, and it only goes one way. Trying to send him any substantive message would be impossible."

Reed's mind began to race. What did Davis do that could only send one letter? He'd wondered about the delivery system before, of course, but the fact that it was only the one letter was a new constraint—and a constraint was like gold to a cryptographer. Now wasn't the time to think about it, though; he filed the information away in his head, and focused on the conversation.

"The point I'm trying to make," said Reed, "is that neither of those two scenarios for a compromised agent applies in this case. He's not sending us deathbed intel or clearly marked lies. He's not even sending us full-fledged lies, which is what he would do if he'd been turned completely to the other side. Whatever's going on here ... I really don't think he's been compromised."

"What about a third scenario?" asked Hogan. "Let's say Longshore was captured and interrogated, but he gave them a bad code. They tried to use it to send us something, and all we got was gibberish."

"That's the first theory yet that can actually explain the gibberish," said Reed.

"And it is my working theory," said Davis. "The Stasi are engaged in a disinformation campaign designed to use our own double agent to feed us lies. Now that we know it exists, our best course of action is to pretend like the messages are real, and let them waste their time and energy sending nonsense to an automated tape recorder."

Hogan stared at Davis for a moment, then flashed a smile so harsh and predatory Reed couldn't help but lean away from it. "As I said to your companion, Mr. Davis: if you were bad at your job, you wouldn't be here."

Reed looked back and forth between the two men, wondering what he'd missed.

"What do you mean?"

"Mr. Reed," said Hogan, keeping his eyes on Davis. "What's the name of your boss's counterpart in the Stasi? The Section Chief in charge of whatever station Longshore is a part of?"

"His name is Konrad Siedel," said Reed, confused. "We have files on all of them—"

"You have files," said Hogan. "What is the name of their lead cryptographer?"

"Jürgen Bauer."

"Their asset handler?"

"Hans Nowak."

"Their researcher?"

"Um, Martin something ... They have two; I think the lead is Martin Vogel?" Reed frowned. "Sir, why are you asking me this?"

"As we've said several times in this meeting," said Hogan, "everything we do, they do. The US and the Soviets are like reflections of each other, and this divided city is the mirror. If you know who the Stasi agents are, the Stasi agents definitely know who you are. So when this message arrived, barely more than an hour ago, and your office dropped everything for an immediate meeting with the State Department, I can guarantee you that they noticed. If your Section Chief was really trying to convince the Stasi that nothing was wrong, and that this message was perfectly normal, he's failed spectacularly."

Reed stared at him in shock. Davis paused a moment longer, then stated, "I'm impressed, Mr. Hogan. You said you weren't a spy."

"I'm worse," said Hogan. "I'm a politician."

"Wait," said Reed. "Are you accusing Davis of ... lying? You can't be serious."

"I'm accusing him," said Hogan, "of not sharing everything he's thinking."

"Then what," asked Davis crisply, "am I thinking?"

"I couldn't say," said Hogan, and here he turned his full attention from Davis to Reed. "What about you?"

Reed blinked. "Do I know what Davis is thinking?"

"Do you know what Wallace Reed is thinking?" Hogan asked. "I can tell when someone's lying to me, but that doesn't mean I can conjure up the truth. You, though, that's your job. You're a codebreaker, and this is a code, so: what's your theory?"

Reed glanced at Davis, who said nothing. Reed swallowed. He had a theory, and had in fact been working it through in his head for some time now, but it wasn't a good one, and he certainly didn't want to share it here. But what else could he do?

"Sir, I … I think it's best if we take this situation at face value: this was a coded message, sent by an agent, containing important information. Exactly what it looks like. Maybe our only mistake, sir, is in thinking that the message was sent to *us*."

Hogan's eyebrow went up. "Who else would it have been sent to?"

Reed grimaced, hating to say it out loud. "Well, sir. I think … I mean, it's like you said. We're reflections of each other. And we have a double agent in the Stasi. So I think we have to consider that they might have a double agent in the Cabin."

West Berlin

"THAT WAS FOOLISH," said Davis, walking back to the Cabin.

"He asked for my opinion," Reed protested, but Davis cut him off.

"And you told him our entire office was untrustworthy. *Obviously* a double agent is the most likely explanation, and *obviously* we're going to try to find him, but that doesn't mean you go and tell the entire State Department we've been infiltrated."

"So you suspected the same thing?"

"Don't insult me," Davis snapped. "Of course I suspected, it's my job to suspect. And I assumed that *you* thought the same way, I just thought you were smart enough not to say it out loud."

"I'm sorry," said Reed.

"You're not just a hobbyist anymore," said Davis, "solving newspaper puzzles in your bathrobe. You're a spy for the CIA; start acting like it. Why do you think I fed him that story about a captured agent? Because we need to handle this on our own, without the State Department breathing down our necks."

"Understood," said Reed, though one question continued to bother him: why had Davis gone to the State Department at all?

They walked in silence the rest of the way back, and when they reached the office Reed sat at his desk with a somber frown.

Frank watched Davis's back as he went into Bettina's office, then beyond it into his own. As soon as he closed the door, Frank looked at Reed.

"Rough meeting?"

"Yeah," said Reed, and blew out a low breath. "I think ... I think I may have caused a big problem for all of us."

"This does not sound good," said Ostertag, leaning in toward the conversation. "What happened?"

"Just a ..." Reed stopped. He wasn't going to make the same mistake twice; if Davis suspected that the Cabin had a mole, then he certainly wasn't going to blab it all over the office. You had to be careful in a situation like this, because you never knew who was listening.

Wait ...

Reed stared at his desk, thinking. Who *was* listening? Which person, inside of the Cabin, was this message intended for? Because the way it was sent didn't make a lot of sense. If the Stasi had the means to give their hidden agent an entire decoding system, sophisticated enough to decrypt a 150-character message, couldn't they deliver the actual message through the same means? Why did they need to use the Longshore frequency at all? It had tipped their hand, and revealed their presence and a portion of their plans, and there was no good reason to do that if you had any other way of passing your message instead. Which meant there wasn't any other way; this was the best and only way that this particular message could be sent.

That implied, in Reed's mind, three possibilities:

Number One: there was no double agent, but the Stasi were trying to make it *look* like there was. They were trying to sow discord in the Cabin, and make them all suspicious of each other—or to make the State Department suspicious of them all. If that was their plan, it was working.

Number Two: it was a deathbed message, like they'd posited in the meeting. Something had gone so wrong, and the need to communicate had become so dire, that it was worth burning an entire communication channel—and a valuable agent—just to get the message across. If there really was a double agent, contacting him so publicly could only possibly end in that agent being discovered, tracked down, and either caught or scared away. Which would make this the beginning of the end.

But ...

But but *but*!

Possibility Number Three: maybe there *was* a double agent in the Cabin, but Message 41 was not *for* him, it was *about* him. Maybe the message had come from Longshore—not a traitorous Longshore, but a faithful one—trying to warn them about a Stasi mole without letting that mole know they were onto him.

Because you never knew who was listening.

Reed mulled over this last one. If he were in the field, with brand-new intel about a double agent inside of the Cabin, how would he go about it?

The first thing he'd do was find a way to send a message that only some of the Cabin officers could read. The garbled Message 41 might fit that bill, provided that someone, at some point, could read it at all. But who, and how? Davis was the only one who even knew who Longshore was, so this might have been a secret message just to him, using a code they'd established before going undercover. Except Davis hadn't privately decrypted it, he'd taken it straight to the State Department. So whoever was supposed to receive and decrypt the message almost certainly wasn't Davis.

Was it possible that the message was intended for someone in the State Department? If it was, this had to be the most convoluted way of getting it there. Why send it here first, unless you were certain it would get relayed directly to Hogan's office? And how could you be certain of that, unless Davis was somehow in on it? But then why involve Reed, and why carry out that whole business of Hogan and Davis distrusting each other? No; it was too big of a mess, with too many variables. Spycraft, for all its twists and secrets, would always default toward Occam's Razor. The simplest explanation was the best.

The message had been sent to the Cabin because Longshore wanted someone in the Cabin to read it. And he didn't want anyone else to be able to.

Reed had a moment of panic when he followed that particular line of thought. Why change the encryption system unless you were specifically trying to hide the code from him, Reed, the man who received them, decrypted them, and read them? And why hide the code from Reed unless *Reed* was the double agent you were trying to expose? Reed knew, of course, he wasn't a double agent or a traitor or a Stasi mole; he had no secret handlers or foreign contacts or really any contacts at all outside of the Cabin. These were his only friends, and essentially his only acquaintances. He knew he was safe.

But did Longshore know that?

I need to focus on the immediate concerns, he thought. The message was sent to someone here in the Cabin. And now he just needed to figure out how that person was supposed to read it.

Occam's Razor came into play here, as well. Longshore had not likely had time or opportunity to establish a new code system with anyone in the Cabin, which meant that he was still using the same code system that was already in place. He was using *Player Piano*. But how? There had to be something Reed had missed.

Reed's eyes went wide. What if they'd missed an entire message?

"Hey, Wally," said Frank, and rapped his knuckles on the desk. "Hey, buddy, you okay?"

"What?" Reed shook his head and focused on the room. Frank, Ostertag, and Lise were staring at him. "What's happening?"

"You tell us," said Frank. "We've been trying to get your attention for five minutes."

"Sorry," said Reed, and stood up. "I need to go back in the room." He walked toward Bettina's office, and Ostertag called after him.

"Mr. Reed! Are you feeling well?"

Reed shut himself in the decoding room, locked the door, and checked his weapon. He opened the safe, pulled out his notes and the hardback novel, and started to work.

A one-time pad encryption system was very fragile; use the wrong pad, and it all fell apart. Decode Message 41 with the wrong section of *Player Piano*—even one letter off—and all you got was garbage. But what if Message 41 was actually Message 42? What if there was an entire previous message that they had missed—something that hadn't been recorded, or maybe hadn't even been sent?

Reed opened the book. Even after forty previous messages, they were only on the second page, starting about halfway down:

gnawed through the insulation on a control wire and put buildings 17, 19, and 21 temporarily out of commission.

The nature of the RT-3 meant that each message came in twenty-five-character segments. If there really was a missing Message 41, Message 42 would start on one of those twenty-five-character points. Reed counted across the line, and made a mark between the O and the N in "insulation." He counted another twenty-five, and made a mark between the L and the D in "building." He continued like this through the next several lines, and then got to work testing each one.

The first segment of the message was a 5. The N at the end of "insulation" was a 14. Five minus fourteen was negative nine; wrapping around the alphabet like a circle, that became a seventeen, which was the letter Q. Reed shook his head; he needed it to be a V, to match the confirmation code. He jumped twenty-five characters ahead to his next mark, the D in "building," and tried again. D was 4; 5 minus 4 gave him 1, or A.

Still no V. Still no good.

"I'm doing this backward," Reed muttered. "If I know I'm starting with a 5, which is E, and ending with a V, what letter is going to get me there?" Going backward from E to V was nine steps, and the ninth letter was I. Reed counted almost the entire page, looking for Is at every twenty-fifth letter, and finally found one near the bottom, in the word "during." If that was the beginning of Message 42, then the missing Message 41 would be several times longer than any other message Longshore had ever sent. That seemed unlikely, but ... maybe that's why Longshore had sent it through a different method? Maybe the missing message was so long that sending it over the radio would have required too much broadcasting time, and given away his position?

Reed started in the new section of the book, and decoded the first few letters of the message: V, X, W, H, L, O, G. Not a word, not an abbreviation, not an acronym or anything else he could use. Just more gibberish.

He counted off several more twenty-five-character sections,

looking for more Is in the right position, but none of them gave him anything resembling a coherent message.

Maybe he was thinking in the wrong direction. Maybe the missing message, if it existed, wasn't larger than usual, but much smaller.

Maybe it was smaller than even the standard twenty-five characters.

Reed shook his head, convinced that this was impossible, but he had no better ideas and knew he had to at least consider it. The first twenty-five characters of this section of the book included two Is:

gnawed through the insulation

He began decoding the message, starting with the first I in *insulation*, and got V, X, O, F, H, S, J. Maybe XO referred to an Executive Officer? Or maybe the X was "of" something? *X of HSJ*. Maybe the HS was "High School"? They didn't even have high schools in Germany, though he supposed Longshore could have been referencing an American. He decrypted the next few letters, just to be sure: M, D, T, W, I, Y.

Nothing again.

He scrapped that plan, pulled out a new sheet of paper, and tried again, starting at the second I in that same section, the one in the middle of *insulation*. He got V, W, P, M, which was still nothing.

"Just keep going," he muttered. "You'll find it sooner or later."

V, W, P, M, F, S—

"Whoa."

Reed stopped abruptly, staring in shock at the letters he'd written on the page. MFS jumped out at him immediately, because it was an acronym Longshore used all the time: *Ministerium Fur Staatssicherheit*. The Ministry of State Security.

The Stasi.

Reed swallowed. If MFS referred to the Stasi, what could the WP mean? An abbreviation? Initials? Who had the initials WP?

Reed whispered it softly, almost not daring to believe that it was true: "Werner Probst."

He dove back into the translation, forcing himself not to rush, to take his time and do it right, and worked out the next few letters: A, G, E, N, T.

Reed shouted in triumph, and smacked the table with his hand. *WP MFS AGENT.* Werner Probst Stasi Agent. A direct confirmation of what they'd been talking about just that morning. Reed kept going, finished the entire message, and then grabbed the paper and ran for the door. He was halfway done unlocking it before he remembered the protocols; he went back to the table, gathered his materials, and locked them all carefully in the safe before retrieving his gun and walking back to the door again. He finished unlocking it, jogged past Bettina without a word, and barged into Davis's office, the paper clutched tightly in his fist.

"I've got it!"

Davis looked up. "Got what?"

Reed closed the door behind himself, catching a brief glimpse of Bettina's surprised face, and then locked the door tightly. He turned back to Davis and slapped the paper down on the desk.

"Message 41," he said. "Or Message 42, maybe. I think we missed one. That's why it didn't make sense before. I was decoding it from the wrong part of the book."

"Keep your voice down," Davis hissed, and then picked up the paper to read it. Reed already had it memorized:

V

WP MFS agent CN Harry Ziegel
MFS new op CN Talon is trying to turn Cabin
officer no ID yet
VVV

"Hot damn," Davis whispered, though his eyes were dark with worry. "Do you realize what this means?"

"It means we missed a message, somehow," said Reed again. "A message twenty-three characters long. That's why I couldn't find it at first, because they're supposed to be in increments of twenty-five, but twenty-three is too long for him to have just started in the wrong place, so he must have done it on purpose—"

"I don't mean that," said Davis. "I mean the message itself. You translated the damn thing, did you read it?"

"I ..." Reed trailed off. "Yes. It confirms that Werner Probst was a Stasi agent, just like we thought he was, and it even gives us his identifier: CN is Longshore's standard abbreviation for 'code name,' so Probst's code name was Harry Ziegel. Then it mentions a new Stasi operation, code named Talon, designed to turn a Cabin ..." Reed's face fell. "Oh, wow."

"Yes, 'oh, wow,'" said Davis, "though I think that's putting it lightly. The Stasi are trying to recruit one of our own officers, right here in the Cabin."

"Doesn't that mean they already have one?"

Davis raised an eyebrow. "This morning you thought this garbled message had been sent to a mole in our office. Now that you've ungarbled it, and that's not what it says, you still think there's a mole?"

Reed swallowed nervously. "I think ..." There was nothing to do but share his suspicions. "I think Longshore got word of a Stasi mole inside of the Cabin, and the missing message is his attempt to warn us. He sent it through some other method, to make sure that whoever that mole is, he wouldn't be able to find the warning, realize he'd been discovered, and get away before the rest of us could stop him."

Davis stared at him for a long time, then sighed and nodded his head. "That does seem like the most likely scenario at this point, doesn't it?"

"I don't want to suspect any of the others," said Reed. "I don't like this at all."

"Then you'd better get used to it," said Davis. "We might already have one traitor, and now they're trying to recruit a second." He scowled. "But yes, trying to figure out who they've turned, and who they hope to turn, will be painful."

"It says 'No ID yet,'" said Reed. "Does that mean the Stasi haven't chosen anyone to turn yet, or just that Longshore doesn't know who it is?"

"Probably the former," said Davis. "He calls it a 'new op,' so they might not even have a target." Davis stared at the message, and suddenly broke into a grin. "Longshore, you beautiful son of a bitch! He's helping us get out in front of it. He's giving us a heads up now, so we can turn the whole thing to our advantage."

"Operation Talon," mused Reed. He thought about the people in the main office, just a few feet away through the wall.

Which one of them was already a traitor?

And which one of them would the Stasi get their claws in next?

Davis stared at the paper a moment longer, then set it down and looked Reed squarely in the face. "Before we move on this, are you absolutely sure that there's a missing message?"

"Not absolutely," said Reed. "But it makes sense."

"Because of the twenty-three characters he skipped in the book?"

"Look at the way this one ends: VVV. That's standard

protocol, padding out the end of a message so it comes to an exact multiple of twenty-five characters. The fact that he skipped twenty-three letters is probably one of the clues: a clear indicator that whatever message he did send, he didn't send it on an RT-3. So he must have sent it through another channel. Maybe he put it in a dead drop somewhere. And now he's relying on us to figure out the message he *did* send, because there's a clue in it."

Davis looked up sharply. "A clue?"

Reed nodded. "I realize that this is a lot of supposition but, honestly, look at the message again, and tell me there's not a glaring abnormality in the middle of it."

Davis peered at the translated message on his desk, thought for a moment, then tapped one of the words: "Ziegel."

"Exactly," said Reed. "Stasi code names are one word each, nice and short for ease of use. 'Harry' fits perfectly, but 'Harry Ziegel' flies in the face of everything we know about Stasi protocol. So either the Stasi have changed their protocol, or Longshore added the word Ziegel as some kind of hidden signal."

Davis scowled at the paper. "But to who?"

"Us, I hope." Reed shrugged. "Possibly to another double agent, if Longshore has turned, but I find that unlikely. It would burn the entire form of communication. If we assume he's talking to us, but in secret, then he's telling us where the missing message is. 'Ziegel' means 'brick' in German, but that doesn't tell us anything by itself. I assume he didn't hide the missing message in a brick somewhere, and just expect us to know which one. Or maybe he did; maybe the analysts can connect this to something that you and I don't know."

"Maybe," said Davis, and hesitated. "If we trust them."

And that, Reed knew, was the whole problem.

Someone in the Cabin was likely a double agent, and yet they needed the help of everyone in the Cabin if they were going to track down and stop that double agent. And if they didn't stop him? Or her? Reed shuddered to think what a GDR operative could do if left unchecked in a CIA office. Raising a wall in the middle of the night was just the beginning; how long before they swarmed across that wall and claimed more territory? How long before another midnight operation saw Grenzers marching through West Berlin in a full-scale invasion? It would be a violation of the Potsdam Agreement—the agreement that had carved up Berlin in the first place—but would that really stop them? The Wall itself was already a violation, more or less.

The GDR was already starting to gather more troops along the border—not a guarantee of an invasion, but a possibility difficult to ignore. If they started to restrict that border as well, blocking out government officials instead of just civilians, then it would become very difficult to draw any conclusion other than invasion. And a double agent inside of the Cabin—or, heaven forbid, two double agents—could only serve to make an invasion easier. How many CIA secrets passed through here in a day? In an hour? How many BND plans did the people in this office know about? Worse yet—how many Stasi secrets could a person in this office bury if they wanted to? For all Reed knew, the invasion plans were already underway, and one of their agents had already sent a warning, but a traitor in the very next room had made that warning disappear.

Reed thought about the ghost stations, hollow and dark, and imagined the whole city under the same heartless control. It made him feel sick to his stomach.

"Twenty-three characters," said Davis, and looked at the wall, as if he could see right through it to the officers beyond. "Whose name fits?"

"'Harald Wagner, MFS agent,'" said Reed, counting in his head. "That's twenty. 'Harald Wagner *is a* MFS Agent' is a perfect twenty-three."

"You think it's Harald?"

"I have no idea," said Reed. "He's just the one I know the least."

"This is dangerous territory," warned Davis, but then paused. "Jannick's name is longer. And Johannes's. 'Johannes Ostertag' has ..."

Reed counted in his head faster than the Chief could. "Sixteen letters. 'Jannick Wohlreich' has the same."

"'Wallace Reed' has eleven," Davis warned.

Reed shot him a wary glance, but continued. "'Jannick Wohlreich MFS ...,' not 'agent,' that's one letter too long. 'Mole?'"

"'Gordon Davis a double agent,'" said Davis. "A perfect twenty-three. I suppose we could sit here all day and find a hundred incriminating sentences for every person in this office, but that's only going to sow paranoia. I shouldn't even have brought it up. We need ..." He shook his head. "We need to be able to trust our people, is what we need."

"What if we bring in the analysts," said Reed, "but we only give them a portion of the message? Not enough to cause damage, but something they can help shed some light on."

"What portion?"

"How about 'Ziegel?'"

Davis laughed, but there was no humor in it. "And if Ziegel is the one word a traitorous Longshore is trying to pass to a Stasi contact? An activation code for an operation, maybe? What then?"

"We could ..." Reed frowned. "We could have the surveillance specialists follow the analysts after, to see what they do—but then the surveillance team will know that something is going on, and any trust our officers have for each other will start to crumble, and—"

"And who knows where such a thing will ever end," said Davis, nodding. "This is the great conundrum, isn't it? Do we trust each other, and possibly enable a double agent to destroy our office, or do we stop trusting each other and destroy the office on our own?" He drummed his fingers on the desk, reading the message again. After a moment he pulled out a fresh piece of paper, and started copying down a portion of the message—the message they were now thinking of as Message 42. "Get Kohler and DeMille in here. We'll show them 'Ziegel' and see what happens—which means we have to *watch* what happens; we'll function as ad hoc surveillance specialists, and observe them ourselves. Which one?"

Reed blinked. "Excuse me?"

"Which one do you want to follow?" asked Davis. "Kohler or DeMille?"

"I'm not trained in—"

"You're a spy," said Davis. "It's not all desk work. Either they do their jobs, or they try to contact a Stasi handler; either way, we learn something—but only if we're paying attention. I almost hope one of them *does* contact the Stasi, because that would make our mole hunt so much easier."

"You don't really want that," said Reed.

Davis sighed. "No, I don't. But I don't see what other option we have."

"I'll ..." Reed hesitated. "I'll watch Lise Kohler."

"Fair enough," said Davis. "I'll take Chuck. Bring them in."

Reed nodded and unlocked the door.

"Bettina?"

The secretary looked up. "Yes?"

"Could you get Lise and Chuck in here, please?"

"Of course, Mr. Reed." She stood to go and get them, and Reed turned back to the office. Davis finished copying the first line of the message, the letters neat and crisp, and then folded Reed's original and put it in the breast pocket of his jacket.

"Hi," said Chuck DeMille, coming into the room. He

carried a pad and a pencil, and Lise was close behind him with the same. "What's up?"

"Ostertag owes you ten dollars," said Reed. "Werner Probst *was* a Stasi agent."

Chuck grinned. "Where's my bookie when I need him? The old DeMille nose strikes again."

"Nose?" asked Reed.

"I can pick a winning horse like nobody's business," said Chuck, sitting down. "I've always been an analyst, Wally, it just hasn't always been for king and country."

Lise looked at Reed, and then at Davis. "Is this about the Longshore message?"

"It is," said Davis. "Have a seat. Mr. Reed, can you close the door, please?"

Reed closed the door, and twisted the bolt to lock it. Lise looked at him again, just for a moment, then sat down next to Chuck. There were no chairs left, so Reed leaned against the wall behind them.

Davis held up the paper. "The message we received today was not number forty-one, it was forty-two. Message 41 has gone missing."

"How do you know?" asked Chuck.

"We don't," said Davis, "but we have good cause to believe it. We also believe that Longshore did this on purpose. We will proceed, for now, on the assumption that he's hidden Message 41 somewhere in the city." He slid the paper toward them across the desk. "Message 42, I suspect, can tell us where."

Chuck took the paper and read it out loud. "'WP MFS Agent CN Harry Ziegel.' Huh." He handed the paper to Lise. "What's Ziegel? It's clearly not part of the code name."

"That's the mystery," said Davis. "What do you make of it?"

"Ziegel is the German word for 'brick,'" said Lise. "Though I assume it is not as simple as 'I hid the message in a brick.'"

"Depends on the brick," said Chuck.

"No," said Reed, "the German matters. He's not talking about a brick, he's talking about 'Ziegel'—that word specifically."

Chuck looked at him. "What makes you say that?"

Reed smiled slightly; he wasn't an analyst, but he knew cryptography better than anyone in the room. "Because 'Ziegel' is six letters, and 'brick' is only five. Space is at a premium in these messages; Longshore never uses extra letters unless he has to."

"Where is the rest of the message?" asked Lise. "The RT-3 sends messages in twenty-five-character segments, and this doesn't add up." Reed said nothing, and Davis stared at her, probably deciding how to answer. He took long enough that she spoke again. "Usually you give us the entire message."

"This one had something we're not fully ready to share yet," said Davis. "Focus on 'Ziegel' for now. Figure out everything Longshore might possibly be referring to, and find that message."

Chuck shook his head. "Chief, even if he did hide a message somewhere, he had to have hidden it on the other side of the Wall. He can't get over here—that's the whole problem."

"Government officers are allowed to cross at will," said Davis, "as part of the Potsdam Agreement. Wall or no Wall, we're still allegedly partners overseeing the reconstruction of the city. Civilians aren't allowed to cross, but ... if you can find that message, I can go and get it."

If they let you, thought Reed.

If this isn't the start of a military invasion.

7:24 PM

West Berlin

REED WORKED LATE, combing through Message 42 for anything else he could find. Were there other meanings hidden in the words? In the numbers? Translated back into numbers again, did the word Ziegel add up to anything—an address or a time or a coordinate? Did it matter that Ziegel was the sixth word, or that MFS was both the second and the seventh? It was just like his earlier attempts to decrypt the radio transmission; purely meaningless until suddenly it would all make perfect sense. Except this time it never made sense.

He finally retired for the night at 7:30 PM, nearly the last person in the building; he locked up his work in the safe by his desk, put on his jacket, and walked to the train station.

The mid-October air was chilly, and he turned up his collar at the wind.

Reed caught the 8:07 train to Gesundbrunnen, and rode it in silence, gripping the pole tightly through the ghost stations. The only light was the faint illumination from inside the train itself, and it barely reached more than a few feet into the darkness.

He got off at Voltastrasse, walked the half block to his building, and fumbled for his key. He walked up the narrow stairs to his apartment, and opened the door.

He heard a noise in the back room.

He froze, and listened. A footstep, and then a scraping sound: wood on wood. A drawer? Someone was going through his things.

Reed still had his gun under his jacket. Had the intruder heard him? He stood in the doorway, locked in indecision. Attack or run? Fight or flight? He heard another footstep, from what had to be his bedroom. He didn't keep anything secret in there, but the intruder wouldn't know that. Was it a burglar? A GDR assassin? A Stasi asset handler come to recruit him into Operation Talon?

Another footstep, and a small *thunk* as something was moved or set down. Whoever was back there didn't know Reed was home yet.

He pulled out his gun, and stepped into the apartment.

Reed's eyes scanned the front, a small living room and kitchen. It didn't look like anything had been dumped out or knocked over. He had a TV here, and a radio, and a collection of books which, while not heirlooms, were at least somewhat valuable. The intruder had gone past them all. Reed stepped over the squeaky spot on the floor, keeping his gun pointed down the hallway toward his bedroom, and glanced at the air vent in the wall behind the living room chair. It hadn't been touched; whoever was here didn't know about his cache of CIA documents, or at least didn't know where it was hidden. Is that what they were searching for in his room? He took another step to the side, glancing into the kitchen; it was empty, and untouched.

There was a kettle on the stove. Had the intruder made himself some tea?

Reed tightened his grip on the gun, holding it in front of

him carefully, and walked into the hallway. There were four doors: a closet, a bathroom, and two bedrooms—one that Reed slept in and one that he used as an office. The closet door was closed. The bathroom and the office were open, but dark; if the intruder had searched them, he had already finished and moved on. The bedroom door was ajar, and a dim light spilled out into the hallway; not the bright light from the fixture in the ceiling, but not the moving beam of a flashlight, either. The bedside lamp, Reed guessed. He held his breath, and stepped closer, placing his feet carefully to avoid the creak in the wooden floor.

A shadow passed in front of the gap, plunging the hallway into a split second of darkness. Reed paused, training his gun on the door, waiting to see if the intruder came bursting out. He heard more footsteps. Nothing happened.

He took a step forward. Then another.

The intruder, whoever it was, was inside the room and to the right. Reed needed to step in, spin around the door, and aim, all in a single motion. He put his foot in front of the door, ready to kick it open, and steeled his nerves.

One.

Two.

Three.

Reed shoved the door open and burst into the room, spinning toward the right to draw a bead on the intruder. He was met with a blur of motion—a glimpse of brown hair and black clothes and bare skin—and then a hand grabbed his wrist and twisted it to the side, wrenching the bones just enough to spasm the muscles in his hand, sending the gun flying into the wall. He stepped back, prepping himself for another blow, and the attacker stepped forward, and then he recognized her.

"Lise?"

Lise Kohler stood by the bed, wearing a black silk slip and crouching in a combat stance. She seemed to have recognized him in the same moment, though while Reed was confused she looked angry.

"Wallace!"

"Lise, what are you ...?"

"I could have killed you, Wally. Why did you have a gun?"

"I always have a gun, Lise, it's our job. I thought you were a burglar!"

She widened her eyes. "I am your girlfriend, dummkopf—"

"Why are you here on a Thursday? You never come on Thursdays. We have a schedule. That's how we hide this whole thing from the rest of the Cabin—"

"Shh," she said, putting her finger in front her lips. She walked toward him. "I missed you. We will be fine."

Reed's heart was still pounding. "I almost shot you, Lise."

She smirked at that. "I worked in the field for six years, Wally; you did not come *close* to shooting me."

"I'm sorry," said Reed, and walked to the bed. He put his hand on his head, feeling the adrenaline still coursing through him, and then sat on the edge of the mattress. "I just ... It's been a day, you know? A really long, hard, paranoid day. I heard footsteps and I thought maybe you were a burglar, or a Stasi agent or something. We spent the whole day hunting an enemy spy, and then I come home and hear footsteps in the darkness, and ..."

Lise stepped toward him again, but this time she stepped closer, sliding one bare leg between his. Her silk slip came barely to the middle of her thigh. She put a hand on his face.

"Not everything that happens in the dark is dangerous."

Reed laughed, and put a hand on her waist. He could feel nothing under the silk but her body.

"If they find out we're seeing each other, it's going to become dangerous quickly."

"I was very good at the office," she said, and bent and kissed him slowly on the side of his forehead. She whispered, "I wanted to do that all day, but no one could tell a thing."

Reed raised his hand from her hip to her cheek, turning her head and lining up her lips with his. He breathed deeply, filling his lungs with her breath, feeling the hollow space between their parted lips, and then kissed her—gently at first, light and probing, and then deep and hungry.

She broke contact, and whispered in his ear: "You closed the door?"

"I ... Damn, I left it open."

"Close it," she said, and took a step backward, and slid one of her straps off her shoulder. "Then come back here, and we can do something productive with all this adrenaline."

———

Half an hour later, spent and cheerful, they lay in bed together, staring at the ceiling. The light from the bedside lamp didn't quite reach all the way to the corners, and Reed imagined it as a full sphere of illumination, sliced into an imperfect cube by the borders of the room. He wondered if there was anything useful behind the mathematics that calculating such a shape would require, and was startled when Lise laughed.

He looked at her, and found that she was watching him. The corners of her eyes wrinkled with delight.

"What?" he asked.

"You have Cryptographer Face again."

"Is that ... bad?"

"It is why I am here, so you decide. I think it is adorable."

Reed watched the light as it reflected on her cheeks and nose, and then chuckled softly and lay back down, staring up at the ceiling again. "Further proof that math has given me every-thing I truly enjoy in life."

"Such a little professor," she said, and snuggled closer to

him, pulling the thin blanket up over her shoulders. The day had been warm enough, but the nights were already growing cold enough to bite. "What do you want to do, when all of this is over? I think you would be good as a professor."

"All of what is over?" he asked. "The Wall? The Soviet Union, as an entity? I don't know if that's *ever* going to end."

"Everything ends. It is very American to think that the way a nation exists today is the only way it will ever exist. Your nation has only ever been one thing."

Reed frowned. "We were an occupied colony before we were a nation."

"Exactly. But now that you are a nation, you think you are perfect. I have read your history books. America is not just a phase in your development, but the grand culmination of it."

Reed glanced at her. "And you think that's naive?"

"I think it is very adolescent, and adolescents hate to be critiqued, so I will not say anything else about it."

Reed laughed. "That's cheating! You can't just say something like that and then refuse to explain yourself."

"I do not have to explain anything," she said, and kissed him on the cheek. "I'm mysterious." She yanked the blanket away from him, wrapped it around herself, then padded across the floor to the hallway, and from there to the bathroom.

Reed pulled the bedsheet tighter around himself, found that it did very little to warm his chest, and leaned across the empty space to grab a sweater from the back of a nearby chair. He pulled it on, and stared at the open bedroom door. He had told Chief Davis he would observe Lise Kohler, to see how she reacted to the snippet of Longshore's message—to see if she did anything suspicious. This was definitely not what Davis had had in mind when he'd asked, but what else could Reed have done? If he'd offered to watch Chuck instead, then Davis would be watching Lise, and it wouldn't take him long to discover their secret relationship. So Reed had to watch her.

Could he do such a thing unbiased? On the one hand, they'd been in this secret relationship for a couple of months now, and he'd gotten to know her—he thought—fairly well. He'd never seen anything to make him suspect her as a Stasi agent.

On the other hand, she'd been a field agent for years before joining the Cabin. If she wanted to make someone trust her, she knew exactly how to do it.

He could drive himself crazy trying to second-guess her and himself in an endless paranoid spiral, but it wouldn't do anyone any good. Better to simply observe, without prejudging, and take things calmly.

Reed looked around the room, and picked up his book from the nightstand: *The Military Cipher of Commandant Bazeries.* He read it once in college, but he knew so much more of the theory now, and had decided to read it again with a new perspective.

"You are lucky," Lise called from the other room. "You have a good position in the Cabin, and you have the ear of Chief Davis. You will get a good promotion from that."

Reed smiled again, half bothered and half amused by her choice of word. "And that's because I'm lucky? Here I thought I was good at my job."

"Very good," she said, coming back into the bedroom. She threw the blanket over his head, and laughed while he struggled to pull himself clear of it. When he did, he saw she was wearing another of his sweaters, and she climbed back into bed. "But you were the one who decoded the transitional message from Longshore, the one where he established his new encryption system. Now, by necessity, you get invited to all the important meetings. We are all good at our jobs, but the Chief sees you being good at your job much more than he sees us."

Reed pursed his lips, thinking. "I suppose."

"I am an analyst," said Lise, and pulled out a book of her own. "Trust me when I analyze something."

"I'm not entirely certain that I want a promotion," said Reed. "Since we're talking about Davis, he's a good example. I wouldn't want his job. He spends all day managing papers and coordinating operations, and I ... I'd rather spend my time doing this." He held up the book. "Cryptography. Codebreaking. This is what I love."

"Nobody stays in the same place forever," said Lise. "Do you not think about the future?"

"We live in the gap between two superpowers," said Reed. "The future is all I think about."

"I mean *your* future," she said. "I used to work in the field, and today I am in the office, and tomorrow I will be doing this." She mimicked his gesture, holding up her book: a solid blue cover with the single word "FORTRAN" in large white letters. "Someday we might not even need human cryptographers anymore, because computers will do everything."

"Never," said Reed.

"Said the horseman to the automobile."

"Computers speak in code," said Reed. "If anything, cryptography will get more useful, not less."

"It is not a code, but a language," she said. "You might as well call German a code, or French."

"In the former case you might be right." Reed laughed when she smacked him playfully on the thigh. "My German is good, aber die Sprache ist sehr komplex."

"German is not that complex."

"Neither is binary," said Reed with a grin, "but you seem fairly proud of yourself for learning it."

"First," said Lise, looking at him seriously, "every German two-year-old can speak German, so it cannot be that much of an achievement to learn it. And your accent is perfect, so what are you complaining about? Second, FORTRAN is a language that lets you program a computer *without* knowing binary."

"That seems like it would take all the fun out of it."

"Some of us do not get to have fun all day," said Lise with a smirk, and opened her book. "Some of us have to work for a living."

Reed laughed again, calling the banter a draw, and looked back at his own book, but found that he couldn't focus on it. His mind was too full of binary.

"Programmers call binary 'machine code,'" he said, closing his book again and looking at Lise. "It's useful for computers because it's very simple for their circuits to process, but for untrained humans it's incredibly difficult to understand. Which means that we might be able to use it as an *actual* code."

Lise cast him a long glance from the side of her eye, then peered in closer, pretending to study him carefully. She nodded. "Definitely Cryptographer Face," she said. "Worst case I have ever seen."

"We've been looking for a code we can use between us," said Reed, growing more excited. "Something to pass messages that no one else would know are messages. What if we used binary? But not with actual ones and zeroes, because that would be too obvious. Ostertag would recognize that in a heartbeat. All you really need is two states: on and off. Empty and full. What if I had to send you a message at work, but all I had was a row of coffee cups—?"

"Coffee cups?"

"Some of them empty and some of them full. In an A-1 cypher, one full cup by itself would be A, and a full cup with an empty would be B, and no this isn't going to work because you'd need up to five characters per letter to do the whole alphabet. I'd have to cover my entire desk with coffee cups—"

"Goodness! I thought I had seen Cryptographer Face before, but this is a whole new level."

"One one zero zero," said Reed, and looked at her with a smile. "That's you. That's the letter L."

"Okay," said Lise, setting down her book. "And Wally starts

with W, which is the number ... 23? Which in binary would be ..." Reed waited while she figured it out. "One zero one one one." She laughed. "That is a lot of full coffee cups."

"Maybe we could tap it out like Morse: a dot for zero, a dash for one, and an empty space between letters. We could send an entire message that looks like Morse but isn't."

"Do you think that Longshore did that with his missing message?" asked Lise.

"I—" Reed blinked. "No." The question confused him, not just because it didn't seem plausible, but because he and Lise had agreed not to talk about the specifics of their work outside of the office. Office politics was fair game, but secret information was, well, secret—and the details of Longshore's messages were definitely secret. Dating another officer was already against the rules; sharing secrets with one was far worse. "Why would you ask that?"

"You just seem very excited about it," said Lise.

"It's a way to send Morse messages without sending Morse messages," said Reed. "How is that not exciting?"

"It is just not very practical," said Lise. "If I tried to tap even something as short as your name in binary Morse, the entire Cabin would know I was up to something."

"Then we find some other ..." Reed paused, then brightened suddenly. "Calendars! A monthly calendar is a five by seven grid; if each column is a five-letter sequence denoting a single letter, you could write a whole seven-letter word on a calendar page just by putting a little mark on some of the days and not others! And no one would ever suspect a thing."

Lise stared at him, her eyes wide, and then laughed out loud. "You are adorable." She gave him another kiss on the cheek. "A cryptographer to the bone."

She looked back at her book, and Reed opened his, but instead of reading he simply watched her. He hadn't said it out loud, and he didn't dare to—not yet, at least—but this was what he *really* wanted from the future. With or without the Wall, with or without the Cabin, even with or without cryptography. He wanted *her*. He wanted to have this easy rapport, this depth of understanding, this ... love. He'd never told her that he loved her. Did she know? She had to know; she was the analyst, after all, and interpreting unspoken truths was her entire area of expertise. And yet she'd never said anything about it.

Maybe she was waiting for him. Maybe it was his job to say it first.

Maybe it had never occurred to her either way.

Their relationship was definitely going to make spying on her more difficult. But there was no way out of it now.

He looked at his book, and tried to read.

FRIDAY, OCTOBER 20, 1961
5:33 AM

West Berlin

THE PHONE WOKE Reed with a strident ring. He fumbled for it in the cold darkness, and almost hit himself with the receiver when he picked it up.

"Hello?"

"Good morning," said a woman's voice. "Do you have any bread today?"

"What?"

"Bread," the woman repeated. "Do you have any bread today?"

Reed's brain finally clicked, and his eyes shot open. Bettina, with a message from the Cabin. "Yes, yes, I have bread today. Do you need it this morning?"

"If you please."

"Of course. I'll put it on your account." Reed hung up the phone, and clicked on the light to look for clothes. Lise stirred.

"Bread?"

"Sorry," he said, and clicked off the light. "This is an unscrambled line, so we use a code when the Cabin calls me. I assume they do the same with you?"

She squinted at the window, then closed her eyes and squirmed deeper into the covers. "It is too early. There is no way it takes you this long to get ready."

"They need me now," said Reed, gathering a full change of clothes as he shivered in the cold. "That probably means we just got a message from Longshore."

Lise bolted upright in bed. "Do they need me?"

"Damn," said Reed, freezing in place halfway to the door. "I hadn't thought of that."

"Do not cover for me," said Lise, scrambling for her clothing. "If they've already called my flat they will know I wasn't home; if they think you know anything about where I've been they will be suspicious. If they ask, I will tell them I spent the night with someone; they don't need to know who."

"Just ... some guy?"

Lise glared at him. "Are you jealous of my cover story?"

"I mean ... what about your reputation?"

"You are such an ass," said Lise, and pulled on her skirt. Reed started to protest, but she cut him off with a glance. "You shower. I have to go home anyway for clothes, so I can shower there. If they call me at all, it will probably be after you translate the message, so I will have time."

Reed watched her, trying to think.

"Go!" she said. He turned and hurried into the shower.

Ten minutes later he was running through the street to Voltastrasse Station, and ten minutes after that he was clutching the train's cold bars, rocking gently back and forth as they rumbled through the ghost stations. He thought once that he saw movement beyond the windows, but it was only a trick of the darkness.

"Guten morgen," said the guard at the Cabin's elevator. Reed showed him his ID, and opened the door to the office.

"Morgen," said Bettina. The main room was empty.

"Thank you for coming in early. The message is in the recorder."

"Thank you," said Reed, and walked past her into Davis's office. How early did *he* arrive in the mornings? "New Long-shore message," said Reed. "What's the confirmation code?"

Davis looked up. "B. Bring it to me as soon as you've finished. It isn't often we get two of them back-to-back, so I'm assuming it's important."

Reed rubbed his eyes. "Yeah, I gathered that when Betty called me at 5:30 in the morning."

"Be quick," said Davis, and Reed nodded.

The rest of the ritual was the same as always. He retrieved the tape from the recorder, threaded in a new one, took the tape and a clean pad of paper into the code room, and carefully locked the door. He laid out his materials, readied his pistol, and unlocked the safe to retrieve the book and his previous notes.

Player Piano. He stared at it, wondering what it was really about. He'd skimmed through the first few pages, finding a story about a man in a factory complex, and something about a dead cat. It didn't make much sense to him, but he didn't have time to read the whole thing in here, and didn't dare to read it at all on the outside. If anyone connected him to the book, and made the leap of logic ... well, it would be a ridiculous leap of logic, but it was safer to avoid it.

Someday when he retired, like Lise had talked about last night. Then he would read it.

For now, he had decryption to do.

He listened to the tape on normal speed, finding six bursts of Morse. Six cylinders on an RT-3 Burst Encoder. The new section of letters for Message 43—assuming there wasn't another missing message—should pick up right where 42 had left off: in the middle of the word 'intercom.'

The first number of the message was 20, and the first letter in the book was R, the 18th letter; 20 minus 18 was 2, which was B, so the confirmation code was correct. Reed smiled. Another normal message. Yet ten minutes later he was back in Davis's office, shaking his head.

"It's not a normal message," he said, and handed Davis the translation:

B

Tsyganov says in meeting in Rennstall Talon op CN Baker not chosen
BBBBBBBBBBBBBBBBBB

Davis frowned as he read it.

"Part of it makes sense," said Reed. "Operation Talon is being led by someone named Tsyganov, who's chosen a code name for their potential double agent but still hasn't chosen the actual agent yet—they don't know which one of us they're going to be able to recruit. That matches what we guessed yesterday. Also, Longshore apparently gained this information from a meeting in a racing stable—that's what 'Rennstall' means. Beyond that ..." He shrugged. "It's very strange."

Davis counted with his finger. "Eighteen Bs," he murmured. "That's most of a cylinder."

"It's a cylinder and a half," said Reed.

"I thought a cylinder had twenty-five letters?"

"This is getting into of the nitty-gritty details of how an RT-3 Burst Encoder works," said Reed. "It has twenty-five slots, yes, but each slot is only capable of producing ten different characters: B, F, G, K, L, M, R, V, W, and 5. Those were chosen because they're all about the same length in Morse, and they're easy to tell apart. I suppose they could have made the Encoder capable of producing the entire alphabet, but it would have been massive—limiting it like this makes it portable, so our agents can actually carry the thing around, and hide it more effectively."

Davis frowned. "I remember reading about this, now that you mention it. The agent uses combinations of those characters to produce all the others."

"Exactly," said Reed. "Every letter and number is produced by a two-character combination of those basic ten. So this message has seventy-five characters, but it took one hundred and fifty characters to send it: six cylinders. And those eighteen Bs took thirty-six characters to send. That's not a full cylinder and a half, but it's close."

Davis frowned. "The confirmation code at the beginning is to let us know the message is real, but the letters at the end are only there to fill out the cylinder. Why send an entire cylinder of placeholders?"

"The cylinders hold twenty-five characters each," said Reed, "so our two-letter code doesn't fit into it perfectly. The final character on any odd-numbered cylinder wouldn't actually mean anything without the first character on the next cylinder to finish it off."

"Surely he thinks we're smart enough to figure out that the message was over," said Davis. He stared at the message a moment, then spoke without looking up. "Has this ever happened before? A message that should only require an odd number of cylinders?"

"Never," said Reed. "I think he deliberately builds them around the constraints of the device. An odd number of cylinders would leave an ambiguous ending, so he adds extra information or abbreviates words to keep the cylinders even."

"And then this time he didn't."

Reed nodded. "If you ignore the eighteen Bs at the end, the message is only fifty-seven characters long. And it's oddly wordy, at that; it seems like he could have easily cut this by enough characters to fit it on four cylinders instead of six." He gestured at the message. "And without eighteen Bs."

Davis stared at the message, one hand on his mouth and the other hand tapping on his desk. "Why did he spell out 'meeting,' like that, all the way? Why not 'M-T-G'?"

"And why bother telling us where the meeting happened at all?" asked Reed.

Davis started counting again. "Abbreviating 'meeting' to 'mtg' would save four characters. Eight in the two-character system. And he'd have saved even more if he'd shuffled the words a bit: 'Rennstall mtg, Tsyganov says ...,' etc. The way he has it now feels almost like he's *trying* to pad it out. It says the word 'in' twice: 'Tsyganov says *in* meeting *in* Rennstall.' But he doesn't really need either of them."

"Obviously we're missing something," said Reed. "Every cylinder he broadcasts increases the chance that the Stasi will trace his signal and find him. Why pad this out, and why pad it out so ... poorly? If he's sending a message anyway, why not fill that extra space with more information?"

"There is one obvious possibility," said Davis, and looked up at Reed. "Assuming we're right about the missing message, this could be another clue about where to find it." He looked at the door and raised his voice. "Bettina, is Chuck in yet?"

"Not yet, sir, it is still early."

Reed glanced at the clock over Chuck's desk; it was barely seven o'clock.

"Tell me when he gets in," said Davis. "And ..." He frowned again at the message. "Yes. Can you call Miss Kohler as well?"

"Yes, sir," said Bettina.

Reed watched Davis, waiting. After a moment, the Chief sighed and gestured to the door. "Can you lock that?"

Reed glanced at him, unsure of what was going to happen next, but closed and locked the door.

"Did you watch Lise Kohler last night?"

Reed tried to keep his face neutral. "I did. I'm not sure what her normal evening routine is, but this.... Nothing struck me as particularly suspicious."

Davis nodded. "I saw the same with Chuck DeMille. We'll keep watching, but ..." He sighed. "Have a seat. I'm going to bring you in on something. I'm starting a new operation, to counter the Stasi's Operation Talon. Right now you're the only other one who knows about Talon, so: welcome to the team."

"You're going to fight Talon?"

"I'm going to *feed* Talon," said Davis. "Yesterday we thought we might be able to get ahead of it, and I started thinking about how. I'm sure they're going through all of our resumes, looking for weak points, trying to find which of us they could blackmail or, more likely, tempt. So I've done the same. And I've found the perfect target."

Reed's eyes widened. "You know who they're going to target?"

"Wally, *they* don't even know who they're going to target." He waved Message 43 in the air. "Longshore just confirmed it. So as long as they're still looking, I'm going to dangle the juiciest worm I can find right in front of their faces. I'm going to help them recruit one of us. I'm going to feed them a triple agent."

Reed nodded. "So they'll think they've turned one of our officers, but really he'll still be reporting to us." He smiled. "You're going to infiltrate the Stasi agents on this side of the Wall. We'll be able to figure out who the other mole is!"

"Exactly."

Reed laughed, but it caught in his throat as a sudden realization hit him. "Wait—you don't mean me! I can't do that. I'm not trained for field work or asset handling or anything like—"

"No," said Davis, dismissing the idea with a wave. "Absolutely no; you'd be terrible as a triple agent."

"... thank you?"

"I need you here, helping me work it from the inside. The actual agent is going to be Frank."

This shocked Reed even more. "Frank? You don't think Frank would turn traitor—"

"I think any of us would turn traitor with the right incentive," said Davis. "But no, I don't doubt Frank's loyalty. If we already have a mole, I'm fairly certain it's not Frank; certain enough to bring him in on this. But yes, I do think I can make the Stasi doubt his loyalty, and push him into their confidence."

"Because he's a ..." Reed tried to think. "He's not a socialist. I don't think he's even a liberal. He's a patriot."

"Everyone here is a patriot," said Davis. "Everyone in the Cabin knows, without exception or doubt, that they're on the right side of this war. They fight for their ideals, and the only way to turn one of them is to convince them there's a higher ideal. Something huge and important; something personal and simultaneously universal. Something which is somehow in conflict with their work here."

Reed saw immediately what Davis was getting at, and the implications turned his stomach. "And Franklin Schwartz is a Jewish man being forced to work with Nazis."

Davis nodded. "We have two former Nazis in the Cabin, and none of us likes working with them, but it's hit Frank worst of all, and with good reason. If the Stasi found a way to ... let's see ... A friendly bump, I'd guess, say in the corridor of his apartment building, or out on the street in front of it. Someone new has just moved in—maybe a single girl, new in the neighborhood and looking for a friend. A few weeks of building trust, never even talking about work much less admitting she's part of the Stasi, and slowly hooking him deeper and deeper. 'You had a bad day? Tell me all about it. Still forcing you to work with those damn Nazis? I hate them, too. Hey, you should come to my anti-Nazi group, we meet every Thursday night, because Something Has Got To Be Done.'"

"That ... could work," admitted Reed.

"That's the kind of thing that will be put into place after they identify Frank as a potential target, as their Agent Baker. Our job now—yours and mine and Frank's—will be to help them to make this identification without ever seeming like we're the ones pushing it. It has to be completely natural." Davis flashed a grim smile. "Some Soviet prick named Tsyganov wants one of my men as a double agent? I'm going to give him a double agent."

Bettina knocked on the door. "Mr. DeMille is here, sir. And Lise says she can be here in fifteen minutes."

"Thank you," said Davis. "Send them both in when Miss Kohler arrives."

Reed pointed at the message on Davis's desk. "Do you want me to recopy that, sir?"

"Why?"

"Yesterday you only showed them the first half of Message 42, and cut out the part that talked about Operation Talon. I ... assumed we'd be doing the same today."

"Analysts are only as good as their information," said Davis. "We need them to find a clue, and while it probably has something to do with the meeting in the stable, it might just as easily be buried in those eighteen Bs. Both parts of the message are equally cryptic. They'll need the whole message if they're going to understand it. But we will continue to watch them, as closely as possible."

Reed felt a pang of guilt.

After a moment he recovered his composure, and nodded. "When should we talk to Frank?"

"This afternoon, I think," said Davis. "I need some time to prepare."

"Sounds good." Reed excused himself, and wandered

through the main office on the way to the restroom; most of the officers were already there. Chuck and Frank were talking in low voices, and Gisela was thumbing through a thick stack of reports. Ostertag was sitting in the window, watching the yoga girl and smoking. He caught Reed's eye and grinned.

"Good morning, Wallace."

"Good morning, Johannes."

"I looked this one up in the library," said Ostertag, pointing out the window with his cigarette. "They have a book about yoga poses—this one is called adho mukha svanasana. Downward-facing dog."

Reed walked over and looked, only to see the girl in the park—maybe twenty, twenty-one years old—bent over on her hands and toes, with her rump stuck high in the air. He rolled his eyes and walked away, headed for the restroom. Ostertag laughed and called after him.

"Come on, Wallace! It is my favorite one!"

Fifteen minutes later, almost to the second, Lise walked into the office, looking showered and dressed and nothing at all like she'd spent the night away from home.

Bettina gathered them up—Reed, Chuck, and Lise—and brought them to Davis's office. Once again, Reed gave the analysts the chairs and leaned against the locked door.

"Good morning," said Davis.

"Morgen," said Lise. "Bettina said you had something important?"

"Another Longshore message," said Davis, and slid the paper with Message 43 across his desk.

Chuck peered at it. "Interesting ..." He pursed his lips, read it a second time, then spoke without raising his head. "What's Talon?"

"A Stasi operation," said Davis. "Ignore it for now, and tell me what you think of the message itself."

Chuck shrugged, still studying the message. Reed saw him counting with his finger before speaking again. "Eighteen Bs."

"Five Bs would have sufficed to fill space on the cylinder," said Davis. "Five and a half, technically. Why send the rest?"

Reed watched Lise, waiting for her to speak, but all she did was stare at the message.

"Maybe he's just trying to be clear," said Chuck. "If he'd truncated the message at five and a half Bs, would we be sitting here having the same worried conversation about why we only got a half a letter? Was he trying to send something else? Was he killed before completing it?" Chuck shrugged, leaning back in his chair. "Or maybe we're reading too much into it."

"Maybe," said Davis. He nodded toward the paper. "What do you think about the rest of it?"

Lise was still silent. Chuck leaned forward again, this time picking up the paper. "They met in a racing stable. Does that mean Tsyganov races horses? Is it a specific stable we're supposed to know about? I've been to most of the local ones, back before the Wall went up, but none of them really stands out as a likely place for a secret meeting."

"Miss Kohler," said Davis. "Do you have any thoughts?"

Lise looked up, like she'd been shaken from a reverie. "Sorry?"

Davis's expression changed, so slightly Reed wasn't sure what to make of it. "I asked about your thoughts on the message."

"Sorry," said Lise again, "I am ... still waking up." She took the message from Chuck's hand. "I cannot help but wonder if the Bs are there to ..." She hesitated. "To get our attention."

"What do you mean?" asked Chuck.

"We thought Longshore might be trying to send a message that only one specific person would see," said Lise. "But now he sends another message so strange, crying out so loudly to be analyzed and studied and pored over, and it is almost like ..."

She laid the paper on the desk, and smoothed it with her hands. "Like he wants as many of us to see it as possible."

Davis leaned forward, looking at the message. "Why do you think he might do that?"

Lise shook her head. "I do not have any idea."

10:15 AM

West Berlin

"THANKS FOR COMING IN, MR. SCHWARTZ," said Davis. "Have a seat. Wallace, would you close the door, please?"

Frank smiled, cheerful but obviously uncertain about why he'd been called in for a meeting with the Chief. "Sure thing. Who do you want me to watch this time?" Frank was a surveillance specialist, and one of the best Reed had ever worked with; he could find ways to watch someone so arcane and yet so effective that the targets gave up more information about themselves than they ever imagined was possible.

"This ... isn't really about that," said Reed. He locked the door, and sat in the chair next to Frank's. "How are the scores today?"

Frank raised his eyebrow. "You locked the door so we could talk about baseball?"

"No," said Reed, shaking his head, "I just ..." He pointed at Davis, head down over some paperwork. "I'm just waiting for the Chief and I'm terrible at small talk."

Frank looked at Davis, then back at Reed, and furrowed his brow. "Spoooooooky. Am I being killed?" He pointed back and forth between the two men. "Are you guys gonna kill me?"

"What?" asked Reed. "No, of course we're not—"

"Relax," said Frank, "I'm obviously just yanking your chain. A locked door meeting with a Section Chief in a Cold War spy bunker? I gotta cut the tension somehow."

Davis finally looked up. "What we're about to talk about is in strictest confidence. You're under special orders not to share this with anyone outside this room."

"I ..." Frank's face grew more serious. "Of course, sir. You can trust me completely."

"We know," said Davis. "That's why you're here. Wally?"

Reed started the explanation. "Agent Longshore has advised us about a Stasi operation to recruit an officer here, inside the Cabin, as a double agent."

"Who?" asked Frank, and then paused. "Wohlreich?"

Davis's face gave nothing away. "Why do you say Wohlreich?"

"I just ..." Frank stopped. "I don't want to speak ill of a fellow officer, sir."

"We're accusing people of treason," said Davis. "The least we can do is speak freely."

"In that case, sir." Frank swallowed. "I just have to say that I've never trusted Jannick Wohlreich, sir. He's ... Well. I've never really trusted him."

"Because he's a Nazi," said Reed.

"Former Nazi," said Frank.

"Does that make it better?" asked Davis, and shot a glance at Reed.

"I mean, it has to, sir," said Frank. "That's the only way we work with them, right? Because they've reformed."

"Not every BND officer was a member of the Nazi party," said Davis. "Ostertag wasn't, or Lise, or Gisela. Wagner and Wohlreich both were, and some of the security guards, and some of the people who hired them, but every one of them has made their *current* loyalties clear. Whether we like it or not, that's who the BND has given us to work with. But no, in this particular case we don't think any of the former Nazis is the target."

Frank raised his eyebrow. "So the Stasi have standards, then."

Reed expected Davis to reprimand him, but instead the Chief smiled. "What did I tell you, Wally? He's a natural."

Reed frowned, not entirely comfortable with the plan. Frank glanced at him, then back at Davis.

"Sir?" he asked. "Who are they trying to turn?"

"The Stasi haven't decided yet," said Davis. "Longshore's given us so much advance warning on this op that we think we can turn it to our advantage."

"You think ..." Frank looked back and forth between them. Reed could see on his face the exact instant that he figured out their plan. "You ... want *me* to become a double agent?"

"Triple," said Reed. "A CIA officer who pretends to feed secrets to the Stasi, but is really just sowing misinformation to help the CIA."

Frank narrowed his eyes. "That sounds dangerous."

"Very," said Davis. "Not at first, obviously. They're not going to introduce themselves as Stasi agents—they'll build up to that, if they ever admit it at all. You'll need to be on the lookout for anyone new that you meet over the next few weeks —maybe a new neighbor in your building, or someone on the train, or in a bar. Even a random hello in the hallway, or a smile across the street."

"You can't possibly expect me to follow up on every person who smiles at me."

Davis raised his eyebrow. "Do a lot of people smile at you?"

"I mean—" Frank frowned. "Well, no, not a huge number. Not that I've noticed, anyway."

"Then, yes," said Davis, "I expect a full list. And I expect you to update that list every morning, here in my office. And I expect you to maintain your normal habits, to the greatest extent possible, so that anybody who might be watching you will have no idea that you've just gained a brand-new source of paranoia."

Frank cast a sidelong glance at Reed. "I'll do my best."

"We haven't even gotten to the fun part," said Reed.

"Through your careful observation," said Davis, "and your complete lack of tells, we hope to identify who your new Stasi handler might be. Once we do, under my supervision, you will begin fostering that relationship. You will go along with any activities he or she suggests, you will visit people and places that he or she takes you to visit, and eventually—with extreme care—you will begin feeding that person secrets. Many, if not most, of those secrets will be true; we're going to start with simple things, too innocuous to do any harm, but which the Stasi can confirm through other sources and thus use to verify your value as an informant. Once they trust you, we'll be able to feed them deliberate misinformation."

"Okay," said Frankly warily. "Or I mean, it's *not* okay, but it's ... an order, I guess, so ... yeah. But. You say they haven't targeted anyone yet." He looked at Davis. "How are you going to make them pick me? Wait." He paused, staring at Davis, and then narrowed his eyes. "You were talking about the Nazis."

"Yes," said Reed.

Davis nodded. "We believe that we can use the former Nazis in our office to give the Stasi the illusion of leverage against you."

Frank laughed, though there was no humor in it. "Why does everyone keep using Nazis for everything?"

"We're going to make you the most appealing target in the office," said Davis. "Nothing overboard, nothing too obvious. We'll make them believe you have cracks in your armor, cracks that they can exploit to ... finesse your patriotism in a subtle, new direction."

"But all of this has to be completely secret," said Reed. "They have to believe that we know nothing about their operation. That's one of the reasons we're being so secretive, even inside of the Cabin."

"*One* of the reasons," said Frank.

Davis nodded. "The other reason is that we're going to use Wohlreich against you."

Frank was stunned into silence.

"I'm very sorry, Frank," said Reed.

"As of Sunday," said Davis, "Jannick Wohlreich will be promoted to Section Sub-Chief. He will be your direct superior. He doesn't know anything about this operation or our plans for you, so the onus will be on you to ... chafe, under his leadership."

Frank looked incredulous. "You want me to fight him?"

"Not fight him," said Reed, "just ... be disgruntled. 'This isn't what I signed up for, why am I working for a Nazi,' that kind of thing."

"Because I'm Jewish," said Frank, "and we're known for our hotheaded insubordination."

"That's not what we're saying," said Davis. "But it is, essentially, the illusion we want to create. We think the Stasi will target you for precisely that reason—not because you're discontented enough to betray your country, but because they will see an opportunity to stoke whatever level of discontent you already have, enough to get you to drop a secret here or there, maybe even without realizing it."

"I would never," said Frank.

"We need you to," said Reed.

"Beginning on Sunday," said Davis, "Wohlreich is going to be your boss. He's already overbearing, so once he has the authority to back that up you should have ample opportunity to complain about his leadership—not necessarily here, but out there in your life. When that handler eventually contacts you, you'll have something real to complain about, which means they'll believe it, and if we're lucky they'll pull you deeper into their trust than they otherwise would. It may be that all they ever do is ply you with booze and try to get you talking, and if that's the case then we can feed you information, as I said. But if you can convince them that you hate working with Nazis to the point that you hate the entire BND, they might bring you into active service. You might have a chance to meet people higher up in the organization, or they might directly ask you for sensitive information—which not only gives us an added chance to fill that information with damaging half-truths, it will give us a clearer sense of what they're trying to learn. The opportunities for intelligence here are amazing."

"And if they realize that I'm playing them?"

"Don't let them," said Davis.

Frank laughed again, harder this time, as if the situation were simply so impossible to believe that he had no other reaction to it. "Well, I suppose it shouldn't be that hard. Because I do hate working with Nazis, and I'm genuinely angry that you —you, of all people—are promoting one, no matter what the reason is. I had relatives who died in the camps. I think the BND is corrupt, from Wohlreich and Wagner all the way up to the top, and every jackbooted thug in between. You're not asking me to play a role, Chief, you're asking me to be myself."

"That's where you're wrong," said Davis. "That's where this becomes not the easiest but the most difficult mission you will ever be assigned. You *will* be playing a role, and that role is almost exactly Franklin Schwartz, but it's not. Ninety percent of it, maybe ninety-five, will be you, and that is why it will work. It will have your truth at its core, your passions and your emotions and, yes, your anger at a bad situation. But that last five percent is not and cannot ever be you. The real Frank

Schwartz would never go as far as the one you'll be pretending to be; he would never hurt his coworkers or endanger his country's plans or actions or intelligence. You need to keep that five percent fixed in the center of your mind—buried deep, so they can't see it, but touching and influencing every decision you make. You need to believe with all your soul that the things you are doing are correct, that they are right and moral, but you also need to know, simultaneously, that they aren't. That you are only doing them to hurt the enemy. That the real Frank Schwartz is always and endlessly loyal to this office, to his coworkers, and to the country that he works for."

"You're asking me to tear myself in half," said Frank.

"I am," said Davis. "I'd offer my condolences, but nothing I say will make it easier. Live the lie without giving in to it, and talk to us if you need to talk."

"No," said Frank. "I'm ... fine. I can do it."

"Good," said Davis. "Don't do anything yet, though, just ... wait for Sunday."

West Berlin

KEEPING secrets in an intelligence office proved to every bit as complicated as Reed had expected. Even more so, if that were possible. Frank knew that the Stasi were trying to recruit a new double agent, but he knew none of the details—not even the codenames Talon and Baker. The analysts, Chuck and Lise, knew about Talon and Baker but had no idea what they referred to, or what such an operation might be about. And Reed and Davis's shared suspicion—that there might already be a double agent among them—had been revealed to no one. They each had pieces of the puzzle, but nobody had them all.

And that was the problem.

The Stasi were working with a man named Tsyganov, and that was concerning because Tsyganov was so clearly a Russian name. East Germany claimed to be a sovereign state, aided but not governed by the Soviet Union; proof that a KGB officer was overseeing a Stasi operation could be a vital piece of proof that the Soviets were far more involved than they claimed. Davis needed to know who Tsyganov was, and eventually decided that the name itself was safe to share. This was the Cabin's whole purpose, after all: not just to gather information, but to interpret it, increase it, and pass it along to those in a position to act on it. Figuring out who Tsyganov was could be a major coup for Western intelligence, and so he put the team to work on it.

"The Stasi have recently met with a man named Tsyganov," Davis told them, leaving out all other details and suspicions. Even the racing stable was a secret. "I want to know everything you can possibly learn about him, as soon as you can possibly learn it."

That afternoon, Gisela Breuer filled them in on the first sparse fruits of her research. "I have found four men named Tsyganov," she said, handing out mimeographed sheets to each officer in the Cabin. "There are presumably more, but these are the ones most likely to have been involved in a meeting with the Stasi."

Reed picked up his copy of the freshly inked paper, wrinkling his nose at the smell.

"None of them lives in Berlin," said Wagner, looking at the list.

"That is right," said Gisela. "Whoever was at this meeting came in from out of town. Out of the country, in fact; they all live in Russia."

"That's pretty damning right there," said Chuck.

"Nothing is damning unless we can prove it," said Wohlreich, taking control of the impromptu meeting as he always seemed to do. "Tell us about the first one."

Reed wanted to say something, but worried he might reveal too much.

"Vasili Tsyganov," said Gisela. "A miner from Monchegorsk. I do not know what business a miner would have in Berlin, but—"

"But Monchegorsk has a Soviet airbase," said Lise. "So his registration as a mine worker might only be a cover."

"Correct," said Gisela. "It is not a big town, and the mines and the airbase are the two main employers. It wouldn't be the first time that a Soviet military officer is registered as menial labor with a nearby factory or mine, trying to throw us off."

"Married," said Ostertag. "Five-year-old son."

"There is certainly a possibility," said Wohlreich, "but nothing jumps out as immediately suspicious. We will look into him. And the second one?"

"Josef Tsyganov, from the city of Kuybyshev," said Gisela. "One of the key sites in the Soviet space program. Josef works in the Progress Plant, where they built the Vostok."

Reed thought that was a tenuous connection at best—there was no way the man they were looking for was an engineer in the space program—but he didn't want to say that, once again out of fear that he would give away something he shouldn't.

Keeping secrets from professional secret finders was a nightmare. How was he ever going to pull this off?

Chuck jumped in and solved the immediate problem, arriving through deduction at the same conclusion Reed had reached through knowledge. "I can't imagine we're looking for someone in the space program. A local meeting would be for a local op, right? If Berlin were suddenly part of the space program, we probably would have heard about it elsewhere."

"Probably," said Wagner. "That does not make it impossible."

"But why would the space program send someone here?" asked Frank. He had an old baseball on his desk that he played with when he was nervous; he was playing with it now. "Why would they have a space op in Berlin, of all places? We don't have any launch sites, or landing sites, or the political stability to risk building one."

"Have you not heard the propaganda?" asked Ostertag with a grin. "The GDR is the strongest nation in the world!"

"It could be a social op," said Wohlreich, ignoring the joke.

"Yuri Gagarin is the biggest hero they have right now—and he stayed in Kuybyshev, by the way, after they recovered his landing capsule. If the Soviet government is taking him on another victory tour, they will absolutely stop in Berlin to win a few more hearts and minds."

"Gagarin already had his victory tour," said Lise. "Plus he was injured last month—his wife caught him with a nurse, and he jumped off a second-story balcony to get away. Read the reports. He landed on his face, and he has a big scar." She drew a long line above her left eyebrow. "They will not be touring him for a long while."

"Chicks dig scars," said Frank.

"But not infidelity," said Lise.

Reed made sure not to look at her.

"Fine," said Wohlreich, frowning at the paper in his hands. "Number Three?"

"Three *and* Four are both from Moscow," said Gisela. "Alexey Tsyganov is a known military officer, a Lieutenant Colonel in the Soviet Army."

"You should have led with him, then," said Ostertag.

"A known officer is far less likely to be involved in a covert operation," said Wagner. "He would be too recognizable."

"By who?" asked Chuck. "You're in surveillance, but most of the people who'd see him on this trip are untrained civilians. As long as he's smart enough not to come in uniform, he could walk from one end of the GDR to the other and nobody would know him from Adam."

"They would hear him speaking Russian," said Wagner, "or German with a Russian accent."

"But that's true of all of these guys," said Frank. He tossed his baseball in the air, and caught it again, deftly. "Lieutenant Colonel Tsyganov wouldn't be any more noticeable here than the others, if he was trying to stay unnoticed."

"We have contacts in Moscow," said Wohlreich. "With

access to army base records. I will ask them if Alexey Tsyganov is out of the country right now—that could answer this fairly decisively."

"If Alexey's still there, then sure," said Chuck, "we'd have our answer. If he's gone, though, that could potentially still mean anything." He looked up. "Unless your contacts can get us his travel itinerary, to prove that he's come here."

"That is unlikely," said Wohlreich.

"Let's move on," said Frank. "I want to hear about this fourth Tsyganov—"

"I'm not done talking about Alexey," said Wohlreich, shutting him down without so much as a look. He was definitely, Reed thought, an overbearing man; he always had to be in control of any conversation. Reed watched Frank to see what he'd do, but Frank merely caught his baseball again and held it, staring at Wohlreich without speaking. Was he planning to say something? Trying to decide if he should? He wasn't *supposed* to start complaining about Wohlreich until Sunday, but would his anger at the situation cause him to jump the gun?

But Frank said nothing, and Wohlreich continued: "What does he do in the army?"

"He's a Lieutenant Colonel," said Chuck. "He commands a battalion—what else? He's got a few hundred soldiers and all the bureaucracy that goes with them; he probably spends most of his time doing paperwork."

"If a whole battalion is coming to Berlin," said Lise, "that is not good."

"We would have heard of it," said Wagner.

"Because they're speaking Russian," said Frank.

"Because we are a surveillance office," Wagner growled. "Hearing about things is our job."

"Maybe this *is* us hearing about it," said Lise. She turned to Reed. "We still don't know what operation Tsyganov is running. A massive troop movement? An occupation force?"

"An invasion?" asked Reed.

"Or reinforcements for the GDR's police force," said Chuck, "to stop their citizens from tearing down the Wall."

"But the Wall is there because the people want it there," said Ostertag, shaking his head in mock solemnity. "It's not there to keep them in, it's to keep us out. It's an Anti-Fascist Protection Rampart! Doesn't *anybody* read the propaganda—?"

"Mein Gott!" said Wohlreich loudly. "Try to take at least one conversation seriously, Johannes, this is important!"

Ostertag only chuckled. "What I am saying is this: can you imagine the propaganda nightmare if the GDR has to defend their own Wall from their own citizens? With Soviet troops, no less? It would expose the lie at the heart of their actions; they'll wait as long as they possibly can before moving in an entire battalion of Soviet soldiers." He smiled at Wohlreich. "The situation is bad, but it's not that bad. They must maintain the fiction behind the Wall, even more so than the Wall itself, if they want to retain their power."

"That," said Wohlreich testily, "is the first helpful thing you've said all day. Maybe start with that next time instead of telling jokes."

"Du wirst zu Amerikanisch," muttered Wagner.

"Oh crap," said Frank in mock terror, "and none of us speaks German! How will we ever know what he just said?"

Chuck shook his head. "Everybody just calm down."

"I assume it was nice," said Frank. "Something really loving and supportive."

"Enough," said Wohlreich. "We are moving on."

"Very well," said Gisela. "Sergei Tsyganov is a mid-level financial officer in Korporatsiya Volskaya. They make drive trains for industrial vehicles. That gives him the weakest connection to the Soviet government, but the strongest justification for traveling to Berlin."

"Which makes him the most likely one to be a spy," said

Ostertag. "Lack of suspicion and freedom of movement are the best two qualities he could have."

"So the Soviets hired him to pass along a message?" asked Frank.

"Or the corporate job is a cover," said Chuck, "just like that first guy's factory job."

"What was the exact wording of the message?" asked Wagner.

Reed shifted uncomfortably in his seat. "That's ... on a need to know basis."

"And we don't need to know?" asked Wagner.

Wohlreich shook his head. "According to Chief Davis, no, we don't. If we knew more about who this man is, and why we're looking for him, then yes, maybe that would make this Tsyganov easier to identify. But our leader has determined that we don't need to know, so we will make do with what we have."

"Always obey the leader," Frank muttered, but if Wohlreich heard him he didn't react.

"So what do we know, then?" asked Wagner. "Nothing."

"We know that whatever Tsyganov is up to—some kind of local operation or reconnaissance—is small," said Lise. "Or it is still in the early stages. If it were bigger, or further along, we would have heard about it before."

Frank frowned. "So it's a small, local op. So then why would Tsyganov, whichever one of these guys he turns out to be, come here from out of town to tell the local Stasi officers about their own op?"

"Well," said Chuck, and then stopped. He looked at Lise; she looked back, but Reed couldn't read her expression. "Well," he started again. "The obvious answer is that Tsyganov is running the op. That makes him almost certainly KGB, no matter what other cover story he ends up having. And the most likely operation for a KGB officer to come in and manage is —counterintelligence."

Reed grew nervous. They were so close to intuiting a truth Davis had tried to keep hidden.

"So he is hunting for a mole," said Wohlreich. "Perhaps even Longshore."

"That, or he is trying to create a mole," said Lise. "Maybe in the US State Department, maybe in the West German government or police. Maybe even in the BND, or the CIA."

"Maybe even here," said Wagner.

Frank looked shocked. Gisela looked sick. Ostertag smiled, but glanced at Wohlreich and bit down on whatever joke he'd been going to make. Reed scanned the other faces in the Cabin and saw them all looking back, all studying each other, all gauging the potential innocence or guilt of their coworkers' reactions.

They have one single name, thought Reed, *and they still managed to pull the truth out of it, like a rabbit from a hat.*

Professional secret finders indeed.

SATURDAY, OCTOBER 21, 1961
9:24 AM

West Berlin

REED SLEPT in on Saturday morning, though it was a fitful rest, and he spent most of it with his eyes pressed into the pillow, telling himself that it was still dark outside long after it was light. He expected the phone to ring at any moment, and for Bettina to call him in for another message from Longshore, and he couldn't decide if he dreaded that possibility or craved it. He didn't get very many days off—the Cold War never rested, so neither did the Cabin—and while he didn't want to go in to work, he didn't really want to stay home, either.

They had two little fragments that might be clues—Ziegel and a meeting in a stable—but they still had no idea how those fragments fit together into anything substantial. He wanted more. It was like he was riding a train, racing through the stations, and each one brought a new piece of intel. He wanted it to stop, or at least slow down, so he could think about each new clue as it arrived, but he also wanted it to speed up, and bring him each new clue as quickly as it could. Instead, he simply held on to the railing, and hoped it didn't crash.

At 9:30 AM he got out of bed, filled his kettle with water,

and set it on the electric stove to warm. He had spent much of the night outside of Lise's apartment building, watching it nervously, hoping that she didn't try to leave. He didn't want her to be guilty; he didn't want her to be anything but the trustworthy friend, lover, and coworker she had always been. It made him sick to spy on her, even in this distant, unobtrusive way, but an order was an order. She could be doing all manner of traitorous activities inside her apartment, and he knew he should be trying to get a closer look. But he told himself that he would look more closely when he could, all the while praying that such an act would never be required.

The kettle whistled, and he poured a cup of tea. While it steeped he wandered through the tiny apartment in a robe and two pairs of socks, curling his toes against the cold. He looked outside; the sun was shining. It would be warmer out there. He should go for a walk. He drank his tea and dressed, being sure to carry his identification and his service pistol, hidden under his coat. He stared at his books on encryption, wondering what kind of code Longshore might be using to send his hidden message-in-a-message.

He wondered who he might be sending that message to, and why it was secret.

He left his apartment and walked down the stairs, only to find Lise coming in from the street.

"Li—Miss Kohler. I thought you were at work today."

"I should be. I told the Chief I was sick."

Reed looked around him nervously, though the building's foyer was empty. "Why?"

"We need to talk. Can we go up to your room?"

Had she seen him outside her apartment? She was a trained field agent; she knew how to spot a tail. He'd tried to be so careful, staying so far away he'd been practically useless, but maybe she'd seen him anyway. He shook his head, and tried to convince himself it was fine. If she was mad at him he'd be able to see it in her face. She must be here for something else.

He hoped.

"People saw you come in," he said. "We're not supposed to be together."

"More people will see us if we stay outside." She started walking toward the stairs. "Come with me, this is important."

Reed followed her back up to his apartment, staying silent while he pulled out his key and let her in. She walked to the center of the sitting room and stood there, not even turning, while he locked the door behind them. He looked at her, still unmoving, and shivered. He turned on the radiator, but didn't take off his jacket. It would take a while to warm up.

"Lise?" he said at last.

"I do not know how to ask this," she said.

"Ask? I thought you had something to tell *me.*"

"Both." Her face was solemn, but also jittery and nervous. She licked her lips; she wrinkled her nose. She was working up her courage.

"Just say it," Reed said, but inside he was wracked with worry.

She nodded, licking her lips again, and then spoke. "I think I know who it is."

That wasn't what Reed had expected at all, and it took him a moment to process. "You think you know who *who* is? Tsyganov?"

"Longshore," Lise said. "I think I have figured out who Longshore is."

Reed's eyes widened, and he walked to the bookshelf—not because he needed something from it, but because he wanted time to think. He was pacing. He stopped.

"Who is it?"

"It is the clues Longshore gave us," she said, deflecting his question. "Ziegel, and Rennstall. I think they are references to signal phrases I used to use, before I moved behind a desk. I think ..." She paused, and then looked Reed right in the eyes. "I think Longshore is a man I used to work with in the field. And if I am right, I think he is not just sending mysterious messages, he is sending them to me. Personally."

Reed nodded, looking at her face, wondering what to do next. The idea that Longshore was sending hidden messages had been his theory—he proposed it and argued for it—but he'd never considered that the messages might be intended for Lise. Should they call Davis? Should they go to the Cabin and sort it all out?

Whatever they did, they couldn't do it together.

"Who is it?" he asked again.

"I do not want to say. I might be wrong. And if I am, I do not want to reveal someone who might still be an active agent in a different operation."

"You don't trust me?" asked Reed, though he felt guilty as soon as he said it. He wasn't telling her everything, either.

"Chief Davis has not told any of us who Longshore is," said Lise. "If he is keeping it secret, then so am I."

"That's ... fair enough." Reed paced again, no longer caring if he looked nervous. "So what do the clues mean?"

"I did not put it together until after the second message. I thought Ziegel was just a brick, but it was also an old warning phrase I used to use with ... the agent. I cannot just keep calling him 'the agent.' We need a name we can use for him." She looked around the room, reaching for a code name, and pointed at the thermometer on the wall. "We will call him Mercury. So: when I worked with Mercury in East Berlin, Ziegel was our word for 'pay attention, this is important.' We could say it in written messages or even in person. But that was four years ago, and I didn't even think about it in the first message. But then the second message had the word 'Rennstall.'"

"A racing stable," said Reed.

"Yes," she said, "but not just any racing stable. Mercury and I used a restaurant called Rennstall as one of our meeting places. We had three restaurants that we used, all over the Soviet sector of the city, but Rennstall was the safest. It was the farthest from the border, and the least likely to have Stasi employees or politicians of any kind. The owners were ... sympathetic to our work. We met there when we needed to talk about something in private."

"You think he wants to meet with you in person?"

"I do not know what I think."

"It might be a coincidence."

"It might," said Lise, "I know. But we know those words mean *something*, because they're the part of each message that doesn't make sense. And each word—Ziegel and Rennstall—is the sixth word of its message. And the only words in German." She paused, as if speaking the next bit aloud was painful, but then she said it anyway: "Unless I'm wrong, and the rest of that message has more German? Or more words in the beginning?"

Reed grimaced, and stopped pacing. "I can't tell you any parts of the message that Davis hasn't shown you."

"I understand that," said Lise, "but am I wrong? Is there anything that makes my guesses false?"

Reed didn't want to answer, but the fact that he didn't correct her was evidence enough. She stared at him a moment, studying his eyes, and then nodded. "So I'm right. They're both the sixth word, and they're both the only words in German."

"Fine," said Reed, "you're very clever. But what does that tell us? Does the number six have any meaning between you and Mercury?"

"No," said Lise. "But it is a pattern."

"Two instances isn't a pattern," said Reed, repeating the word as if eager to believe it. "Until it happens in a third message it's still technically just a coincidence."

"That is why I am here." Lise stepped toward him, then

apparently thought better of whatever she'd been planning, and stepped back. "Message 43 had eighteen placeholders, probably to make sure that we knew there was a clue. 'In a meeting in Rennstall' is an odd thing to say in a message, but if not for the placeholders we might have glossed over it completely. The long string of Bs drew extra attention to the wording, to make sure that Davis called in the analysts, and to make sure that when he did I saw the pattern: the sixth word is German, and it is a place I used to visit. Mercury made sure that I, personally, would see the clue he left for me."

"You don't know that for sure."

"I do not," she said, and she stepped forward again, closing the distance between them. This time she didn't step back. "Usually we get to see all of the messages, but Davis only showed us a portion of Message 42. I have my own suspicions as to why, but whatever the reason, something very big is happening. If we are right about Tsyganov, it could be as big as a military action. And if Longshore really is my old friend Mercury, then he is sending secret codes directly to me, because he thinks that this is the only way to stop the bad thing from happening. But I ..." She put a hand on Reed's arm. "I cannot guarantee that Davis will show me any of Longshore's next message, let alone the full text. You are the only one who—"

"Whoa," said Reed. "You want me to ..." He stopped. "You want me to show you a classified message?"

Lise looked at the floor, then lifted her eyes to meet his gaze. "I was awake all night trying to work up the courage."

"I can't show you any document that Davis hasn't cleared," said Reed. "I've already told you that."

"It may be against the rules—"

"You say that like there's a caveat."

"It is not against the spirit of our job."

The sentence fell like a weight on the floor.

Reed opened his mouth, not sure how to respond.

Lise spoke again. "Why would Longshore send one of his messages in a strange, nonstandard way, unless he is trying to prevent the wrong person from seeing it? And why would there be a 'wrong person' inside the Cabin unless one of us is a double agent?" Reed's face must have given something away, for she nodded at him. "I assume that this is the secret you and Davis have been keeping from the rest of us. I am an analyst; it is my job to figure these things out. My guess is that Longshore found out who the double agent is, hid the secret somewhere, and is now hiding clues in the rest of his messages, trying to lead me, specifically, to that missing message." She stared at Reed a moment. "I did not set out to uncover your secrets, Wally. All I did was look at the evidence and draw the most logical conclusion."

Reed was supposed to be watching Lise, to see if she did anything suspicious, and now here she was asking him to go behind Chief Davis's back. It was too much to take in.

"I ... can neither confirm, nor ... deny ..."

"Please, Wally. You are the worst liar I know. It is written on your face as plain as day. But now ask yourself: if Davis can redact the messages before the 'wrong person' sees them, why does Longshore have to hide this secret? He knows who we are —we have files on the Stasi, and they have files on us. So why not simply tell us who the mole is, and let Davis see it, and let him deal with the traitor right there? Why go to all this trouble? Unless ..." She trailed off waiting for Reed to fill in the rest of the logic.

When he did, he shook his head in shock.

"You can't possibly think Davis is the traitor?"

"I do not know who it is," said Lise, holding up her hands in protest. "It could be Davis; it could be you." She put her hand back on his arm, curling around his triceps. "I do not want it to be. And I do not want it to be Davis, either, but ... why hide the message, if not from him?"

"He's not a traitor—"

"Neither am I," said Lise quickly, "neither are any of us, as far as I know, but we still keep secrets from each other. You know that better than any of us. You were the one working cryptography when the transitional message from Longshore came in; that means you are the only one who knows the new encryption system, so you are the only one Davis uses in any talk about Longshore. A different day, maybe even a different hour, and it would have been Ostertag, and now he would be the Longshore expert and you would be working all the other codes that he has now." Her hand tightened on his arm. "This is the same thing, isn't it? You and I are the only ones who know about Mercury, and about the true meaning of the clues that Longshore is trying to send us, so why bring in extra people until we are sure? It is strictly in the spirit of the Cabin and its rules to keep this between us for as long as we can."

Reed looked at her for a moment, then looked away, blinking, trying to think. It made sense, in a way. What if Davis was a double agent? He could disrupt their process, ruin their plans; he could corrupt their information, hide key snippets of it, and point them off in wrong directions.

But then why bother with the investigation at all?

Because Reed had forced it. He'd mentioned the possibility of a double agent to Michael Hogan in the State Department, and now they *had* to investigate, and Davis had been furious. And there were plenty of *good* reasons to be furious about that, Reed knew. Davis's anger and suspicion could be entirely justified by right and moral reasons.

But they could also be consistent with the behavior and plans of a double agent.

Reed shook his head, grabbing himself by the hair. He took

a deep breath, smoothed his hair again, and restarted his pacing.

"What would you need to see in Longshore's next message?" he asked. "Just the sixth word?"

"I think so. If we are right about this, the sixth word of Message 44 will also be in German, and that will be the sign that it is another piece of the puzzle."

"Ziegel warned you to pay attention," said Reed. "Rennstall confirmed that the messages were for you—maybe—and that they were coming from a known associate; from Mercury. What will the next one say? An offer to meet in person?"

"That would be too dangerous," said Lise. "It's very likely that whatever he needs us to know is in the missing Message 41."

"You're right," Reed said. "He'd need to use some sort of dead drop, then tell us where to find it. So if we're right, the clue will be in the sixth word of Message 44."

"Exactly," said Lise. "And it will say it in a way that only I can understand. Which means it will not be just any dead drop, it will be one of the ones that Mercury and I used when we passed each other messages in the field."

Reed stopped pacing, licking his lips and shaking his head. He didn't like this; he didn't like any of it. But it made sense, at least for now. And how much could giving her one word hurt?

It made him feel guilty even to think that. It made him feel even worse to believe it.

"When the next message comes in I'll look at the sixth word," he said. "If it's in German, I'll tell it to you later." He turned to face her. "But you can't tell anyone else about this. Not anything."

"I would get in just as much trouble as you. Maybe more." She took a deep breath, and then stuck out her hand to shake. Reed hesitated, looking at it.

A double agent in the Cabin would be bad enough if it was one of the officers—if the GDR or the Soviets were planning a military action, a double agent could obscure the details, and make it harder for the Cabin to identify the threat and warn the Western governments. But if the double agent were Davis? He was the Section Chief—he could do so much more. He could actively support an invasion, enabling it from the inside. He could create a false threat and send all the troops to the wrong place, effectively leaving the door unlocked for a Soviet army to march in unimpeded.

Reed had to find the double agent, or the city of Berlin could be lost in a heartbeat. Maybe the entire Cold War.

"I promise," said Lise, her hand still extended. "I will never tell anyone."

Reed took her hand, agreeing to help her and echoing her promise. "I'll never tell anyone."

Lise stared at him for a moment, before stepping in closer, breaking the handshake, and wrapping her arms around his chest.

She kissed him, slowly and deeply, then led him toward the bedroom.

5:58 PM

West Berlin

"TWO MEN," said Reed, reading from a puzzle book, "meet again after many years. James has three children. The oldest is a boy, and the other two are girls. John asks how old they are. 'The product of their ages is seventy-two,' says James, 'and the sum of their ages is today's date.'" Reed looked at the cover. "If this was a daily newspaper that would mean something, but since it's in a monthly puzzle book, published without a date, it means something completely different."

"Mm, hmm," said Lise.

"What it means," said Reed eagerly, "is that the exact date doesn't matter, but the idea that it *could* be a date does. John says that this formula doesn't help him, which means—"

"Mm, hmm," said Lise.

Reed looked up from the book in his lap, pencil in hand, to find Lise staring at the clock on his living room wall. "Lise?"

She answered without looking at him. "Yes?"

"You seem preoccupied."

"5:59 PM," she said, watching the second hand click over past the twelve and begin a new revolution. "One minute left."

Reed frowned. "What happens at 6:00 PM?"

"Bettina goes home. Not exactly on the minute—not every day—but most of the time. And when Bettina goes home, the Cabin is effectively closed for the day." She stared at the clock a moment longer, then shook her head and turned away. "Longshore can send us a message any time he wants to, day or night, but we will not know about it unless it comes while someone is in the office. If it does not come right now—" She looked back at the clock, and watched in silence as the second hand moved around the circle and back up to the twelve again. "We won't know until tomorrow."

Reed frowned. "Is that ... why you've been hanging around my apartment all day?"

"And because I am nervous," she said, still staring. "I did not want to be alone." She paused, then shook her head and looked at Reed. "I am sorry, I make myself sound heartless. I am not using you, Wally, I just ... You help me feel calm. Thank you for being here for me."

Reed set down his pencil. "I ...," he started, but didn't finish. Of course she'd been nervous about the message—he was nervous, too—but it changed things, somehow, to know that she'd been so completely focused on it. He'd spent a pleasantly lazy Saturday with her, or he thought he had. Had she spent that time not with *him*, but with his proximity to the Longshore messages?

Was Lise the mole?

She looked at him. "Yes?"

"What?"

"You started to say something."

"I was just going to say that we don't know for sure what's happening in the Cabin. Maybe the message is coming in right now, and they haven't decided to call anyone about it yet."

"You are making me anxious." Lise rose to her feet, pacing

idly in the cramped apartment living room. After a moment she turned to him. "Tell me about your puzzle. The three men."

"Three children," he corrected automatically.

"Three children," she said. "Two girls and a boy. And we need to calculate their ages?"

Reed had the distinct and unsettling feeling that she was trying to distract him. Was she? He didn't know how to press the issue without pressing too hard. He looked down at his book. "The product of their ages is seventy-two, and the sum of their ages is today's date."

"October 21," said Lise.

"This was published a few months ago in the States," said Reed, "and it's a monthly, so there is no date, which means the exact date doesn't matter."

"Then you cannot find the ages," said Lise. "There must be many groups of three numbers that multiply together into seventy-two."

He did the math in his head. "There are twelve sets of numbers that multiply to produce seventy-two. The date restriction makes some of them obviously false, like 1 and 1 and 72; I suppose it's possible to have children with those ages, but their sum is 74, and no months have 74 days. I think there's only"—he did some more mental math—"nine combinations that add up to a number in the proper range. No, wait: 1 plus 3 plus 24 is only 28, so that fits. There are ten."

Lise glanced at the clock, and Reed's eyes followed. 6:03 PM.

"How long are you staying?" he asked.

"What?"

He nodded toward the clock. "How long are you staying here tonight? Are you here for a while? Should I make dinner?"

"Only Americans eat dinner at six o'clock."

"Until eight, then? Nine? Or ..." He hesitated, and then

said it. "Are you only staying until you're sure that I won't be called into the Cabin?"

Lise moved her head, as if considering him from another angle. "You seem upset."

"I'm a little frustrated, yes."

"I'm listening to your puzzle."

"It's not about the puzzle. The kids are 3 and 3 and 8. This is about you. It's about whatever reasons you have for being here."

Lise paused again, looking at him closely. "I thought I was spending a Saturday with my boyfriend."

"I thought you were, too."

She raised her eyebrow, and then her expression turned cold. "Then why am I here?"

He hesitated again, but it was too late now. "Because you want to hear the next message."

"So do you."

"Of course I do."

"So what is the problem?"

"The problem is—" He stopped, and then looked down at his puzzle book. He didn't know what the problem was. Or maybe he did, and he didn't want to name it. If she was only spending time with him as a way of getting access to the Longshore messages, then—

He shook his head, refusing to follow that line of thought any further. "The problem is nothing," he said. "It's me. I'm just nervous, is all. Going behind Davis is more than I'm ready for."

"You agreed that it was a good idea."

"I agreed to *do* it," he said, looking up at her again. "That doesn't mean I'm happy about it."

"Do you want to back out?"

Reed pursed his lips, trying to probe his own feelings. Did he want to back out? Yes. But not as much as he wanted to know what was really going on. And either way, he didn't dare leave Lise to work on this alone—if he was with her, he could at least see what she was doing.

"I want the truth."

"Good," said Lise, "because we need to get to work." She shot a final glance at the clock. "It is 6:10 PM. Bettina is gone, and most everyone else in the office, too. Davis will still be there —who knows when he goes home?—but it is safe to assume that they are done for the day. We are not getting a look at any new messages until we go to work tomorrow morning. Which means that if I am still here, I am here for you, and you can drop this petty jealousy."

"Or you're just staying later to prove my jealousy wrong."

"This is not an attractive look on you, Wallace."

"Some of us don't—" He stopped himself. "I'm just nervous. I told you that."

Lise stared at him in silence for a few more moments. Reed pretended to focus on his puzzle.

"If we want to find out what is going on," she said, "we need another avenue of investigation."

"What do you mean?"

"I mean that we cannot simply wait for another Longshore message. What if he never sends one? What if they have caught him and killed him?"

"Don't—"

"We need another angle of attack," she said again. "There may be a double agent in the Cabin, and we have to root him out. By whatever means are necessary."

"I'm not breaking into the Cabin."

"Neither am I," said Lise. "But remember our goal: ultimately, we are not looking for a new Longshore message, we are looking for an old one. Message 41."

"We can't just go pick it up," said Reed. "It's in a dead drop somewhere."

"Maybe. Or maybe it's somewhere else. We are still only working on theories, remember, so here is a new one: what if Longshore is passing messages to Davis through the same method Davis uses to pass messages to him?"

Reed frowned. "You mean the confirmation codes?"

"Davis sends him a new code every day," said Lise. "They obviously have some kind of channel they use to communicate."

"But it's only one way. It basically has to be, or we'd be using that instead of—" Reed stopped himself, terrified at how close he'd come to saying 'Player Piano.' He collected himself. "Instead of the system we're currently using."

"Maybe. Maybe not. It is worth looking into, at least?"

Reed felt that sick feeling in his stomach again. "Now we've moved beyond hiding intelligence from the Chief. You're talking about spying on him."

"I am talking about finding a hidden message that might identify a dangerous double agent," said Lise. "That is a threat to Davis, to us, maybe to the entire Western alliance. If breaking one rule means doing that much good, it is obviously our duty to do it."

"Even if it is, the system they use for confirmation codes can't possibly be the answer we're looking for."

"You don't know that—"

"Message 41 has twenty-three characters," he said, interrupting her, "and Davis can only send one letter at a time."

Instantly Reed knew that he'd said too much; he'd just shared two pieces of top secret information, with a person he still wasn't certain he could trust. The gaffe made him stop short, dumbstruck by his own mistake.

Lise furrowed her brow in concern. "You look like you have seen a ghost. What is wrong?"

"I shouldn't have said that."

"That he can only send one character?" asked Lise. "That is not damaging intel."

"But it is," he said, and now his prudence was at war with his professional eagerness. Cryptographer Face. "It's a limitation, and every limitation we discover in a system tells us more about it. It's like ..." He looked around the room, and his eyes lit on the puzzle book. "It's like this puzzle," he said at last, tapping the thin pages. "There are twelve sets of three numbers that multiply into 72, so we need more restrictions to tell us which set is the correct one. Listen to it again: James has three children. The oldest is a boy, and the other two are girls. John asks how old they are. 'The product of their ages is seventy-two,' says James, 'and the sum of their ages is today's date.' John says this formula doesn't help him. James says he has all the information he needs."

"James sounds like an ass," said Lise.

Reed ignored the jibe. "Limitation number one: the sum of the ages is a date—a day of the month. That cuts out two options, because their sum is higher than thirty-one, but mostly it just points us at the next limitation: John says that knowing this formula *doesn't help him*. And why wouldn't it help him? Because two of our number sets add up to the same sum: 6 plus 6 plus 2 is 14, and 3 plus 3 plus 8 is 14. All the other sums are unique; if it was one of those, then the formula *would* help. But because of this limitation—that knowing the formula doesn't lead directly to the answer—we know that it has to be one of those two sets."

"But that still doesn't tell us the final answer," said Lise. "Which of the two sets is correct?"

Reed smiled. "It's right there in the puzzle."

"Now *you* are being an ass."

"Fair enough," said Reed, and tapped the second line of the puzzle with his pencil. "In most codes, the key that brings it all together is usually something completely innocuous, that doesn't look like a clue at all."

"Their ... genders?" asked Lise.

"Close," said Reed. "The genders are a distraction; the real clue is in the way they're presented. 'The oldest is a boy, and the other two are girls.' Which means there's an oldest, which means it can't be the set of 6, 6, and 2."

Lise smiled. "Another limitation."

"Exactly," said Reed. "So the only answer left is 3, 3, and 8."

"So," said Lise, "we have two limitations for the confirmation code delivery system. One: it has to go out every day. And two: he can only send one letter at a time."

"Maybe three limitations," said Reed. "I'm still pretty sure that the system only goes one way."

"Pretty sure," said Lise, "but not completely."

"No."

"Then that is our next job," said Lise. "We will divide our labor and move on two fronts. I will talk to Bettina, to see what I can learn about Davis's daily routine. Does he go somewhere every day? Does he change the arrangement of flowers in his window? If he does something every day, she has to have noticed it. Your job is simpler: you have his ear and his trust, so use it to learn what you can."

The thrill of explaining the number puzzle evaporated like mist, and Reed felt the reality of the situation crashing back down on him. She was asking him to spy on an officer of the CIA.

"Lise, I ..." He didn't know how to finish that sentence.

"I know it's hard," she said. "I know it feels wrong. But you're the only one who can do this. You're the only one who can get close enough."

And then it hit him—the terrible question he'd felt circling him earlier, now lunging out of the shadows for the kill:

Was Lise only with him because of his access to Longshore and Davis?

Was their relationship a lie?

"Wally?"

He didn't answer. Instead his mind was focused on one single fact, looming so large and so abruptly in his mind that he couldn't think of anything else. He and Lise had only started seeing each other about six weeks ago. Two weeks after the Wall went up. One week after the transition from the old one-time pads to the new *Player Piano* system. Before that, it was just occasional flirting at office functions. Before that, he hadn't had anything of specific value to offer her. Now he did.

And she was taking it.

"Wally?" she said again, and her voice had become more playful. "You have Cryptographer Face again."

He didn't want to believe his own conclusion. There were any number of reasons she might have chosen to start seeing him, and most of them were completely innocent. But which was more likely? That an experienced, beautiful field agent would be attracted to the quiet cryptographer with no social skills? Or that she was using him to get information?

She was using him just like Operation Talon would try to use Frank. Get close, build trust, and then ask him to betray everything he stood for.

But no. The other explanation also worked: maybe she genuinely wanted to help find a Stasi double agent. Reed couldn't let his own lack of confidence accuse a woman who might be completely innocent. If he removed his poor self-image from the equation, the side that said to trust her held just as much evidence as the side that said to run away. Which side should he trust?

For now, he couldn't trust either. He needed to gather more information.

And that meant he needed to wait.

SUNDAY, OCTOBER 22, 1961
8:04 AM

West Berlin

REED PASSED the ghost stations in silence, too caught up in his fears about Lise, and Longshore, and everything else, to pay much attention to the gloom or the emptiness or the chance of being trapped. He made his transfer, walked to the Cabin, and tried to find some way of saying hello to the security guard without looking guilty.

The guard checked his ID, asked an idle question about the weather, and waved him through without comment.

Reed walked in the door, greeted Wagner with a polite hello, and then gave the same to Lise. She smiled back, signifying nothing but professional courtesy. Suddenly worried that someone might think he was talking to her too much, he then said hello to Frank, only to find that this was just as awkward. Reed was hiding a secret about him, too, and also about Wohlreich, and every time he addressed any of them worried that he was giving away vital information about those secrets. He saw Ostertag, sitting in the window, and practically ran to him as an oasis of guileless small talk.

"Guten morgen, Wallace." Ostertag took a pull on his

cigarette, and then blew the smoke out of the window in a smooth, gray cloud.

"Morgen," said Reed, and looked out the window. "How's your girlfriend?"

"Deep in the physical and spiritual cleansing that only the Eastern Arts can provide."

Reed scanned the park—not crowded, given the late October temperatures, but still dotted here and there with walkers and dog owners and groups of children kicking a ball. The yoga girl was standing in profile, her legs spread wide, one arm up and one arm forward. She projected an almost eerie stillness. "Virabhadrasana," said Ostertag, and smiled mischievously. "'The Warrior.'"

"Do you ever feel bad?" asked Reed. "Just ... watching her like this?"

"Bad?"

"Guilty," said Reed, and then clarified further. "Dirty."

"We are spies," said Ostertag. "Every second of every hour we are watching people, listening to people, ascribing to them motives and meanings so intimate it would make them blush to know that anyone was paying attention. My Aphrodite, at least, is doing what she does in public, where everyone can see. Which does not mean she that demands to be watched. Perhaps she simply likes the park, or finds that her energy flows more purely with her bare feet planted in dirt and grass. But it means that she is not *opposed* to being watched. She makes her choice actively. How many of our subjects can say the same?"

Reed frowned. "I suppose. But watched or not, she's probably opposed to whatever you're thinking about her."

Ostertag smiled again. "And now you have reached the limits of my redeemability." He blew another cloud of smoke into the air, and looked back into the park. "My explanations sound noble, but they only go so far."

Reed waited, standing by the window, watching the smoke

curl and dissipate, and when he didn't move away he realized that he wasn't just waiting, he was waiting for *something*. He was waiting for Bettina to poke her head around the door and tell him about another Longshore message.

He watched the door to her office, but she didn't appear.

"This one is called the Tadasana," said Ostertag, but Reed shook his head.

"I have work to do."

Reed walked to his desk, said good morning to Chuck and guten morgen to Gisela, and sat down to read his stack of daily reports. He finished, and Bettina didn't call for him, so he read them again, paying closer attention this time, forcing himself to think about new things—any things—and not about Longshore. There had been another skirmish by the Wall, though no one had been harmed. Another pair of refugees had crossed into West Berlin, in such a way that they were questioned by the West German police instead of disappearing into the city, and the Head Office had requested Lise and Chuck to read through their reports. Ostertag thought he had cracked part of the mystery behind Mother Goose, one of the Stasi's more mysterious numbers stations in the city, and wanted Reed to check his math. He set that one aside to work on later, and then sat and waited again.

Five minutes. Ten minutes. Still nothing new from Longshore.

He wanted to look at Lise to see what she was doing. Was she nervous? Was she staring at Bettina's doorway? He didn't dare to turn.

Bettina stepped into the room and walked toward him. He started gathering his pencils and paper, but she walked past him to the next desk, and smiled at Jannick Wohlreich.

"Do you have a moment? Chief Davis would like to see you."

The promotion. Of course. Reed watched Wohlreich

frown, stand, and follow Bettina into her office, toward Davis's beyond. This path led his eyes past Frank, who gave no sign that he noticed or cared.

Reed picked up the papers with Ostertag's notes on the Mother Goose numbers station. It was a statistical analysis of more than a year's worth of broadcast numbers, cross-checked against the letter frequency in English, German, Russian, and French. It was exactly the kind of thing Reed loved, but he couldn't concentrate. Where was the new message? Longshore could send them at any time, it was true, but they typically came in the early morning, and they almost never had a gap of two days between them. Was he trying to gain more information before he sent something? Was he trying to send it, but something was stopping him?

"Hey, Wally." Reed looked over to see Chuck standing up, holding a small stack of papers in his hands. "Can you join me in the back room? Lise, you too."

Reed frowned, not sure what this was about, but he and Lise followed Chuck into a filing room just off the main office. Chuck closed the door most of the way, keeping an eye on the gap, and spoke in a whisper.

"I think I've got something on the racing stable," he said. "I don't think anyone else knows about that part, so I'm keeping it just between us for now—in case there's a ... you know."

Lise nodded. Apparently Chuck had arrived at the same conclusion she had—that Longshore's current messages, and the secrecy around them, suggested the presence of a mole in the Cabin.

"There are only two racing stables that survived the war," said Chuck. "Only two big ones, anyway. And one of those is right here in the American sector."

"That's Mariendorf," said Lise. "My father used to go there."

"It's a great one," said Chuck. "I go all the time. But the

only reason I can do that is because it's on our side, and that means it's probably not the scene of a secret Stasi meeting with a KGB overseer. Or at least if it is, we're all very bad at our jobs. The other major horse track in town, though, is the Hoppegarten, which is technically just outside of town, but still within what I would call the Greater Municipal Area. And very much inside the cozy confines of the GDR."

"Is it still in use?" asked Lise. "Even a lot of places that survived the war are just sitting empty and abandoned."

"I went to a race there just a few days before the Wall," said Chuck. "It's about a forty-minute train ride from my apartment; if the Wall had gone up a couple of days earlier I'd have been trapped on the other side."

"They would have let you come back," said Reed. "You're American."

Lise looked at him, one eyebrow raised, and Reed frowned.

"They wouldn't have let him back?"

Lise shook her head.

"I'm an American in West Berlin," said Chuck. "That means I almost definitely work for the CIA or the military. They'd strap me to an interrogation chair and lose the key."

Reed swallowed. "Remind me never to cross the Wall, then."

Lise bit down on a laugh.

"Hoppegarten is not the only stable in the East," said Chuck, "but it's the biggest by far, and if Longshore is just casually referencing a rennstall like we're all supposed to know what it is, the odds are very good that he's talking about Hoppegarten."

Reed wondered if the Rennstall even had any meaning anymore. Was it just a restaurant, mentioned only to grab Lise's attention, and the entire Cabin was chasing an empty lead? How many resources were they wasting by refusing to share their secrets?

If the alternative was a Soviet invasion, it would all be worth it.

If.

"Do we have any agents who can look into it?" asked Lise. "There's only so much we can learn without actually visiting the location."

"Wohlreich has contacts on the other side," said Chuck. "It's never easy to get them a message, but he might be able to do something. We'll have to wait until he—speak of the devil."

Chuck had been keeping his eye on the crack in the door, and now he opened it, revealing the main room of the office. On the far wall the door to Davis's office creaked open, and Wohlreich emerged with a smile.

"Achtung," he said. "May I have your attention? Section Chief Gordon Davis has just asked me to serve as Section Sub-Chief of the Cabin. I will continue my ongoing duties as asset handler, while also helping to manage the office and increase productivity. This is a great honor, and I promise you all that I will serve humbly and professionally to make this listening station the best in Germany. Thank you!"

"That's weird," Chuck said.

"That he got promoted?" asked Reed.

"That he announced it himself." Chuck shrugged. "That's Wohlreich for you, I guess."

Harald Wagner stood, and walked to Wohlreich to shake his hand. "Glückwünsche."

"*Ja*," said Lise, nodding at him from across the room. "Glückwünsche, Jannick. You've earned this."

"Congratulations," said Reed, and the others in the office echoed the same. All but Frank, who furrowed his brow.

"Section Sub-Chief?" he asked. "I didn't know we had Sub-Chiefs."

"The Cabin has been under increased scrutiny from the Head Office," said Wohlreich. "Davis doesn't know why, but he suspects—and I agree with him—that we've been doing good work lately, and the leadership of the CIA and BND might want to duplicate our organizational system in other Sections. Because of that, I won't be changing anything, simply making sure that our existing systems function as efficiently as possible."

"Okay," said Frank, and nodded. "Okay. I guess that makes sense." He looked back at his work, and Reed couldn't help but watch him, waiting for the other shoe to drop. A few seconds later, it did. Frank began his career as a disgruntled underling with gusto. "I guess any organization that can execute that many people is a pretty good go-to source for efficiency."

"Excuse me?" Wohlreich was halfway to his desk, but stopped cold.

"Hmm?" Frank looked up, as if confused. "Did I say something?"

"I did not execute millions of people," Wohlreich protested.

"Of course not," said Frank. "I'm just saying that the people who trained you did, and by all accounts they were pretty damn good at it, and whatever ... organizational prowess made that possible must have rubbed off at some point." He looked at Chuck. "Did you know they found entire crates full of wedding rings in some of those death camps? Entire crates! You could just sift your hand through them—"

"Frank," said Ostertag, but Frank ignored him.

"I mean, to kill that many people, and dispose of all their bodies, and then still save all their stuff, is just impressive as hell is all I'm saying—"

"Frank!" Ostertag shouted, and Frank finally stopped.

Bettina smiled from her doorway, though it looked more strained than cheerful. "Chief Davis would like to announce that we are all invited to a celebratory meal at Richardhof, for lunch. He is buying."

The Cabin was silent for a moment, and then Frank

nodded again. "Good. Great. That sounds like fun." He looked back at his work. "Congratulations again, Jannick, that's great."

The rest of the morning passed like that: tense and quiet, and filled with uneasy looks. Reed tried not to make eye contact with anyone, but Chuck caught his eye once, with a look that meant ... what? Probably that he was worried. Reed couldn't argue with that. Who wouldn't be?

By the time lunch finally rolled around the mood had calmed, and Frank chatted amiably with Reed as they walked together to Richardhof, a *biergarten* that claimed to have been around since 1464. A lot of places in Germany were like that, but only some of them had survived the war. This neighborhood, called Neukölln, had survived much better than the actual city of Köln, which had lost everything but its cathedral, and that only survived because the Allied pilots had used it for navigation.

Reed tried not to think of the destruction—of life, of infrastructure, of history itself. Most people didn't. It was numbing, after too long, and all you could really do was move on. Europe had bars, like Richardhof, so old they'd been serving beer for two generations before the people drinking in them had gotten up and sailed across the sea and settled Reed's continent. The sense of time here was so different to him it felt alien. And it had all been wiped away.

Frank talked about baseball, his usual obsession, but the conversation felt different to Reed than usual. More determinedly cheerful, like Frank was trying to force it.

"So Whitey Ford goes out there," Frank was saying. "Game four—World Series!—and just blows them away. You have no idea. Strike after strike; you've never seen a pitcher this good. Reds didn't know what hit 'em."

They reached the antique building, and Reed held the door while his coworkers filed through it. Bettina had called ahead for a table, and Davis gestured to it. "Lunch is on me." He winked. "And so is the booze."

There was a general cheer from the officers as they all found seats, and the server began taking orders. Reed ordered maultaschen, which was basically German ravioli, and there was another round of laughter.

"It is not Easter," said Wohlreich.

"Maybe he is Schwäbisch," said Gisela with a smile.

"Are these just an Easter thing?" asked Reed. "They're wonderful, why would you only eat them at Easter?"

"And why would you only eat roast turkey at Thanksgiving?" asked Ostertag.

"We eat turkey all year," said Reed.

"Not roast turkey," said Chuck. "Not with dressing and gravy and cranberry sauce."

"Look," said Reed, "it's on the menu—" but Wohlreich only laughed and slapped him on the back.

"Order what you want," said Chuck. "In fact, you know what?" He looked at the server. "Maultaschen for me, too. I love those little bastards."

The others made their orders: schweinbraten and weisswurst and rouladen, rich meats and potato salad—the German kind, mixed with vinegar instead of mayonnaise, though Reed had never quite gotten used to it. The first round of beer appeared, and Davis offered a toast to Wohlreich, wishing him luck with his new job.

"Prost!" said the officers, and even Frank joined in. Alcohol was the great equalizer, and Davis knew what he was doing in presenting it as a peacemaker to soothe the Cabin's nerves. As the lunch wore on, though, Reed began to realize that Davis knew what he was doing in much darker ways. A lunch party gave Frank a chance to get more and more inebriated, raising the chances that he would say something more about Wohlreich's past, and bring the argument out into the public where other people could see it, hear it, and spread rumors about it.

"I'm thinking of getting a cat," said Gisela, cutting a bite of meat from the corner of her schweinbraten.

"Pass the wine, please," said Reed, and Gisela handed the bottle across the table.

"A cat?" asked Lise. "I love cats. What kind?"

"Orange," said Gisela. "It does not matter what breed, I just want a cat."

"I'm more of a dog person," said Frank. "Wine?"

Reed handed him the bottle, and took another bite of his salad. Too much vinegar.

"A dog is a simpleton," said Wohlreich. "A cat does not need you, or maybe even want you, and that is what makes them interesting."

"Wine," said Wagner.

Frank passed it toward him. "Hand this back when you're done. Okay, Harald? I need a little more."

Wagner took the wine and grunted.

"Do you build all of your relationships that way?" asked Ostertag, looking at Wohlreich with a sly grin. "With women, perhaps? You only love the ones that do not love you back?"

"A woman is not an animal," said Wohlreich.

"You are seeing the wrong ones," said Ostertag. Wagner glared at him, and passed the wine bottle back to Frank.

"Save some for the rest of us, huh, Frank?" Chuck held out his wine glass, wiggling it slightly in front of Frank's face. Frank poured him some, and then poured a little more himself.

"I had a dog when I was a boy," said Davis, setting down his fork. "And two cats. And two hundred head of cattle, though I only named one of them."

"You grew up on a farm?" asked Reed.

"Ranch," said Davis. "Wyoming."

"Please tell me that you named her Bessie," said Ostertag.

"Tulip," said Davis. "Some wine, Frank?"

Frank poured Davis a serving. Then another for himself.

"I did not know that people named cows," said Lise.

"Most people don't," said Davis. "I learned why when we slaughtered Tulip for steaks in the winter."

Lise's eyes went wide. "She was your pet."

Davis shrugged. "We were hungry."

"Pass the wine," said Wohlreich.

"We never had a cat when I was kid," said Frank, "but there was a neighborhood cat, like an alley cat, who came around from house to house and purred for food. I used to set out a little saucer of milk for her every night at dinner. Drove my mother nuts."

"The wine," said Wohlreich.

Frank reached across and poured him a tiny splash. "We had a name for it—all the neighborhood kids. We called it Moshe—"

"A little more," said Wohlreich, and suddenly Frank whirled on him, eyes fierce with irritation.

"What is it with you and the wine, huh?"

"You are the one who has drunk half the bottle," said Wohlreich.

"Oh, I'm sorry," said Frank, in a voice that sounded anything but. "Am I taking more than my share? Not a great start to the Wohlreich regime; I apologize." He reached out with the bottle and poured it into Wohlreich's glass, far more than was proper, filling the glass to the top until it curved up above the rim, jiggling slightly, held in place by nothing but a weak cohesive force.

"You are drunk," said Wohlreich.

Reed almost reached out, almost put his hand on Frank's shoulder, almost said "easy there, buddy, calm down." But he didn't. He had to let this happen.

"Believe it or not, there are some things you're still not in charge of," said Frank, and poured the dregs of the bottle into his own glass. "Sorry."

"Come on," said Chuck, filling in where Reed would not. "Everyone just take it easy, okay?"

Frank drained his entire glass, maintaining eye contact with Wohlreich the entire time.

"Frank," said Chuck, but Frank turned on him now, snapping out a question like a knife strike.

"How many of your family died in the war?"

"My ... uncle," said Chuck, taken by surprise. "Two of my cousins on the other side. My school teacher."

"Soldiers?"

"Every one."

"Then how can you sit here," said Frank, "and drink wine and talk about cats, with the same damn Nazis who killed them?"

"Mr. Schwartz," said Davis sharply.

"They've changed," said Chuck. "We have to do the same."

"Easy for us to say," said Frank, and pushed his chair back from the table. "We're the ones who lived."

He stood up and walked away.

Reed looked at his food, tapping it uncomfortably with his fork in the heavy silence that hung over the table. After a moment he looked up, and saw that most of the Cabin officers were doing the same, avoiding each other's eyes while they picked at their potato salad or peered into the corners of the room. Lise caught his eye, holding it for longer than Reed expected before looking away again.

Gisela was the first to speak. "You were only a child in the war," she said, looking at Wohlreich. "We all were."

"I was a Wehrmacht officer."

"Only because all the adults were dead," she said. "You were a boy of nineteen."

Wohlreich looked ready to speak again, but Davis spoke with an air of finality.

"We've all been people we didn't want to be. I assembled this team because I trust who you are today; who you were fifteen years ago doesn't matter."

Wohlreich closed his mouth, and they finished the meal in quiet contemplation.

Reed couldn't help but run his eyes across the other tables in the restaurant, wondering which of the other patrons had heard them, and what they thought, and if any of them had been eavesdropping on purpose, reporting to the Stasi for Operation Talon.

When they returned to the Cabin, Frank wasn't there, though he eventually arrived about forty minutes later. He smelled like he'd been drinking the entire time, but he didn't start any more arguments, and worked sullenly at his desk. Reed did his best to work as well, checking Ostertag's Mother Goose decryption numbers with his slide rule, making notes in the margins where he thought the figures diverged too widely from the conjectures Ostertag was attempting to draw. Most of it was sound, though, using a mathematical theory Reed had only read about and never used in practice, and—

"Mr. Reed!" said Bettina, loud in his ear.

Reed looked up, startled. "What? What's wrong? Did something happen?"

Ostertag laughed.

"I have been trying to get your attention," said Bettina, her cheeks coloring slightly. "You were very deep in your work, and I am sorry to interrupt."

Reed looked at the clock; it was nearly four. "Is everything okay?"

"A message just came in," said Bettina. "It's still coming, actually."

For all his nervous impatience in the morning, it now took Reed a moment to shift his mental gears and realize what Bettina was talking about. "A message. A Longshore message! Of course." He gathered his notepad and pencils and stood—stopping to arrange the other papers on his desk into some semblance of order —then picked up his notepad again and hurried after Bettina. Davis gave him the day's confirmation code—Q this time. Reed stood in front of the large reel-to-reel recorder, watching as it turned in circles. At the moment it was recording nothing; it responded to radio signals, lying dormant until it heard something, and then recording that frequency for several minutes to be sure it got it all. Since the actual message came in tiny bursts, each separated by a minute or more, most of the tapes were dead air.

An odd patch of static sounded softly on the speaker, here and gone almost before Reed knew it was there. He looked at Bettina. "Is our antenna broken?"

"I think that is the message," she said. "He's using the three-second option. I almost didn't recognize it as a message when the recorder first started going."

Reed looked back at the recorder again, silently spooling more empty tape from one reel to another. It made sense; the RT-3 Burst Encoder had a fast option, sending each cylinder in three seconds instead of eight. Longshore had never used that option before, but if he was sending this in the middle of the day, where he might be seen, he needed to be as fast as he could. Was he sending from home? From the restroom of a bar or restaurant? Holed up in the closet of a Stasi office building somewhere? Reed counted the seconds, imagining Longshore reading the code off a pad of paper and rapidly setting the sliders on the cylinder. At fifty-two seconds—remarkably fast, even for Longshore—another three-second burst croaked out of the speaker. At this rate it wasn't even discernible to the naked ear as Morse code: eight letters per second, with as many as five pulses each. He'd have to slow it down even more than usual to try to interpret it.

"That's the fourth burst," said Bettina.

Reed said nothing, listening intently and counting the seconds. Fifty-five seconds later the speaker squawked again, and after another fifty-eight seconds it squawked a sixth time. Reed kept counting, and held his breath when he reached the fifties. Fifty-eight, fifty-nine, sixty. No burst.

Sixty-five, seventy.

Eighty.

A hundred seconds.

A hundred and twenty. Two minutes with nothing.

"That's probably it," said Bettina.

"Probably," said Reed, but he let the machine run anyway. It would record for a full five minutes after the last signal it received, and he let it have the full time, not wanting to risk losing a burst if another came in while he was switching out the reels. The timer expired, and the recorder stopped, and still Reed watched it, listening and waiting.

"Mr. Reed?"

"Yes," said Reed, and picked up another reel. He took a deep breath, steeling himself to do it, and then switched the tapes as fast as he could, threading the new one through the machine as quickly as he could without doing it wrong. No more bursts.

Six bursts, he told himself. Standard message. 150 characters, down to 75 after decoding. He locked himself in the private room, set his loaded pistol on the table, and opened the safe. The next section of *Player Piano* was marked with a pencil:

it now, sir. Ten, fifteen minutes, I promise."
**Doctor Katharine Finch was his secretary, and
the o**

Reed scanned the rest of the paragraph, reading the next few lines: "and the only woman in the Ilium Works. Actually, she was more a symbol of rank than a real help, although she was useful as a stand-in when Paul was ill or took a notion to leave work early." Once again Reed wondered what the book was about. Why did the man have a doctor as his secretary? What was she a doctor of? He'd gathered from the first page that the Ilium Works was some kind of factory, so maybe she was an engineer? And a good one, apparently, if she was able to do her boss's job every time he couldn't be bothered to do it himself. The rest of the paragraph seemed to imply that the world had become so automated that even a job as a secretary was scarce; machines did everything. Maybe Lise was right, and this was the future, and he should study computers as she was.

He listened to the tape carefully, slowing it down and recording each dot and dash exactly. He listened to the recording a second time, double-checking his transcription, then triple-checking it just to be sure, then dove into the translation. Q. That was a good sign. O, P, T, A, L, O, N. Operation Talon. Everything was working smoothly.

What would be the sixth word? If Lise was right, it would be German, and another clue she could use to find Message 41. If Lise was a double agent, it might instead be a code phrase that her handler was using to send her instructions. And Reed was making sure the instructions were delivered straight to her; the thought made him sick. Or maybe Lise was innocent, and Davis was the double agent? Or anybody? He still wasn't sure what to make of Wagner, and Ostertag definitely had his quirks. Could Chuck be the traitor? An American? It wouldn't be the first time; Davis wouldn't be using Frank as bait if the Stasi didn't have a history of corrupting American citizens.

Maybe the Stasi had officers in the upper ranks of the CIA? How much did Reed really know about his superiors? A corrupt hiring officer in the CIA or BND could have filled the listening station with double agents. For all he knew he was the only person who *wasn't* a traitor.

Reed closed his eyes. These were his friends. Lise was his closest friend—the woman he loved, or thought he did. He didn't want to suspect any of them.

But what else could he do?

He concentrated on the message: OP Talon. Baker. Shandler. No, the S belonged to the previous word: *Baker's Handler.* CN, meaning codename, and then the sixth word: Weiss. "Operation Talon, Baker's handler codename Weiss." The sixth word was German, right on cue.

But ... something about it didn't sit right. What were the odds that the exact German word Longshore needed in order to pass his secret message to Lise just happened to be the codename for Baker's handler? Unless Longshore had known this all along, and had planned his messages around it.

Or Longshore was so highly placed in the Stasi that he could choose his own nicknames, and chose this one because he needed it to make his code work.

Or the entire message was a lie, and Longshore was making the whole thing up just so he could put his secret code in the sixth word slot.

Reed translated the rest of the message, and when he was done he sat there for several minutes, staring at the code, and the tape, and the door. And the gun. Should he tell the sixth word to Lise, as he'd promised? Should he even show it to Davis? He had no idea who to trust, or how to figure such a thing out. On the other hand, everyone knew he was in here. Everyone knew that a message had come in, and that he had decrypted it, and that any minute now he would open the door, walk into Davis's office, and show it to him. If he did anything else, he'd be breaking the law. If he refused to share the message he'd be branded a traitor—and rightly so—and locked away in a CIA cell. The wheels were in motion, and Reed had to move or be crushed.

He put his things away in the safe, holstered his pistol, and unlocked the door.

Wohlreich was discussing something with Davis. "Do you want me to come back later, sir?" Reed asked.

"Not at all," said Davis. "Come in. Close the door."

"With—" Reed looked at Wohlreich. "With Jannick inside?"

"Yes," said Davis. "He's Sub-Chief now, and we need another head in these meetings anyway. I've been catching him up on some of the details, and I'd like his thoughts on whatever Message 44 has to offer." He put an odd emphasis on the words 'some of,' and Reed got the hint that Wohlreich didn't know everything. He was certainly still in the dark about Frank's counter-op against Talon, and his own unwitting role in it. Reed wondered what else the man didn't know, and determined to say as little as possible, just in case.

Reed closed the door, locked it, and sat next to Wohlreich. He pulled the decoded message from his pocket, hesitated, and then handed it to Davis.

The Chief read the message in silence:

Q
OP Talon, Baker's Handler CN Weiss
Erich Gunter Anselm
GDR to demand ID at border entry
QQQQ

It was Reed's biggest fear, made explicit by Longshore: the East Germans were closing the border. By demanding ID they were breaking the Potsdam Agreement, and from there it was only a small step to a full military action.

The Cold War was about to heat up.

"Interesting," said Davis.

"Have you ever heard of the man he mentions?" asked Reed.

"I haven't."

"What is the name?" asked Wohlreich. "I can ask Gisela to look him up."

"Not yet," said Davis. "Let's ... No. I'll look into it myself. The fewer people who know the name, the better."

Reed nodded. There was no guarantee, after all, that Wohlreich himself wasn't the Stasi mole. Telling him the name of another Stasi contact might tip him off that they'd already discovered Talon.

"Should I leave?" Wohlreich looked visibly frustrated. "Whatever the contents of that message, you are clearly not comfortable sharing it with me."

"Not the first part, no," said Davis. "The second part I definitely want your thoughts on. Wally. You add all the spaces and punctuation yourself, correct?"

"I do," said Reed. "Is there a problem with it?"

"Only that I think you've overreached this time," said Davis, tapping the message. "You've put the name on a separate line. But if you group everything together, the meaning seems obvious." He showed Reed the words:

Baker's Handler, CN Weiss: Erich Gunter Anselm

"I'd considered that," said Reed, "but then I thought ..." Actually, he didn't know what he'd thought—he'd been distracted by the German word. But no; that was only partly true. Really he'd been distracted by Lise, and his ongoing indecision. Should he tell her? Should he not?

"What were you saying?" asked Davis.

"Nothing, sir."

"You're obviously concerned about something," said Davis. The Chief's eyes flicked to Wohlreich, then back to Reed. "Is there something about the ... other matter?"

"I should get back to my desk," grumbled Wohlreich.

"No," said Reed, "really, it's nothing. I guess I was just thinking that maybe ... maybe we should get the analysts in on this." There. He'd said it. If Davis agreed that showing the message to Lise was fine, then Reed didn't have to feel guilty about it.

"I don't want too many people involved," said Davis.

"Clearly," muttered Wohlreich.

Reed's heart sank. Now it was worse than before; Davis had directly ordered him not to share the message, or any words in it, with anyone else.

"But Chuck and Lise have already seen some of the related messages," he said.

"They've seen some, but there's no reason to show them everything," said Davis. "And you know why. For now, we're going to keep information limited to as few people as possible. Even among the three of us; there are things you know that Jannick doesn't, and vice versa. It's the only way to do this safely." Wohlreich looked at Reed, then back at Davis. "What is in the part of the message you *do* want to show me?"

"'GDR to demand ID at border entry,'" Davis quoted. "That's sobering news."

"It is," said Wohlreich. "Do they mean the diplomatic checkpoints? Dreilinden and Friedrichstrasse and those?"

"No one's allowed to cross the border anywhere else," said Reed, "so I assume it's at the checkpoints. But ... even that would be a violation of the Potsdam Agreement. Military and diplomatic officials are supposed to be able to travel freely in the city, even across sector borders. I mean, we're allegedly allies. The Soviet Union has been pushing the limits for years, but are they really going to push them this far? Turning their back on Potsdam would be the biggest change yet. Bigger than the Wall, maybe."

"The *Soviets* wouldn't dare," said Davis. "Or at least not if their fingerprints were on the orders. But if it's the GDR doing it, they could potentially get away with it. Russia's gone out of its way to brand the GDR as a distinct political entity, and maybe this is why. It's all been building toward a total closure of the border."

"Or maybe they are opening the border again," said Wohlreich, and Reed was shocked to hear a note of emotion in his voice. "Maybe they will demand ID because the people crossing will be civilians. Maybe the city is uniting again." He spoke with passion, and Reed realized that this rare show of emotion shouldn't shock him at all. Berlin was Jannick's city; he'd been born here, and had returned as soon as the war was over. He probably had family in East Berlin; almost everyone did. If there was even one glimmer of hope that the city might be reunited again, who wouldn't be emotional?

Which is why it pained Reed so much to have to argue against Wohlreich's theory. "Longshore chooses his words with precision. In this one he doesn't call it a border 'crossing,' he calls it a border 'entry.' He had enough room to say 'border crossing' or 'border traffic' or even 'open border,' but he said 'border entry.' People entering East Germany. It ... doesn't say anything about people coming out."

Wohlreich sighed. "I know. I knew before you said it. But every now and then, I allow myself to hope."

"Every step they take toward closing the border leads to only two possible explanations," said Davis. "One is that they're trying to keep their own people inside—East Germans

are fleeing in massive numbers, and the GDR is doing everything they can to stop it. But the other explanation worries me
even more. And they're not mutually exclusive; they might
both be true. Maybe the East Germans have given up on the
Potsdam Agreement completely. Maybe they're going to
declare the Soviet sector of Berlin to be a fully autonomous
nation, separate from the rest of the city, and cut off from our
ability to see what they're doing."

"They could be gathering troops," said Wohlreich.

"They could be," said Davis. "There's nowhere in the
world that the Soviet Union can get an army this close to vital
Western territory; cutting off our access could be a prelude to
invasion, to war, to who knows what military action." He
looked at Reed. "Longshore is one of the only agents the CIA
and BND still have over there. The only one, as far as I know,
actually inside of the Stasi. He's the one eye we'll have left if
they go through with this border closure, and that makes him
more vital than ever. We have to keep him safe—and that
means we have to—" He stopped abruptly. "Jannick, I believe
it's time to excuse you."

Wohlreich looked displeased, but Reed supposed the man
would rather leave than sit through another conversation full of
exclusions and veiled secrets.

"See what you can learn about this border issue," said
Davis. "Feel free to use anyone on the team you need; this is a
priority, and we want to know everything we can about it
before the GDR puts their plan into action."

"Understood," said Wohlreich, though he still walked out
in a cloud of wounded pride.

Reed closed and locked the door behind him, and Davis
lowered his voice.

"We need to protect Longshore," he said, "and that means
we have to find this double agent before he can discover our
secrets, give up Longshore's identity, and blind us completely."

Reed nodded. "I agree."

"Then find that mole," said Davis. "Or you'll be eating borscht for breakfast this time next week." He sighed, and looked back at the message. "I'll send word of this border business to Hogan and the State Department; a nice way to remind them, double agent or not, that we're a vital link in the intelligence chain, gathering intel nobody else can get. As for this stuff with Weiss ..." He frowned, staring at the words on the paper. "I want to know who I can trust, Wally. I can't run an intelligence office if I can't actually use anyone in it. So I'll figure out who Weiss is, where he is, and everything else we can learn without letting him know that we're watching. We'll keep the others in the dark until we have something to tell them that won't instantly give everything away."

"What about Frank?" asked Reed. "We're trusting him."

Davis pondered that for a moment, then nodded. "Yes, but not until after we find this Erich Gunter Anselm. If Anselm is the handler codenamed Weiss, Frank will have to interact with him anyway—and if Frank is already a mole, our triple agent op is already ruined. Anselm will be our litmus test for Frank: if he bolts, we'll know Frank tipped him off because he's the only one who knew about it."

"And nobody else," said Reed.

"Chuck and Lise have some of the other bits and pieces, but Erich Gunter Anselm is a whole new level of sensitive intel." Davis shook his head. "No one else in the office can know anything about this—about Talon, Baker, Weiss, none of it."

Reed felt himself deflate slightly. The ball was back in his court. If Lise was going to find out about the code word, it would have to be because he told her himself. In what was, now, a direct violation of orders.

Davis continued, "I wish there was some way to ask Longshore for clarification. For all I know we're on the wrong track completely—maybe Anselm isn't Weiss, and Longshore is pointing him out for some other reason. For all we know it's another hint about where to find Message 41. Does Anselm have it? But why would Longshore trust a stranger over us?" He closed his eyes, and pinched the bridge of his nose. "Maybe the next message will say more."

This, Reed realized, was the perfect opportunity to ask about the confirmation codes. How did Davis send them? How much, precisely, could be communicated through them? Lise had told him to ask, but he still wasn't sure how much he trusted her. He waffled, then forced himself to make a clear decision.

"What about the confirmation codes?"

"What about them?" asked Davis.

"Obviously you can communicate with Longshore some-how. Is there any way we could send a message that way?"

"It's only one letter at a time," said Davis. "Even if ..." He hesitated. "No, there's no way."

"Are you absolutely sure? This is my specialty, after all; maybe there's something I could—"

"The method I use is sensitive," said Davis. "I don't want to put anything at risk. If worse comes to worst, the method is on file in the State Department computers. So it won't die with me, but I'll have to die for anyone else to get it. Hogan won't give access to anyone but the Section Chief."

And if the Section Chief changed, Reed realized, it would be because Davis was dead.

And Wohlreich was now the next in line to replace him.

5:22 PM

West Berlin

REED WALKED to the train station with his head down, thinking. What should he tell Lise? He wanted to trust her, and a part of him knew that he'd be happier if he did. To open himself completely, to share everything, to tell himself that she was as innocent as he had always believed her to be. To tell himself, perhaps most important of all, that her feelings for him were pure. That their relationship was motivated by mutual interest, and not the convenience of espionage.

Another part of him, quiet and insidious, told him that he was a fool.

He rode the C1 train from Neukölln Rathaus to Hermannplatz, and transferred to the D. He sat in a bench near the right-hand window, and settled in for the ride. Three stops before the ghost stations.

The first stop was Schönleinstrasse, where a handful of new passengers trickled in. Reed ignored them, but one of them —a woman—sat behind him on the opposite bench, and whispered softly.

"Get off at Kottbusser." Reed recognized Lise's voice instantly. "Take the B2 to Warschauer."

Reed forced himself not to turn around. He and Lise had never contacted each other this close to the Cabin, and he didn't know who else might be watching. He stared forward, pretending not to hear, and wondered. What did she want now? He debated simply ignoring her, but decided the least he could do was to hear her out. Taking a different train was, in itself, still perfectly allowable.

Kottbusser Tor was the very next station, and when the train pulled to a stop he stood up, turned, and followed the crowd out onto the platform. Most of the passengers exited here—with so many stations closed, this was the last transfer before the end of the line—and he lost sight of Lise almost immediately. He followed the signs for the B2, and stood on the platform marked "Richtung Warschauer." Someone had scrawled over it in sloppy black paint, changing it to "Richtung CCCP." There were a handful of other riders waiting with him, but he couldn't see Lise.

Maybe Lise is Weiss, he told himself. *Maybe I'm Baker, and our whole relationship has been Operation Talon. She's been bending me, bit by bit, toward the Stasi, and now she thinks I'm ready to meet her leaders.* The thought left him feeling surprisingly peaceful; if this was Talon, then going along with it just made him a triple agent, like Frank was. He could talk to Lise, learn what he could, and report back to Davis with a clear conscience.

The B2 came, half-full of people, and he stepped in and grabbed a strap on the top bar. The train rumbled through two more stations, but at the second one, Schlesiches Tor, it emptied completely. Reed stood alone, holding the strap in an empty train, and the conductor walked by.

"Letzter halt," he said.

Reed frowned. "Last stop? What about Warschauer?"

"It is on the other side of the Spree," said the conductor in broken English. "A ghost station. We do not go there."

Reed stepped off onto the now-empty platform, and walked to the stairs. This station was raised instead of underground, and he caught a brief glimpse of the Spree River as he passed the windows. Lise appeared as if out of nowhere, and fell into step with him as he walked down the stairs to the street.

"Follow me," she said. "It's a short walk."

"Where?"

"Two blocks up. Number 10, Köpernicker Strasse."

Reed nodded. Not a secret meeting with the Stasi, then, unless Lise and Davis were in it together. They exited the train station, and Reed could see to the northeast a small park, and beyond it a wide, double-decker bridge that crossed the Spree river, bristling with regal arches and medieval towers. It was only about a block away, close enough for Reed to see the barriers that had gone up at the edge of it, barring anyone from crossing.

Reed nodded toward it. "Another piece of history that managed to survive the war."

"The Oberbaum Bridge?"

"That's the most gothic piece of architecture I've seen here yet."

"It is a lie," said Lise. "The bridge is barely sixty-five years old." She turned away, and led him to the left.

Reed quickened his pace to catch up. "So, um. Davis wouldn't tell me about the confirmation codes." He supposed he could tell her that much, at least, and it would earn some trust to tell her that he'd tried.

Lise nodded. "That is fine. I think I may have found a clue. I talked to Bettina. She is an angel, and smart as an owl, but she is only the secretary so people ignore her. She was happy to chat with me. I told her about you. Not by name, obviously, I just said I had a boyfriend, and gossiped a bit about all the annoying little things he does. How you never wash your dishes until you do not have any clean ones left; just little things. Girl talk. Bettina says she does not have a boyfriend—though I think she does, and just didn't want to tell me—but she did have quite a bit to say about Gordon Davis. 'Like taking care of a child,' she says. For example, did you know that he calls his laundry lady every day?"

"Is that so strange?" asked Reed. "Even I have a laundry lady. What single man in the CIA doesn't?"

"Maybe," said Lise, "but what single man generates so many dirty clothes that he needs his laundry done every day?"

"Good point," said Reed. "A lover, then?"

"Men with secret lovers don't call them every day from work," said Lise. "And men with no secrets do not pretend their lovers are laundresses." She stopped in front of an old apartment building. "He is not hiding his relationship with the woman, but she is obviously doing more than laundry. So he is definitely hiding *something*."

Reed looked at the number on the building: 10, Köpernicker Strasse. "You think he's sending her the confirmation codes, and she's passing them on to Longshore?"

"I think it is likely, yes," said Lise, and opened the wrought iron gate to the building's inner courtyard. "She lives in number 3512. Let us see if we can find her."

They walked into the courtyard, and then through an arch at the back that led into a smaller courtyard, surrounded by a tall ring of walls and windows above them. They followed the next arch to a third courtyard, then slipped into a side door and climbed five flights of stairs. Apartment 3512 looked identical to every other door. Lise straightened her jacket and knocked on the door.

An old German woman answered, gruff and impatient: "Gruss Gott."

"Hallo," said Lise, and proceeded to tell her in lilting,

almost musical German that they were new in the neighborhood, and someone had mentioned that she washed laundry. The old woman furrowed her brow at this, obviously angry, and demanded to know who.

Lise described someone generic, brushing it off as no big deal, but the woman only grew more agitated: "Ich mache keine Wäsche," she kept repeating, over and over. She didn't do laundry.

This made Reed nervous. What if she really wasn't a laundry lady at all? Two people showing up and asking about what was supposed to be only a cover story would look incredibly suspicious.

He looked past her to a window beyond, seeing a small apartment balcony and what was very clearly a clothesline filled with shirts. He didn't have time to point it out before the old woman closed her door. He could hear her slide the latch closed to lock it.

"Was she just grumpy, or was she lying to us?" Reed asked.

"Both," said Lise. "I asked around before we came here. She is definitely known as a laundry woman. But she certainly didn't want to talk about it with us." She started walking slowly back to the stairs. "Maybe there is a message in the clothing itself. Maybe he hides something in the pockets, or writes it under the collar, and she collects it that way. We could try to intercept the handoff when she gets them from Davis—"

"Or we could just try to look at them here," said Reed, not eager to raise the stakes even further by stealing. "I didn't get a good look at the shirts, but they're right outside."

Lise paused, considering it. "Maybe can talk our way onto the balcony above her," she said, and started going up the stairs instead of down.

"No good," said Reed, and Lise stopped. "The clothesline was too far back from the edge. The only way to get a clear view would be from the—oh." He froze, and then closed his eyes as the realization hit him. "Oh my word."

"The river," said Lise, picking up instantly on the same line of thought. "The only clear view of that laundry line is from the other side of the river—in East Berlin."

"It's a visual code," said Reed. "The two sides of the city can't talk to each other but we can see everything. She could write her message on a sign if she wanted, and just let him read it."

"It's got to be more subtle than that," said Lise, and started back down the stairs. "Maybe we can see her balcony from the courtyard."

They reached the ground level, and stepped out into the wide-open space at the base of the building. Beyond them was the river, at least a hundred yards across, and on the far side was another open space.

"Train tracks," said Lise, staring across the water, and then she pointed to a large building slightly to the left. "That is the Ostbahnhof—one of the biggest train stations in East Berlin. A hundred trains pass through there in a day, maybe a thousand, and any passenger on any one of them could see these balconies."

"Then whatever the code is, it's got to be big," said Reed. "Big enough to see from all the way over there. If Longshore pulled out binoculars every time he rode the train, he'd look far too suspicious." He turned and looked up at the side of the apartment, seeing row after row of windows and balconies. He backed up, all the way to the edge of the courtyard, where a thin iron railing stopped him falling straight into the water. He looked down; the building's foundations had been built directly into the river. He looked up, counted the floors, and identified the exact balcony of Davis's mysterious laundress. A line of white clothing billowed slightly in the breeze.

"Even the trousers are white," said Lise, staring with him. "I have never seen Davis wear white trousers."

"You sneaky bastard," Reed muttered, staring at the clothes. "Those aren't Davis's actual clothes, they're Morse code. Look at it: shirt, shirt, trousers, shirt. Dash dash dot dash."

"That is ... Q," said Lise, frowning as she recalled her Morse. "What was today's confirmation code?"

"Q," said Reed. "I suppose it's possible the dots and dashes could be reversed, but that's today's code, and that's too big of a coincidence to ignore." He looked at his watch: 6:27 PM. "If we hang around, we can be here when she changes it to tomorrow's code. How consistent is Davis in the timing of the calls? Every night at seven?"

"Bettina didn't say," said Lise.

Reed looked around, and found a row of benches. "Do you have any other plans?"

"I can think of nothing I'd rather do," said Lise, smiling slightly. They sat on one of the benches as if they were nothing more than two lovers on a date. They looked out across the water, huddled together in the October chill, and only occasionally glanced up to see if the code had changed. Reed watched East Berlin with quiet fascination: so similar to West Berlin that they looked, from a distance, completely indistinguishable. The same people, the same styles, the same habits. They weren't sister cities but a single organism, cleaved in half and wincing from the pain of it, like the endless ache of a phantom limb.

The more he looked, though, the more he saw evidence of one major, glaring difference: Grenzers. The border troops were everywhere, watching for runaways.

Or planning out avenues of attack.

Seven o'clock came and went without a change in the code. Seven thirty. Other people came and went, watching the city or murmuring softly. By eight it was almost too dark to see, but most of the windows had lights inside, including 3512. *You could use lights to pass Morse code as well,* Reed thought idly. *If you had enough of them in a row. Five, so you could do numbers as well as letters. But no, because turning lights on and off wouldn't be enough. You'd need three states: dot, dash, and nothing. If you can't distinguish a signal from an empty space it doesn't work—*

"I am hungry," said Lise.

Reed looked at his watch, barely visible in the moonlight. "Eight ... nineteen. Wow." He looked back up at the clothesline, but it still said Q. "You want to give up? We might be wrong about all of this."

"No," said Lise, standing up. "Stay and watch. I will get us something."

"It's dark," said Reed, standing with her. "Are you sure you're safe?"

She gave him a disappointed smirk, and he remembered how easily she'd disarmed him the other night. She was a trained field agent; she'd be fine. He sat down again, still watching, and at eight thirty Lise returned with a pair of sausages in thick, crusty rolls. She held them out, one in each hand.

"Weisswurst or bratwurst?"

"Weiss," said Reed, struck by the sudden memory of Message 44. "So take it then," said Lise, holding it toward him. He took the sausage from her, smelling the mix of pork and sweet mustard, but didn't take a bite. He wanted to tell her about Longshore's latest code word. Either she was innocent, or he could play the triple agent, like Frank. Either way, telling her could earn her trust, and give Reed more information to work with.

He made his decision.

He gestured with the weisswurst. "That was the sixth word today: Weiss."

"So we were right," said Lise, covering her mouth as she

chewed. "The sixth word is always German, and that must mean something. If Longshore is my old partner Mercury, then this is his way of telling me where to find Message 41. In a dead drop, I assumed, but ..." She shook her head. "We had three, maybe four different dead drops that could conceivably be called 'white.' He needs to send us another clue to help narrow it down."

"Can't we just check them all?" asked Reed.

"We will be lucky if we can check any," said Lise, and pointed at the lights across the water. "They're over there."

Reed took a bite of his sausage, and thought about the Wall.

Nearly forty-five minutes later, he glanced up to see someone rearranging the clothesline.

"Kind of late for laundry," he said.

"Kind of late for Davis to be calling from the office," said Lise.

The old woman worked swiftly in the light from her windows, but all she did was take down a single shirt: the one farthest to the left. She went inside and closed the sliding door, but left the lights on.

"Dash dot dash," said Reed. "That's K. Or R if I have it backwards."

"Then tomorrow we wait for a Longshore message," said Lise. "If the confirmation code is a K or an R, we will know we have found Davis's system."

"For all the good that does us," said Reed. "We still can't use it to talk to Longshore, and there's no way he can use it to talk back to us."

"All information is useful," said Lise, standing up. "Even if we don't know how yet."

They walked out to the street, and from there back to the train station. Reed stopped in a pool of shadows, away from any streetlamps, and pulled Lise in close for a kiss. She kissed him back eagerly, her tongue brushing gently at his lips, and then pulled away.

"I cannot come home with you tonight," she said.

"I know."

She kissed him again, and then they stepped away from each other. He went into the train station and she disappeared into the shadows. Reed rode the B2 back to Kottbusser Tor, and transferred to the D. The train was practically empty as he passed through the ghost stations, and he shivered involuntarily at the sepulchral feeling of it. He got out at Voltastrasse, walked home, and heard his phone ringing.

"What?" He checked his watch; it was nearly 10:30 PM.

The phone rang again, and he fumbled with his key to get in. He raced across the living room and picked up the receiver just in time.

"Hello?"

"Damn it, Reed, where the hell have you been?" It was Chief Davis, practically shouting into the phone.

"I was ... on a date," said Reed, scrambling to find his bearings. "What's going on?"

"It's the checkpoints, Wally, just like Longshore told us. They stopped Allan Lightner at the border—the damn Chief of Mission—and turned him back. Kennedy's screaming, the State Department's barely keeping their heads on, and General Clay sent a whole damn military parade through Checkpoint Charlie just to prove we couldn't be bullied. And you're out shtupping some German girl in a beer garden bathroom!"

"I wasn't—I didn't know!" shouted Reed. "I didn't hear anything about this! I'm here now, though. What do you need me to do?"

"I don't know if there's anything you *can* do," said Davis, "I'm just trying to find everyone in the Cabin and make sure we're all alive." He paused, just for a second, and Reed knew exactly what that pause meant: Reed had disappeared in the middle of a crisis, and now Davis was suspicious. "Where were you?"

Reed told the half-truth: "I was on a date."

"So you said. Where?"

"Do you think I was talking to the Stasi, Chief?"

"I think it shouldn't be this hard for you to tell me where you were tonight."

"It was an Italian restaurant," said Reed, and said the first name that popped into his head. "The Kalamata."

"That's Greek."

"I ordered pasta."

"What was the girl's name?"

"Ana."

"Last name."

"For Pete's sake, Chief—"

"Last name!"

"Gorman," said Reed. It was the name of his landlord. He spun out more details, lying as fast as he could, listening to the words coalesce from nothing on his lips like sugar in a cotton candy machine. "Ana Gorman. She's ... a little young for me, honestly, barely twenty years old, so I didn't want to tell you—"

"Damn it, Wally." Reed heard Davis breathing, half a gasp and half a sigh. "I'm sorry, Wally. You know I trust you."

"It's ... a hard time," said Reed, wincing at the blandness of his own words. "It's okay."

"Have you heard from Lise?" asked Davis. Reed tensed, but of course Davis would have been trying to reach her, too, and wouldn't have been able to. There was no reason for anyone to suspect she and Reed had been together.

"No, sir," said Reed. "Is she gone, too?"

"And Harald Wagner."

Reed shook his head, gritting his teeth, cursing himself for lying to his Chief but having no other way to get out of this. "Lise has a boyfriend. She might be there."

"You're supposed to be following her."

"Her boyfriend is clean," said Reed, trying to think faster than he spoke. "When she's with him she's fine."

"You don't know that—"

"I can't just ... live under her bed," snapped Reed. "If you want twenty-four-hour surveillance we need a whole team, not just me." He shook his head at his own outburst, knowing that he'd just made several bluffs stacked on top of each other, and praying that Davis didn't call any of them.

The silence on the phone dragged on, far longer than Reed was comfortable with.

"I know," said Davis at last. He paused again, then: "What about Harald?"

"I ... well, I told you before: I don't know him well."

"Nobody does," said Davis, and paused, but if he was going to say anything else about Harald he decided against it. "Keep your ears up and your eyes open—and your bloody gun loaded, for all the good it'll do you. We're on the brink of war, and you saw how the last war ended. We don't shoot bullets anymore, Wally. We drop atomic bombs."

MONDAY, OCTOBER 23, 1961
7:00 AM

East Berlin

THE TRAIN STOPPED.

Reed jerked forward, nearly falling off his seat as the train lurched to a sudden halt. The other passengers did the same. "Scheisse," somebody muttered.

They were halfway between two ghost stations, in an unlit tunnel. Reed looked out the window, seeing the dull gray wall barely a foot or two away.

"Was ist passiert?" asked a man by the door.

"I don't know," said Reed, forgetting in his shock that he should answer in German.

"You are American?" asked the man. He wore a blue suit with a shabby brown hat.

"Yeah."

"They closed the border last night," said a woman across the aisle. "Are we trapped?"

"My brother was trapped," said another man. He wore a pair of coveralls. "He was out late drinking with his friends when the Wall went up. They won't let him come back."

Another woman wailed.

"We're not ... we're not trapped," said Reed, trying to sound more certain than he felt. "They blocked one diplomat at the border and it almost started a war. They wouldn't dare block an entire train car full of people."

"He is an American," muttered a man in the back, and then raised his voice so that everyone could hear him. "He is probably military. He is probably why they stopped the train."

"I'm not with the military," said Reed, "and I'm not a target. I'm a businessman, just like all of you." It was the CIA's standard line, though Reed felt completely transparent as he said it.

"Our city is not a battleground for your pissing contest," the man snapped.

The door at the front of the train car opened, and a man from the next car relayed a message from the driver: there was a problem with the track, and they had to wait.

"See?" said Reed, trying to convince himself as much as anybody else. "It's nothing sinister."

The man in the doorway looked at him, then looked back at the Germans, and told them to pass the message to the next car. He started to close the door again, but Reed stood up.

"Wait!" He was too flustered to think in German. "What does the conductor say? Der Fahrer? Do we just wait here? Can we walk out?"

"This section of track connects to Alexanderplatz," said the man in the hat. "Four other train lines intersect with it. We would be run over and killed."

"Back the other way then," said the woman. "No one uses that track but the D Train."

"It's miles," said Reed.

"You wouldn't walk miles to find freedom?" demanded the man in the back.

"The driver says we need to stay calm and wait," said the man in the doorway. "Workers are coming to fix it. Tell the other cars." He closed the door, and Reed and the other passengers looked at each other.

No one moved. Finally, the man in the coveralls grumbled, and moved toward the back of the train car. "I will do it." He forced the door open, and relayed the message to the next group of people.

"We should get out and walk," said the woman. "Back to Voltastrasse; it is better than waiting here."

"That's miles," Reed repeated, "through pitch black tunnels and three ghost stations. And they're patrolled by the GDR. If we stay here they know we're West German, but if they catch you out in the tunnels they might think you're a runner, trying to escape from the East."

"They could do the same to us here," said an older man. "They could collect us all for processing, and take us to ask questions, and then never give us back. Political hostages."

"We don't know that," said the man in the hat.

"We don't know who is coming for us, either," said the angry man, speaking loudly as he walked toward them. "Workers, he says. Are they *our* workers? Would they let West German workers into East German tunnels? This close to Alexanderplatz, never!"

"This close to Alexanderplatz," said Reed, "an obstacle on the tracks will affect dozens of trains. They'll fix it in a couple of minutes at most."

"Unless the obstacle only affects our track," said the woman. "If we are not allowed to fix it, and they do not have to fix it, we could be here for hours."

The man in the coveralls came back. "The passengers in the next wagon are even more nervous than we are."

The old man snorted. "The man from the front car probably said the same thing about us."

"How long do we wait?" asked the woman. "I am willing,

but for how long? Ten minutes? Thirty minutes? Do we sit here for an hour before we do something?"

The door at the front of the car opened again, but this time it was the conductor himself. "Achtung!" he said loudly, and made an announcement in tense, fearful German. He had received an explanation on the radio:

The delay was being caused by a body on the tracks.

The passengers gasped.

The conductor continued, walking the length of the car as he urged them to be patient and wait for help. He reached the back of the car and started working on the door; the man in the hat started to speak, but the conductor stopped him. "Keine Fragen." He opened the door and stepped into the next car. "Achtung!" The door closed behind him.

"A body on the tracks," said the woman.

"A refugee, maybe," said the angry man. "Someone tried to flee to the West." He looked blankly at the floor, then shot Reed a furious scowl. "One oppressor for another." He turned and stalked back to his seat.

Nobody asked about getting out after that.

The passengers waited in silence, checking their watches and staring at the floors or the windows or the doors. The conductor had gone back to the front of the train, but the look on his face warned any further questions away. Reed closed his eyes, controlling his breathing, feeling the walls and the tunnel and the full weight of the city—of the entire GDR and the Soviet Union—pressing in on him like the ruins of an earthquake. He felt trapped and short of breath.

"Stop panting," said the man in the coveralls. "We have plenty of air; you will make yourself sick." Reed slowed his breath further.

The conductor announced that he was turning off the lights to save power, and the train was plunged into blackness. Minutes ticked away into nothing.

How will it come, when it comes? Reed found himself looking at the windows and the doors, expecting at any minute to see Stasi officers appear in the glass, shining flashlights in their faces and hauling them to the surface, to some interrogation where they could be debriefed and deprogrammed and disappeared. The other passengers, barely more than shadows in the darkness, kept looking at him, probably still thinking that this was somehow his fault, or that his status as an American would get him special treatment they wouldn't receive. And they were right; the Germans would eventually, probably, get to go home. As soon as they discovered Reed was a CIA spy, they'd throw him into the deepest hole they had.

A light flickered through the window, distant but shocking after so long in the dark. Reed's heart quickened, and he gripped the bar tightly. Was this it? Were they coming?

The lights in the train car came back on, one by one, humming and buzzing as they struggled awake. Reed looked at the doors, both at the ends of the car and on the sides, leading out into the tunnel, but nobody opened them.

Abruptly the train lurched forward; once, twice, three times, building up speed. The woman across the aisle closed her eyes and started praying.

Reed waited until they'd passed through Alexanderplatz—until he recognized that they were still in the right tunnel, instead of rerouted into some East German detour—before finally closing his eyes and relaxing. The train pulled into Moritzplatz, the first stop after the ghost stations, and as soon as the doors opened the passengers poured out like water from a broken bowl, spilling into the station and rushing upstairs to air and light and freedom. The walk from here to the Cabin was long, but Reed didn't care. He sat on a bench, quivering, then bought a coffee and drank it in a single, gulping pull. His hands were shaking.

He found a bakery, gripped the counter, and flagged down one of the clerks.

"Ja?"

"Telefon?" The clerk shook his head. "Es gibt kein telefon."

"Look," said Reed, and pulled out his American ID. "I'm an American officer, working with the State Department. Let me use your phone, now."

The clerk paled, but waved him behind the counter and into the back room. The heat in the kitchen was oppressive, but the phone was in a side office, and Reed followed the clerk gratefully and dialed Davis's number as fast as he could.

"Hallo," said Bettina, and gave the name of their false corporate facade: "Schultz Fabrik."

"Bettina, it's me," said Reed. "Give me Davis."

"We heard about the train," said Bettina. "Ein moment."

The phone clicked, then clicked again, and Davis growled on the other end. "You can't catch a break, can you Reed?"

"You heard about the train?"

"Body on the tracks," said Davis. "We think it was a runner. Two cars got stuck in there. We figured you had to be on one of them."

Reed closed his eyes. "Scared me to death."

"Where are you?"

"Moritzplatz," said Reed. "I can get to you in ... half an hour, maybe."

"Take a taxi," said Davis. "We need you here now."

Reed opened his eyes, startled. "Another Longshore message? What's the confirmation code?"

"Easy," said Davis, "this isn't even a secure line. There's nothing new from our friend, but we've found ... someone. I can't say who. I want you here *now*."

"Understood," said Reed. *Was it Tsyganov? The mole?* "See you soon." He hung up the phone, and shivered again. The adrenaline rush from escaping the tunnel was starting to crash, and he needed food. He walked back to the front, fairly certain that the clerk had been listening to the conversation, but too shaken to care. He gave the man a mark for a bag full of brötchen, and ordered another coffee from the cafe next door while he tried to flag down a taxi. The cab came before the coffee, and he made it wait, one foot in the open door, until the waiter brought his order in a thick paper cup. He gave the man another mark, not bothering to wait for change, and collapsed in the back seat, not even drinking his coffee, just letting it warm his hands.

It felt like the world was falling apart.

The cab let him out at the Cabin, right next to the Wall. A Grenzer on the Eastern side watched him get out, pay, and hurry into the building. Reed finished his coffee in the elevator, showed his badge to the guard, and was greeted by a chorus of voices when he walked into the office.

"Wally!" said Frank.

"Mr. Reed!" said Ostertag.

"I am glad you made it," said Wohlreich. "That must have been unsettling."

"That's an understatement," said Reed.

Gisela grabbed him in a hug, and then Lise as well—no more personal or intimate than was appropriate for an office. "I am glad you are safe."

"Thanks," said Reed, and set his briefcase and his bag of bread on his desk. "If anybody wants a piece of bread, I, um ... thought I was buying scones."

"Wally!" said Davis from his office. "You're here. Frank, bring him in, and let's have our meeting."

Reed was still trying to find his feet after the whirlwind race through the city, but Frank took him by the shoulder and led him into the office. Davis locked the door and sat.

"We've found Anselm," said Davis.

"Anselm! How do you know?" Reed asked.

"He was at Richardhof," said Frank. "He had lunch there today."

"Lunch?" asked Reed. "But it's barely ..." He checked his watch, and then checked it again against the clock on Davis's wall. "It's one in the afternoon."

Frank smirked. "Time flies when you're trapped in a communist subway tunnel."

"I found Anselm last night," said Davis. "This is the best photo I managed to take." He slid a surveillance photo across the desk, and Reed studied the man in it—about his age, about his height, with blond hair and a broad German face. He looked familiar. "Then today I went to lunch at Richardhof, and I saw him again, right there at the bar. The waitress treated him like a regular; she knew his name and his 'usual.' Richard-hof, Wally—at least one person from this office is in there almost every single day. I've probably seen him a dozen times or more in the background of my memory, and just never thought anything of it."

"That's ..." Reed nodded. "Definitely suspicious."

"I guarantee he's watching us, looking for a target to recruit," said Frank.

"Anselm lives in a neighborhood called Spandau," said Davis, "in the British sector. He works here in Neukölln, though, in an advertising office, so he is perfectly placed to keep an eye on the Cabin."

It sounded suspicious, but Reed tried not to jump to conclusions. "If he works nearby, he could have any number of completely innocent reasons to be a regular at Richardhof."

"Normally, yes," said Davis. "But when a man gets mentioned as a Stasi agent in a secret communique from one of our own spies, I'm a lot less likely to hand out benefits of doubts. Even if by some miracle Anselm is not watching us, he's in a prime position to do so, and we will treat him as a suspect until we prove that he is not one. We are officially declaring

Erich Gunter Anselm to be the Stasi operative Agent Weiss. I left the restaurant immediately, and came back to brief Frank."

"Anselm has lived in his current residence for almost ten years," said Frank, looking at a thin dossier. "He has a wife and six-year-old daughter. My guess is that the Stasi converted him sometime in the last few years, though in theory it's possible that they've had him placed as a sleeper agent for much longer."

"This is ... all good intel," said Reed, shaking his head. "But ... why am I in this meeting? You've got research, surveillance—why a cryptographer?"

"Because a longtime agent on this side of the Wall is in the same situation as Longshore on the other side," said Davis. "He's communicating, either in or out, and given what we know about Operation Talon I have to assume it's both. I want to know what he's saying and how he's saying it."

"I'm working on a way to grab his garbage," said Frank. "He's probably more careful than that, but you never know when he might accidentally throw away a bit of code on a piece of scratch paper or something. But the main communication—"

"—will be over the radio," finished Reed. "You're thinking that he might be running one of the numbers stations here in the city, or that his handlers are."

"Precisely," said Davis. "I know Ostertag is already working on the numbers stations, but I don't want to expand this team any more than I have to, so: now you're both working on them."

"I'm already reviewing his numbers on Mother Goose," said Reed. "I can get up to speed on the others pretty quickly."

"Mother Goose?" asked Frank.

"Some of the numbers stations use Morse," said Reed, "but others just read the numbers into a microphone and broadcast across the city. The numbers station designated 2377 is one of those, and he begins each broadcast by reading a nursery rhyme. And since Mother Goose is more memorable than 2377, it stuck."

"American accent, or German?"

"British," said Reed. "Our friends in the British sector say that it sounds most like the Manchester accent, though with enough of a hitch in it that it might be a foreign speaker who just lived there for a while."

"Don't take the job *away* from Ostertag, Wally," said Davis, "but stay involved with it. I'll let him know to give you a full rundown on the project, but first gather everyone in the Cabin. It's time for another party."

Frank frowned. "We're in the middle of a crisis—and not just this triple agent problem. The border guards at Checkpoint Charlie are practically at each other's throats. You've got the whole office working to figure out if this is just GDR idiocy or if the Soviet Union is trying to orchestrate a war. This is hardly the time for—"

"A party," said Davis, "at Richardhof. If we go there now, Anselm will be just finishing his lunch, and if he suddenly finds an excuse to stick around for another hour or so, well, that's all the more proof that he's watching us. I consider that a valuable use of our time. We can work on the border issue when we get back."

"Well," Frank said, "I guess I know what my part in this is supposed to be." He took a slow breath, then shrugged. "Time to go alienate all my friends."

West Berlin

"AND THAT," said Gisela, pointing with her fork, "is how you get into a closed archive."

Lise laughed, covering her mouth with her hand, and Reed chuckled along with her, shaking his head.

"That's incredible. And they actually let you in?"

"What else were they going to do?" asked Gisela. "I had the birds right there in front of them—one each hand, like this." She held out her hands, miming a grip on two fat, green parrots. Lise started laughing all over again. "They didn't want to take them, and they didn't want me to leave them right there on the floor, either, so they had to let me in."

Reed grinned, and took another bite of his lunch: schnitzel with noodles, just like in the song.

"What I don't understand," said Ostertag, "is why they let you in through the door in the first place."

"I think it short-circuited their brains," said Gisela. "A strange woman barging through the door of the library's special archive, holding a parrot in each hand and screaming like a lunatic, and they had no idea what to do. Is she dangerous? Is she crazy? Should I stop her, or help her, or—wait! Are those *birds* in her hands? Bzzzt! Short circuit."

Reed shot a glance across the restaurant, catching a brief glimpse of Erich Gunter Anselm at the bar, nursing a beer. He didn't look like he was watching them, but he'd been on that same beer for half an hour. He was definitely listening in on somebody.

"So they let you in," said Reed, "because they knew the parrots had to go back to their cages, but they didn't want to have to take them themselves."

"And once I was in," said Gisela, "and the birds were home again, then of course I had to wash my hands, and I had to clean up my shirt—just feathers, but so many—and it was just easier to let me stay. And they were so eager to tell the other security guards what had happened that they left me alone for an hour while they told the tale of the crazy bird woman."

Reed and Ostertag couldn't help but laugh. Lise was practically in tears by now, and some of the other Cabin officers were starting to pay attention, trying to see what was so funny.

Wohlreich had been listening enough to interject. "Which library?"

"Humboldt," said Gisela. "Special collections. They had an old plan of the city, from the middle ages, showing an early layout of the sewer system. I was able to find an old drainage system under a Soviet military office."

"Wait," said Ostertag, sitting suddenly straighter. "The Freistadt job? That was you?"

"That one small part of it was me," said Gisela, pouring herself another glass of water from the bottle in the center of the table. "This was, what, five years ago? Four?"

"Four and a few months," said Lise. "BND agents were able to plant listening devices all over that office thanks to the access door they found in that old tunnel. The Stasi has since found it and sealed it, but still."

"I have heard of that mission," said Ostertag, and nodded appreciatively. "I had no idea that was you."

"Never underestimate the power of a research librarian," said Gisela.

"Wait a second," said Reed. "The Humboldt University library?"

Gisela nodded, swallowing a mouthful of salad.

"But that's in the Soviet Sector."

"This was four years ago," said Wohlreich. "The Wall was not up yet."

"I know," said Reed, "I guess it just ... well, it spooks me a little, is all. Even before the Wall I never went over there much."

"You missed out," said Lise, and nodded toward his plate of food. "The best schnitzel in Berlin was right there downtown."

"Nordland?" asked Ostertag.

"Guido's," said Lise.

Ostertag nodded. "Yes, that was excellent. I miss Guido's." He looked at Reed. "When this Wall comes down again, go to Guido's."

"And go quickly," said Lise, "before it fills up with desperate West Germans who haven't eaten there in months."

"Years," said Ostertag, and swallowed the rest of his wine. "Let us at least be realistic."

Reed looked at Ostertag, keeping an eye on Anselm hunched over the bar behind him. "What did you do before ..." He gestured with his finger. "All this."

Ostertag copied the gesture with a smirk. "All this? Do you mean today's lunch, or the Wall, or the Cabin, or Berlin in general? Before my life, Mr. Reed, I was nothing but a twinkle in God's eye."

"I mean before the Wall," said Reed. "Or maybe before the Cabin, I don't know. Gisela was a research librarian, Lise and Wohlreich were in the BND. What did you do with yourself before you broke codes for a living?"

"I created them," he said, and picked up a nearby newspaper, neatly folded in thirds. He held it up with a smile. "Crossword puzzles."

"You wrote crossword puzzles?" asked Gisela.

"For nearly two years," said Ostertag. "Combine that with two years in the Cabin, and I was just penning my first professional puzzle when Gisela was thrusting birds into the faces of the Humboldt Library Security Team."

"I love crosswords," said Reed.

"Our cryptographers both love puzzles?" asked Lise dryly. "I never would have guessed."

"Seriously, though," said Reed. "I do them all the time. Including the German ones, so I probably did some of yours. *Morgenpost?*"

"*Kurier,*" said Ostertag. "But thank you for assuming that I could get a job at a real newspaper."

Gisela looked surprised. "Isn't the *Kurier* a GDR paper?"

Ostertag gave a mischievous smile. "What our Soviet overlords don't know can't hurt them, right? A failed writer in the American Sector could never have gotten a job at the *Zeitung,* but at the *Kurier* we went out of our way to poke the overlords in the eye. Every day, now, I ..." He hesitated, his mirth evaporating. "I expect to hear that the editorial staff has been executed." He shrugged. "Looking back, I am glad I got out when I did."

"You sound a lot more regretful of that than I expected," said Reed.

"Perhaps I simply enjoy poking overlords in their eyes." Ostertag shrugged again, and took a bite of his meal.

Reed looked down the table at the other officers, engaged in a lively debate about ... fish? "Are they arguing about fish?"

"Seafood," said Lise. "Harald likes it, but Davis thinks it is terrible."

"It's not that bad," said Reed.

Lise smiled. "The word 'abomination' was used."

"I love seafood," said Gisela. "But I'm from Bremen, so how could I not?"

"The Nordsee," said Lise.

"The Schlamm See," said Ostertag.

"Schlamm?" asked Reed.

"Mud," said Ostertag. "Miles and miles of it, as far as the eye can see."

"It's one of Germany's most popular vacation spots," said Gisela, indignant enough that Reed was fairly sure she was serious.

Ostertag sighed. "Imagine how terrible the rest of our country must be, that we all go on vacation to mud fields."

Gisela punched him in the arm.

The fish conversation was growing more heated, and Reed cocked his head to listen.

"... not about management," Frank was saying, "it's about control. The German government doesn't need those fishing rights —no one's going to starve if the government doesn't have them—but the fishermen might literally starve if they don't get them back."

"You are a socialist," said Wohlreich.

"I'm a capitalist," said Frank. "Business rights should stay in the hands of businesses, because that's who creates jobs and cash flow."

Lise caught Reed's eye. "This is the third time they have fallen into an argument," she explained softly.

"About fishing?" asked Gisela.

"About everything they try to talk about," said Lise. "Chuck keeps changing the subject, but Frank and Wohlreich just end up yelling at each other again."

"And poor Harald, caught in the middle," said Ostertag.

"Poor Bettina," said Lise. "Harald is as bad as the rest of them."

"I'm worried about Frank," said Gisela softly. She leaned in, trying to keep her voice low. "He's been so angry the past few days, don't you think?"

Reed froze, not sure how to answer. What would help their operation more? What did Anselm need to hear? That Frank's anger was new, implying that something recent had affected him, but leaving open the possibility that he was altering his behavior on purpose? Or that he was always like this, implying that Frank was consistent but hard to work with? The latter seemed like the more recruitable quality, from a double agent perspective.

"I wonder if something happened to him," said Lise. "At home, I mean—did he get bad news about his family in New York?"

"Maybe," said Reed, choosing his words carefully, "but you know Frank. He's always been on a hair trigger when it comes to politics. He has very particular ideas about things, and when they don't line up he ... cusses out Wohlreich over fish, I suppose."

"I suppose," said Gisela. She and Ostertag looked at Frank, but Lise kept her eyes on Reed. Analyzing.

Reed looked away.

"Do not speak to him that way!" growled Wohlreich, suddenly loud. "He is your boss!"

"And what the hell does that have to do with anything?" asked Frank. "We're not allowed to disagree with our bosses anymore? Is that some new rule I wasn't aware of?"

"Everyone is staring at us!" hissed Wagner.

"Or maybe it's an older rule," said Frank. "From back in the old days—"

"Don't you dare," said Wohlreich.

"—with your good buddies the Nazis," Frank finished. He stood up and looked around, seeing the rest of the restaurant's patrons and staff all staring at him. "How about the rest of you, huh? Any other former Nazis in the house or is it just my own damn middle manager?"

"Frank," said Davis, reaching toward him.

"Don't touch me." Frank jerked away so harshly he knocked over his chair. "Damn it!" He bent down to pick it up, and Wohlreich started talking, and faster than he could understand his own reaction Reed stood up, put a hand on the fallen chair, and tightened his grip. Frank pulled against it, but only once, then let go and stormed away, out of Richardhof and into the street beyond.

"I should go after him," said Chuck.

"No," said Davis, "just let him cool down a little."

In the corner of his eye, Reed saw Anselm. He looked like he'd been one of the first in the restaurant to turn back to his own business.

Reed realized he was still holding the wooden chair. He turned it upright, and set it by the table. He sat down, and realized his hands were shaking.

"Lucky you were there," said Gisela. "I think he would have hit Jannick with that chair if you had not been holding it."

"I was ... just helping him pick it up," said Reed.

"Never underestimate an obsequious cryptographer," said Ostertag.

Lise only looked at him—the tiniest glance, impossible to read—then turned and looked at the door.

Look at me, thought Reed. *I'm a mess, and I wasn't even in danger. Two of my coworkers started yelling at each other, and I stopped one of them from hitting the other, and now I'm shaking like I was in a gunfight.*

What am I going to do if I ever have to do any real field work?

There were several answers to that question, but only one of them made sense.

I'll die.

West Berlin

REED AND LISE sat in the courtyard, and watched the laundry lady's balcony. It still showed the Morse code for 'K' or 'R.'

There had been no new message from Longshore, so there had been no way to know if the previous day's confirmation code was correct. So they were back to see tomorrow's code, and hope for better luck.

"Maybe it's the standoff at the border," said Reed.

The East German government had spent the day making announcements over the radio, loud and clear for the entire city to hear: Allied personnel attempting to cross the Wall without a uniform or papers would be denied. The West German government had responded with an outright refusal to accept the new policy, and sent four tanks to Checkpoint Charlie.

"The border guards are still staring at each other," said Reed, "with their fingers on their triggers. Maybe Longshore didn't have time to send us a message because their office spent the whole day doing the same thing ours did: trying to prevent a nuclear war."

"Probably," said Lise. "They do not want a war any more than we do."

"Are you sure about that?"

"We are both just trying to ... push as far as we can without pushing over the edge."

"God help us," said Reed. He glanced up again at the unchanged clothesline. "We don't have to sit here the whole time. We could just go somewhere, and come back after she changes the code."

"If we sit here and occasionally look around, we are just two lovers." Lise leaned in and gave him a kiss, but he didn't know if it was genuine or just for appearances. "If we come and go, people will notice us." She paused, picking at the wooden bench. "I am worried about Frank."

"I know how you feel," Reed said. Frank's blowup at Richardhof had been exactly what they'd needed for their counter-op to Talon, but ... But all Reed could see was Frank's rage, all too real, and Wohlreich's devastating blend of pain and superiority in response. The op was working, but what would it cost?

"I can see Frank's side," said Lise. "If I were Jewish, I would not want to work with Jannick, either—I mean, if I were Jewish, I would not even be here to work with him. I would have been killed in the war. But I *am* here, and I have seen Wohlreich's file. He was part of the German retreat—too young to join until 1944, and all he did was defend his country from invaders. Not kill Jews."

"You think that makes it any easier on Frank?" asked Reed.

He wasn't much younger than Wohlreich—too young to fight in the war, but old enough to remember every news report, every dark discovery and development, every grainy photograph of carnage and destruction that ran in the papers and horrified his mother. He'd grown up in a world where the Germans were the enemy, and now he was living with them, working with them, even sleeping with one of them. Governments came and went, ideologies came and went, but the people were always the same old people.

"How long," he asked, "before Russia becomes our greatest ally?"

"The Soviet Union is different," said Lise. "The Americans allied with Germany and Japan after the war because you were helping to rebuild them. If you ever have to rebuild Russia, you will be just as destroyed as they are. That is your strategy, is it not? Mutually Assured Destruction."

Reed looked at the canal. "Do you think they'd really do it?"

"I do," said Lise. "But I guess the question is, would they do it over a tiny little border checkpoint on Friedrichstrasse?"

Reed looked up at the clothesline, just in time to see the old woman, six stories up, changing the shirts that hung on it. She pulled them down, and hung up two more: a shirt and a pair of pants. "Dash dot," said Reed. "Or dot dash. N or A."

"Good," said Lise. "If we get a message tomorrow with N or A as the code, we will know we have it for sure."

"And then what?" asked Reed. He looked across the canal to the city beyond, slowly growing darker as the sun went down. "We can't use this system to talk to Longshore, or he to us. We could send him a message at one letter a day, if we could suborn the process somehow, but even if he noticed the confirmation codes were spelling something, it would take a week to spell out even a single word." He frowned, and looked back at the side of the apartment, and the giant wall of balconies. "Maybe if we had the entire building, we could put a letter on each balcony. But even that might be too noticeable. One clothesline is nothing; you see a hundred of them in a day. If you know it's a code you can read it, and if you don't it's completely innocuous. A whole building covered with carefully spaced white trousers would stand out so clearly that any trained Morse operator could probably read the thing by accident."

"It needs to be subtle," said Lise, nodding.

"What drives me crazy is how *close* it all is," said Reed. "If we want to get a message to an agent in Moscow it takes days, maybe weeks, with a dozen different links in the chain, any one of which could fail. If we want to get a message to East Berlin we could just ..." He laughed. "I mean, we could literally just throw a paper airplane out the window of the Cabin, right? We're thirty feet from the other side."

Lise looked incredulous. "A paper airplane?"

"It wouldn't be the most secure system," said Reed. "There are always Grenzers standing around who would see it. But it wouldn't even need a message written on it; it might be just as a signal to start an action, or a confirmation that you've received something. Just open your window and throw a paper airplane."

Lise looked up at the balcony, and then out over the canal, and her voice became soft, almost wistful. "We used to use a system like this. Not a paper airplane or a clothesline, but a TV antenna. We had a man in the Soviet sector, back when Mercury and I worked there. Pollard Rapp. A grumpy old man, but a true German patriot, and eager to help us. He had an apartment near the border, in sight of the American sector, and we used him to send information to our bosses. We had a whole network of messengers like that, but we used him for troop movements: where are the Soviet soldiers going, when are they going, how many of them are there. That sort of thing. We'd find the information, new every day, but even before the Wall it was too dangerous to just give it to the BND directly. We would be seen. Far safer to pass it to Rapp in a dead drop, and let him go up and adjust his antenna."

Reed grinned. "Just an old man, angry about his bad reception. That's brilliant. Not Morse, though, I assume." He cocked his head to the side. "Semaphore? You could do the full alphabet with the right TV antenna."

"Similar," said Lise, "but we used our own code to make it faster. One position to mean Stasi, another to mean Soviet; we had the numbers and directions and all of the key cities all worked out. He'd set the antenna one way, go down to see if the signal had improved, and then come back up and set it again. Back and forth. It only took five or six changes to send a whole message, though as slow as he was on the stairs even that might take a half an hour." She laughed, but it was a sad laugh, which seemed to Reed to be full of old memories.

He asked his question softly. "What happened to him?"

"To Herr Rapp?" She shook her head. "Nothing. But my ... His wife, Michelle, was taken by the police, during a protest against the government. We told her not to go to the protest, but she was too like her husband, I guess." She smiled again, covering her sadness like a mask. "And too like her son. German patriots."

"What happened to the son?"

Lise only stared across the water, watching trains come and go like strings of lights in the darkness.

Reed waited, but if she didn't want to talk she wasn't going to talk. A person "taken" by the Stasi was, more often than not, never seen again. A protestor especially. And the tears that brimmed at the corners of Lise's eyes seemed to hint at a deeper story, or at a deeper relationship, perhaps, between Lise and the woman. Or maybe the son. Whatever the young man meant, and whatever had happened to him and his mother, Pollard Rapp would have fallen under suspicion as well: guilty by association. Even if nothing happened to the old man directly, Lise and her partner would have had to stop using him for anything, just to keep him safe.

Which turned on a light in the back of Reed's mind.

"That's why Davis is being so careful about this laundry-line code system. He doesn't want anything to happen to the old woman." He looked up at her balcony again. "I wonder if she's a friend, or the mother of one."

"I do not think it matters who she is," said Lise. "Davis protects people; that is his job."

Reed shot her a glance from the corner of his eye. "Does this mean you trust him?"

"Do I still think he might be the mole, you mean?" Lise sighed. "I do not know what I think. Except that I think it is safer not to trust anyone at all."

"You trust me," said Reed.

"Of course I do," said Lise, but something in her voice gave him that same odd feeling he couldn't identify.

He wondered if it was guilt.

TUESDAY, OCTOBER 24, 1961
7:45 AM

West Berlin

THE MESSAGE FROM LONGSHORE, when it came, was short, meaningless, and devastating:

N
Tsyganov not in meet at bank
N

It didn't seem to mean anything—Reed knew nothing about a meeting in a bank, so knowing that Tsyganov wasn't a part of it raised far more questions than it answered.

Worse still, the sixth word was in English. Bank. Reed stared at it, his heart sinking. Their whole hidden-message theory, completely out the door. He checked his figures and his transcription a second time, just to be sure, but it was all correct.

What was wrong? He didn't *like* funneling secret messages to Lise, but at least he understood it. But this message broke the pattern, which meant that maybe he didn't understand anything at all.

If Longshore wasn't warning Lise about a double agent, then ... what was really going on?

He longed for a simple explanation. Something that made everything make sense—something that said his friends were all innocent, and everything would be okay. But that was impossible now. He'd glimpsed a side of Lise and Frank and Wohlreich and even Davis that he'd never known was there, and double agent or not it would still be there no matter how this crisis ended; ignorance had hidden it, but nothing could erase it.

The worst part, he knew, was that they couldn't turn back now. Even if there was no double agent, and all they were chasing was a ghost, they had to keep chasing it. It was better, in the long run, than allowing a double agent to run rampant through their office.

As much as he didn't want a traitor in the Cabin, part of him prayed that there was one, simply because that was the only way this investigation would ever end.

He packed the book and his notes into the safe, and took the message to Davis.

Davis looked up from his desk. "You don't look happy. Bad news?"

Reed closed the door, and handed the message to the Chief. "It's not that he sent us bad news, it's that I have no idea what he's talking about. Which is, yes, very bad news."

Davis read it, and frowned. "Another mention of Tsyganov, who we still know nothing about. Gisela's narrowed it down to three, but that's a far cry from a positive identification."

"Her list was only four to begin with."

"Exactly," said Davis. "We know nothing." He read the message again. "The military officer from Moscow is still in

Moscow, so we know it's not him. The businessman, maybe? Is that why they're meeting in a bank?"

Reed closed his eyes. "Let's think it through. We know the Soviets are behind the change in the border controls, right?"

"We *think* we do," said Davis. "If we knew it for sure we'd have some kind of leverage on the GDR to stop it."

"So what if Tsyganov is a part of that?" asked Reed. "We've assumed he's part of a counterintelligence op, but what if he's here from Moscow to encourage the GDR to inhibit Allied travel? And this is being decided in meetings, which are being held in key places, and if we ..." He trailed off, frowning at the discarded message. After a moment Davis hit a button on his intercom.

"Bettina, can you send Gisela in here, please? And the analysts?"

"Yes, sir," said Bettina.

Davis continued to brood, and Reed thought again about the sixth word: bank. Every other sixth word had been in German, and they'd thought it was a pattern, but this one was in English. Bank. Why "bank" and not—

"Holy mother of—"

"What?" asked Davis.

Reed snapped his head up, staring at Davis with wide eyes. "What?"

"You were cursing," said Davis. "And you had that look on your face that means you were working through a problem in your head."

"Oh," said Reed, caught off guard. "Yeah, Lise calls that—" He froze. "I mean, she has a desk near mine, and she's commented on the same thing. She calls it Cryptographer Face."

Did I give us away? he thought. *Did I slip up and reveal too much, and now he knows that Lise and I are sleeping together? Did I just ruin everything?*

"Whatever you call it," said Davis, "you just did it and cursed, which means you've thought of something."

"I ..." Reed didn't know what to say. "It's just that I ... well, yes." He couldn't think of a lie, so he gave the simplest version of the truth that he could think of on short notice. "The strange words in each message, the ones that stood out so bizarrely, were all in German: Ziegel, and Rennstall, and Weiss. And it just occurred to me that this one has German as well."

Davis looked at the message again, read it, and nodded as the realization dawned. "So it does. The German word for bank is 'bank'—they're pronounced differently, but they're spelled exactly the same." He pursed his lips, thinking. "Do you think it means something?"

"I think it has to," said Reed, trying to sound curious and cautious, but in his head he was practically leaping with joy. "Count them; every one of those words is not just in German, it's the sixth word in the message."

Reed ran through them in his mind: Ziegel for 'pay attention,' Rennstall for 'hey, Lise, it's me your old partner,' and then the location of the message: Weiss Bank. The white bank. Was white its name or its color? How could they know which he meant?

Would anyone be able to find it aside from Lise?

It occurred to him, not for the first time, that this message—in fact, the entire string of messages—might be completely fake. That Longshore, or a Stasi officer who had captured him, might very well be fabricating Tsyganov and the meetings and even Operation Talon itself, all to serve as a delivery system for those four code words. Instructions, or even an activation order, for a sleeper agent in the heart of the Western intelligence system.

Ziegel. Rennstall. Weiss. Bank.

A knock on the door interrupted him, and he realized with a start that Lise was right there, about to come in. It was now or never. If Reed was going to betray her to Davis, and tell him all his suspicions that Lise might be a traitor, now was his last chance; ten seconds later and she'd have the information. Anything her Stasi handler might be trying to tell her, she would know.

"Reed?" asked Davis, staring at him. "Can you get the door?"

Reed looked at him, not knowing who to trust.

Davis frowned. "Wally?"

Reed stood up, turned around, and opened the door.

"Morning," said Chuck, coming into the office. Lise and Gisela trailed behind him. "Another Longshore message?"

"Yes," said Davis. "Kind of a maddening one this time. Close the door, would you?" Reed closed the door, and he and Chuck let Lise and Gisela have the two chairs. Davis looked at Gisela. "Miss Breuer, have you been able to discover anything new about Tsyganov?"

"A little. Jannick's contact in Moscow says that the military Tsyganov is still there, so we know it is not him; I assume you saw that report already. I used a cover identity at NASA to request the Kuybyshev Tsyganov to speak at a space science conference in Tokyo, but we haven't heard back yet. As for the factory worker and the businessman, there is not much more I can do without somebody on-site in their locations." She held up a stack of papers. "I am digging up all the background I can, but it is mostly birth records, and things like that. Nothing that can tell us which one of them is in Berlin right now talking to the Stasi."

"That's still helpful," said Davis. "Stay vigilant, but ... put it on the back burner for a while. I need you on something else." He straightened the fallen message, and turned it to face them. "'Tsyganov not in meeting at bank.'"

"What meeting?" asked Gisela.

"What bank?" asked Chuck.

"Exactly," said Davis. "There's a whole series of meetings

here that Longshore seems to think we know more about than we do: first the racing stable, now a bank. I want all three of you working this, top priority, starting now. If you have other projects too important or time sensitive to set aside, talk to Wohlreich and see if he can delegate something. I want these meetings found, and I want them found yesterday."

"Yes, sir," said Chuck.

Lise still hadn't spoken, or looked at Reed, but she'd seen the German word "bank," and she had to have recognized its significance. He could practically watch the wheels turning in her head. There were only a few "white" dead drops, she'd said; knowing that it was also a bank must have made it shockingly obvious which one Message 41 was hidden in. Was it on the other side of the Wall? How could they reach it? Was she already making her plan?

And was Reed a part of that plan?

Davis excused them, and the four officers walked back to their desks. Reed kept an eye on Lise, not suspicious so much as wary. What if she ran off on her own to get the message, without taking him? Was he one hundred percent certain she wasn't a traitor?

Maybe eighty percent, he thought, *at the most.* That was a dangerously low number in the field of international security.

Reed did his work for the rest of the afternoon, keeping a close eye on the others in the office. Frank went to Richardhof for lunch, presumably planning to sit near Erich Anselm and mutter just-audible complaints about the Nazis in the office. Lise stayed in for lunch, so Reed did, too, keeping an eye on her, though he hadn't brought anything to eat. By three in the afternoon his stomach was growling loud enough for Ostertag to hear it, and the German cryptographer laughed at him.

"I am sharing my desk with a bear," he said cheerfully, and growled back, curling his fingers into claws. "Do you need food? Some berries, perhaps, or a wild deer?"

"I'm fine," said Reed. "Just ..." He trailed off, staring at Lise's desk.

She had moved a calendar to the edge of it, perfectly placed to be visible from his chair. Today—October 24—had an X on it, and some of the other days as well, but not in any immediately obvious pattern. October 10, October 11; the fifteenth, the seventeenth, the nineteenth. 24, 25, and 30, and then the first two days of November. It was strange, but it wasn't *noticeably* strange. A casual observer probably wouldn't have paid it any attention it at all.

But Reed was not a casual observer.

This was the binary code they'd talked about in his apartment.

How had they set it up? He cast his mind back, trying to remember. There are twenty-six letters, and the number 26, translated into binary, was 11010, so in an A-1 cypher you needed up to five spaces per letter. *That's right,* he thought: *each column was a letter, so a month gave you up to seven letters.*

The first column on Lise's calendar, the Sundays, had one X, on the fifteenth. 00100. That was a 100, which was a 4, which was a D. The second column was even easier: 00001. The letter A.

He calculated the rest of the letters quickly, working from memory and doing all the work in his head. He didn't want to be seen staring at her desk, and he didn't want to leave a printed record that someone else could find and ask about. The third column was N. The fourth was K, and the fifth was E.

D, A, N, K, E.

Danke.

She was thanking him? What for?

He looked up, and realized with a shock that she wasn't there.

He stood up immediately, looking around the room with wide eyes. Lise was gone.

"Wallace," said Ostertag. "Is everything alright?"

Reed looked down, and saw that everyone was staring at him. "I was ..." He stammered, but gave up. He didn't have time for excuses; he had found the final code word, he'd suspected Lise, and he hadn't done anything about it. He'd let Lise into Davis's office and given her the final piece of the puzzle.

And she had thanked him secretly and disappeared.

"I need to talk to Lise," he said. Every word was a struggle. "Is she in the ..." He pointed, though not really at anything.

"She just left," said Wohlreich. "She said she had a lead on Tsyganov."

"Damn," said Reed, and grabbed his pencil. He set it back down. "I need to talk to her." He walked to the hat rack in the corner, and grabbed his coat and hat. "I'll ... be back."

"Are you okay, Wally?" asked Frank.

Reed looked at him. "I'll be back," he repeated, and jogged out the door.

He ran to the first corner, saw nothing, and then ran to the second one. He recognized her dress about a block ahead, and breathed a sigh of relief—she hadn't disappeared yet. He followed her for three blocks, when suddenly she sat down in a sidewalk cafe, facing away from him, and waited. Who was she waiting for? He watched her for a moment, half a block away, not knowing what to do, until finally she turned around and looked in his direction. He froze. Was she looking at him? She was. She beckoned to him, her eyes unreadable behind a pair of sunglasses; he gave up all pretense of hiding, and walked up and sat at her table.

"It is insulting enough that you are following me," said Lise sharply. "Do not make it worse by thinking I am so stupid I did not notice."

"I'm sorry," said Reed, "I just ... where are you going?"

"You know where I am going."

"No, I don't. I know there's a white bank somewhere but there are probably dozens of those in the city. You're the only one who knows which bank has the message."

She raised her eyebrow, surprised by something, but recovered quickly and shook her head. "And you thought I would try to get it without you?"

"I'm not a field agent," said Reed. "I never have been. It doesn't make any sense *not* to go without me."

"Then why are you upset about it?"

"Because I—" He didn't know how to answer without insulting her, but Lise finished his sentence for him, insults and all.

"Because you think I might be the double agent. I asked you to break protocol. I asked you to spy on the Section Chief. I did a hundred suspicious things, but dammit, Wally, I also trusted you. I took you everywhere I went; I told you everything I found. The least you could do is trust me back."

"If you're as good of a spy as you say you are, how could I *not* distrust you?" asked Reed. It was his greatest fear, spilling out unplanned and unchecked. "How do I know you're not just working me, like any other asset, to get what you want?"

Lise paused, staring at him, but her anger had drained away, replaced by ... Reed couldn't tell. She took off her sunglasses, and he instantly saw that it was sadness.

"Wally, I know that I ..." She stopped, and sighed. "I know that I do this sometimes, and I do not do it on purpose. They train us so thoroughly in psychology, and manipulation, and yes, even seduction, that sometimes I fall into the patterns whether I mean to or not. And sharing vulnerability is one of a spy's best tricks for assuaging suspicion, so you cannot even be sure that what I am saying right now is genuine or part of the lie, and I hate that, Wally, you have to know that I hate it. Sometimes I feel like the only way I can ever live a real life again, with real relationships and a real ... love ... is to throw this whole thing away and start over, with someone who does not know I am a spy, and does not know I ever was one, and does not have any reason to think that everything I say is a calculated facade designed to extract information or compliance. But even then, I would be building a real relationship with someone I would be lying to. And I know it cannot work that way."

Reed started to feel sorry for her, but didn't know if he should allow himself to feel that way or not.

"I am not a traitor, Wally. And I am not a double agent, and I am not just dating you to get closer to Chief Davis and his secrets."

"But you didn't start dating me until I had access to secrets you needed."

"That is a coincidence, Wally, I promise you. I did not know I needed those secrets until barely this weekend."

"Do you love me?"

The question hung in the air like an invisible singularity, pulling all sound and focus until it seemed as if nothing else existed.

"I ..." She paused. "I do not know. I ... like you, certainly, but love is ... that is not a fair question."

Reed felt something inside of him grow stale and brittle; not shattering, but ready to at the slightest nudge.

He nodded. "Okay then. I retract it. But I replace that question with two others, and you have to answer them honestly."

Her eyes were wet, but her voice was studiously controlled. "It is the least I can do."

"First," said Reed. "Where's the missing message? Where's the white bank?"

The shadow of a smile played at the corner of Lise's lips. "It is not a bank, Wally. The German word 'bank' has two meanings: bank, and bench."

Reed raised his eyebrows. "It's in a white bench?"

"Close," said Lise. "Mercury and I used to love to use park benches as our dead drops, because you can sit on one for hours. You can drop things under them, you can pretend you dropped something and bend down to pick it up, you can 'accidentally' leave a bag or a purse or even a piece of garbage when you get up to go. We had one we used a lot, in the park called the Weissensee, and that is where the message is. I guarantee it."

"Good," said Reed. He hadn't expected a bench, but it made sense, and it tracked perfectly with everything else she'd told him about the clues and their possible meanings. But it still had one big problem. "That's on the other side of the Wall."

"We knew it had to be."

"There's no way we can get to it."

"Is that your second question?" she asked. "How are we going to get the message?"

"We can figure that out later," said Reed. "First we're going to prove that you trust me as much as I've trusted you. I've told you everything, I've shared classified information, I've kept no secrets. So here's my second question: now that you know for sure it's him, I want you to tell me who Longshore is. Your old partner, Mercury; I want his name."

"No."

"You promised."

"It could compromise his cover and his life—"

"I'm compromising everything," said Reed. "I'm putting my job, my life, and everything else I have at risk for you; I've given you information I never should have even hinted at, let alone divulged in full. You've kept his name secret because you didn't know who to trust, but this is where we are now: you have to trust me, or I don't know if I'm able to trust you."

Lise looked at him, though he couldn't tell if she was

studying his face or thinking about her options. Either way, she eventually pursed her lips, and nodded, and opened her bag.

"His name is Dietrich Böhm," she said, rooting through her purse. Reed had never heard the name. She found an old wallet, the kind with a slim wooden shell that clipped shut with a metal clasp. She pulled it out, opened the clasp, and folded the wallet open like a book. It was filled with photos, some sepia, some in glacial black and white. She sorted through them, found one, and handed it to Reed. It showed three people in a bar, holding tall glasses half-full of beer. "This was taken in 1955. In Rennstall, as a matter of fact. We had just started working together, under cover as university students." She pointed at the figures. "That is me in the front. This one here, in the cardigan, is Böhm."

The Lise in the photo was younger, of course, but more than that she was ... happier. More lively, with an open-mouthed smile and an inescapable twinkle in her eye that made her look as if the camera had caught her mid-laugh. Maybe it was a truly joyful event, or maybe she'd grown more jaded now, but Reed didn't think he'd ever seen her that happy.

Dietrich Böhm was tall, though not inordinately so. Young and handsome, with a wide, German face, and a haircut so unmistakably '50s that he could have been one of the Everly Brothers. He wasn't as vivacious as Lise, but he was clearly happy as well.

The third man was also young, with bright blond hair and a dashing smile. He had his arm around Lise, and she had hers around him.

"Who is this?" asked Reed.

"Another student."

"Pro-Soviet? Anti-Soviet? Who were you infiltrating at the time?"

"He was ... just a student," said Lise. Reed noted the hesitation, but didn't say anything. "The university was our cover, not our mission. Tobi was ..."

"Also cover?" Reed could tell that she'd had feelings for the man, perhaps strong ones. He shouldn't even be asking about him—he should be focusing on Dietrich—but he couldn't help himself.

"At first," she said. "Eventually he became a liability."

"Because you loved him?"

"Because he loved his country."

Reed didn't know what that meant, but he had already tread too deeply into her private memories. He studied the photo, ignoring Tobi and staring at Dietrich's face, concentrating as if he was trying to memorize it. Maybe he was. "They had to have done a background check on Böhm when he started work with the Stasi," he said at last. "If they know that he used to pal around with a woman who currently works for the BND, they have to suspect him."

"He will have a new name now," she said. "And a new life, created by the BND as a part of his infiltration. We have their names, after all: the Stasi officers who work against us. None of them is named Dietrich Böhm."

"We also have photos," said Reed. "Gisela and Frank collected photos of everyone they could."

"I ..." She took back the college picture, tucking it gently into her wallet. "I have never looked. Even before I suspected that Longshore was Dietrich, I worried that it might be someone I knew. I have too many friends from the old days, still working in the field. I did not want to ... react ... if I learned that Longshore was in danger." She clipped the wallet closed, and slid it back into her purse. "I was reassigned two years after this photo was taken, and lost track of Dietrich. I heard he was still working in the Soviet sector, but honestly I had not thought about him in years, until the word 'rennstall' showed up in Message 43."

Reed nodded. "Do you still think the mole is Davis?"

"I ..." She paused. "I do not know."

"But you don't think it's me."

"I observed you, after I told you my suspicions, to see what you would do." *The same thing that he had done to her,* Reed thought. She smiled again, sad and apologetic. "Still working an asset, and I apologize. You did not do anything a trained agent would do, with his cover so close to being exposed, so you are either innocent or much, much better at espionage than any of us realized."

"Or very bad at it," said Reed. "That's far more likely." He stared at the street for a moment, watching cars and people pass. "Do you want to look at the photos?"

Lise frowned. "Of the Stasi officers?"

"Your suspicions are already confirmed. No one but Dietrich Böhm would point you to a bench in the Weissensee." He looked at her. "Do you want to see a current photo? Find out which of the Stasi officers is your friend in disguise?"

"We cannot go back to the office," she said. "It is already suspicious enough that one of us left early, let alone two."

"We don't have to go back," he said, and stood up. "I have a stack of CIA files in my apartment, for some after-hours work on an old project. Including copies of the Stasi personnel files."

9:28 PM

West Berlin

REED UNLOCKED HIS APARTMENT, opened the door, and
let himself in. He left the door ajar while he put away his coat
and retrieved a small screwdriver from a drawer in the kitchen.
A moment later Lise arrived; they'd come by separate routes,
just to be sure. She closed the door behind her, and locked the
bolt.

"It's in here," said Reed. He pointed at the air vent in the
wall, and started dragging a fat, overstuffed chair so he could
stand on it to reach.

"No," said Lise, "like this." She picked up one side of the
chair, gesturing for him to do the same, and together they
carried the chair instead of dragging it. "I have always known
you hid something in that vent," she explained, and pointed to
the hardwood floor. "Dragging chairs leaves scratches in the
floor."

Reed looked at her suspiciously. "You knew? Did you ever
look?"

Lise scowled. "I only noticed something, Wally; I do not
spy on you."

"That's fair," he said. "Sorry." He stood on the chair, unscrewed the vent, and handed it down to Lise. Sitting inside the duct, pushed back a bit so it couldn't be seen from the room, was a pair of thick folders, each stuffed full of papers. He pulled them out, blew away the thin layer of dust, and climbed down from the chair. He set the folders on the table, and opened one to search for the Stasi personnel files.

"How long have you had these?" asked Lise.

"A few months," said Reed. "Longshore gave us all these names, back when he first went undercover, and he keeps us updated every time they lose an old officer or hire a new one. Davis wanted me to memorize as many of the files as I could, to make it easier to recognize the names when Longshore uses them. Then the Wall went up, and this project mostly got lost in the shuffle. I still pull them out now and then, though, as you ... noticed from my floor."

Lise gave a wry smile. "I am starting to believe we need some basic spycraft lessons for Cabin officers—not all of you have field training, and it is becoming too dangerous not to know certain skills."

"Here," said Reed, finding the first page. "Konrad Siedel, the Section chief of the Stasi's main listening station. This is Jürgen Bauer, their lead cryptographer, and this is his colleague Frida Baumann." Each officer had a single page with a brief biography, and a black and white photo attached with a paper clip. Many of the pictures were photos of photos, snapped in secret by a field agent leafing through the Stasi's own files. Others were taken from a distance, live and candid with a tele-photo lens; those were likely all from Frank. Reed laid the pages out on his table, covering it like a grid. "This is Martin Vogel, he's one of their researchers, I think, and this one's Otto Koch. He's an ..." He read the file. "Asset handler." He set it down next to the others. "You can tell I haven't really done a great job at memorizing them."

"That is surprising," said Lise. "You are usually very quick to remember things."

"Only numbers," said Reed. "Remembering that the other asset handler is ... Hans Nowak ... is a little harder. Wait." He'd almost set Nowak's file on the table, but pulled it back up toward his face. "Do you have that photo of Böhm handy?"

"Let me see," said Lise, and took the file. Her eyes widened when she saw it. "You are right," she said, and set it down, reaching for her purse and wallet. "This looks like him." She pulled out the old college photo and laid it gently next to the photo of Nowak. The man in the latter was noticeably older—a little thicker in the face, a little colder in the eyes—but even at that, the similarities were undeniable.

"That's him," said Reed. "Hans Nowak is Dietrich Böhm. And Longshore. And Mercury. And who knows how many other fake names and identities."

"He left me a message," said Lise, and her face turned from cheerful recognition to grim determination. "I need to go get it."

"But Weissensee Park is on the other side of the Wall," said Reed.

"We still need it."

"Maybe someone else can go get it for us," said Reed. "Davis can cross the Wall—he's high enough rank that he—"

"Do you trust him?" asked Lise. "Fully?"

"I ... I don't know."

"That is why I have to go myself."

"No," said Reed. "It's too dangerous. What about ..." He wracked his brain for any other option. "What about Rapp?"

"Rapp?" asked Lise.

"Pollard Rapp," said Reed. "The old man you used to work with; the one who did semaphore with his TV antenna. Can you contact him?"

"Probably not," said Lise. "He is not a spy, he is an old man;

even if he had the equipment to receive a message, he does not have the training to do anything about it."

"All he needs to do is get a message out of a hole in a bench," said Reed. "He doesn't even need to bring it to us. He could use the old semaphore code to just tell us what it says."

Lise shook her head. "Even if that were possible, I have no way of contacting him. And like I said before, he is *old*. He was old when I worked with him, and that was four years ago."

"Somebody else, then," said Reed. "You have to have other contacts over there, right? What about that kid from college? Tobi? You said he loved Germany. And obviously there was something between you, but no matter how badly it ended—"

"He died," said Lise. Her voice was soaked in bitterness.

Reed pulled back, devastated. "I'm sorry."

"I knew so many idealists back then," she said, "but the GDR is a fascist state, Wally. All the idealists are either dead or hiding. Michelle and Tobi and so many others—everyone I knew who was willing to risk their life for this already did. And the Wall went up anyway. There is nobody left to fight."

"That can't be true," said Reed.

"You have never been over there," she insisted. "It is an evil empire."

"Evil empires create heroes," said Reed. "Like antibodies, fighting off an infection; somebody is always going to stand up to them."

"I pray that you are right," said Lise, "but ... that does not help us now, for this problem. If any new heroes have come, we do not know who they are or how to get in touch with them. We are on our own."

"There has to be a better way—"

"There is not," said Lise. "Message 41 is the name of a Stasi agent infiltrating a CIA/BND office. I am sure of it. Even in the right hands that information could get people killed; in the wrong ones it could be catastrophic. You've seen the troops lining up by the checkpoints—this could be the prelude to invasion. Finding that double agent is more important now than ever. So we can go back and forth like this all night if we want, but sooner or later you will have to accept it: no one can get that message for us. I have to get it myself."

Reed shook his head. "That's … insane."

"It is dangerous," said Lise, "but it is possible. The Wall is designed to keep East Germans in, not us out. Why would anyone cross *into* the GDR? They are not even watching for us."

"Keeping us out is *exactly* what it's designed for," said Reed. "They call it an Anti-Fascist Protection Rampart; its entire stated purpose is to keep us out."

"*Stated* purpose," said Lise. "In practice, it is all about containment. They have been losing tens of thousands of people per year since the war, and every increase in border security has been an attempt to stop that tide."

"They're demanding IDs at the checkpoints," said Reed.

"Then I will not go through a checkpoint," said Lise. "They cannot watch every part of the Wall all of the time, right? It is miles long."

Reed remembered the D train, stopped for hours in the tunnel, and shivered involuntarily. "They would never let you out again. But with official sanction—"

"Look," she said. "We cannot do this officially, because there is a GDR informant in our office and they will know we are coming. But if I go in, alone, in the dark, I can get the message and get out before they know I am there."

"You say that like it's easy."

"The best way in is on Bernauer Strasse." Lise leaned forward, sketching imaginary maps on the table with her finger. "It is just a few blocks from here; we could go look at it now if you want. There is a long stretch of road there where the Wall is literally just the side of a building. That made it impossible to patrol, so people started climbing out of their windows to flee to West Berlin. Hundreds of them. The Stasi came through a few weeks after the Wall went up, evacuated those buildings completely, and then bricked up the windows. If this goes on much longer they are probably going to tear those buildings down altogether, because they are a massive security issue. But for now they are still up, and they are still impossible to patrol effectively. So I should be able to walk right up to them, unseen by any guards, and knock a hole through the bricks in some basement window. That is how I get in, and that is how I get back out."

"Even if the GDR can't patrol the back wall of those buildings," said Reed, "you know they'll be patrolling the front. The whole street, probably. And what if they've bricked up the front doors, too? You'll be in East Berlin, sure, but you'll be trapped in a derelict building."

"So *you* cause a distraction," she said.

Reed's eyes opened wide. "Excuse me?"

"Nothing dangerous," said Lise. "Just loud. You go to the nearest open stretch of wall and pretend you are drunk. Start raving about how much you hate the Wall, or the communists, or anything you want, and any Grenzers in the area will come over to see what the trouble is. Smack the Wall if you have to; maybe wave a pair of garden shears around, like you want to cut the razor wire. They're not going to shoot someone on the Allied side of the Wall, especially not with tensions like they are right now. The American State Department is ready to storm Checkpoint Charlie with a tank brigade, so everyone will be extra careful not to start any wars."

"Except for us, apparently."

"You are not going to *do* anything," said Lise, "you are only going to draw their attention. And if you draw enough of it, no one will see me at all."

Reed thought about it, and about Lise, and about the

twenty-three-character message hidden in a hollow in an East German bench. He thought about the Wall, and the East German police officer who stood watch over it across from the Cabin. He thought about Werner Probst, shot dead in the canal.

He thought about his own mother, at home in the States.

"No," he said at last.

"Wally!" growled Lise. "We have to do this—"

"Exactly," said Reed. "*We* have to do this. We're in this together, and if you're going, I'm going."

"You are not trained for field work."

"And you're not trained for decryption," said Reed. "You need me to translate the message."

"You can translate it when I get back."

"*If* you get back," said Reed. "On your own in enemy territory, that's hardly a guarantee. With two of us you have backup, and we increase the chance that at least one of us makes it out."

"You are taking a very defeatist view of this mission."

"It's not defeatist to plan for failure," said Reed. "Planning for failure is how you overcome it. If you don't at least recognize that the *Titanic* might sink, you understock it with life boats and everybody dies."

Lise pursed her lips, looking at him. It seemed like ages before she finally spoke again.

"You are right, I think, about backup. If something happens to me and you are not there, you will have to come in after me—which will be even worse. This way we double our chances of getting the message back out."

Reed tried to smile, but the reality of what he'd just insisted on was starting to sink in.

"Besides," she said, "one person in a park after dark is suspicious, but two of us are just lovers out for a stroll. The GDR is strict, but they do not yet have a curfew; we can walk a few blocks from the empty buildings on Bernauer Strasse, and take a taxi from there."

"We'll need East German marks," said Reed.

"We have plenty at the Cabin," said Lise. "Wohlreich picks them up from the refugees as they come over the Wall; they are practically worthless, so he doesn't even catalog them. I can take some tomorrow and no one will miss them."

"Just like that?"

"Just like that," she said. "And we will need to arrange another distraction at the Wall, if you will not be staying behind to do it."

"The woman down the hall has a teenage son," said Reed. "He and his friends are always getting into some kind of trouble. If I buy them beers they'll make plenty of noise for us, and we can even tell them where to do it."

"Better not to use people who know you," said Lise. "If somebody asks, we do not want this coming back to us. We will find some kids on the street, maybe right there on Bernauer, and have them do it."

"Good idea," said Reed. His stomach seemed to churn. "So. When do we do this?"

"As soon as I get the money from the Cabin," said Lise. "If we are lucky, tomorrow night."

West Berlin

"ACHTUNG," said Bettina. She stood in the doorway to her office, holding a piece of paper, and the officers in the Cabin turned to look at her as she read. "Memo from the US State Department: 'US Commandant General Watson has spoken to Soviet Commandant Colonel Solovyev, telling Solovyev that his men are not doing their part to maintain order and respect during delicate peace negotiations. He has demanded that Soviet authorities take immediate steps to remedy the situation.'"

Bettina lowered the paper and stepped back into her office; apparently that was all.

"'Immediate steps,'" said Wohlreich. "I wonder what that means?"

"It means we want them to stop checking papers at the border," said Chuck.

"And why is it such a problem to check papers?" asked Wagner. "Military and diplomatic personnel are allowed to cross, but no one else. It seems logical that they would check to make sure the people crossing the border are allowed to do so."

"The Potsdam Treaty says that travel throughout the divided country must be unimpeded," said Gisela. "When they stopped Allan Lightner, they broke that treaty."

"And the State Department followed that up with a squad of armed soldiers to force him through," said Frank. "That doesn't violate the treaty, but it's not exactly 'maintaining order and respect,' either."

"Are you on the Soviet side now?" asked Wohlreich.

"I don't know," said Frank. "How many Nazis do they employ?"

"Obviously he's not on the Soviet side," said Chuck, stopping that line of argument before it could go any further. "Geez, Frank, can you calm it down for one damn day?"

"Everyone get back to work," said Ostertag. "I am trying to do maths in here, but you are as noisy as a hen house. Tock tock tock tock tock!"

The Cabin went silent again, and Reed looked back at his work—more of the same math that Ostertag was doing, analyzing the statistical distribution of data from the various numbers stations in the city. It was hard to focus on anything, knowing that just a few hours later, when night fell, he and Lise would be breaching the Wall to enter East Berlin. He found himself staring at the clock, or at the windows, far more often than he should have been.

The Cabin's building had a sister building on the other side of the Wall, practically identical; they faced each other like a man and a mirror. Over the years, Reed had learned to ignore it, but today all he could do was stare at it, a mere fifty feet away. You could play catch from window to window, high above the street; looking straight out, instead of down, you couldn't even tell that the Wall was there at all.

Focus, Reed told himself. *You look guilty and suspicious. Everyone is staring at you.*

He looked back at the numbers in Ostertag's report. It was

a number-frequency analysis of Mother Goose, one of the more active numbers stations in the city; Ostertag was trying to determine what type of encryption Mother Goose was using. Reed tried to focus on the puzzle of it, hoping it would draw him in. The numbers station itself was simple. Once every two or three days, a man would broadcast on a specific frequency; he began by quoting a nursery rhyme, and followed that with a series of two-digit numbers. Ostertag's theory was that these numbers used a one-time pad encryption system, and his math seemed to agree.

A truly random one-time pad would produce patternless junk, a flat field of numbers with no clear peaks or valleys. Every number—and therefore every letter in the encoded message—would show up just as often as every other. Ostertag had transcribed the entire Mother Goose archive, added up the numbers, and found no significant peaks or valleys.

There were some hills—odd little bumps in the data—but they weren't strong enough to mean anything. In both English and German, eight letters accounted for almost two-thirds of the written language. In English, they were E, T, A, O, I, N, S, and H. If E was enciphered as, say, 22, then 22 would show up a statistically noticeable number of times in any significantly large sample size. The Mother Goose archive included well over a hundred broadcasts, most of them with dozens of letters; it was a large enough sample to find any meaningful trends in the data, if they existed. Ostertag claimed that they didn't. Reed checked and rechecked Ostertag's math, going over each calculation, but always found the same.

"Johannes," said Reed. The two cryptographer's desks were facing each other head to head, making it easy for them to confer.

Ostertag answered without looking up. "Tock tock tock," he said, though his tone was only mockingly angry. "What do you need, little hen house?"

"This is good work," said Reed, tapping the stack of papers. "You're right about the statistical frequencies. This is definitely a one-time pad."

"I am delighted to have your approval," said Ostertag. Reed couldn't tell if he was being sarcastic or not. "What do you recommend for the next step?"

Reed stared at the data a moment longer. "Hypothesize for me. There is a total of ninety two-digit numbers, and Mother Goose uses all of them. That's far more than a standard number/letter cipher would ever need. A one-time pad system, if you don't wrap around like we do, would at most use fifty-two. So: how are they encoding a plaintext message in such a way that they end up with ninety possible outcomes for every letter?"

Ostertag kept working. "I thought you had read my report."

"Of course I read it," said Reed, "I've been checking your math all day."

"You have read my thesis and my methods," said Ostertag, and here he finally deigned to look up; he wore a small smirk. "You have not read my projections."

"I ..." Reed flipped through the report, finding a page near the end labeled "Projections." "You're right, I haven't." He skimmed the page, and nodded. "You think Mother Goose is inserting random numbers into his broadcasts to pad them out?"

"It is only a theory," said Ostertag, going back to his work. "But it is a theory I like."

"But why would they—?"

"Tock tock tock," said Ostertag. "Some of us are working."

Reed grumbled, but fell silent. He read Ostertag's projections again, more closely this time, and he had to admit that the theory had merit. Random numbers inserted into the message would be obvious to the intended recipient—if they were expecting them—but added untold amounts of noise into the code itself, making it that much harder to break.

Except ... Why would they need to make a one-time pad system harder to break? If the pad you used was truly random, then the system was already unbreakable. Why complicate an already perfect process?

It was a dead end; Ostertag had already analyzed and reanalyzed everything Mother Goose had ever given them, and this was as far as they could go. Reed hated dead ends, because there was only one thing to do: start over at the beginning, retrace every step, and see if you'd taken a wrong one somewhere. Reed had already checked Ostertag's math—it was all perfect—so now it was time to go even earlier in the process. Had Ostertag transcribed the messages properly?

Reed looked at the clock: 11:34 AM. It was almost lunch time, but he didn't think he could eat a bite. He was too nervous. He sighed and stood up; at least starting from scratch would give him something to fill the time while he waited for night. And for the dumbest, most dangerous thing he'd ever done in his life.

He walked into the back of the Cabin, past the break room to the archive. Here they kept all of their records, including tapes of every coded broadcast they received—Mother Goose, Longshore, and everything else. He found the box of Mother Goose recordings, dug through it for the earliest—*June 4, 1959*—and threaded it through an audio player. He sat down with a pen and paper, and pressed *play*.

The sound was different from what he was used to with Longshore. It was full audio, instead of Morse code blips, so there were scratches and thumps that he didn't usually hear. After a moment, a voice appeared: male, British, impassive.

Jack Sprat could eat no fat, his wife could eat no lean.

"Hey, Wally," said Frank. Reed hit *pause* and looked up,

seeing Frank leaning in through the door of the room. "I'm going to lunch. You wanna come?"

"I ... No thank you. I need to finish this first, and then I've got some numbers I need to run past the Chief."

"Right," said Frank, and grinned. "And you wanting to be here the absolute second another Longshore message comes in has nothing to do with it."

Reed glanced at the clock, then back at Frank. All the nerves and worry of the issue came rushing back to him. "Right," he said, and tried to smile. "Nothing at all."

Frank frowned. "You okay?"

"I'm fine," said Reed, "just ... indigestion. Eating would only make it worse."

"It's all this heavy German food," said Frank. "It's a wonder we're not all sick. I found a good Chinese place, though, if you ever want to give it a try."

"Sometime," said Reed. "Have a good lunch."

"Suit yourself," said Frank, and he stepped back into the hall. "Johannes! Lunch?"

Reed tuned out the rest of their conversation, and hit play on his recording again.

And so, between the two of them, they licked the platter clean. 15, 30, 88, 22, 42 ... It continued like that for a few more seconds—citing fifteen numbers—and then ended. Reed dutifully transcribed the entire thing, and then played it back to make sure he'd gotten it right, and then he even wrote down the nursery rhyme, just in case. Introductions like that were usually meaningless—they were just a way to identify the numbers station, and to make sure the intended audience was listening—but you never knew.

"Achtung," said Bettina in the other room. Reed looked up, then walked to the door and peered in. The rest of the office looked as confused as he was.

"Memo from the US State Department," she continued. "'Soviet Commandant Colonel Solovyev has sent a letter to US Commandant General Watson calling the American use of armed soldiers across the sector border an open provocation, and the use of tanks at the border checkpoints a direct violation of GDR law. Quote: "I am authorized to state that it is necessary to avoid actions of this kind. Such actions can provoke corresponding actions from our side. We have tanks, too. We hate the idea of carrying out such actions, and are sure that you will reexamine your course."'" Bettina's calm look faltered, and she looked at the floor. "That is ... all it says." She turned again, and walked back into her office.

"'We have tanks, too'?" repeated Ostertag. "What the bloody hell is that supposed to mean?"

"It means they're calling our bluff," said Chuck, and scowled. "At least they're not raising yet."

"I don't understand these terms," said Wagner.

"It is an American card game called poker," said Lise. "He means that the Soviets are matching our threat of force with a similar threat of their own, but they are not yet escalating to an even more dangerous level."

"They do not need to escalate," said Wohlreich. "The two most powerful nations in the world have tanks pointed at each other in the middle of our city. Who needs to escalate?"

"We're one itchy trigger finger away from a war," said Chuck.

Davis appeared in the doorway, his voice an angry snarl. "Damn these bullying bastards."

"Commie pricks," said Chuck.

"Ours are no better," Davis snapped. "Both sides are posturing, trying to pretend we're not afraid of the single most frightening thing in the world."

"What else can they do?" asked Wohlreich. "Just let the GDR get away with whatever they want?"

"Of course not," said Davis. "That's the worst part of the

whole affair. We have to do it, and they have to respond, and there's only one way that any of it can end." Ostertag started to speak, but Davis silenced him with a shake of his head. "Johannes and Wally, have you cracked that Mother Goose code yet?"

"We're not even close," said Reed.

"Keep working on it. Gisela, Chuck, Lise: have you found Tsyganov?"

"Not yet," said Chuck, answering for all three.

"Find him," said Davis. "And Wagner, keep watching—damn it, you're not the one watching him."

"Watching who, sir?" asked Wagner.

"None of your business," Davis snapped. He looked almost instantly apologetic. "I'm sorry, that was uncalled for. I'm just tense. And I know you're all working hard, but ... we have to work harder. We can't waste a second. No lunch breaks for anyone; Bettina can bring food in."

"Mr. Schwartz has already gone to lunch," said Wagner.

Davis paused, frowning. "That's ... Jannick, tell him when he gets back."

"Yes, sir," said Wohlreich.

Davis turned and went back into his office. Reed followed him.

"Excuse me," he said, hurrying to catch up. "Chief! Can I have a minute?"

Davis looked at him for a moment before nodding his head. "Sure, come on in." He sat at his desk, and Reed followed him into the office, closing and locking the door behind him. Davis paused at that, then looked at Reed with renewed interest. "What is it?"

"It's ..." Reed faltered, not sure how to bring this up. He'd been thinking it ever since he'd learned about Longshore's real name—ever since he'd been forced to see him as a real person, with a real past, and not just a nameless agent who sent secrets through the radio. He couldn't exactly say all of that, though, so he dropped the preamble and just asked his question straight out: "How much longer? For Longshore, I mean: how much longer do we risk him before we pull him out?"

"As long as we can," said Davis.

"But he's ...," said Reed, and stopped. *He's Dietrich Böhm,* he thought. *Knowing that Lise knew him, and liked him, and misses him ... that changes everything.* It was exactly what Lise had been afraid of: that knowing Longshore's real identity would make her soft. But Reed was softer than Lise had ever been, and he couldn't help but ask. "He's our agent. That means he's our responsibility."

"I understand that you may have ..." Davis paused, searching for the right words. "Developed a kinship with him. You've been reading his messages and interpreting his mindset every day for months. You probably feel like he's talking directly to you, and I understand that; that happens. But we are also talking about the very real possibility of invasion and nuclear war. Every day Longshore stays over there—every minute—he is providing a service and communicating intel that can help us end that war before it ever begins. So if it comes down to pulling him out, or leaving him there for just one more day, I will leave him there for one more day. And one more day. And one more day."

"There's always one more day," said Reed.

"You think I don't know that? You think I don't want to keep him safe? Of course I do. But I will sacrifice him or you or anyone else in the office—I will sacrifice myself, and gladly—to avert this war. Do not forget that, and do not underestimate it."

Reed nodded, his throat too dry to swallow. "I understand," he said, but then he paused. "Does this mean you don't ever intend to pull him out at all?"

"I'll pull him out when having him over there stops being useful."

"He won't stop being useful until he's discovered," said Reed. "That's an awfully small window before he just gets executed."

"Longshore is a professional," said Davis. "He knew what this job entailed when he agreed to do it."

"When he agreed to do it he wasn't trapped on the other side of a barbed wire barrier."

"That only changes the logistics," said Davis. "Not the mission."

A knock sounded loudly on the door. "Chief!" It was Frank's voice.

Davis looked at the door, then back at Reed. "This conversation is over. Longshore and everyone else here will do what they are asked, when they are asked." He nodded at the door. "Let him in."

Reed turned to the door, trying to hide his frown. He didn't like the Chief's callous attitude, but ... was the alternative any better? Would Reed, in the same situation, trade one man's life for the lives of millions? He was certainly supposed to. It was his job to do so.

For the hundredth time in the last few days, he wondered how suited he really was for that job.

The knock sounded again, loud and urgent, and Reed opened the door. Frank was on the other side, practically sneering at Jannick Wohlreich as the Sub-Chief chastised him harshly.

"We are in the middle of an international crisis," said Wohlreich. "I don't care how hungry you are, or how tired, or how sad you are. You have a responsibility to this office, and to your superiors, and yes, even to me, and if that means I tell you to work through lunch—"

"Because Arbeit Macht Frei, right, Jannick?"

"Shut them up and get him in here," said Davis. Reed took Frank by the arm and pulled him in; Wohlreich watched him go, then turned back toward the main office as Reed closed the door.

"Try to behave like a damn professional," snarled Davis. "We have work to do."

"I'm doing what you told me to do!" Frank whispered loudly. Reed worried that even with the door closed, everyone would hear them.

Davis scowled. "I didn't tell you to sass off to a superior officer!"

"You're going to call that Aryan bastard 'superior'?"

"You know damn well what I meant," snapped Davis. "Don't play this game with me, I'm the one who told you how to play it. You're supposed to chafe against him publicly, for a specific purpose and outcome, not drag it back into the Cabin and ruin our entire operation."

Frank glared at the Chief, then sighed and closed his eyes. "You're right," he said. "You're right." His eyes snapped open again, bright and alive. "And it's working. Anselm talked to me today."

Reed's jaw dropped. "What?"

Frank nodded. "That's what I was trying to tell you before that ape tried to crawl down my throat."

"He's your supervisor," said Davis. "He was doing his job."

"And I was doing mine—" started Frank, but Reed cut him off.

"Tell us about Anselm. He actually spoke to you?"

"Yeah," said Frank, finally calming enough to hold still. "He didn't say anything important, obviously, but he sidled up to me at the bar, told me he was having a rough day. We commiserated, he bought me a round, didn't talk about a single thing to make anyone suspicious. If I hadn't known he was a Stasi agent I wouldn't have thought twice about it. He's a smooth operator, I'll tell you what. But we dangled the bait and he snapped it up. Five bucks says he finds me again tomorrow."

"Be slow," said Davis. "You can't just jump straight into asking him about his anti-democratic proclivities."

"You're assuming we have time, sir," said Reed. "This city could be a war zone in days—maybe hours."

"I can't infiltrate a spy ring in hours," said Frank.

"With Wohlreich's help you might," said Reed.

Frank stared at him, eyes wide in a mixture of shock and fury. "Wohlreich? Are you kidding me? After everything he's done, you want to bring in *Wohlreich*?"

"He's our asset handler," said Reed, "this is literally his job. He knows better than anyone in this office how to build a relationship with an adversary. He could teach you exactly what to say, and how fast to start reeling Anselm in."

Frank closed his eyes, shaking his head. "You can't possibly be serious."

Reed kept his voice soft. "Bringing him in is our best chance—"

"No," said Davis. He stared at both men solemnly. "Wohlreich could be invaluable for this, but I'm not convinced he's right for this job."

"Because of—" said Reed, but then stopped himself.

"Because I'm a hothead?" asked Frank. "Because he's a Nazi and I hate him too much to do my job? Damn it, Davis, come on—you know I'm better than that." He closed his eyes again, screwed his face into a snarl, then composed himself. "I can do this. You want to bring in Wohlreich? Let's bring in Wohlreich. He has asset experience that I don't; don't let me be the weak link that keeps us from doing this right."

"That's not what I'm talking about—"

"That's exactly what you're talking about—"

"I mean that's not why I'm leaving him out of this op," said Davis. "I trust him, I just ... don't trust him with this."

Frank stared at him, then glanced at Reed, trying to read his face. He looked back at Davis, then back at Reed, both men saying nothing. Reed looked away, not wanting to meet his eyes, and that seemed to be the clue Frank needed to figure it out.

"Oh, hell," he whispered. "We have a mole."

"Frank," said Davis.

"We have a mole in the Cabin," said Frank, looking at the ceiling. "'Trust him but not with this.' Why not? Because we're trying to fool the Stasi—because if the Stasi know that Frank Schwartz is a triple agent, the whole op goes down the toilet. And the way they find out is by one of us talking." He looked at Davis. "You think someone in the office is a mole."

"Frank," said Reed, but Frank plowed on.

"You don't know who it is yet—if you did then we'd either trust Wohlreich or we wouldn't. But here we are trying to do both at once, so it might be him or it might be one of the others; literally anyone outside of this room."

"One of these days," said Davis, "I will figure out how to keep a secret in an office full of spies."

"I don't think the others have figured it out," said Frank. "I'm the surveillance expert, for crying out loud—watching people is my whole job—and I didn't know a damn thing."

"Lise might suspect it," said Reed. He wanted to talk about her, and about his suspicions, but only if he could find a way to bring it up without making himself look guilty.

"You've seen something?" asked Davis.

"Are you spying on Lise?" asked Frank. He shook his head again. "What the hell is going on in this office?"

"She's an analyst," said Reed, "and we've given her information—not the same stuff you have, Frank, but different pieces of the same puzzle. I think she's figuring it out because it's her job to figure it out."

"Then the fewer pieces we give her the better," said Davis. "Same with Chuck—same with everybody."

"What is this doing to the Cabin?" asked Frank. "Does

everyone have a little piece of the puzzle? Is everyone slowly starting to realize that their friends all might be traitors?"

"Lise has field experience," said Reed. "She's worked with assets before, just like Wohlreich—she'll know skills and techniques that we don't. She could teach Frank how to reel this guy in—"

"I *said* the less information the better," said Davis. "Do you think this is a game? Do you think we can just tell everybody everything and all our problems go away? There is a Stasi agent somewhere in the Cabin—the instant that person figures out what Frank is doing, or why we're looking for Tsyganov, or hears the name Erich Gunter Anselm, everything we have falls apart. Our counter-op destructs. Our contact disappears. Every lead we've managed to come up with turns to ash in our fingers. So, no: we don't tell Lise, we don't tell Wohlreich, we don't tell anybody about anything. We do our jobs and they do theirs; we trust each other explicitly.... Except for when we don't."

Frank looked back at him, nodding, and after a moment he laughed. "This is insane."

"I hate it," said Reed.

"This is espionage," said Davis. "If you can't fragment yourself into at least two people, you're never going to survive here."

"I can do it," said Reed quickly, snapping the words out more aggressively than he'd intended to. "I just hate it."

Frank clapped him on the shoulder. "Welcome to the CIA."

"So solve our problem for us, Wally," said Davis. "If you can do the job, do it. How do we hook Anselm, and how do we do it as quickly as possible?"

Reed mentally kicked himself for his vocal bout of confidence. He had no idea how to attract an enemy asset, so he wracked his brain for anything he might have learned or seen the other officers do. Every time he did, though, his brain kept circling back to the same person, over and over.

Lise.

It had been two months, more or less, since he'd first started to suspect that she was interested in him. He hadn't known how to react, or what to do or say, but had eventually settled on a tactic that might work here.

"Let him come to you, Frank," said Reed. "We still don't know if Anselm is trying to build a relationship with you or not —but if he is, he'll pursue it. He won't expect you to. Too much eagerness from you—too much interest, too much action— might tip him off, or make him suspicious. But if it really is his job to become your friend, let him do his job. If they're planning the kind of thing that would put us on a deadline, it means they're on a deadline, too. He'll move at exactly the speed he needs to, and as long as they don't know we're onto them, that'll be the same speed we need as well. So let him come to you."

It bothered him to realize that his courting strategy had been so weak and reactive.

It bothered him even more to realize that Lise's behavior tracked so perfectly with that of an enemy asset.

Davis watched him for a moment, then nodded. "Not bad. You might be more cut out for this job than I thought you were."

Reed frowned. "Thank you?"

"But we need a secret, too," said Davis. "Something you can drop in a casual conversation, like a kind of down payment—a sign that investing in you as a potential informant will pay off in a big way sometime down the line."

"That's easy," said Frank. "Someone we're surveilling. The Stasi might not know about the bug we planted in the Happels' house. That's the neighbor of the Stasi chief, so it seems like a big deal, but we never really learn anything from it. We could give it up without losing anything valuable."

"We *never* learn from it?" asked Davis. "Or we *rarely* learn from it?"

Frank hemmed and hawed for a moment before shaking his head. "Rarely," he said. "We still do occasionally get something good."

"We'll need something else, then," said Davis.

"Complain about me," said Reed. The two men looked at him in surprise, and Reed steeled his courage. It was another idea he'd gleaned from Lise, the same thing she'd talked about the other night in bed, but much more dire in the new context. "The next time Anselm talks to you, say something about favoritism: that Wohlreich likes me more than you, and lets me get away with stuff, because I'm the only one who gets to see the Longshore messages. They know who we all are anyway, right? I mean, maybe don't say Longshore, but do you see what I'm saying? Pretend that Wohlreich is passing you over for ... vacation time, promotions, rewards, whatever, because I'm important to this office, and to the Chief, and your evil former Nazi boss thinks I have the Chief's ear."

"That's good," said Davis. "That tells them that Wally is the only one who decrypts secret messages, which they almost certainly already know. It's perfect."

"I'll do it tomorrow," said Frank.

"Excellent," said Davis. "Just ... be careful. And for the love of all that's holy, be discreet."

The meeting adjourned, and the officers returned to their desks. Reed glanced at the clock: still only barely past noon. Only half the day gone. His nerves were wound so tight he felt sick to his stomach. He walked back to the archive room, sat down with his pen and paper, and transcribed more Mother Goose broadcasts. He fell into a rhythm, concentrating all his attention on the voice and numbers, and it helped him ignore the clock and his nerves and the agonizing slowness of time. He looked up with a start when he felt a hand on his shoulder; it was Wagner.

"Harald," said Reed. The Cabin was strangely quiet. "What's … going on?"

"It is nearly six o'clock," said Wagner. "Most of the officers have left. I thought perhaps you had become lost in your work."

Reed looked around, wide-eyed, like he'd just woken up from a nap. Cryptographer Face. "Yeah, I think I did." He shook his head, as if he were trying to clear it. "Wow. Um. Thanks."

"You seem as if you are under a lot of stress," said Wagner. "I suppose we all are."

"I think you're right." Reed had just started on a new recording; he made a note of which one it was, then pulled it from the player and tucked the reel back in its box. "I suppose I can finish this up tomorrow." *If I'm here tomorrow,* he thought. *If I'm not a prisoner in an East German cell. Or dead.* He looked down at his notes, now hours of them, spilling onto page after page. He stacked them carefully, squaring the corners, but then he wavered. Should he take them home? He might never have a chance to look at them if he didn't. Or should he leave them here, for someone else to study?

In the end he left them, a neat stack next to the recorder, like a monument.

"Are you feeling alright?" asked Wagner.

"It's been a strange day," said Reed, walking toward the main office, but then he froze. "Did a message come in from Longshore today?"

Wagner shook his head. "They would have come for you immediately." He followed Reed into the large, empty room. "Are you busy this evening, Mr. Reed? I am alone for dinner, and it looks like you could use a companion."

Reed looked at Lise's empty desk, and shook his head. "I can't. I mean, thank you, obviously, that's very kind. But … I promise I'm doing okay, and I'm afraid I have something pressing I need to get home to. Thank you for your help." He waved. Wagner gave a small, hesitant wave in response, and Reed grabbed his coat and hat and slipped out the door. In the corner of his eye he saw Davis, still sitting in his office; he was beginning to think the man never went home. He waved again, at the security guard this time, and then hurried out the door, down the stairs, and out into the cold October twilight.

Part of him wanted to get home as quickly as possible—he was going across the Wall tonight, and he needed to be ready. Another part of him, equally strong, wanted to delay for exactly the same reason.

He was going across the Wall. Tonight. The wrong way.

He didn't want to talk himself out of it, so he ran to the train station, bit his tongue through the ghost stations, and then ran home. When he got to his apartment, he began gathering supplies: black clothes, a warm coat, a hammer to break through the bricks in the Wall. He paced the floor. He cleaned his pistol; he cleaned his kitchen. Anything to use up his nervous energy. He pulled out the personnel files again, and studied their faces: Dietrich Böhm, and Konrad Siedel, and Frida Baumann, and all the rest. Distorted reflections of himself and his friends. He put them away again, and inventoried his equipment, and paced the floor again.

The longer he waited, the more he worried; not about the mission, or at least not directly. What he worried about were the Mother Goose papers he'd left at the Cabin. He'd intended them as a gift, so that Ostertag or whoever else could finish the work he'd started in the event that Reed never returned. The more he thought about it, though, the more it felt like an omen —that by leaving the papers he was assuming his own death, and accepting it. That he was, in some superstitious way, ceding his right to survive and come back. *Better to have taken them*, he thought, *so that I have to come back to finish.*

It left a sour feeling in his stomach, and the wait only made it worse.

At ten o'clock Lise arrived, but the look on her face was grim.

"We are not going tonight. I could not get the money."

"What?"

"We need East German marks if we're going to get anywhere. Davis locked them up—I don't know why."

Reed paled. "Does he know?"

"How could he know?" Lise shook her head. "I have an old contact I went to this evening, but he didn't have any either. I have one more option I can try tomorrow."

"Which?"

"I will break into Davis's safe."

Reed's jaw fell open. "Are you joking?"

"Not at all. You will cause a distraction, and I will crack Davis's safe."

"Absolutely not," said Reed. "We'll just go without the money."

"We need the money."

"Not if it means breaking into our boss's safe!"

"You would rather scrap the entire plan?"

"We don't scrap a plan over a few lousy marks—"

"Weissensee Park is six kilometers from here," said Lise. "We can walk it, but not quickly, and the longer we spend on the other side the more we risk our lives. We need money for taxis, and maybe for bribes, or we risk being late, being caught, being seen, being recognized—even being talked to could ruin everything. We need those marks because the surest way for this to fail is if we do not plan ahead. I know what I'm doing, Wally. Do you trust me?"

"I used to."

"What changed?"

"You *know* what changed! You're asking me to break into the secured safe of a Section Chief of the CIA!"

"Keep your voice down," she snapped, glancing at the

walls. "Listen, Wally. This is the same plan as before, the same plan you agreed to—the same plan you forced me into. Do you want me to go alone?"

"It would be too dangerous."

"Then follow my lead. You are our best cryptographer, but I am our best field agent. I have been working operations like this since before you even came to Berlin. You demanded trust from me, now return it. I will give you the signal, and you will cause a distraction."

Reed closed his eyes. He didn't want to do it, but he didn't dare not to.

"Wally?"

"Fine," he said. "I'll do it."

He went to his bathroom, and threw up in the sink.

THURSDAY, OCTOBER 26, 1961

9:38 AM

West Berlin

ANOTHER DAY GONE.

Military police stared at each other across the Wall. Officers in the Cabin peeked at each other across their desks, drawing invisible battle lines between those they trusted and those they didn't. Wallace Reed very deliberately didn't look at anyone.

Though he watched the clock like a man awaiting execution.

Inside the Cabin, tensions rose, without anything to release them. No new message from Longshore or Mother Goose. No new visit from Erich Gunter Anselm. No new data on the man named Tsyganov, or any of his meetings. The officers kept their heads down, tugging fruitlessly at a Gordian knot of secrets and unknowns and politics and threats, hoping against hope that this cord, that this bend, that this line might be the one they could pull that would finally give them an in.

Nothing worked, and nothing helped.

Outside the Cabin, the city seemed restless, watching the Wall more intently and more nervously than they had ever watched it before. A silence seemed to hang in the streets, as if the buildings themselves were holding their breath. Who would shoot at whom? What would happen when they did? Berlin was a watched pot, perpetually on the edge of boiling, and nobody dared to watch anything else for fear that it would boil over.

Reed tried to work, but the clock was right there, ticking so loudly he thought it would drive him insane.

What did it mean, another day gone? Another day without bad news, but another day without good, either. They solved no mysteries, but started no wars. They survived, but all survival bought them was a slow craw to the next, inevitable crisis. Another day gone, and another night coming.

And that night, Reed was crossing the Iron Curtain.

He had distracted himself all morning the same way he'd done it yesterday, studying the Mother Goose transcripts, though this time he stayed at his desk, analyzing the numbers he'd recorded the day before. He found the same range of numbers that Ostertag had found: 10 to 99. Every two-digit whole number. Ninety separate ciphers. They couldn't stand for letters, there were too many of them. Syllables, maybe? Or key phrases? Number 24 might mean X, or it might mean A, or it might mean 'Stasi' or 'kill' or 'observe' or even 'capitalist dog.' If they were working from a code book, each individual number could mean anything. And the only way to figure out what would be to find the code book.

"But the numbers appear too often," he mumbled. He flipped through the transcripts, well over a hundred of them, some of them with hundreds of numbers each. "There is no phrase they could possibly need to repeat this often. Words, maybe, but even that ..." It wasn't enough to double-check Ostertag's transcriptions, he needed to double-check the number frequencies as well. He pulled out a clean sheet of graphing paper, split it into columns, and numbered the rows from 10 to 99. Then he started at the beginning of the transcripts and made a tally mark for every number he found. 15, 30, 88, 22 ...

He worked through lunch, so absorbed in his work he didn't notice his hunger until his stomach rumbled, loud and insistent. He looked up, shocked at this sudden awareness of the growing ache in his gut, and his eyes found the clock: 3:27 PM. Ostertag caught his eye, and smirked.

"Yesterday a clucking chicken. Today another growling bear."

"Yeah," said Reed, looking down at his work. "I was ..." He'd done a full frequency analysis, with page after page of handwritten calculations. "Kind of distracted." He stared at the numbers, shocked by what he saw.

There were no peaks in the data, just like Ostertag had said.

But there were definitely valleys.

He'd have to graph it to be sure, but it looked like a series of bumpy plateaus, interspersed with deep, narrow pits. He'd never seen that kind of distribution before. What did it mean? He pulled out another sheet of graph paper, ready to draw a chart to see the data more clearly, when he realized that Lise was gone from her desk. He looked around, saw her nowhere, and then looked back at her desk. Papers were scattered across it, almost purposefully haphazard, but there in the middle was her calendar—the same October calendar she'd used for the binary message. Now more dates were marked, overlaid on top of the previous code; instead of Xs in the squares, certain numbers had been circled in pen. The same blue pen had drawn several musical notes in the corners of the page.

October first. October tenth, eleventh, and twelfth. Twelve numbers in all, going as far as November third. Reed fixed the image in his mind, not wanting to be caught staring, and then did the binary calculations in his head.

A six-letter word, starting with P. A. L. Then O. M. A. *Paloma?*

Reed frowned. That wasn't a German word, or an English one; it was Spanish. Paloma meant "dove." He only knew that because of a song—an old Spanish folk song that had become an old German folk song, of which a new recording by Freddy Quinn had spent the entire month of September on the top of the German radio charts. In America they had "Take Good Care of My Baby" by Bobby Vee, but here in Berlin it had been "La Paloma," ad nauseum. Not that Reed had minded—it was a catchy song, and a classic for a reason—but why was Lise referring to it now? The musical notes in the corners made it obvious that she wasn't talking about a street or a restaurant or an actual dove; she definitely meant the song.

Was this the distraction she wanted? For Reed to sing a song?

He didn't look up. He didn't know how long the calendar had been there; how long she'd been waiting for him to sing. He wanted to ask where she was—it wouldn't do any good to cause a distraction while she wasn't in place—but he worried that asking such a question directly would be suspicious. He would do it another way. He kept his eyes on his desk, tapping his papers with his pencil, and then spoke without looking up:

"Hey, Lise, have you figured out which of Gisela's Tsyganovs is our man yet?"

Silence, and then a hesitant syllable from Frank: "She's—"

"Do not tell him," said Ostertag. "I like to see his face when he realizes what is happening."

Reed looked at him. "Realizes *what's* happening?"

Ostertag only grinned, saying nothing but watching him intently.

"Ms. Kohler is not at her desk," said Wohlreich. "She is in the Chief's office; she has been there for quite some time."

Slough it off, thought Reed. *Don't let them know that it matters.* He looked at Wohlreich. "Do you know?"

"About Tsyganov?" asked Wohlreich. He shrugged—an uncharacteristic gesture for him. "We do not *know*, but we are fairly certain it is the businessman from Moscow. Sergei Tsyganov. He has been in East Berlin for a week, according to Aeroflot passenger records—that does not prove he is a KGB officer, but it does place him in the right places at the right times."

"Great," said Reed, and nodded. "Thank you." He looked down at his desk.

This is it, he thought. *She's in place. I don't know how "La Paloma" is going to help her, but if she thinks it will ...*

Very quietly, so quietly it couldn't possibly be a useful distraction, he began to sing: "Ein Wind weht von Süd und zieht mich hinaus auf See ..." He trailed off, losing the words and humming the tune. After another line he forced himself to start singing actual lyrics again, more loudly this time: "Mein Herz geht an Bord und fort muss die Reise geh'n."

"Wally," said Gisela. "I didn't take you for such a sentimentalist." She paused, shooting a glance at Chuck DeMille; he'd started humming along. "What, you too?"

"Give me a break," said Chuck, "this song is practically all I ever hear on the radio anymore. It's stuck in my head like a virus." He looked at Reed, who was still singing softly, pretending to work. "And thank you very much for getting it stuck there again, Wally, I hadn't thought about it for almost the entire morning."

"Some of us are trying to work," said Wohlreich.

"Vor mir die Welt!" sang Wagner loudly, his bass voice booming through the room. "So treibt mich der Wind des Lebens!"

Chuck pointed at him, joining the song with mock enthusiasm, and Reed could watch the tension in the room begin to splinter, crack, and break. Days of nervous energy—weeks of it, really, if not months—had built to a head and now came tumbling down as, one by one, more people joined in the song. It didn't bear any significant meaning, as far as Reed knew, but it was simple, and it was catchy, and it was heartfelt, and this was a room full of intelligence officers who went out of their way not to feel anything too heartily. A song that everyone knew, that everyone could sing together, was like a breath of air at the bottom of the sea.

"La Paloma: ohe! Einmal muss es vorbei sein!" Bettina and Gisela and Ostertag sang with them, and Wagner went so far as to stand up, and Reed felt as if the Cabin had become suddenly a biergarten, with an accordion and a giant barrel of beer, and everyone singing and raising their steins to the smoke-stained ceiling. Reed let himself grow quieter, watching the song in fascination, and saw that Frank wasn't singing at all. Instead he watched the others with a look that could just as easily been bemusement or disgust.

The Cabin officers pressed forward into the second verse. The song was about a sailor who loved the sea too much to stay home with the people who loved him on land. Reed had often wondered if he could ever love anything so much he'd leave his whole life behind for it, but watching a roomful of intelligence officers belting it out with vigor he realized that each of them, in their way, had done the same for this job. For this cause.

Reed would be doing it again tonight, leaving everything he had gained to set out into who knew what.

Another voice joined the singing, and Reed turned to see Davis standing next to Bettina in the doorway. The distraction had worked, but for how long? How long did Lise need? Reed stood, trying to add more animation to the room, but he felt immediately foolish, like he was presenting a paper in school, and knew he had to go further. Participation wasn't enough—a group song like this needed energy and motion. He couldn't think of anything else to do, so he began to sway. It wasn't long before all the others were swaying with him.

"La Paloma: ohe!"

Chuck walked toward Frank as he sang, and began needling him and poking him, trying to get him to join the impromptu folk festival. Reed glanced at Davis, still swaying in the doorway, and thought about Lise. Right now she was in Davis's office, ignoring them all and trying to open the safe. What had she talked about with Davis, to stay in his office for so long? What else might she take from the safe, besides East German marks? Part of him wanted to call it off and report her for stealing; another part of him was sickened by such cowardice.

Wasn't this his plan, too? Wasn't he just as guilty as she was? Either way, it was a reality now. The only way out was to back away, to say no, to either turn her in—and himself with her, after so much collusion—or to let her go alone.

He didn't dare to do either.

He'd come this far, swallowed this many theories, compromised this many principles, and now he was actively aiding a theft from the US government. There was no turning back. If Lise turned out to be a double agent, he had to be there to stop her when she tried whatever it was that she tried; if she was innocent, then he had to be there to help her stop whoever wasn't. Longshore was trying to send them a message, and whether it was out of kinship, or inertia, or simply stubborn curiosity, Reed was determined to find out what that message said.

He looked back at his singing coworkers. Friends, though he may have just betrayed them. How long until he left the office? How long until Lise met him at his house? How long until they paid for another distraction, broke through the bricks in a basement window, and left the free world behind? The ghost stations were disconcerting, but they were a part of a system, and when that system took Reed through them he could surrender his responsibility, knowing that it wasn't him; it was the train. Grab the railing and hold on tight, and if there's a problem it's the train's fault. This was different. This was a conscious choice. But even so. He felt strapped into the machine, watching it move and helpless to stop it.

The song ended, only to be followed by "Muss I Denn," another German folk song, though this one derailed into friendly competition when Chuck and Davis—and eventually even Frank—began to sing Elvis Presley's "Wooden Heart" instead, which had the same tune. Lise joined in on that one, singing as if she'd been there all along, so Reed assumed that she'd gotten what she'd needed. And, once again, he hadn't turned her in. Every time, he chose not to, and every time he felt guilty. Eventually the singers laughed and dispersed, though the rest of the afternoon was peppered with outbursts of other folk songs, with everything from "Der Erlkönig" to "O Susanna" to something in Yiddish that Frank called "Hu-tsa-tsa," which nobody else recognized. At 5:32 PM, Reed left the Cabin; as a good luck charm he took seven or eight of the Mother Goose papers, folded them reverently, and tucked them into the breast pocket of his shirt. It was a deal he made with the universe: bring me back, and I'll finish my work. At 5:57 PM, he boarded a train, and rode the ghost stations home.

At 6:21 PM, he arrived at his apartment. At 9:07 PM, he was still there, staring at the clock, when Lise knocked on his door.

She came in without speaking, and locked the door behind her. "Are you ready?" she whispered.

"No," he said. "But we've got to do it anyway."

"You do not have to come."

"Yes, I do."

They prepared their things: dark coats and hats to help hide in the shadows, but not so suspicious they couldn't wear them in public. Quiet shoes. East German marks, direct from the Cabin safe. They pulled their West German marks out of their wallets, and left them in a pile on the bed, along with anything else that might identify them as Westerners: no IDs, no U-Bahn passes, even the business card of a nearby coffee shop got left behind.

"Weapons?" asked Reed.

"Bring your pistol," said Lise, "but not the holster. We'll be more likely to discard them than fire them."

"But we might *need* to fire them."

"Pray that we don't."

Reed put the High Standard pistol in his pocket, and also grabbed a hammer and a wad of old shirts to help muffle the sound of breaking brick. Lise took Reed's shopping basket from the closet and filled it with every bottle of alcohol he had. It wasn't much, mostly different brands of half-empty wine, so they grabbed some West German money after all and stopped at a store on their way to Bernauer Strasse. They spent it all on bottles of beer, filled the basket, and left it by the Wall, in a pool of light from a streetlamp, in the gap of what used to be an open street. They hid in the shadows, half a block away, waiting for barely five minutes before a group of young men happened on the booze and cheered at their good luck.

Reed and Lise walked further along the darkened street, past a long row of empty buildings. Here the buildings were the Wall, their edges pressed tightly together, and their doors and windows filled with bricks. They found a small window near the ground. Lise held the wad of old shirts against the bricks to muffle the sound, and Reed held the hammer tightly in both hands, ready to swing. He glanced around nervously, wondering who was watching. Could anyone even see them? Would anyone even care? Down the street, leaning against the Wall while East German policemen watched them closely, the young men were laughing and singing and passing around the bottles. Reed hoped it was enough. He swallowed, adjusted his grip, and swung the hammer. It hit with a barely audible thud. He swung again, and then again, over and over, trying to break through the bricks. Lise stopped him occasionally to look at the Wall behind the shirts, measuring their progress; Reed was certain that at any second, someone would come to stop them or arrest them. The teens joked and brayed, seemingly oblivious. It took nearly an hour to knock a hole large enough to fit through. When they finally had it, Lise crawled through first, then Reed. The apartment inside was half-ransacked, as if the family had only had a few moments to grab what they needed and go. Reed wondered if they'd fled to the West, or been forced further into the GDR. He and Lise did their best to reassemble the broken wall, though many of the bricks were pulverized. They shoved a bed against the hole, hoping that it would make the patch more stable or less noticeable. They walked through the home quietly, not knowing how close the East German guards might be on the other side. They found a front window, haphazardly covered with boards, and peered out between the cracks to find a street just as dark and empty as the one behind them. The window still had glass, which would be too loud to break, so they looked for another way out. The front door was sealed with a heavy link chain on the outside, and when they tried to open it —slowly, quietly, barely daring to breathe—they found that it would only pull in a few inches before the chain stopped it. "Not far enough," said Lise. "Maybe the windows on the upper floors are open."

"Go look," said Reed. "I'm going to try to find tools." He was nearly blind in the darkness, but started in the kitchen while Lise went upstairs; he opened each drawer carefully, probing delicately in case any of them held knives. The objects scraped loudly across the wood as he sifted through them, and he was certain that someone outside would hear and come looking. He found a junk drawer with an old screwdriver just as Lise came back downstairs, shaking her head.

"They were thorough. Every window is nailed shut." She pointed at the screwdriver in Reed's hand. "That is not going to help."

"This is for the door," he said, and led her back to the front. The chain would stop anyone trying to get in, but only because the people outside couldn't reach the hinges. On the inside they were perfectly accessible; he worked the flat head of the screwdriver under the pin in the bottom hinge, and slowly levered it up and out. The pin was nearly four inches long, and scraped through the metal rings that held it in place; he had to remind himself that it only seemed loud because he was nervous. He hoped he wasn't lying to himself. He started on the second hinge; it scraped out more slowly than the first, and Reed wished he could see through the door. He imagined a pair of East German soldiers simply standing on the other side, listening to their clumsy fumbling with amused smiles, ready to arrest them both as soon as the door opened.

He pulled the pin out of the second hinge, and started working on the third. Lise seemed to be thinking the same thoughts, for she had pulled out her High Standard pistol. When the last pin finally slid free, she licked her lips and pointed the gun at the doorway, bracing herself for whatever was on the other side. Reed moved the door slowly, pulling it loose from the hinges to pivot on the chain. He opened it just wide enough for Lise to peer out.

Lise looked, then nodded. "Alles klar." She stowed her pistol in the pocket of her coat, and together they slipped outside, reached back in, and propped the door as well as they could in the doorway. They were in East Berlin.

Their abandoned house had also, technically, been in East Berlin, but it had felt like more of a no-man's-land, cut off from either side. Even the ghost stations were a gray area, tolerated by both sides but belonging to neither. This, though, was real; visually identical to the city they'd just left, but somehow, impossibly, a million miles away.

The street in front was more of an alley, a kind of walkway between this row of houses and another that didn't touch the border and thus hadn't been evacuated. They crept silently through the darkness, skirting the edges of dim, glowing circles where light pooled outward from curtained windows. When they reached the street Lise took Reed's arm, holding it familiarly, like lovers out on a date, and the simplicity of the action twisted at his heart. In West Berlin, wary of being seen, they had rarely ever walked so closely or so casually together. Only here, in enemy territory, could they be themselves in public.

The more they walked, the more the shocking sameness of East Berlin chafed at his senses. It was enemy territory, perhaps, but only because his enemies were the people who ruled it. The Stasi. The Grenzers. The Soviet Union, and those GDR officials who went along with their commands, either because it helped them personally or because they saw no way to resist. Everyone else who lived here—the fathers and mothers, the children, the butchers and bakers and brewers and shopkeepers—they were just normal people, as German as anyone on the other side of the Wall, barely fifty feet away. The Wall wasn't even three months old, and before that this had been one city—four sectors, with stricter and stricter rules every year, but still one city. Reed had always thought of the people trapped on the Eastern side as prisoners, straining under an oppressive regime, but walking among them now shattered every illusion he had ever held. Voices drifted down from open windows. Cars drove in the distance. Couples, dressed almost identically to him and Lise, walked quietly down each street, holding hands or talking. People laughed. Televisions droned. A cat sat on the rim of a high wooden fence and watched them go by.

Lise guided him subtly, passing from smaller streets to larger, until they reached the thoroughfare of Torstrasse. They were practically downtown now, and while the city was quiet, it wasn't asleep. People laughed in cafes, or sang in bars, and cars filled the streets with light. They stood on a curb and hailed a cab, and Reed let Lise do the talking:

"Der Weissensee, bitte."

"Ja," said the driver, and took them back out into traffic, deeper and deeper into the GDR. Lise slipped Reed some of the East German marks, and when they reached the park he smiled and paid and helped Lise chivalrously from the car. He worried about his accent, but he'd lived in Berlin for years, and practiced the language daily, and the taxi driver didn't bat an eye. They stood on an asphalt walkway that ringed the park, and watched as the cab drove away.

"You speak well," said Lise.

"Danke," said Reed. She took his arm again, and leaned close and kissed him. "Is that for luck?" he asked, "Or for courage?"

"For both, and for anyone watching two people go walking into an unlit park in the middle of the night."

Reed nodded, and let her lead him into the trees. It was just past eleven.

The Weissensee Park was a narrow ring of trees around a small, dark lake, flat and black but glittering in the faint starlight. Lise led him left, past a shuttered food stand, along a narrow path that skirted the edge of the water. A tiny jetty reached out into the lake, lined with rowboats carefully chained to metal rings. They walked slowly, as if Lise were remembering the area piece by piece, getting her bearings after years of being away. They walked further, past a locked restaurant and tiny junctions with other paths. At one point Lise paused, frowned, and led them backward, finding one of the junctions and taking a different direction. Eventually they reached a row of benches, looking out through the trees at what Reed assumed would be a picturesque view of the lake during the daytime. At night it was dark, and isolated, and Reed felt lost and exposed at once.

"Lass uns sitzen," said Lise, not loudly but cheerfully, still keeping up the pretense that they were simply lovers on a date. She cuddled close to him, and kissed him again, and when her lips pressed up against his cheek she whispered softly in his ear. "I do not think we have been followed. Let us wait a moment and see."

She kissed him again, though he found that any thrill he may have gotten from it was deadened by his anxious nerves, and by the disconcerting theory that she was only kissing him as part of an op; that Lise wasn't kissing Wallace Reed, it was only her nebulous cover identity kissing whatever passed for his. He wondered, all over again, how real their relationship had ever really been. A minute passed, and then another, and soon she nodded. "We're alone." She set her purse on the ground by her feet, and then on the pretense of retrieving it she reached under the bench, probed gently with her fingers, and sat back up. She was clutching something tightly, and Reed saw a triumphant smile on her face.

"Dietrich," she said giddily. "You son of a bitch."

"Did you find it?" She turned her hand over, and opened her fingers, and there in her palm was a tiny metal canister, no bigger than a cigarette. She picked it up, and pulled on one end, and the tip slid off like a tiny metal cap. She set the cap aside, tipped the cylinder into her hand, and a tiny roll of paper fell out. Her whisper was practically reverent:

"Message 41."

East Berlin

"WE HAVE SOME TIME, WALLY," said Lise. "Decode it here, and then we will both know what it says. If something goes wrong on our way back, we will have twice the chance that one of us will be able to deliver it."

Reed plucked the paper from her hand, and carefully unrolled it. It was a string of numbers, carefully written by hand in a firm, black pen. Reed counted exactly twenty-three numbers. This was definitely the missing message. *Gnawed through the insulation,* he thought, remembering the appropriate section of *Player Piano.* He began the translation, found that the first letter was B, and stopped in worry.

"This isn't right," he said. "The confirmation code that day was V—the first letter should be V."

"Maybe he did not use the confirmation code," said Lise. "Try a few more letters."

Reed decoded the second letter—R. The third letter worked out to Q; the fourth and fifth to V and L.

"This is all wrong," said Reed. "It's gibberish." He laughed at the absurdity of it. "We finally find the real Message 41, and it's just more gibberish."

"Maybe you are decoding it wrong."

"I know what I'm doing."

"That is not what I mean," said Lise. "You are the only one who knows the Longshore codes; you and Davis. But Dietrich is not expecting you or Davis to be here. He sent these messages to me, specifically, and he is expecting me to be the one to decode it."

Reed frowned. "Okay, but then ... why skip twenty-three letters from the one-time pad if he isn't actually using them?" He knew the answer as soon as he said it out loud, and shook his head at his own foolishness. "Because that's the only way to let us know there was a missing message. He skipped the letters to get us all looking, but he can encode this in whatever method he knows you can decipher—and you don't know about the code I use." He looked at Lise. "So. What encryption systems did you use when you worked with him?"

"Nothing fancy," said Lise. "Our messages were small, and usually not vital enough for extensive encryption. We used English, and then sometimes ROT13."

Reed almost winced. "Please don't tell me that the safety of the free world was being protected by ROT13."

"I told you, our messages weren't usually vital. Meeting times in public cafes, that sort of thing, and then anything important we said in person. ROT13 was perfect, because even if we were caught we would not look like spies using BND codes, but like college kids, asking each other on dates in silly ways."

"I guess that makes sense," said Reed, but it still bothered him. ROT13 was one of the most well-known ciphers in the world. It stood for "rotate the alphabet thirteen places," so all you did was take A=1 and move it to A=14. If anything, ROT13 was even less secure than A=1; if you turned them into letters instead of numbers, the first half of the alphabet mapped perfectly onto the second, and vice versa, so the encryption and the decryption methods were identical. A=N and N=A. It was fun for hobbyists, but dangerously insecure for anything else.

The first number of the message was 9. The ROT13 for 9 was V. The confirmation code was correct.

Reed closed his eyes. "I can't believe the hidden message we've bent our entire lives around is in ROT13."

"Just decode it," said Lise.

Reed scratched out the other letters with his pen and started over.

V

R

E

E

"Damn," he said, seeing where this was headed. He swallowed, and wrote the fifth letter next to the others: D.

R, E, E, D.

"Your name," Lise whispered.

"I know," said Reed. His heart was racing. Why was his name in this message? "I'm not a double agent."

"Of course you are not a double agent," said Lise, though he could hear the fluster in her voice. "We only *assumed* this message was about a double agent; it could be anything. He could be telling us you are in danger."

"Then dragging me into the heart of the GDR is bad way to tell me."

"He had no idea you would be here," said Lise. "Just ... just finish it. It might not even be your name, once we see the rest of the letters."

Reed nodded, and continued the translation.

I, S, N, T—

"Thank goodness," he breathed. He hoped that 'isn't' was a good thing.

"Hurry," said Lise.

B, A, K, E, R.

"'Reed isn't Baker,'" said Lise. "Why hide this? If he knows who Baker is, why not just tell us straight out?"

"Because he doesn't know who Baker is," said Reed. "He told us as much in his other messages." This made him frown. There was only one reason it would be necessary to say, now, and in this message, that Reed wasn't a specific Stasi agent: to differentiate him from another Stasi agent.

He didn't want to keep going, but he was in it now. Sit down, grab the rail, and hope the train didn't crash.

He decoded the next letter: A. And the next letter: L. Then R, E, A, D, Y. *"Already?"* he wondered. *"Already what?"* Lise wasn't speaking; she was barely even breathing. *"Does she see the same possibility I'm seeing?"* he thought. *"Where this looks like it's going? But it ... It can't possibly be true."* There were only three letters left, and as soon as he decoded the first, he knew what the rest would be:

M

He licked his lips.

"This is wrong," he said.

"Wally," said Lise softly. "Finish the code."

MF

S

The Stasi.

Reed isn't Baker, already MFS.

Barely a second after he wrote it down, Lise was standing up, backing away from him, the pistol in her hand glinting dully in the moonlight through the trees. A Walther P38, with a suppressor attached.

"Drop the pad and paper."

"It's not true," said Reed.

"Drop them."

"Lise, you know it's not true—"

"Just drop them!" she barked, and Reed let the pad and paper fall to the ground, raising his hands above his head.

"Take off your coat."

"Can we talk about this?"

"You have a gun in your coat pocket," she said. "And a hammer, I think, because I did not see you leave it at the Wall. So, yes, we're going to talk, but first you are going to take off that coat, and leave those weapons out of reach, before we say anything."

Reed nodded slowly, trying to figure out what he could do or say. "If I set down my gun you have to set down yours."

"That is not how this works."

He was innocent. He knew he was innocent, and she had to know it, too. She was just being cautious. If he could talk to her, surely she'd understand. He started to stand, but she stopped him immediately: "Nein. Stay in your seat, keep your hands above your head, and pull your sleeves off one at a time."

Reed complied, slowly and without any threatening movements. The October air was cold, and he shivered as first one sleeve came off, and then the other. "Why would I translate that message in that way if I were a Stasi agent?" He dropped the second sleeve, and the coat fell limply on the bench behind him.

"I don't know," said Lise. "Now stand up, and take ten steps over there, to the middle of the path." He stood, and stepped slowly away from the coat and the weapons. She rotated with him, maintaining a careful distance; always out of reach, always with her pistol trained squarely on his torso. She reached his coat, rifled through the folds, and slipped the gun from his pocket to hers. The hammer came next, disappearing into another pocket of her coat.

"Tell me what this means," Lise said.

"It means Longshore is wrong."

"Prove it."

"You *know* me," said Reed. "You know that I'm not a traitor or a double agent."

"I know that you never *seemed* like one."

"Do I seem like one now?"

"No." She paused, watching him shiver in the cold, and then shook her head. "No, you do not. But I cannot ignore this."

"Somehow Longshore is wrong," said Reed. "We can find an explanation—"

"Not together," said Lise. "You need to understand. We're in enemy territory, with no backup and no resources and no way of proving anything. So either I let my guard down, making myself vulnerable to a man our most trusted asset thinks is a traitor, or I find another way. You have to know that I cannot let my guard down, right?" She sounded desperate. "You have to understand that."

"But I'm not a traitor."

"But you have to know that I can't ignore this, right?" She was pleading with him now. "You have to."

"You keep saying that."

"It is true!"

"It's my word against his," said Reed. "Do you really trust him more than me?"

"I ... If I trust you and I am wrong, I die."

Reed choked back a shout, composed himself, and spoke. "So you're going to let me die instead?"

She stared at him in silence, and he saw the glint of tears on her cheeks. "I do not want to," she said at last.

"Then don't."

"Then what? What do you want? What do you expect me to do?"

"I'm not a double agent!"

"How can I possibly know that?" Her voice was trembling. "You insisted on coming here with me—against all logic, against all of your alleged expertise. Is that because you knew what it would say? You knew that you couldn't let me read this message alone, so you came here to kill me and take a different message back to the Cabin?"

"If that was my plan I'm doing a pretty bad job of it."

"Yes, you are."

"So why?" he demanded. "If I really had some grand plan to overpower you, why didn't I do it?"

"Because you never respected me," she said, and there was more pain in those words than in anything she'd said to that point. "I was a field agent for years. I infiltrated Stasi buildings; I passed secrets over the most tightly controlled border in the world. One time I wrestled a KGB operative for ten minutes until I finally choked him unconscious. I am a decorated professional, Wally, and you have always treated me like a frail little girl who does not know what she is doing."

"I ..." Reed trailed off, shattered, and realized it was true. "I'm sorry."

"You thought you could get here—if this is true, I mean— you thought you could bring me here and gloat over the message and defeat me like that." She snapped her fingers.

"Does that really sound like me? I'm a cryptographer, Lise: I'm a mathematician who likes puzzles. I'm a terrible intelligence officer and useless as a spy, and you *know* that. You know *me*. I didn't think you were weak because you're a woman, or because I'm arrogant, or anything else, I just ... I just assumed you couldn't do things because *I* couldn't do them. Because *I'm* weak." He paused. "Lise. What's more likely? That I'm a Stasi mastermind, or that I'm a bookworm in over his head?"

"The bookworm," she said instantly. "By a mile." She shook her head. "I want to believe you, but you have to understand that I cannot. Not here."

"You keep saying that."

"Not until I am safe." She paused, swallowing, but kept the gun trained on his chest, and when she spoke again her voice was harsh. "Maybe I am just a silly little girl. Too stupid to see past your awkward mumbles and your friendly manners and your ... Cryptographer Face." She spat the last two words like they were poison; like they were good friends she'd trusted, and then they'd betrayed her.

"Just put down the gun," said Reed.

"Look at this from my side," said Lise. "You might be innocent. You probably are. The only suspicious things you have ever done in your entire life are the ones I talked you into. But now there is a note." Her voice broke again. "Now there is an accusation, and even if it is false I cannot ignore it. You have to see that, right? If it is true, you kill me, the first chance you get. Or you leave me alive, and I take you back to the Cabin, where every officer there and half the US State Department are searching for this message and the double agent it reveals, and ... what? We tell them we found it, and it says the traitor is you, but you said you were innocent and I just believed you? No one would ever trust me again. Or worse: we do not tell anyone, and no one ever finds the message, and then a year or a month or even just a week later, when I am fully and completely guilty of hiding a potential double agent, you tell me that it is true, every word of it, and threaten to blackmail me if I do not help you pass secrets to the Stasi. And then, like before, no one ever trusts me again and they will be right not to." She shook her head. "I am in this too deep already, Wally: the lies, and the spying on Davis, and now stealing from his safe. We sneaked across the Wall. And even if we had not done any of those things— even if we had sat back and let all of this pass us by—we have still been hiding an illegal relationship from the CIA and the BND. For months. The one and only way we could ever recover from any of this is if that piece of paper had someone else's name on it. Any name at all. We could take it back, expose the traitor, and be heroes." She was crying now.

"But it is your name. And true or not, that name has destroyed us."

"You could take me in as a prisoner," said Reed. "They'll lock me up for a while, but they won't find anything, and we'll both be exonerated."

"How could I possibly take you back as a prisoner?" asked Lise, exasperated. "Think this through, Wally: if you are really a traitor, you will take the first opportunity to attack me, so I need to either keep this gun on you or knock you unconscious. Do you really think that in either of those scenarios we can just stroll out of this park, hail another taxi, and flee the wrong direction across the Wall?"

"I won't attack you."

Lise shook her head. "I have learned two things in my life. First, anyone who spends his energy telling you he is trustworthy, is not. Second, when an enemy goes out of his way to show you how weak he is, that's the one you kill first."

"You don't ..." Reed felt his knees start to weaken. "You don't have to kill me."

"But I cannot let you follow me. If you are part of the Stasi I cannot let you warn them I am trying to cross the Wall."

"You're going to leave me here?"

"What other choice do I have?" She reached up with her free hand, and wiped the tears from her face. "If you are guilty, then the fate of the free world rests on my shoulders to stop you. Even if you are innocent, I cannot take the risk of letting you go. But if you are innocent ... Wally, if you really are innocent, please: lay low. We will find a way to prove it, and bring you home."

Reed took a step toward, but she stopped him cold with a gesture of her pistol.

"I know it is hard. If my name was on that message, you would do the same to me."

"I ..." He hesitated again. "No, I wouldn't." And then he said out loud what he'd never dared to say before. "I love you."

Lise stared at him for a moment, drawn out into an eternity in the dark, empty silence of the park. He stared back.

She angled the gun down, and shot him in the foot. Even suppressed, the noise of it exploded through the empty park, and Reed fell to the ground with a grunt, clutching his foot while a cacophony of pain screamed through his skull.

"People will be coming to investigate the shot," she said. "Get out of here, try not to leave a blood trail, and lay low. If you are innocent, we'll get you out."

Reed tried to answer, but all he could manage was her name, screamed out in heartbreak and betrayal:

"Lise!"

She turned away, and disappeared into the night.

FRIDAY, OCTOBER 27, 1961
12:03 AM

East Berlin

REED GRITTED his teeth against the pain, trying to concentrate. He needed to ... something. *Pain.* His foot was all he could think about. Bolts of pain stabbed up through his leg and into his thighs and back, and he found himself writhing in the dirt of the path.

No, he thought. *I have to ... what?*

I have to move.

People are coming. I have to get out of here.

He bit down hard, clenching his teeth together. He was lying in the dirt, partially smeared with it. His right foot was bleeding, a red tide pooling out through the bullet holes in his shoes—mostly on the bottom, but even the hole in the top was oozing red. He needed to wrap it. With what? His coat. His heavy wool coat was still draped on the bench, a black hole in the darkness of the park. He dragged himself toward it, using one hand and his one good foot, keeping his left hand clamped tight on the wound to try to stanch the flow of blood. He dragged the coat down to the ground. It was a trench coat, calf-length, with a tie for the waist. He wrapped his foot in the folds of it, around and around, and used the tie and his own leather belt to cinch it down hard. It would stop most of the bleeding for now; he could do better when he got clear of the danger.

Reed paused, clenching his fists to distract himself from the pain, and tried to listen. Was that voices? How close were they? The gunshot wouldn't go unnoticed; people would come. He needed to hide, but he didn't know where. Which way was the road? He'd gotten so turned around by the message and the argument with Lise and the pain. Did she really think he was a Stasi agent? Had she really shot him?

There was no time to dwell on it now. He had to move.

He grabbed the bench and heaved himself to his feet, putting all of his weight on his left leg. The lake was behind him; during their walk to the bench, it had been on their right. If he kept it on his left, he would be walking back to the main road, and he didn't want that. He had no money for a taxi, his foot was a giant ball of wool, and his hands and arms were covered with blood. He needed to stay hidden. He kept the lake on his right side, and started hobbling along the path, deeper into the park.

Every step was agony. His foot felt like it was on fire, and any pressure—on or off—sent spikes of excruciating pain rocketing up his legs. He clenched every muscle in his upper body, not just his hands but his arms and his elbows and his shoulders, tightening his chest and flexing his jaw, using the exertion as a distraction from the pain in his foot. He passed the first tree, then the second, then the third. He could definitely hear voices now, off to the left. He glanced down and behind himself, looking for the telltale glimmer of blood on the path, but there was nothing. The layers of his coat were stopping it for now. He kept walking. A fourth tree. A fifth.

All he wanted to do was lay down. They couldn't find him if he laid down, right? But of course they could. He was wearing a white dress shirt; he practically glowed in the dark.

And once the police found blood they'd bring dogs, and then it wouldn't matter what color he was wearing. He had to get far away, and he had to move faster than whoever was looking for him.

He needed a car.

Streetlights ahead of him beckoned him onward; he was nearing the far side of the park, or at least he could see it now. The park seemed to go on forever, but he knew that was probably just an illusion brought on by the pain, and the slow speed of travel.

Where could he get a car? Could he risk just ... introducing himself to someone? Hi, I'm an American intelligence officer on a secret mission. I need you to hide me. East Berlin was full of Western sympathizers, but what were the odds he could find one? And on his first try? Even one GDR loyalist, or one fence-sitter too frightened to defy the Stasi, and Reed would find himself arrested before he could do anything about it. Could he steal a car instead? Could he even drive one? The bandage on his right leg would make the pedals almost impossible to use, let alone the wound itself.

The path reached a clearing; the lake on his left, and a wide lawn with an empty parking lot on his right. He set out across the grass, keeping to the trees as best he could, and skirted the open area with slow, agonizing steps.

He passed another restaurant on his right, closed and empty for the night, and then a dark house on his left. He was nearly at the edge of the park. The road here was lined with parked cars, and he started trying the handles of each one, hoping to find one open. Some of them were, but none had keys in them. He was out of the park completely now, walking between two apartment buildings; some windows had lights, but most were dark. He paused, leaning against a wall to take pressure off his foot. A car drove past on the road ahead, and

Reed pressed himself more fully against the wall, trying to blend in and disappear.

The road was empty again, and Reed dragged himself along the wall, hopping on his good foot. None of the cars would work. How close were the pursuers behind him? He looked back, but didn't see anyone. Had he gotten away? He heard dogs baying in the distance; he didn't know if they were police dogs or not, and didn't want to risk finding out. He crossed the street to another tall building, though this one was clearly not an apartment, and didn't look like an office building. He hobbled to the nearest window, peered in, and saw rows of desks. It was a school, probably a high school by the size of it. That gave him an idea, and he clenched his teeth against the pain and hopped around the periphery of the building, looking for the main entrance. He found it, and sure enough, it had a bike rack nearby with a pair of forgotten bicycles. One of them was unchained. Reed said a quick prayer of gratitude, newly convinced that God might be real, and pulled the bike out onto the sidewalk. He threw his bad leg over the seat, took a deep breath, and launched himself forward. He whimpered out loud as he pressed down on his right foot, trying to use the thick wrapping of his makeshift bandage to work the pedals, and rolled away into the night.

He didn't know where he was going.

His first priority was to get away from the scene of the shooting, and deal with his other problems when he had more time. He coasted through empty side streets, putting distance between himself and the park, and catalogued those problems now. For starters, he was bleeding to death. The bandage on his foot was keeping his blood off the ground, but he suspected it was doing very little to keep that blood inside of his body. His increasingly light head and woozy sensations only added to that fear. He needed to find a pharmacy soon or, at the least, any collection of fabric he could use to bind his wound more tightly.

A clothing store might be better than a pharmacy, he decided, because his other immediate problem was his shirt, with its sleeves stained from blood. They would make him stand out far too easily anywhere he went.

And that was the biggest problem, wasn't it? Where to go. He needed to cross the Wall. Assuming he could even make it to the abandoned homes on Bernauer Strasse, was that route still open? It was hard enough to believe that one agent could make it back through the way they came in, let alone two, let alone with one of them injured. How, then? The Berlin Wall was, as Lise had said, the most closely watched, tightly controlled border in the world. Werner Probst, and dozens like him, had been shot for even *trying* to cross it; Reed couldn't just stroll up and do it, and he certainly couldn't do it alone.

But who could he turn to? The only contact he had in the GDR was Longshore, and Longshore apparently thought Reed was a Stasi agent.

He reached a row of darkened storefronts, and slowed his bike to peer into them. A bakery, a grocery store, a bookshop, another bakery. He turned a careful arc in the road, and rolled down the other side of the street. An electronics shop. A real estate agent. A sewing shop. He stopped at this one, leaning on his good leg. The window was full of mannequins, but behind them he could see walls lined with shelves, all of them filled with bolts of fabric. It would be perfect, but how could he get in?

As was common in Germany, the stores were the bottom floor of a much larger building, and the upper floors were almost certainly homes and apartments. Breaking the window would make noise and attract attention. He kept his bad leg draped over the bike, and hopped alongside it around the side of the building, looking for another way in. An alley led to the building's rear, where a couple of cars shared the narrow space with a series of garbage cans. He heard music drifting down

from an open window above, probably a record player; he heard
no voices, but stayed as silent as possible just in case. He
counted the back doors, trying to calculate which would be the
rear entrance to the sewing shop. He made his best guess,
leaned the bike against the wall, and studied the small glass
window in the door.

Would anyone track him this far? Would some enterprising
police detective connect the shooting in Weissensee Park to the
mysterious thefts of a bicycle and some fabric? Would they
connect any of it to a rogue CIA officer, abandoned on the
wrong side of the Wall? He was running out of time, and
couldn't waste any more of it on theories and extrapolations.
He leaned his back against the window, dampening the sound
with his body, and slammed his elbow into the thin pane of
glass. It shattered, and Reed held his breath, listening for a
response. No one seemed to have noticed. He reached his hand
through the broken window, turned the knob, and let
himself in.

In addition to the main store area, the shop included a
storage room, a tiny restroom, and a small back room, more of a
break room than an office. This had a woman's jacket hanging
on a wooden coat rack, and he put it on gratefully. He grabbed
a bolt of thick cotton, a pair of heavy scissors, and a small
cushion bristling with pins, and went into the restroom. It was
barely more than a toilet and a sink, though the floor was tiled,
and the wall had a spigot that they probably used for mopping.
He took a long, ravenous drink from the sink, then collapsed on
the toilet and allowed himself a single, luxurious minute to rest.
It was one of the greatest sensations he had ever felt. Even with
the jacket on he was shivering, from cold and from loss of
blood, and something in the back of his mind told him to just
give up—to stay here, relatively warm and no longer running,
and just let whatever happened happen. He listened to that
voice longer and more intently than he should have, practically

in tears at the pain and exhaustion he was feeling, both physical and emotional.

Just wait, he told himself. *Stop running and just wait.*

No.

With more effort than he cared to admit, he forced himself to lean forward and undo the belts that held the coat to his foot. The wool coat loosened, and he unwrapped it slowly; the inner layers were soaked with blood, and he let the coat fall in a dark, pungent pile in the corner. Next came his shoe, and he groaned in agony as he loosened the laces and then pulled the thing free of his foot.

The sight of his foot, and the hole through the middle of it, almost made him pass out.

He dropped his head between his knees and took deep breaths. When he thought he could move again he started unrolling cotton sheeting from the bolt; he took about two yards, and then got to work cutting it into strips of bandage with the scissors. He wanted to wash the wound, but worried that the pain of it would be too strong. More than that, though, he was simply bleeding too much to let the wound go unwrapped even one second longer. He shoved a wadded bandage into the hole, gritting his teeth at the pain that burned through him at the touch, and then began winding more bandages around his foot, stretching them as tightly as he could.

When he finished, he secured the bandage carefully with pins from the cushion, and then collapsed back onto the toilet again. Two problems dealt with, and if he kept the jacket he was wearing that made three. Now he just needed somewhere to go, as he doubted the shop's owners would take kindly to him breaking in and stealing their things. He wished he had something to repay them with, but he'd left everything of value in his apartment.

But where could he go? Who, in the vast city of East Berlin, would take in an American spy? He didn't know anybody here—

Wait.

He hauled himself to his feet and limped back to the front of the store. He'd seen a phone behind the counter, which meant that there might be ... yes. A phone book. He set it on the counter, and flipped to the Rs.

He didn't know anybody here, but Lise did. Her old contact, Pollard Rapp.

He found the address, and looked it up on the map in the back of the book. Three miles away; not easy to get to, by any means, but not impossible, either. He tore the map from the phone book, and hobbled outside to the bike.

2:21 AM

East Berlin

POLLARD RAPP LIVED IN A SQUAT, gray house on a street
called Mittelsteg. It was a quiet neighborhood, full of houses
instead of apartments, each with a small yard and tall pine
trees. *It was probably a peaceful neighborhood,* Reed thought,
but he was too exhausted—and too terrified—to feel anything
but dread. Every tree seemed to loom over him like a phantom;
every home seemed to house Stasi surveillance and KGB
informers. Reed found Rapp's house, read the number twice to
be sure he'd gotten it right, and pulled his bike behind the small
car that sat in the narrow driveway.

He dragged himself to the door, driven more by desperation
than any actual remaining strength, and rang the bell.

A moment passed in silence, and he rang it again. Three
times, to be sure the old man could hear it.

Reed watched the other houses nervously, and the shadows
and the formless silhouettes, certain at any moment he would
see police and soldiers pouring out of the darkness to arrest
him. He rang the bell, and then he rang it again, and then again
and again and again, horrified now that the neighbors would

hear it and come looking, but too horrified to stop. Finally, he heard footsteps behind the door, and shouted curses.

"Drecksau!" The door opened, and an old man stood in the entryway, wearing a robe and slippers and scowling in a fury. "Verflucht noch mal! Das ist halb drei am morgen! Wer bist du!"

"Please," said Reed. He clutched the railing for strength. "Ich brauche ..." He couldn't remember his German, and switched to English, though he felt like he could barely remember that, either. "I need your help. Medicine."

"Gott im Himmel," whispered Pollard. He stared for a moment, then started to close the door, but Reed shuffled forward, trying to keep it open with his hand.

"Please," he said. "I'm a friend of Lise Kohler." Even if it wasn't true anymore. He took a ragged breath, and zipped open the stolen jacket to show the man the bloodstains underneath. "Please."

Pollard looked at him a moment longer, then took Reed by the arm and pulled him inside. He took one last, careful look at the empty street outside, then closed and locked the door, and led Reed to a couch.

"Sit here. What medicine?" He pointed at Reed's foot. "You are hurt?"

Reed collapsed on the couch, closing his eyes in relief. "Shot. I was on a mission with Lise. It ... went bad."

"Wait here," said Pollard, and Reed heard the floor creak as the man went to get something.

The next thing he knew, sunlight was peeking through the curtains.

"Guten Morgen," said Pollard.

Reed opened his eyes; he was laying on the old man's couch, in a tiny living room rimmed with knickknacks and photos. He tried to sit up, but the motion made him woozy and he sank back down.

"Sun," he said. His throat felt raw. "What time is it?"

"A quarter for eight," said Pollard. "I gave you drugs, and cleaned your foot."

"Eight," said Reed, grimacing. "I've slept for hours."

"Not long enough," said Pollard. "You need rest."

"I need ..." Reed trailed off. He didn't know what he needed.

Reed raised his head just enough to look down at his legs. His foot was wrapped in a different bandage; the wraps had frayed edges, and a hint of a faded floral pattern. Probably old sheets. He moved it, gingerly, and found that while it still throbbed, the strident fury of the pain was dulled.

"You cleaned it?"

"It is not good to leave a wound dirty."

Reed laid his head back down on the couch, and closed his eyes in amazement. "I don't know how I slept through that, but thank you."

"I have Ischias," said Pollard, reaching his hand to point at his own back. "I do not know the English word. Back pain." He smiled. "I have good pills."

Reed nodded. "You saved my life."

"Maybe." The old man shrugged. "You are still in East Berlin." He glanced at the window, though the curtains made it impossible to see outside.

"I know this must be dangerous for you," said Reed. "Risking yourself for me like this. I want you to know that I'm incredibly grateful. I don't know how, or even when, I'll be able to repay you."

"We have always done what we can for Germany," said Pollard, and looked at one of the photos hanging nearby on the wall: a younger Pollard, with a woman and a son. He stared at it a moment, then looked back at Reed. "You are not supposed to be here?"

"I am not. I was on a ... secret mission, I guess. I'm a spy, for the West."

"And you know Lise Kohler?"

"She was my partner, sort of." Reed frowned, and tried to weave a better-sounding version of the truth or, at least, a more confident one. "Not permanent partners, but last night we were. She used to talk about you, sometimes, so when we got separated I came here."

A look of concern clouded Pollard's face. "Is she shot, too?"

"Not as far as I know," said Reed. "When she left me she was fine. I assume she got back over the border again, but ... I don't know for sure."

"The Wall is right behind us," said Pollard, pointing toward the back of his house. "I do not think you can get out through here, though. Too many Grenzers."

"That's what I figured." Reed tried again to sit up, and this time managed to pull himself upright though, even then, he had to rest his head flat against the back of the couch, feeling too weak to support his own weight. "I don't know how I'm going to get out. I just needed somewhere to hide."

"You stole that bicycle," said Pollard.

"Yes."

"It is a girl's bicycle," said Pollard, nodding sagely. "And your jacket."

"The police might be looking for them," said Reed. "When I leave again, I can't take them with me."

Pollard frowned. "Surely the jacket will be less familiar than your face."

"The police haven't seen my face."

"Then how were you shot?"

Reed didn't answer for a long while, trying to come up with something. Finally, he settled on a version of the truth that seemed to explain things without incriminating himself.

"Lise and I were looking for a message, left in secret by an agent we've been working with. We found it, and translated it, but then somebody found us. The shot was wild; that's why it hit my foot instead of something vital. Just bad luck that it hit me at all, really. Getting the message back to the West was more important than saving me, so Lise ran one way and I ran the other. I ... drew them off and got away." He couldn't resist adding that last part, assuring the old man of Lise's safety, and of his own heroism, but saw immediately that it was a mistake. Pollard's forehead wrinkled in concern, and he looked at the window again, leaning forward to peek through the gap at the edge of the curtain.

"Are you sure they did not follow you?"

"This was miles away," said Reed. "I promise, no one knows where I am."

Pollard didn't look convinced, but he settled back into his chair. He looked at the floor for a moment, then back at the dark curtain. "Where do you go now? Can your government get you out?"

Reed felt himself deflating inside, his eroding hope starting to crumble in bigger and faster chunks. "Probably not. It was a very ..." He didn't even know how to finish that sentence. *It was a very illegal mission,* he added to himself, *completely unsanctioned by his office or the government, and instead of good intel it had resulted only in getting me accused of treason.* If Lise had made it back safely, she would already be in Davis's office telling him the entire story. It might be that he could never go back at all. "I don't know what to do," he said. "You want the truth? I'm not a field agent; I'm a cryptographer." He reached inside the jacket to the breast pocket of his shirt, and pulled out the Mother Goose papers. "See? This is the kind of stuff I do: letters and numbers. I'm just a ... mathematician, with delusions of grandeur." He dropped the papers on the couch next to him. "I came on this one mission because we needed my one specific skill set, and now everything's gone wrong and I don't know how I'm ever going to get back home again. Maybe I can't."

"Lise will find a way," said Pollard. "She was always very good at her job."

Reed nodded, more in resignation than agreement. Lise being good at her job was part of the whole problem right now.

If only he could talk to her again. If only he could talk to Davis. Davis knew he wasn't a traitor, right? Unless Davis was the traitor, and used this as a perfect opportunity to frame someone else. He thought about it for a moment, and wondered if there was anyone in the Cabin he could be completely certain *wasn't* a double agent. Wohlreich? Wagner? Frank? Frank was pretending to be a traitor, but that didn't mean he hadn't already been one for real. If he was such a prime candidate for shifting his loyalties, who's to say the Stasi hadn't already turned him? And now Davis had given Frank the perfect cover for passing secrets to the enemy. They'd literally ordered him to do it.

The more Reed thought about it, the more he realized that the only person he trusted—the only person he was one hundred percent sure of—was Lise. If all she'd planned to do was get rid of him, she'd have done it. Why leave him alive? No. It was far more likely that this was all real—that Longshore really was her old partner Dietrich Böhm; that Böhm really was trying to warn her about a double agent; that Lise really had been just as surprised by that message as Reed. If there was anyone in the Cabin he could trust, it was her.

But how could he get her to trust *him*?

"Do you have a car?" Reed asked. "I mean, I'm sorry. I saw a car in your driveway. Can you take me somewhere?"

"Can you walk?" asked Pollard. "There are places in the country where the border is less closely patrolled, but you would have to walk for miles even to reach it, and you would have to be very lucky to cross."

"We're not going to the Wall," said Reed. "Or I guess we are, but we're not going to cross it. Not today. I'm going to try to send Lise a message."

"I can loan you some clothes," said Pollard. "Where are we going?"

"To Neukölln," said Reed. After all, the Cabin was barely ten feet away from the Wall there. People talked across it all the time. Why not Reed and Lise?

Pollard went into the back of the house, the old floors squeaking as he shuffled through the halls, and after a few minutes he returned with a pair of trousers, a button-up shirt, and a pair of boots tall enough to hide the bandage on Reed's foot. Reed changed, gingerly, doing his best to keep his foot from flexing, while Pollard went back into the bedroom a second time. When Reed was dressed, Pollard returned with a coat, a hat, and a cane. Reed accepted them with audible relief, and together they walked out to the car. Pollard was almost as slow on his feet as Reed was, and Reed tried to stop him and give back the cane.

"Please. This is yours; I can't take it."

"Michelle, my wife, would want you to have it," said Pollard, and handed him a bottle of pills. "These also. Two more now, two more tonight, but do not take too many." He smiled. "You will start to see pink elephants."

Reed smiled back, took the bottle, and swallowed two pills dry.

The drive was long; south past the French Sector, then through the city center on their way toward Neukölln. But they had only gone a few kilometers toward the center when traffic slowed nearly to a stop. They sat in the car for several minutes, inching forward at a glacial pace, when Pollard finally rolled down his window and shouted a question to a driver who was inching north in the opposite direction. Reed couldn't hear the exchange, and waited for Pollard to lean back into the car and roll his window back up.

"The American army has stationed a tank division in Friedrichstrasse," said Pollard. "Every soldier and Stasi officer in the city is heading in to respond." Pollard frowned at the traffic. "He said he thought they might start shooting."

Reed looked at the street ahead, concerned. "It can't be a real attack. I mean, I can't imagine it would be. We'd have heard something, or they'd be routing cars out of the combat zone."

"Maybe they are," said Pollard. A few blocks later they found a police officer waving all the southbound cars onto another road, detouring them away from the city center. Pollard drove in silence, his face solemn, and Reed craned his neck to peer down each new side street, trying to see any signs of fighting. There was no smoke. No sound of guns or bombs. Were they really fighting? Or just escalating the showdown?

How much further could it escalate before it exploded?

It took them over an hour to reach Neukölln, and then they drove down Elsenstrasse toward the Wall. They could have driven right up next to it—they could have rammed it if they'd wanted to—but the Grenzers were still watching, and Pollard pulled to a stop about a half a block away.

"Here?" he asked.

"Here," said Reed. "Thank you for the ride. Can you wait?"

"I am retired," said Pollard, "and you are trying to stop a war. Do I have anything better to do?"

Reed smiled, gripped the old man's arm, and then stepped out of the car. The experience was surreal; the same neighborhood he saw every day, the same skyline, the same sounds, even some of the same people, but all from the East side of the Wall. It was like looking through a mirror, knowing you were trapped on the wrong side of it. He felt unsettled and ... wrong, like a stranger in his own skin.

He walked to the end of the street, leaning heavily on his cane, his foot throbbing with pain, and then there it was: the Wall, topped with barbed wire, and beyond it the tall building that housed the Cabin. A similar building faced it from across the Wall, like twins separated at birth. Reed stopped by the corner of the building, watching the Cabin's door, wondering if anyone would see him, wondering what he would say if they did. He didn't really have a plan, despite all the time he'd had to come up with one. He looked up at the fifth-floor window, hoping to see someone he knew, and there was Ostertag, leaning on the windowsill and smoking, staring into the park. Even though Reed had hoped to see someone—had expected to see someone—it still shocked him. His friend and coworker. So close and yet so unreachable.

Reed looked around again, and spotted a Grenzer; there was always at least one, this close to the Wall, and probably far more. Reed swallowed, steeled his courage, and waited. As soon as the Grenzer looked away Reed waved to Ostertag, but the man didn't seem to notice. He was probably staring at the yoga girl, Reed realized, and he looked toward the park to see if he could see her. Maybe if he walked up next to her, right into Ostertag's field of view, he could get his attention and pass him a message. Reed gritted his teeth and started walking.

How could he do it? Ostertag was a cryptographer, so there should be any number of ways to send a message that the man would understand. Morse code, maybe just by moving his hand up and down. Or semaphore, which was literally designed to be read by one cryptographer looking at another. But, no, that would be too obvious. Everyone in the park would see what he was doing, and know that he was sending a message across the border. He had to find a more subtle way of doing it. But how could you send semaphore subtly, so that no one could tell that's what you were doing?

And then he saw the yoga girl, standing in the park, her legs spread wide and her arms held firmly to the sides, straight out like the arms of a cross.

It was a perfect semaphore R.

Reed froze, staring at the girl. It couldn't possibly be. Could it?

She held the pose for several seconds, and then moved to another—the same pose Ostertag had pointed out to Reed before, with her hands and feet on the ground and her backside pointed high in the air. It had seemed so salacious at the time, with Ostertag leering, but now all Reed could see was two arms pointed at downward angles.

The semaphore signal for the letter N.

He glanced up at the window, but Ostertag wasn't looking at him; he was staring at the girl, and Pollard's borrowed hat, he supposed, made Reed unrecognizable from above. He stepped under a tree, just to be sure he stayed hidden, and watched the girl move into another pose: sitting on the ground, right leg pointed out to the side, with her body bent over it and her left arm pointed up at an angle. Another yoga pose, probably designed to stretch the lower back. And also, if you looked at the leg as an arm, a perfect semaphore O.

She moved into the reverse of the same pose: W.

She had just spelled the word 'now.'

She balanced on her hands, and spread her legs wide: probably a U.

Then something he wasn't sure of, but could have been an S. Or a D. Some of the letters were more obvious than others, and in some poses he couldn't tell if he was supposed to pay attention to the arms or the legs.

Next came an obvious E.

"Son of a bitch," whispered Reed. *Something-R, Now, Use.*

The girl in the park was spelling a clear, readable sentence, right under their noses.

And Ostertag was the double agent.

East Berlin

REED STEPPED CLOSER to the trunk of the tree, his eyes wide, his hands trembling as he clutched the cane. What was the full message? She was telling someone to use something, something with an R at the end of it. Baker? Wagner? Kohler? She moved into another pose—what he now knew was an S— and then a C, and then ... something he couldn't figure out. She squatted on her fingers and toes, looking for all the world like a frog, and then slowly rested her knees on her elbows and lifted her feet off the ground, balancing all her weight on the palms of her hands. Maybe from Ostertag's perspective it looked like something, but Reed couldn't tell what it was.

She finished the pose, and as she moved to the next one she glanced at Reed, and he realized he was staring. He turned away immediately, hoping that he looked like just another lecherous man caught staring at a pretty girl in the park; it made him feel disgusting, but it was better than looking like a spy. When he turned he saw that another Grenzer had arrived, watching the yoga girl just as closely as Reed had been.

Another lech? Or her Stasi handler? Reed stepped to the left, putting the trunk of the tree between himself and the cop, and saw Pollard walking toward him.

"Morgen," said Pollard, looking like an innocent old man on a walk.

"Morgen," said Reed, and then fell into step beside him and whispered: "Walk with me. Pretend like we're talking."

Pollard immediately launched into rapid-fire German, describing his morning and his breakfast and his back pain, and Reed pretended to listen while he stole glances at the girl doing semaphore. She spread her legs apart, one straight down, and one off at an angle, and then stretched her arms high above her head. If he looked at one arm and one leg, it would be a D, but if he focused on the legs alone it was an A. He nodded at something Pollard said, and watched as the girl broke the pose, shook her limbs a bit, then went back into the same one. Not an A, then; no word had two As in a row. S-C-something-D-D. But that didn't make sense either. Maybe the double letters were the end and beginning of two different words?

They walked far enough that the girl was no longer in view, and Reed turned them with a subtle hand on Pollard's elbow. The old man kept talking. Reed's foot was on fire. They were heading toward the police officer now, but Reed ignored him and looked back at the girl. She broke out of her maybe-D-maybe-A pose and did another sideways stretch, planting her left foot on the ground and reaching her right foot far to the side in a long, downward diagonal. Her right arm she stretched up and over her head, bending down until she was pointing it far toward the left. One down and one up: it was the letter L. S-C-something-D-D-L?

"No," he whispered, and it all clicked into place. That double letter *was* an A, because there *was* a word that had two As in a row. It just wasn't in English.

S-C-something-A-A-L. The 'something' was an H.

Now. Use. Schaal.

Bettina Schaal.

The Chief's own secretary, the gatekeeper of every secret and every decision in the Cabin. Who knew more about more topics than Bettina? Who could access more files, and in more ways? Even Lise had used Bettina when she needed to spy on Chief Davis. But Bettina was "only" a secretary, and none of them had ever even considered her as a possible target.

Ostertag was using Bettina Schaal to spy on Davis, and Reed needed to warn the Cabin. Hadn't Bettina told Lise she had a secret boyfriend she didn't want to talk about? What bigger secret than a forbidden office romance?

They walked past the police officer, and Pollard gave him a friendly "Morgen!" while Reed kept his head down. *What's my next step? How do I warn them without immediately outing myself as a spy?* He looked across the park to the wall, and the Cabin barely twenty feet beyond.

All I have to do is get a message twenty feet over, six stories up, and encoded in such a way that Davis can understand it but Ostertag can't. All without letting this Grenzer, or the woman doing yoga, or any other Stasi agents hanging around in the park, know what I'm doing.

Reed laughed, desperately, and then muttered under his breath. "Easy."

"What is easy?" asked Pollard.

"Sending a code," said Reed. *I don't have to get a code to Davis,* he thought, *I have to get one to Lise. She's always more capable than I give her credit for, and she knows one code Ostertag doesn't.*

Our secret binary message system.

He looked up at the apartment building on this side of the wall, practically a twin to the one with the Cabin, and facing it directly. He needed to reach the fifth-floor windows.

Reed did his best to hurry, always careful of his foot, and walked back around to the corner of the apartment building. The buildings were farther apart than he'd given them credit for, maybe sixty feet. Too far to pass this code with the same old calendar system they'd been using before; a series of Xs in one window wouldn't be easily distinguishable from the all the way across in the other building. Plus he needed to send more than one word. He looked up at the apartment building again, walking to the front so he could see the windows. But maybe the windows themselves would work? Each apartment had six windows, all in a row, though they were probably spread out across several rooms. Each window had its own shade. If he raised them and lowered them—one and zero, on and off—he could spell anything he wanted to. And Lise—if she was watching—would understand it perfectly.

A woman came out of the apartment building, and Reed hobbled toward the door as fast as he could, grabbing the edge just before it closed and locked. "Let's go in here," he said to Pollard, and walked inside, toward the elevator, trying to compose a message in his head. Whatever it was, it couldn't have too many characters; he could barely walk, and if he had to move among five different windows, raising and lowering the shades, each letter was going to take him ... five seconds? Ten? Two seconds per shade made it ten in total, plus three or four seconds to pause between letters, plus two more seconds to walk back to the first shade and start over. Sixteen seconds per letter, give or take. If he could keep his message to thirty or so characters, he could send the whole thing in ... Eight minutes? Probably longer, as his leg was likely to hurt more and more after so much use, forcing him to slow down toward the end.

He pushed the elevator button, and waited. The message he needed to send was both long and complex: *Ostertag is a Stasi agent receiving orders through semaphore, using Bettina to steal information from Davis.* He had to compress that into as few characters as possible.

The elevator came, and they got in.

"What are we doing in here?" asked Pollard when the doors closed.

"I'm still figuring that out," said Reed. "Lise and I work in the building directly across from this one. I'm going to send her a message."

"Be careful," said Pollard. "If you just shout it out, the Grenzers will be on you in seconds."

"Exactly," said Reed. "I think I have a way to send it silently."

The elevator stopped, and the doors slid open. Reed stepped out and then closed his eyes, trying to see the building's layout in his mind's eye. Which side faced which direction, and which windows sat directly across from the Cabin? He made his best guess, walked to the proper door, and knocked. Apartment 5E.

"Don't be home," he whispered. "Don't be home."

Nobody came to the door. He knocked again and waited, barely daring to breathe.

Nothing.

Lise would be able to pick the lock, or figure out some other way to open it quietly. Reed had to make do with the blunt approach. "Go downstairs," he said to Pollard, "and stand by the doorbells. Every time anyone looks up at the windows, ring the bell for this apartment. 5E. Can you do that?"

"Ring the doorbell?"

"Every time anyone looks at these windows," said Reed. "I need to know if I've been spotted, while I still have time to get out."

"I will do it," said Pollard, and headed back toward the elevator. Reed waited until he was gone, and then turned his shoulder toward the door. This was going to be loud. He slammed himself into the door as hard as he could. It shook with a boom, but didn't budge. He pulled back and slammed it again, and this time something cracked, and the door flew open. He rushed inside, nearly screaming as he put too much weight on his injured foot, and quickly closed the door again as soon as he was through; the edge of the door was cracked, but it was small enough that a curious neighbor probably wouldn't see it if all they did was open their door and scan the hallway. He leaned against it, listening, and sure enough he heard a door open. A moment later there was a second one, and two neighbors muttered questions to each other. Reed listened closely, catching only some of the words through the door: they'd heard a noise, but they didn't know what it was. Eventually they blamed it on "Inga's son," whoever that was, and closed their doors again. Reed breathed a sigh of relief, and looked around at the apartment he'd just broken into.

Three of the windows were in the living room. He hobbled toward one and peeked out; the Cabin was right there, though most of the windows were closed and dark, and he couldn't see through them. Ostertag was just getting up from his perch in the one open window, flicking the stub of his cigarette down into the street. Apparently, the yoga message was finished. Reed walked into the next room over, finding a small kitchen with two more windows. That was all five that he needed; the sixth window was a bathroom but he shuttered it and ignored it. While he was walking back into the kitchen the doorbell rang—a signal from Pollard—and he looked up in shock. Had he been seen already? It couldn't be; he waited, holding his breath, and nothing more happened. Must be just a passerby. He found a notebook and a pencil by the phone, and sat down at the dinner table to compose his message.

What would Lise believe?

She had abandoned him mere hours ago. Abandoned him and shot him. But she wasn't convinced he was a traitor; she just wasn't convinced he was innocent, either. That tiny window of uncertainty was his only hope. If he could convince her that he'd found something real, she might be able to act on it and save the Cabin.

He wrote the message as sparingly as he could, using every abbreviation he could think of without going overboard into undecipherable nonsense. Then he translated the entire thing into binary, and then reversed it; it needed to read left-to-right from Lise's point of view, not from his. When he had everything ready he walked to the window in the center of the living room, opened it wide, and stepped backward. No one could see him now, from anywhere other than inside of the Cabin. He started waving his arms.

The windows of the Cabin were tinted, so Reed couldn't tell if anyone was looking at him, but he had to trust that eventually they would. The human eye latches onto movement. Even across the Wall, through a window in a strange apartment building, if he kept waving long enough someone was bound to see him from the corner of their eye.

He kept waving, wondering how long it would take, when suddenly a face appeared in the Cabin's open window. Wohlreich. Reed wanted to shout, but didn't dare, and bit his tongue to keep from calling out. Instead he changed his movements, trying to attract more attention, and then pointed at his face. Wohlreich stared, scowled, then recognized Reed and froze in shock. His eyes widened, his jaw dropped, and he stared dumbly, probably trying to parse how Wallace Reed—boring, fragile, milquetoast Wallace Reed—could be standing in East Berlin. Reed kept waving, and pointing at the windows as if that would somehow help Wohlreich to understand what was about to happen.

A moment later Frank joined Wohlreich in the window, and then Gisela, and then another window opened, and then another, and Reed saw Chuck and Wagner and Lise and

Ostertag and even Bettina and Davis, all staring at him in surprise.

The audience was ready. Reed held up his finger, gesturing for them to wait, and one by one he closed all the window shades.

Then he looked at his notes, bit down against the pain in his foot, and began to open the shutters again, one by one, in a careful, predetermined sequence.

Open, open, closed, closed, open.

Pause.

Open, closed, closed, open, closed.

Pause.

He clenched his teeth and walked back and forth through the apartment, from living room to kitchen to living room to kitchen, opening and closing the shades and gripping his cane while his foot burned inside his borrowed boot. The walk from one room to the other, to reach that fifth window, slowed him down, and he paused even longer between letters just in case.

The doorbell rang, but only once.

He walked on his heel, trying to keep the pressure off the wound in his foot. He walked until the pain medication started to wear off, and he took another dose with a shaking hand, trying to open the bottle and swallow the pill without breaking his rhythm. This shade up. Take a step. This shade down. Walk to the kitchen. Back and forth and around and around, crafting his message letter by painful letter:

Lise

Ostertag MFS

Yoga semaphore

O use Schaal get info D

Forty-six characters. Even at top speed, it would take him more than twenty minutes. Lise's name wasn't strictly necessary, but he worried that Lise might miss the first few letters while she figured out what was happening, so a few unnecessary letters on the beginning might help. Helpful or not, it took him over a minute to spell her name and then launch into the actual message.

And all the while, the threat of attention and police response loomed over him like a storm cloud.

Halfway through the word "MFS" the doorbell rang. Halfway through "semaphore" it rang again. After "Schaal," it rang twice, and then almost every word was punctuated by a ring; loud, strident, and worried. Reed finished the message and started it over, wondering how much of it he'd be able to get through before fleeing. Soon the bell was ringing nonstop, a constant barrage of clanging noise, and Reed gritted his teeth and ignored them, trying to get through as much of his message as he could. He had just finished 'MFS' again when something white sailed out of the Cabin's window, streaking through the air and fluttering slightly in the wind.

A paper airplane.

Reed grasped at its most likely meaning—"message received"—and left the windows instantly, grabbing his cane and hobbling out the door. He had to trust that Lise had understood the message; with so many warnings from Pollard, he didn't have time to wait and see for sure.

The hallway had a stairwell at each end, and an elevator in the middle. The elevator was little better than a cage in this situation, so Reed walked to the stairs and started down them, one step at a time, biting down hard against the pain and gripping the handrail until his knuckles turned white. Halfway down the first flight of stairs he heard voices, and loud footsteps coming up. He hurried faster, reached the next floor, and shuffled down the hall as quickly as his injured foot could go. He reached the second staircase just in time, ducking down and out of view just as the police stormed up the first staircase toward the top floor. Reed kept walking, down each step with a grunt, trying to be quiet and fast all at once. He had gone nearly two more floors when he heard more footsteps behind him, the police coming down now, realizing that their quarry had escaped. He reached the second floor and limped through the hall, shuffling as far as he dared before stopping and knocking on the nearest door.

He couldn't escape before the police found him, so he needed to look like he belonged inside. This was his best shot.

An old woman opened the door. "Gruss Gott."

"Oskar?" asked Reed. It was the first name he could think of.

"Kein Oskar," said the woman—*No Oskar here*—and tried to close the door.

"Ein moment," said Reed, and started patting his pockets, trying to look like he was searching for an address or a card. He could hear the police getting closer, and needed to keep the woman talking. "Ich habe die Adresse."

Three police officers came down the stairs, saw the two of them conversing, and shouted brusquely: "Hast du jemanden hier gesehen?" *Have you seen anyone go by?*

Reed looked at the old woman. "Du?"

"Nein," she said grumpily.

Reed looked back at the police, and shrugged. "Nein."

Time seemed to freeze, as if Reed's entire life were hanging on that one single word. Had it worked? Had they believed him? Had he kept his accent as good as he could make it? He wasn't even sure if the police were staring at him, or if he was simply so scared he was perceiving a lifetime of detail in one single moment.

"Mach weiter," said one of the police, and they turned and ran down the stairs.

Reed let out a breath he didn't even know he'd been holding.

"Kein Oskar hier," the woman repeated, and closed the

door. Reed clenched his teeth against the pain, and started walking again.

At the bottom of the stairs Reed saw the same police officers, talking to another resident. He nodded to the officers, and they nodded back, and he hobbled out the door.

East Berlin

REED PICKED a direction and started walking, not caring where he was going, just desperate to put as much distance between him and the apartment as he could. Pollard found him about a block away, driving slowly in his car, and pulled to the side of the road so Reed could get in.

"Where are we going next?" Pollard asked.

Reed closed his eyes, feeling the adrenaline drain away, and his arms and legs grow shaky. His injured foot throbbed, though the painkillers made the pain—and everything else—feel distant and fuzzy.

"They need to catch Ostertag," he mumbled.

"That is them," said Pollard. "What about us?"

"I need to get out," said Reed. "Maybe we could try a ... distraction? I don't know, that was Lise's plan. You could go to one part of the Wall and make a bunch of noise to attract the Grenzers, and then I could go just around a corner and make a break for it."

"You think no one has tried that?" asked Pollard. "The Grenzers have learned—they never let their guard down."

"Then we ... I don't know," said Reed. "Maybe I just wait? They know I'm here, now; if they catch Ostertag, and prove he's a double agent, maybe they'll ..." *Maybe they'll believe that I'm innocent, and find a way to get me out.* He kept the last part quiet, remembering that Pollard didn't know about any of Lise's suspicions.

"Your colleagues could come over to talk to you," said Pollard, trying to be helpful even with only a portion of the truth. "Government officials are allowed to cross freely, correct? They are doing it today, even with the tanks at the checkpoint."

Reed shot him a look. "People are crossing the border?"

"I talked to one of the old men in the park," said Pollard, waving his hand in the vague direction of the Wall. "There are soldiers with guns, on both sides of the wall, and they have orders to shoot but only if they get shot at first. And no one is shooting, so no one is shooting back, and instead they are just ... walking."

"Just walking freely?" asked Reed. "On their own sides?"

"On this side," said Pollard. "American soldiers and East German soldiers just ... walking around each other, watching. Doing nothing."

"That doesn't make sense," said Reed, but then he stopped himself. "Yes it does. Shooting would start a war, and demanding ID might start a war, so instead they're just in a holding pattern. Almost *anything* they do might start a war, so they're not doing anything." He paused, and thought, and stared out the window of the car. "That's how I get out."

"How?" asked Pollard. "Just ... walk out?"

"Why not?" asked Reed. "I don't have any government ID, but I'm obviously American. Any other day—any other spot in East Germany—that would be a huge liability. I'd get thrown in an interrogation room for the rest of my life. But today, at that checkpoint? I can find a group of Americans, make it obvious that I'm one of them, and walk right out. The Grenzers wouldn't dare to stop me, because the Americans would take it as an act of war."

Pollard nodded. "Then I will take you to the checkpoint."

"Yes," said Reed, and nodded. "Let's go. But maybe ..." He put a hand on the steering wheel, stopping Pollard from driving. They were on the East side of the Wall—how many times had he been frustrated, in the last week alone, that he couldn't get certain intel or follow certain leads because the answers were on the East side of the Wall? There were dozens of things the Cabin needed to know, and had no good way of discovering, because they couldn't do the one thing Reed had already done. Now that he had already crossed the Wall, shouldn't he take advantage of that? His mind filled with other possibilities—but it also shook with fear. He didn't want to stay. "Damn it, no! I want to leave! I *have* to leave!"

"Then you leave," said Pollard. "I will take you to the border, exactly as you said. What are you talking about?" He peered at Reed's face. "How many of those pills have you taken?"

"It's not that, it's just ... There's a man we have to find—a man we haven't even been able to look for properly, because he's in East Berlin. Now ... I'm in East Berlin, too. I can do work here that we can't do in any other way."

"You need to get to a hospital—"

"And I will. Later." Reed closed his eyes, barely even believing the words coming out of his own mouth. "I have to do something first."

"We do not know how long the border will stay like this," said Pollard. "If you do not leave now, you might never be able to."

"And what if this is a prelude to war?" asked Reed. "The GDR is blinding us; it's restricting our movement and our intelligence. For all I know they're planning a war. If I can find out what's going on, on this side—who Tsyganov is, what he wants, and everything else—we might be able to stop it."

Pollard's voice held a tinge of wariness. "Tsyganov?"

"Have you ever heard the name?"

Pollard shook his head. "Only enough to guess that it is Russian."

"We think he might be a KGB officer," said Reed. "And we think he might have met with the Stasi in a restaurant called Rennstall."

"That one I know," said Pollard, gesturing with his finger. "My son Tobi would visit it, with Lise and the others."

"Then let's go," said Reed. Pollard nodded, and pulled away from the curb.

Away from downtown, and away from the Wall.

Away from freedom.

Pollard kept driving, but lowered his voice. "We will need to be careful. Rennstall used to be a haven for students and rebels, but if the Stasi are using it to meet with the KGB, it could be very different now."

"All the Stasi are downtown," said Reed. "They've got an American tank division on their doorstep; this is the perfect time to visit their other haunts." But even if he learned something valuable at Rennstall, there was no guarantee that anyone in the Cabin would believe what he told them, assuming he was even able to report it at all. *It all depends on Ostertag,* he thought. *If he runs; if they catch him; if they can prove he's a double agent. I might get my life back.*

They arrived at the restaurant, and Reed saw that Rennstall was every bit as old and weathered as Richardhof. They stepped inside, expecting to see a busy crowd for lunch, but they were the only two customers there.

Pollard found a booth, and gestured for Reed to sit down. "I will find a server. Rest your foot."

Reed waited, and nearly three minutes later Pollard came

back, grinning from ear to ear. He had one of the servers with him, an older woman in an apron, and he gestured for Reed to scoot over. He did, and Pollard sat next to him. The woman sat on the other bench, facing them grimly.

"This is Ana Kluck," said Pollard. "A fellow sympathizer. She used to work here when the students would come, talking of revolution." He saw the look of uncertainty in Reed's eyes, and nodded reassuringly. "We can trust her."

Reed looked at Ana. "It's nice to meet you."

"It is nice to have good people in here again," said Ana. "These days it is only Stasi, and Grenzers, and secret police. They pay well, but ..." She shook her head. "We are not fascists."

This made Reed nervous. "Are all your customers Stasi?" He looked at the door. "Should we go?"

"They are all at the Wall today," said Ana. "Friedrich-strasse. The Americans are starting a war."

"I sincerely hope that they're not," said Reed. "Do you remember a ..." He paused. There was no reason to ask about Lise, so he stopped himself, and cut all proper names out of his question. "Do you remember any of the old students?"

"So many students," said Ana, dismissing the idea with a wave, "and so many years. I do not know names."

"How about a recent customer, then," said Reed. "A Stasi agent named ..." *What was Longshore's new identity again?* "Hans Nowak."

"This man I know," said Ana, and scowled. "He is the one who brings the Stasi here."

Reed chose his next words carefully.

"How about a Russian man? Tsyganov."

"Him I also know," said Ana, and tapped the table. "The first time he came was ten days ago, I think. Maybe eight. Three days in a row he comes here, *boom boom boom*. Then never again."

"A businessman?"

"Secret police. Like the others."

"Everyone he met with was secret police?"

"Everyone," said Ana. "And every conversation was the same. Spying on the West. Betraying friends. Corrupting good people to be more spies."

"I—" said Reed, but then stopped. Did Ana hate the Stasi for what they did, or just for how they did it? He'd never heard of an informant so disgusted by the idea of informants. Didn't she realize that the West was every bit as dirty and underhanded as the East?

He paused, and rephrased, and asked another question. "I realize this is a long shot, but did you ever happen to overhear him talking about a man named Johannes Ostertag?"

She thought for a moment, then shook her head. "No."

"Erich Gunter Anselm? Operation Talon? An agent named Baker?" She only shook her head. "Does any of this sound familiar at all?"

"No," she insisted, "nothing like that."

Pollard sighed. "They must have kept their conversations private."

"Not private," said Ana, almost offended. "I hear everything—I listen to everything. Nobody pays attention to the servers. But these names, no. They did not speak of them."

"But you *did* overhear Tsyganov's conversations?" asked Reed, perking up a bit. "Do you know who he met with?"

"I know them all," said Ana. "Siedel, Weber—all the names."

"He met with Konrad Siedel?" Reed knew that name; he was the chief of Longshore's Stasi intelligence office.

"Not Siedel," said Ana. "Siedel is their leader, yes, but Tsyganov met here only with the workers: Gerhard Weber, Jürgen Bauer, Hans Nowak. Boom boom boom, three meetings three days."

Pollard leaned in closer. "And he said the same thing to all of them?"

"Same," said Ana. "'We have spies in the West.' So many spies."

"Wait," said Reed, sitting up straighter. This felt wrong. "He said 'spies,' plural?"

"Yes," said Ana, "spies. He names three of them; I listen, and they do nothing. I am only the server."

"Do you remember the names?"

She thought for a moment, furrowing her brow, and then said: "Jannick, like my nephew."

This surprised Reed. "Jannick Wohlreich?"

"Stimmt." Ana nodded. "You know him?"

"It's my job to know everyone," said Reed, hoping it made him sound more important than he felt. "And the others?"

"A woman's name. Elsa? Elise?"

"Lise?"

"Yes," said Ana. "Lise Kohler."

This shocked him. Lise was the one person in the Cabin he was certain wasn't a traitor. But Tsyganov said she was? To Longshore? So why hadn't Longshore given the Cabin any of this information?

"The last one was American," said Ana. "Walter, I think. No, Wallace. Wallace Reed."

Reed looked at Pollard, realizing the man had never introduced him by name. Ana had no idea who she was talking to.

And here, again, he stood accused.

What's going on? he thought. Reed knew he wasn't a double agent, so then why was Tsyganov telling people he was? And why had Longshore passed along Reed's name in Message 41, but not the others?

If Longshore had turned—if he had gone too deep undercover, and become a loyal agent of the Stasi—and if Lise was also a part of the Stasi—then this almost made sense. Almost.

Longshore might very well try to feed her information to kill an innocent man. But ... if Longshore believed Tsyganov, Reed *wasn't* an innocent man. He was an ally. And yet two alleged Stasi agents had all conspired to kill a third? It didn't make sense. There had to be another explanation.

He looked back at Ana. "And Tsyganov gave all of these names? Three times, in three meetings? Boom boom boom?"

"No," said Ana, and tapped the table again. "One meeting, one name. Each officer hears a different thing."

And just like that, it all clicked into place.

"We're bait."

For the first time since that first, garbled message, everything made sense.

"Bait?" asked Pollard.

"We have an agent inside of the Stasi," said Reed. "They don't know who it is, but they've narrowed it down to three suspects. Then a KGB officer comes in—some shadow man from Moscow—and sets a trap. He takes all three suspects aside, one by one, and tells them about another double agent: a Stasi informer working inside the CIA. And none of it's true—they're all innocent—but that's the whole point. He *wants* them to go back to their CIA handlers and report the agent's name. Then Tsyganov and Siedel and everyone else just waits and watches." He looked at Ana sharply. "What name did he give to each man? Do you remember?"

"What do you mean?"

"He told Gerhard Weber that who was a spy? Jannick, Lise, or Wallace?"

"Jannick."

Reed nodded. "So if anything happens to Jannick—if the CIA and the BND suddenly fire him, or imprison him, or he disappears completely—then the Stasi know that Gerhard Weber is their traitor. That he's the one leaking information to the West. Or if something happens to Lise, they know the leak

is Jürgen Bauer, or if something happens to Wallace Reed ..."
His voice fell, suddenly void of all energy. "Then they know it's
Hans Nowak."

And Longshore dies, he thought to himself.

Pollard looked at Reed, watching him with sad, ancient
eyes.

Reed stared at the table. "I need—"

"Wait," said Ana. "How did you know it was Nowak they
told about Wallace?"

Reed looked back, worried that he'd given too much away.
He kept his voice even, and looked her in the eyes. "It is my
job," he said again, "to know everything."

Ana frowned, swishing her hand at him and looking away.
"Spies," she muttered.

"Can you bring us wine?" Pollard smiled at her. "And some
for yourself." Ana pulled herself to her feet, and walked back
into the kitchen. Pollard watched her go. "We need to get you
home, Wallace."

"Careful," said Reed. "Everything we say here, the wait
staff will know."

Pollard nodded. "Nobody pays attention to the servers."

"And they're obviously reporting to somebody," said Reed.
"Some new resistance movement. Nobody remembers this
much detail unless they've been coached."

Pollard looked offended. "A new resistance, and they didn't
ask me?"

"You're a known sympathizer," said Reed. "Your wife and
your son both died for this cause."

"Sometimes I think I need to join them."

"Don't," said Reed. "They need you alive. Ana's clearly
been trained in surveillance, but not in discretion. We're two
strangers off the street, and she told us everything. That's why I
don't want to tell her any more than we have to."

"You're American," said Pollard. "We can always trust an American to oppose the Soviets."

"Then it'll only take one bad American to get everyone in this restaurant arrested," said Reed. He was going to add "Or executed," but Ana Kluck returned with a bottle of wine and three glasses. She stayed on her feet while she opened the bottle, and poured a small portion for Pollard and Reed. Only then did she sit with a grunt, and pour a small glass for herself.

"May we ask you more questions?" Reed ignored the wine; he was already feeling light-headed enough from the medicine.

Ana raised her glass. "Prost."

Reed took that as a yes. "You swear you've never heard the name Johannes Ostertag?"

She thought for a moment, then nodded firmly. "I swear."

"Agent Baker?"

"A baker? Someone who bakes bread?"

"No," said Reed. "Clearly you haven't. How about ..." What else did he have? "Mother Goose?"

"Is that another restaurant?"

"It is folk tales," said Pollard. "We have the Brothers Grimm, but the English have Mother Goose. She tells bedtime stories."

"Mostly, yes," said Reed. He hesitated, then reached into his shirt pocket and pulled out the small sample of Mother Goose papers he'd brought from the Cabin. What could it hurt? They were public broadcasts, available to anyone who cared to listen, and all Reed had done was transcribe them. He kept back the frequency graph, but unfolded the others and laid them on the table; a smear of dried blood in the corner lingered from last night, adding a sudden, heavy weight to the meeting. "This is a segment of a coded broadcast originating somewhere here, in Berlin. Does it mean anything to you?"

He handed them each a piece of paper: an English nursery rhyme and a string of nonsense numbers. The two Germans looked at the papers, but shook their heads helplessly. Reed knew they couldn't possibly understand them—the best minds in the CIA and BND had failed to understand them—but then again, one of those minds had been a Stasi agent, corrupting their work from the inside. The whole analysis was compromised. Maybe Ana and Pollard, coming to it fresh, would see something Reed was missing.

While they sifted through the papers, Reed thought more about Ostertag. The two cryptographers had checked each other's worked almost constantly, on every project. Reed had never found a discrepancy before, but now, here, on the Mother Goose papers, he had. Slight differences between Ostertag's original transcriptions, and Reed's new ones. Knowing that Ostertag was a traitor, these differences looked suddenly and suspiciously like sabotage—the transcription discrepancies had been carried forward into the statistical distribution, and now called into question the entire study. And the only reason for Ostertag to start such sabotage now was if these Mother Goose messages were especially important—or, at least, especially important to Ostertag. Maybe they were messages from his handler, or maybe they just mentioned him and his position in the Cabin? Either could be enough to damn him, if the Cabin ever managed to crack the code.

If Reed could crack it now, he might be able to find Ostertag's Stasi contact.

And exonerate himself in the process.

"This one makes no sense," said Ana, handing one of the papers back. "A woman who cannot eat lean meat? Only fat? It is impossible."

"That's ... not the point," said Reed. Apparently she understood far less about a numbers station than he'd hoped. He sighed, and started gathering the papers. "It was a long shot anyway. Thanks for looking."

Pollard set down his paper as well. "There are too many

numbers to be an alphabet cipher. It has to be a phrasebook code, like I used to use."

Ana looked surprised. "You used to be a spy?"

"Of course I did. You are not the only one!"

"I am *not* a spy—"

"Bah," said Pollard. "Maybe you do not *send* messages, but you certainly *listen* to them. You are a spy."

"Maybe it's a combination," said Reed, thinking out loud. "It can't be a phrasebook, because the number frequencies and the message lengths are all wrong for it, but it can't be an alphabet either, like you said, because there are ninety numbers in the cipher. So: what if it's a hybrid system? Some of these numbers represent letters, and some represent words or key phrases."

"Does that make it easier to decode?" asked Pollard.

"It makes it a lot harder," said Reed. "But it would be nice to know, either way."

"What is a cipher?" asked Ana.

Reed raised an eyebrow.

"I take it back," said Pollard. "You are definitely not a spy."

"You ... really are a lot more inexperienced that I thought," said Reed. He set the papers back down. "You're going to need to know this if you're going to keep spying on the Stasi. Do you work with someone?"

Ana stared at him, as if the conversation suddenly terrified her.

"You're clearly observing the Stasi and reporting on their conversations," said Reed. "Who are you reporting to? An American, like me? A German agent? A civilian resistance?"

Ana looked away, suddenly refusing to meet his eyes. Such a clear avoidance of the topic could only mean that he was right.

This is exactly what he'd hoped would happen—what he'd told Lise would happen. The people were fighting back. An oppressive empire was a disease, invading this country like virus, but the country was creating antibodies to defeat the virus: sometimes with brave young students, and sometimes with frail old men and tired old women. Ana didn't know how to be a spy, and she didn't even want to be one. But she knew that something had to be done, and that she was in a position to do it.

Ana stayed silent, and Reed nodded. "That's good: don't tell me everything just because I ask. But I am on your side, and I'm here to help you. Whatever you're doing, knowing a code or two can help protect you. A cipher is an easy one—it's like a second alphabet, where one thing means another thing. This one, for example, comes from a Stasi agent we've named Mother Goose. He reads the numbers over the radio, broadcasting from somewhere safe, and then whoever he's working with listens and writes them down and knows that 27, for example, stands for Q. Or whatever." He pointed at the paper she'd discarded. "15-30-88 might mean T-H-E, or D-A-S, or 'Please send help,' or ... anything, really. We don't know, which is why a cipher is so helpful to a spy organization like yours."

Ana stared at the papers for a long time before answering. "So ... How do you know what the numbers mean?"

"We don't know what they mean," said Reed, "that's the whole problem."

"Not you," said Ana. "Mother Goose. This Stasi spy who is talking to his friend. When the Stasi man says 27, how does the other man know what he really means instead?"

"Because they both have the same book," Reed told her. "Like a code book, or even just a list. I can help you set up a code system, similar to this one, to help pass messages to whoever you're working with. It doesn't need to be complex, but anything is better than nothing."

"Perhaps," said Ana softly, her eyes still on the table. "Perhaps just one of those books you mentioned. A code book."

"It's ... not a real book," said Reed. "That's one of the first rules to keeping a code secret—guard the code with your life, especially if you've written it down somewhere. If anyone finds that, you don't have any secrets left."

"But you can help me to get one?"

"I can help you create one," said Reed. "And then you can share it with the others, and hide it from everyone else. How complicated do you want it to be?"

"As simple as possible," said Pollard. "Five minutes ago she didn't even know what one was."

"Bescheuert!" Ana growled, and took any angry swig of her wine.

"We'll start with a substitution cipher," said Reed. "They're easy to break, once you figure out the trick, but I can give you a few tricks that are pretty hard to figure out. You start by assigning one letter to each number, one through twenty-six."

"Thirty," said Ana.

Reed glanced at her, then nodded and apologized. The German alphabet had the same twenty-six letters as English did, plus three extra vowels with umlauts, and a kind of super-S called an Eszett. English speakers tended to write these out by adding extra letters—the Eszett becoming a double S—but Ana was a native German communicating with other Germans; it made more sense to include the full German alphabet in the cipher. He added them in, numbered them, and explained how to encode a message with a rolling substitution—by shifting the cipher between every letter, it becomes much harder to crack.

"And the Stasi won't be able to read what we write?"

"It'll take a while for them to figure it out," said Reed, "but yes: a good codebreaker will be able to read it. If the messages are long enough, I could probably crack a code like this after only ... four or five of them."

"Even though one number could connect to several different letters."

"I'm afraid so," said Reed. "And the Stasi cryptographers are just as good as I am." He gestured to the Mother Goose papers on the table. "Probably better—they designed *this* thing, and I can't crack it at all."

Ana thought about this for a moment.

"What if we go the other way?" she asked. "With one letter that can connect to several different numbers."

"What?" asked Reed.

"There would be no point," said Pollard. "You are using the numbers to hide the letters, not the other way around."

"More numbers help the letters hide," said Ana. "It's like a rabbit in a bush: if there are three bushes, you don't know which one has the rabbit."

Pollard shook his head. "But if three different bushes all connect to the same rabbit, then the rabbit is easier to find, not harder."

"Ah," said Ana, "I see."

Reed saw, too. Revelation slammed through his mind like a tidal wave, and he felt a growing sense of elation. "No, you're right." He looked at Ana, his eyes wide. "That's brilliant."

"Does 'brilliant' mean what I think it means?" asked Ana.

"It used to," said Pollard, obviously grumpy that Ana's espionage skills had been praised. "But suddenly I'm starting to doubt it."

"It does," Reed assured her, "it absolutely does." He picked up the Mother Goose frequency graph, feeling like he'd just received a prophecy from an angel. "Multiple numbers that all point to the same letter. It's absolutely *brilliant*."

Pollard frowned. "But the rabbits—"

"Exactly," said Reed. "But you have to look at this like a cryptographer. When we're trying to decode something, we don't see the bush as a bush, we see the bush as *the reason that you chose the bush*. Does that make sense? No, it doesn't—let me put it another way. Let's say that the rabbit is the letter E, right? And it's the most common type of rabbit in the entire forest—letter-E rabbits are hopping around everywhere. And they can create a bush to hide in, different from any other kind of bush. So a smart hunter can look at the forest and count all the bushes and say 'there are more number 5 bushes than any other kind, so that must be the letter E rabbit.' And then he knows exactly where they are." Reed picked up the frequency graph and waved it front of their faces. "That's what this is supposed to find, right? The most common bushes, which we know are hiding the most common rabbits. But these rabbits are smart." He smoothed the paper on the table and laughed with eager relish. "These Stasi rabbit bastards figured out how to hide the E behind a bunch of different numbers: maybe four or five or I don't know how many. We'll figure that out. And the slightly less common letters, like a G or an O, still get two or three numbers, and then the last stragglers, the ones we barely ever use at all, get just one number each. It's a polyalphabetic system, but only partly. They've statistically corrected the distribution of letters so that no single number stands out. There's no peaks and no valleys, just plateaus." He slammed his hand on the graph. "I've got you now, you sneaky little—"

"He's forgotten us," said Pollard. "He's talking to himself now."

"I'm glad I'm not the only one who didn't understand that," said Ana.

"Do you have any paper?" asked Reed. He could do this. Once you knew the trick, a cipher was easy to crack—and Reed had just figured out the trick. Thirty letters spread across ninety different numbers. "Do you know what the letter frequencies are for German orthography?"

"I don't even know that word," said Pollard. Ana got up to retrieve more paper.

"The most common letter is E," said Reed. "All by itself, that one letter makes up about sixteen percent of the German written language. N is somewhere around ten, S and R are about seven, and so on, all the way down to Y, X, and Q, which make up about three hundredths of a percent each—they're practically nonexistent." Ana returned with a couple of old, cardboard menus, flipping them over to show the blank backs, and set them on the table in front of him. "Thank you," said Reed. He started writing the alphabet on one of them, leaving plenty of space by each letter. "Do you realize the difference between sixteen percent, and point-oh-three percent? It's huge. For every one time a German text includes the letter Q, it includes the letter E about five hundred times, give or take. That's a massive difference—far more than this ninety-character cipher can account for. So. They've smoothed out the peaks, making it harder to spot the Es and the Ns and whatever else, but they couldn't smooth out these pits." Reed finished writing the alphabet, and stabbed his finger at the frequency graph. "*That's* the crack in the armor. These four numbers: 10, 11, 48, and 56. Those are J, Q, X, and Y, I guarantee it. And they're going to break this code wide open."

"Which number is which?" asked Pollard.

"I don't know the bottom three yet," said Reed, "but this one is J." He pointed at the shallowest of the four pits on the graph. "J, while still incredibly rare, is about ten times less rare than the others." He grabbed the menu, and wrote "56" next to the letter J. He smiled at Ana, feeling such a rush of happiness he felt manic. "Remember when I said how easy it was for a good cryptographer to crack a code? This is how: it's all math. Watch and learn."

He started scanning through the Mother Goose messages, looking for the number 56. He found three, and wrote 'J' above each of them. The German J appeared almost exclusively at the beginning of words—ja, Jahr, jetzt, jung—though never at the end and never in a consonant cluster. This meant that the numbers before it were *probably* in different words, and the numbers after it were almost certainly vowels. The numbers that followed each 56 were 23, 47, and 80. He marked these on his menu as 'A/E/U,' and then searched through the messages and marked them there as well, every time they appeared. He continued like this, deducing what he could, using each discovery to intuit the next, chipping away at the cipher piece by piece.

This was what he loved. This was why he'd joined the intelligence service—not to spy on his friends, not to root out traitors or skulk through enemy territory. Certainly not to get shot. He did this because he loved to solve puzzles. To pit his mind, his creativity, and his wits against another cryptographer; to start with nothing and, through sheer intelligence, wrest meaning from the chaos. It was thrilling in a way that few things could ever hope to be.

It was his life.

Letter by letter he unraveled the code. Between two vowels he found what was almost certainly an Eszett, the double S. It sometimes appeared at the end of a word but never at the beginning, and never—as with J—in a consonant cluster. From this he found more potential vowels, and from these he found what might have been one of the many numbers that stood for the letter S. From this he learned a likely candidate for R, and from that he started to narrow down the many consonants that often clustered with R: T and D and H and G and of course a second R. Each new letter he auditioned in different words and places, seeing what could fit here and what might work better over there; what words he could form, and how they looked next to the words or half-words that he already knew. He had called it math, but it was really a combination of math, linguistics, and art.

Sometimes he showed a word to Pollard or Ana, asking their opinion; sometimes he worked it out himself. At some point food appeared beside him, potato dumplings with pork and gravy. He ate without thinking, focusing all his attention on the words and numbers that danced before him.

The statistical tricks made the work take longer than it would have otherwise; he discovered relatively early that 30 was an R, but knowing that several other numbers could also be an R meant that he couldn't just plug it in and go. He had to start making leaps of logic that he'd never encountered before: if 37 and 54 were both B, was that *all* the Bs or were there more? B represented about two percent of the written German language—was two numbers out of ninety just right, or too many? The letter U was about four percent, which was twice as common as B. Did that mean it would have twice as many numbers? Would N, at 10%, have twice as many again?

Slowly, letter by letter, the very first message in the Mother Goose archive began to take shape: 15-R-I-N-Z-55-90-S-20-R-A-ß-E-W-D. A short string of fifteen characters that Reed was increasingly certain was an address. The 20 was almost definitely a T, which would spell 'Straße,' or 'street.' But which street? And what did the 'W-D' mean at the end?

He reached for his fork, but it was gone. He looked up and saw that the table was empty, and Pollard was asleep on the bench, and the shadows had shifted to the other side of the room. Hours had passed.

"What time is it?"

"Half fourteen," said Ana. "Your food was cold," she added, "so I took it."

Two thirty in the afternoon. Reed shook his head, as if clearing away cobwebs, and muttered: "Cryptographer Face."

"What?" asked Ana.

"Can you come look at something for me?" She came to the table, and Reed showed her the half-formed word: 15-RINZ-55-99

"I only know of one word with RINZ," she said. "*Prinz*."

"P!" said Reed, scrambling to check it against his other

messages. "I should have seen it. And then I assume the last two letters would be EN, for 'Prinzen.' So this says 'Prinzen-straße.'" He nodded. "There's a Prinzenstraße right by the Moritzplatz train station. This is definitely an address. But then what does WD mean? Have you seen an address like this before? WD?"

"Never," said Ana.

"Maybe it's not an address," said Pollard, yawning as he sat up. "Maybe it's an abbreviation. 'Welchst du,' or something like that."

"'Which one are you,'" said Reed, trying out the phrase. "Prinzenstraße, which one are you? Is it asking for an address, instead of giving one?"

"That's not how you ask for an address," said Ana. "More likely he is giving one, but never with WD. Apartment D would make sense, but you still need a street number."

"93," said Reed, and his face broke out in a smile. "You sneaky little Stasi. Prinzenstraße 93 D. I had 93 as a W, because of another message, but in this one he's just using it as a number. That's ..." He tried to remember the street numbers near Moritzplatz, but couldn't recall them. "I don't know where it is, but I can find it. And when I do, I'll have Ostertag's handler." He stood up. "This is my—ahhhh, that's not good." He sat back down again, wincing at the pain in his foot. "I forgot about my foot."

"Your foot?"

"He was shot in the foot," said Pollard.

Ana's eyes went wide. "How can you forget that you were shot in the foot?"

"Cryptographer Face," said Reed. "Better than medita-tion." He gathered the messages, folding them carefully, and then held up the menu. "Can I take this?"

"You have written all over it," she said. "What good is it to us?"

"Nothing," said Reed, "it'd get you killed if the Stasi ever found it." He folded the menu in quarters and tucked it into the pocket of his pants; that piece of cardboard was as valuable as it was dangerous. "You're going to want to burn these napkins, too. You saw how easy it was to make them; you can make more. But keep them hidden, and never use them here. No one ever finds the secrets you hide—they find the ones you forget about and leave on a table."

"We are going?" asked Pollard.

"We are," said Reed. "To the Wall." He gritted his teeth, and stood up carefully, gripping his cane for support. "I'm going to cross it." He grinned. "And the Stasi are going to help me."

2:42 PM

East Berlin

REED LIMPED outside to the car, and Pollard followed. "How quickly can you get us downtown?" Reed asked.

Pollard thought for a moment. "You are certain they will not ask for ID?"

"Not one hundred percent, but enough to bet my life on it." Reed stopped, and put a hand on Pollard's arm. "Come with me. I owe you that much, at least, after everything you've done for me."

Pollard shook his head, and started the car. "Nein, nein." He pointed forward, toward the West and the Wall. "That is my country, but so is this. Here I have my home and my memories. I will fight to protect them, yes, but I will not leave them."

Reed nodded. "That's good." He didn't know what else to say, so he said it again. "That's good. It's good that you ... I mean, someday that Wall's coming down, right? And it'll be people on both sides who do it."

"That is my prayer," said Pollard.

They drove downtown, but the roads were just as slow now as they were in the morning, and the journey seemed to take hours. Police kept waving the traffic onto detours, routing most —but not all—of the traffic around the city center. It wasn't until nearly five in the afternoon that Pollard simply refused to turn, and drove right up to one of the cops and asked if the area was closed.

"Nur lokaler," said the officer. *Locals only.*

"Wir leben dort," said Reed.

The cop didn't even ask for proof, just waved them through with a warning about tanks on Friedrichstrasse.

"Danke," said Pollard, and drove past him.

"Friedrichstrasse is Checkpoint Charlie," said Reed. "Get us as close as you can."

The center of East Berlin was surprisingly normal, given all the madness in the area around it. Businesses were still open, people were still walking around, and life still went on. And right there, in the middle of it all, twenty tanks and scores of soldiers waited for orders to start shooting. The tanks were on this side of the wall.

"The GDR did not have tanks here earlier," said Pollard. "This is new."

"It's escalating," said Reed, feeling anxiety clench at his stomach like a fist. "Maybe we waited too long." Or, worse yet, maybe it didn't even matter. With tanks on both sides now, maybe it had escalated so far that a war was inevitable, and he'd be a casualty of war no matter which side of the wall he was on.

Pollard parked a few blocks away, on Mohrenstrasse, and they walked along it until they came to Friedrichstrasse. Even before they reached it, they could see the crowds gathered to watch. It almost looked like they were watching a parade, and when they rounded the corner they saw a cruel parody of one. A line of tanks and armored transports, weapons loaded, pointed south toward the Wall, and across the Checkpoint in West Berlin a similar grim procession pointed back the other way. Reed had estimated twenty tanks, but saw now that there might be as many as thirty. Soldiers lined the sidewalks, crouching in storefronts or squatting behind sandbags. Gun barrels bristled from every side. Strangest of all, people seemed to be walking freely between them.

"Are those civilians?" asked Pollard.

A woman standing near them answered. "They are officers of the armies. Both are walking free."

"Thank you," said Pollard.

The woman tilted her head to the side. "Why are you speaking English?"

"Optimism," said Reed, giving it his best German accent. He tugged on Pollard's sleeve, and pulled him south toward the tanks. "Let us get closer." As soon as they were out of earshot he stopped, turned, and took Pollard's hand. "Herr Rapp, you've saved my life—at least three times, and probably more."

"Anyone would do as much," said Pollard.

"If that were true there wouldn't be any tanks here." Reed smiled slightly. "And I'd be out of a job."

"Then I pray that you will lose your job soon."

"That's a prayer I can pretty much guarantee," said Reed. He looked at the tanks and the soldiers, then back at Pollard. "Are you sure you don't want to come?"

"Someone has to feed my cat," said Pollard. "And to be there for the next lost spy."

"I'll tell Lise you said hello."

"Tell her Michelle says hello as well," said Pollard. "And Tobi. They are always with me." He squeezed Reed's hand, then let him go, and disappeared into the crowd.

Reed took a breath, gripped his cane, and walked.

Past Mohrenstrasse came Kronenstrasse, and there the crowd began to thin, though by the time he reached Leipzigerstrasse the crowd was back again. There were soldiers, like the woman had said, but also people from every walk of life—old and young, workers and students, all gathered to watch this physical manifestation of the Cold War. Tanks filled the streets —where they met at the border they were barely ten yards apart—and soldiers eyed each other warily. Many of the soldiers were looking at Reed, but he hobbled forward boldly, confident that here, in the GDR's greatest show of strength, they wouldn't dare to touch him.

American officers mingled with German—not talking, but simply eyeing each other warily. It was as if the Wall had swollen and mutated into a tumor of military presence, bulging out into both the American Sector and the Russian. Both sides had live ammo and orders to fire if fired upon, but both sides also had orders to test the other's limits—to push across the border and challenge each other's authority, and see who would break the Potsdam Agreement first. Until somebody did it was a tense political limbo—the Third World War, always on the verge of starting, while everyone held their breath and prayed that it never did.

Reed hobbled further south, closer to one of the GDR tanks, and saw that the symbol on the side had been painted over. He looked around warily. The only reason to paint over a symbol like that would be to hide the tank's origin—which meant that these were Soviet tanks, not GDR. Everything they tried to present was an image of joyful, voluntary communism: "the East Germans aren't trying to flee, they're happy here!" But twenty Soviet tanks blocking the border would make that lie even harder to believe, so they hid them behind a thin coat of paint. Even the soldiers manning them wore black, unmarked uniforms. Were they Soviet as well? The thought made him sick. The East Germans were prisoners in their own country, kept here by hostile foreign soldiers, using an excuse so flimsy they didn't even dare to acknowledge their own actions.

Reed kept walking, past American officers and German officers and silent, stony-faced men who could only be Soviet soldiers. One of the East Germans bore a Stasi symbol on his uniform; he looked up, saw Reed, and broke off from his conversation to start walking toward him. Reed angled to the side, cursing his bad leg, and reached a group of Americans just three short steps before the Stasi.

"I'm American," he whispered. "Get me out of here."

"Excuse me," said the Stasi man loudly. "I do not believe that you belong here."

"Mr. Banner!" said one of the soldiers, and shook Reed's hand firmly, diving straight into the deception as if he'd been expecting it. "We've been looking for you."

"Sorry," said Reed, letting as much of his American accent come through as possible. "I had to check on some things. Did you know these are Soviet tanks?"

"They belong to the Deutsche Demokratische Republik," said the Stasi man. "Who are you?"

"Mr. Banner's one of our diplomats," said the soldier. "He was looking at the tanks for us." He gestured to the south, toward the American side of the Wall. "Let's get your report back to the Captain, okay?"

They started walking, the American soldiers forming an impenetrable perimeter around Reed. The Stasi officer watched them go with a grim frown.

"Who are you really?" asked the American soldier quietly.

"CIA," said Reed, and pointed at his limping foot. "Undercover mission went bad. I'm going to need a car—and a phone." What he really needed was a medic, but he didn't have time for that. He had to get Prinzenstrasse 93 D, to find Ostertag's handler as quickly as he could, and he had to get backup first. He didn't know what the Cabin thought of him—they were as likely to throw him in jail as help him—but it was a chance he had to take. He couldn't do this on his own.

"The phone we can do," said the soldier. "Our vehicles are all kind of busy right now."

"This is a matter of—" Reed paused. There was one more Stasi officer between them and West Berlin, and Reed fell silent as he approached, not wanting to give anything away. The officer heard them, turned to face them, and Reed's entire world seemed to stop.

The man had a face so immediately familiar that Reed lost his breath, staring at the man in shock.

It was Hans Nowak.

Dietrich Böhm.

Agent Longshore, in the flesh.

A thousand thoughts and emotions warred in Reed's mind. Every Stasi agent in the city was here, they'd said. Reed had known it, and acknowledged it, but he hadn't considered the implications. First, that this was the man who'd sent him a message every day or so for months. The man whose mind Reed had come to know so intimately he felt like a brother. Davis had called it a kinship, and Reed could feel that kinship now, a bond so strong it was all he could do not to shake his hand or embrace him.

But this was also the man who'd accused Reed of treason, and by the shocked look on his face he had recognized Reed, and knew who he was. He knew that this was the man he'd been told—by the KGB itself—was a secret Stasi agent infiltrating the CIA. Dietrich knew—or thought he knew—that right here, right in front of him, a Stasi traitor was fooling yet another group of hapless Western soldiers. A vile deceiver, on the verge of escaping his reach—but not there yet. Not quite. Dietrich could still do something to stop him.

Would Dietrich shout? Would he shoot? Would he stop Reed with a black-gloved hand, using his power as a Stasi officer to mete out vengeance on a traitor to the CIA? Would he detain him, or ask him for papers, or call in a dozen other soldiers—a hundred—to stop Reed from crossing the border? Doing so might start a war. Would he start one to save his own country? To save his partner Lise? Or would he simply watch, helpless, as the traitor escaped?

Reed wanted things, too. He wanted to grab Dietrich, to pull him toward the far side of the Wall, to tell him that this was his chance—maybe his last chance—to come back home and live a real life again. To drop the pretense, and the paranoia, and the brutal moral compromise that came from the life of a double agent. To tell him that he'd served his country well, and that with forty more steps, maybe only thirty, he could be over the line and free.

Reed could save this man's life.

Unless Dietrich's position, like Davis had said, was too important to lose. Unless he decided to stay. If Reed talked to him, and he didn't come, Dietrich would have to answer to his Stasi bosses—men who already suspected him enough to feed him false intel as a trap. He'd be marked as a traitor, and surveilled or questioned or killed. On the other hand, if Dietrich tried to stop Reed, a platoon of American soldiers with ten heavy tanks and three armored personnel carriers would come down on him like the wrath of God. And a thousand more tanks behind them, with ten thousand more soldiers, and planes and boats and guns and the terrifying specter of atomic bombs.

A word from one of them might kill the other; a word from the other might kill the whole world.

The soldier behind Reed bumped him, and he realized that the eternity of indecision he'd just experienced had only been a fraction of a moment. The world was still turning. The men were still walking. Reed walked with them, but he kept his eyes on Longshore, and Longshore kept his eyes on him, and the man's face was a maelstrom of fear and anger and suspicion and despair. He wanted to act. Reed wanted to act. But the machine was in motion, and they couldn't stop it, and they couldn't jump off. Reed kept walking, and Longshore kept staring, and everyone and no one got exactly what they wanted.

"Welcome home," said the soldier. They were through the checkpoint, across the Wall in West Berlin. "Glad we got you back."

"Yeah," said Reed, looking back into the East.

Longshore had disappeared.

3:30 PM

West Berlin

THE WESTERN SIDE of the Wall was every bit as chaotic as the East, with soldiers and police and tanks and gawkers. Snipers crouched on rooftops, and every brick corner and outcrop had become a machine gun nest. Reed hobbled toward the nearest American officer.

"I need a phone."

The man frowned at him. "Where did you come from?"

"I'm a CIA intelligence officer, returning from a botched mission on the other side. I need to call my Section Chief *now*."

"Do you have ID?"

"Do you think undercover agents carry ID? Just let me call my boss, he can explain everything."

The officer pointed at one of the soldiers who brought Reed through the checkpoint.

"Take him over there and sit on him until I have time to deal with this. The rest of you with me—I want every eye watching these commies like they were skin flicks, you hear me? Let's move."

The officer left with the small group of soldiers, jogging

toward the Wall. The last soldier pointed Reed toward a small cafe on the left, which the army had turned into a makeshift control center. Reed limped into it, collapsed into a chair, and gasped for breath.

"Are you okay, sir?"

"I'll be fine," said Reed. "Can I use the phone?"

"Not right now, sir, we have to wait for orders."

Reed nodded. It had been worth a shot. But he didn't have time to wait; he needed to leave, and he needed to do it now. Moritzplatz was only a few blocks away—longer than he wanted to walk on this foot, but still reachable in an emergency. And this was definitely an emergency. He just needed to get rid of his guard.

"How about a medic?" Reed asked, and bent down toward his foot.

The soldier looked worried. "Are you injured?"

Reed clenched his teeth, raised his leg, and pulled off Pollard's boot in a long, agonizing motion. The bandage had held fairly well—this wasn't the first time, Reed thought, that Pollard had wrapped a wound—but blood had still seeped through it, and the cloth bore a dark red stain and the strong stench of copper. The young soldier's eyes went wide, and he swallowed as he backed toward the door.

"Of course, sir, I'll be right back, sir!" The soldier ran back into the street, and Reed slid his foot back into the boot with a pained grunt, clamping it down again before it swelled too much to fit.

"Are you okay?" asked one of the other officers in the control center. "Have they started shooting?"

"This is from last night," said Reed, climbing to his feet. He clutched the cane like a lifeline. "Tell that soldier I couldn't wait." He limped toward the back of the cafe, and nobody tried to stop him. They were in a crisis, with bigger problems than one wounded man. Reed slipped through the kitchen and into the alley beyond, and hobbled as fast as he could around the nearest corner. He forced himself to hobble faster, air hissing between his teeth as he bit down against the pain in his foot, racing to yet another corner. How long did he have? How quickly would the soldier find a medic and return? Reed thought about just stopping, sitting down and letting them find him, letting the medic give him drugs for his injury and take him to a hospital. It would be so easy, and feel so good. But he couldn't. He had things to do.

Reed grunted again, almost a roar of defiance, and raced to the next corner. He ducked around it and leaned against the wall, ignoring the questioning looks of the other people on the street. A police car went screaming past, sirens wailing, but it wasn't looking for him. He listened for running feet behind him, but heard nothing. He closed his eyes, breathing deeply, refocusing his mind against the pain. Where was he? He opened his eyes again and found himself standing in front of a dry cleaner's storefront. Did they have a phone? A flash of movement caught his eye, a bright beige car with a yellow sign on the roof, and he practically threw himself into the street, waving frantically for the taxi that was passing by. It stopped, and he climbed in with relief.

"Prinzenstrasse 93," he said, without even the presence of mind to say the number in German.

"You are American?" the cab driver asked as he pulled back into traffic. "You are okay?"

"Yes," he said. The cab turned a corner, driving right past the young soldier as he scanned the street; Reed ducked low in the taxi, and the soldier missed him completely.

"Are you okay?" the driver asked again, glancing into the back seat.

"I'm with the CIA," said Reed. They were on Kochstrasse, driving east. After the first half block he sat up straight again.

"As soon as you drop me off, I need you to go directly to the police, and send them to the same address. Can you do that?"

"The police, or the American base?"

"Either," said Reed, watching out the window, "though I have a feeling you're going to choose the police." The road curved, becoming Oranienstrasse; he could see Moritzplatz just a few blocks ahead.

"Why the police?" asked the driver. "What's going on? Are you with the military? Is there going to be a war?"

"I'm with the CIA," said Reed again, and then, thinking the driver might not know what that is: "The BND. I'm a spy."

"A spy!" shouted the driver. He reached Moritzplatz—a massive intersection, filled with a wide traffic circle—and turned right onto Prinzenstrasse. "What's going on?"

"I just escaped from East Berlin about five minutes ago," said Reed. "Stop here." 93 was on the next block, but it was all apartments, and he needed a phone. "This gas station."

"East Berlin? But ..." He spluttered, searching for the words. "What's going on? Why do you need the police?"

The car stopped, and Reed got out. "Because I don't have anything to pay you with," said Reed. "Prinzenstrasse 93; every policeman you can find. Go!" He banged his hand on the top of the taxi, and turned and hobbled toward the gas station while the cab driver shouted behind him. Reed ignored him, and pushed open the door with his shoulder. His feet burned at every step.

"I need your phone."

"Kein Englisch," said the clerk, eyes fixed on the radio. He was listening to live coverage of the standoff, barely seven blocks away.

"Dein Telefon," said Reed. "Jetzt."

The clerk looked at him, as if realizing for the first time that he was talking to an American—which, as often as not, meant military. His question was the same as the driver's: "Is there going to be a war?"

"Not if I can stop it," said Reed, exaggerating only slightly. "Give me your phone."

The clerk pulled a fat rotary phone from his desk, setting it on the counter. Reed thanked him, picked up the receiver, and dialed the Cabin.

"Hallo," said Gisela.

"It's Wallace Reed," said Reed. "I need to talk to Davis immediately."

"Wally!" Gisela shouted. "What? How are you ... *Where* are you? You're across the Wall!"

"I'm back now," said Reed, turning to face the window. Prinzenstrasse had only a few people, but all of them were nervous, jittery, walking quickly or clustered around a TV screen in a shop window across the street. Watching their greatest fears, broadcast live. "Can I get the Chief, please?"

"He's gone," said Gisela, "everyone's gone. He has them all combing the streets for Johannes."

"He escaped?"

"He left just a few minutes into your message," said Gisela. "We were all so shocked by it, staring across the road, that we didn't even see him slip out."

Had Ostertag cracked the code? Reed hadn't expected that, though Ostertag had always been a capable cryptographer. Or had he simply put two and two together, assumed he'd been discovered, and stepped out just in case? Reed shook his head. It didn't matter why he'd left, only how quickly they could catch him again. Ostertag's guilt was the only proof of Reed's innocence.

"But Lise translated the code?" asked Reed. "You know that he's a traitor?"

"We do," said Gisela. "And Bettina is in custody—Wally, is she a traitor, too?"

"I ... don't know," said Reed. "Ostertag's contact told him to 'use' her, but I don't know if she was a willing participant or a hapless mark. Is she okay?"

"She was weeping," said Gisela, "but the security guards have her isolated now. I don't know how she is doing at the moment."

"Scheisse!" said the clerk, and Reed looked up.

"What?"

"They are raising their weapons," said the clerk. "Do something!"

"Gisela!" Reed shouted in the phone. "I found Ostertag's handler—Johannes might be with him. Is there anyone in the Cabin at all? Do you have any way of contacting them?"

"They are all gone," Gisela insisted. "I don't know where they are."

"Find them," said Reed, "or find anyone else that you can. Cops, soldiers, the State Department—whoever—send them to Prinzenstrasse 93 D. Wait!"

Looking out the window, Reed's jaw fell open.

Johannes Ostertag was walking right past the gas station, his collar turned up, and his hat pulled low over his eyes.

Before he had time to make a conscious decision, Reed found himself turning and crouching on his one good leg, trying to stay out of sight. "He's right here!" he whispered into the phone. "Walking north on Prinzenstrasse, toward Moritzplatz. He's left his safe house, probably trying to get to the train station."

"Get him!" said Gisela.

"I can barely walk," said Reed. He glanced out the window again, just catching the tiniest glimpse of Ostertag's back as he walked out of view. "I'm injured, and I'm unarmed. I need backup."

"I'll send whoever I can," said Gisela. "Follow him!"

"I'll try," said Reed, and hung up the phone. He limped to the window, and peeked out onto the street.

"You need help?" asked the clerk.

"Stay here," said Reed. "I'm chasing a federal fugitive, probably armed." He opened the door, and said it again. "Stay here."

The street was full of nervous energy, people hurrying through the city as if afraid to be caught in the sun. Reed gripped his cane tightly, and limped forward as fast as he could go. Ostertag was about thirty yards ahead, walking quickly. Reed pulled his own hat low as well, hoping that it and the limp and the unfamiliar clothes would disguise him if Ostertag turned around. He fixed his eyes on the man's back, and tried not to lose him in the crowd.

All around them people were running, or turning, or stopping cold, moving as if they didn't know what to do: run toward the Wall, or away from it? Go to work or go home? Stay inside or outside? There were tanks in the city, and maybe a war, and their terrified indecision had gone past "frozen" into "frantic chaos." People ran one direction, only to stop, think, and run off in another. Mothers with children jogged past him, headed home; others piled their families into cars, probably thinking that the best thing to do was to flee—but there was nowhere to go. West Berlin was an island in the middle of the GDR. There was no way out for anyone. Only Ostertag and Reed moved with purpose, heads down, never wavering, straight toward the train station.

As he moved through the crowd, Reed heard whispers and muttered warnings all around him:

"They are going to attack."

"There is going to be a war."

"The Grenzers are going to move the Wall—we're barely a block away from it here."

"They can sneak over it in the night and drag us from our beds."

"This is not their country—not the Soviets, and not the Americans."

"They are going to drop a bomb."

Reed was falling behind; his foot burned, and his legs ached from the effort of moving out of sync. He pulled out Pollard's bottle of pills, and swallowed three more—if he couldn't catch Ostertag then it didn't matter if he overdosed or not. He hoped they kicked in quickly, and he watched Ostertag's back without wavering. For one brief moment he thought the man was turning to the side, but he continued straight: past the railing, down the stairs to the train station, and out of sight. Reed gritted his teeth, practically dragging his injured foot, and hurried to catch him.

The stairs went down to a large, tiled room, filled with people just as agitated as the ones above; on the sides, more stairs plunged down to access the platform itself. Reed had to slow down on the stairs. He realized he was sweating profusely, despite the cold; whether from the exertion or from the drugs, he didn't know. He scanned the crowded room wildly, desperate to catch a glimpse of Ostertag. Instead, he saw several men in hats and coats—it was late October, after all—and couldn't tell at a glance which one of them was Johannes. He stayed a few steps up from the bottom of the stairs, giving him a better view, and as he searched the room a face stood out to him abruptly.

Not Ostertag.

Erich Gunter Anselm.

Anselm was leaning against a wall on the side of the room, facing toward Reed and deep in conversation with another man; the stranger had his back to Reed, so he couldn't recognize him, but he could tell at least that it wasn't Johannes. Reed stared, dumbstruck, wondering if this was why Ostertag had been coming to the train station. Was he trying to make contact with a fellow Stasi operative? Or was this purely a coincidence? He watched in fascination, and his eye caught the movement of a figure in the crowd—a hat-and-trench coat man suddenly changing course, weaving through the mass of people in a direct line for Anselm.

It was Ostertag.

Reed clutched the railing, feeling a wave of dizziness wash through him. The drugs were kicking in. He watched Ostertag's back, trying to parse this new set of wild possibilities. Reed couldn't have overpowered Ostertag as it was, and now that the man had backup it was even more dangerous to approach him. Should he cut his losses and back away, or try to follow them both to some other safe house? And who was the third man with them? A meaningless civilian? Another Stasi agent? Sergei Tsyganov himself?

Ostertag had almost reached the pair of men, moving directly into Anselm's eye line, and Anselm's reaction caught Reed by surprise: not recognition, not understanding, but sudden, abject fear. Why fear? He was clearly not expecting to see Ostertag here, but ... why did his sudden appearance make Anselm afraid?

And then the third man turned around, and Reed understood.

It was Frank Schwartz.

Bettina had said that everyone was out to look for Johannes. Frank, it seemed, had tried to use his brand-new relationship with one Stasi agent to try to find the other. And it had worked perfectly—perhaps too perfectly, for the meeting was so sudden that it surprised all three of them. Frank's reaction was slow. He goggled at Ostertag for just a second—just a pair of heartbeats—but that delay gave time for Ostertag to fumble in his coat, scrambling backward into the crowd. By the time Frank reacted, surging toward him for a tackle, Ostertag had managed to pull out a pistol: a Walther with a long suppressor, standard issue for the BND. He fired, and the shot echoed through the room—not deafening, but loud enough to cause the crowd to stop in its tracks. The shot went high, cratering the tile in the wall behind, but the second shot hit Frank's shoulder just as he slammed into Ostertag. Both men went down, out of Reed's sight, and the screaming crowd started running in every direction at once.

A rush of people charged straight at Reed, desperate to escape the gunshots by running up the stairs. He pulled himself closer to the railing, turning sideways to let the crowd go by, but they were panicked and careless. One man bumped him, nearly knocking Reed down, and as he tried to right himself another man stepped on his foot. Reed screamed, but more from instinct than from actual pain. The overdose of painkillers was working at full force now, and he felt the impact more intellectually than physically. He was still dizzy, though, sweating like a racehorse and growing more nauseated by the minute.

More gunshots echoed through the station, and then the crowd cleared and Reed caught another glimpse of the fight itself. One body was down, though he couldn't tell if it was Anselm or an innocent bystander, and Frank was rushing toward the stairway, clutching his bleeding shoulder with one hand and drawing his pistol with the other. He had a suppressed High Standard, just like the one Reed had lost in East Berlin. Reed pushed through the few remaining people, fighting his way down the stairs, and as he rounded the corner to the next set of stairs he heard another gunshot. Reed flinched away, but the bullet wasn't meant for him; Frank and someone else were trading shots down below on the platform.

Reed wished he still had his pistol. Instead, he clasped the railing in one hand, and his cane in the other, wielding it like a club as he crept down the stairs toward the battle.

The platform wasn't as crowded as the room above, but it still had people, and they, too, were running and screaming and scrambling for cover. It was a standard platform: northbound track on one side, southbound on the other, with pillars and benches in a row down the center, directly in front of the stairs. Ostertag was using the pillars for cover, working his way slowly toward the north end of the platform, firing backward every now and then to keep Frank from following. Frank had stationed himself behind one of the pillars as well, looking for a clean shot and shouting for the civilians to get down.

Reed hobbled up behind him, crouching low, stepping over and around the discarded shopping bags and jackets that the panicked crowd had dropped. He worried for a moment what Frank would do if he revealed himself—he still didn't know if Lise had told the others about Longshore's accusation, or what they thought of it—but this indecision lasted only a moment.

"Frank," he said.

"What?" asked Frank, turning to glance over his shoulder, and when he saw Reed he did a double take. "Wally? What in hell are you doing here? What's going on?"

"Ostertag's a Stasi mole."

"Yeah, we got your message." He looked back north again, keeping his eyes on Ostertag. "Then Johannes confirmed it by ghosting right out of there before we could even figure it out. But how did you get across the Wall? Twice?"

"Later," said Reed. "Where's Anselm?"

"I lost him in the fight; I think he ran away."

"Cover blown, I guess."

"Hell if I care," said Frank, "Johannes betrayed us. He spied on us for years, and then he shot me. I want his head on a spike." He fired his pistol—*tunk! tunk!*—missing Ostertag by inches and forcing the man back behind cover. Frank winced at the recoil. "Damn this shoulder!"

"Stop shooting," said Reed. "There are no more stairways over there: he's trapped."

"Sure he is," said Frank with a growl, pausing to reload his pistol. "Obviously he's not going to use those big giant tunnels to get away."

Reed looked again, realizing what Frank had already deduced: the only way out was the subway tunnels. Ostertag was going to make a run for it, down on the tracks. Reed glanced at the clock. This was the D train, the train he rode to work every day, and he knew the schedule by heart.

"There's a southbound coming in about a minute," said Reed. "If he jumps in behind it and runs north, he'll have ten full minutes before the next one."

"Where can he get in ten minutes?" asked Frank. "The next station?"

"Everything north of here is closed," said Reed. "These are the ghost stations—nothing but empty tunnels for nearly six kilometers. He can't reach—" And then in a flash he knew what Ostertag was doing. "He's going home—back to East Berlin. He's going to use the ghost stations to get back across the Wall."

"I thought they were bricked up."

"Some are only chained," said Reed. "He's had all day to make contact. He'll have someone waiting for him, ready to let him through."

"We've got to stop him. Now!" said Frank, and raised his pistol again, but before he could fire, another gunshot sounded from behind, and Frank went down with a scream. Reed whirled, lashing out with his cane. Erich Gunter Anselm was standing behind them; he stepped back, easily dodging the blow, but in doing so he stepped on a fallen purse. It slid beneath him, his foot moved, and he fell backward, arms pinwheeling helplessly as he tried to keep his balance. His hands clenched reflexively, pulling down on the trigger, but the shot went wild, exploding a fluorescent light above Reed's head. When Anselm hit the ground the gun clattered away. He and Reed both lunged for it, but a woman huddled behind a garbage can saw her chance and kicked it, knocking the gun off the platform and down to the tracks.

"Wait!" shouted Reed, but Anselm jumped after it, desperate to recover the weapon. He landed with a grunt, his feet shifting in the gravel, and reached for the gun. Reed shouted again, but it was too late: the gun was too far, and Anselm leaned too far to reach it, and he brushed the third rail. Electricity shot through him, and he collapsed in an unconscious heap.

A roar approached from the tunnel. The train was coming.

Reed didn't think; he dropped his cane, laid down on the platform, and rolled off the side.

"Nein!" screamed the woman behind him, but Reed didn't stop. They needed Anselm for questioning; the information he could give them would be invaluable. The man's body had fallen away from the third rail, so Reed could touch him without danger, but lifting him was another matter. A limp, unconscious human was fiendishly difficult to raise or control, even for someone who wasn't crippled and wracked with vertigo.

"Der Zug!" a man yelled. "Komm da raus!"

"Englisch!" said a woman. "The train's coming! Give me your hand!"

Reed looked up; he could see the headlight from the train, barreling into the station. He didn't have time to lift Anselm, but he might have time to save him. He rolled him over, flopping him into the corner like a fish. Was that far enough to avoid being hit? He prayed that it was, and he took the woman's hand; she and the man and a whole group of bystanders lifted him up and onto the platform just a few yards before the train hurtled past, horn blaring and brakes screaming.

"Who was that?" asked the woman. "What is happening—?"

But Reed didn't have time to talk. He grabbed his cane and crawled toward Frank; the surveillance officer was clutching his shoulder with one hand and his leg with another, and a group of civilians was trying to stop the flow of blood.

"I'm fine," growled Frank, his teeth clenched in obvious pain. He looked at Reed with fierce, furious eyes. "Get Johannes."

Reed pulled out the pain pills and gave them to a woman by Frank's shoulder. "Give him two of these, but no more—zwei—and then get him to a hospital. Ein Krankenhaus. As fast as you can." And then he pulled himself to his feet, lifted the cane, and ran.

His foot throbbed, feeling more like a dead weight than a limb. His legs felt heavy and hollow at the same time; his head buzzed, and his vision swam before him. He saw Ostertag standing by the back of the train, trying to squeeze through the mouth of the tunnel—the train had stopped early, leaving only a slim opening. Johannes looked up, saw Reed, and fired his pistol, but all it did was click on an empty chamber. He threw it, shoved against the train with both hands, and slipped through into the gap.

Reed stumbled, the platform seeming to ripple before him, but kept his feet, reached the back of the train, and squeezed through after him.

The first twenty or thirty feet of the tunnel was dimly lit by the train's rear lights, but beyond that it was black as pitch. Reed saw the dim outline of a man sprinting away into the darkness, and followed as quickly as he dared. The tunnel was narrow. On the far left, a wall with the third rail; the two normal rails in the center; and on the right a series of pillars separating this track from the northbound side. Reed's eyes adjusted slowly, helping the light reach farther, but soon even that was gone, and Reed was blind. He stumbled on the tracks, and knew that he needed some way of staying in a straight, safe course. So he moved to the left side of the tunnel and kept his left hand against the bricks, stretching out as far as he could, trying to use the wall for balance and navigation without getting too close to the third rail. He remembered the sudden, helpless twitch in Anselm's body, electrified by the powerful current, and stepped out even farther from the side.

At this distance he was straddling the second rail, one foot on either side; the ground beneath him was uneven and dangerous, heavy railroad ties interspersed with a bed of thick, fist-sized gravel. His toe caught the lip of a wooden tie and he tripped, pushing himself away from the wall as he fell, trying to land as far away from the electrified rail as he could. The sharp rocks sliced at his hands, and the wooden beams bruised his legs. He paused, groaning, but then stopped and held his breath to listen. In the sudden silence, without the sound of his own footsteps, he could hear Ostertag ahead of him, moving slowly and carefully. Reed had nearly caught up to him before falling; another few yards and he might have crashed right into him.

"Johannes!" he shouted. "Come back! Tell us what you know and we can help you! We'll give you amnesty!"

Ostertag ignored him, and his footsteps started moving faster.

Reed struggled to his feet, blind in the old brick tunnel, and cautiously reached out his hand again for the wall. He felt it, and started walking again—slower than before, but faster, he hoped, than Ostertag. What was he going to do when he caught him? He didn't know, but it didn't matter. He couldn't stop now. He had to catch him before he got away.

The next stop on the line—the first of the ghost stations—was Heinrich-Heine-Strasse. It was only a few blocks away on the surface, but there in the black, empty tunnel it felt like an eternity. Reed jogged forward, his breath increasingly ragged, and realized that he could see Ostertag's outline, just ahead. Had his eyes adjusted? No; a light was coming. He heard the roar of a train, and looked behind him in fear, but it was on the other track; northbound and southbound, he remembered, shared the same tunnel, with a series of pillars in between them. The train's headlight drew nearer, its glow growing brighter, and Reed used the illumination to sprint ahead. Ostertag did the same, and Reed chased him up the track. The northbound train passed on their right, shrieking past like a dragon in the dark; the light from its windows spilled out, still bright enough to run by, and Reed saw a quick, strobed slide show of faces staring out at them. Reed ran as fast as he could, but his foot throbbed and Ostertag was uninjured. The traitor pulled ahead, and then the train was gone; the taillights faded into the distance, and the light dimmed once again to nothing. The two men slowed back down to a walk, a slow motion pursuit of the blind.

"Just stop," Reed called into the sudden quiet. "Just come back. You don't want to live in the East. We can keep you safe, I promise—"

"Tock tock tock," said Ostertag, his voice drifting back through the tunnel. His breathing sounded as labored as Reed's. "What does a little bird say in America? Cheep cheep!"

Ostertag didn't want to stop, and he didn't want to talk. Reed was too out of breath to talk much anyway. He kept his hand on the wall, and his feet away from the third rail, and tried to estimate how long they'd been running. He knew this tunnel too well; the station at Heinrich-Heine-Strasse couldn't be much farther. How long had they been in here? Three minutes? Five? He had no idea. Time seemed to disappear in the dark tunnel, the same as everything else. And then the wall curved away from Reed's fingertips, just slightly, as the tunnel opened up into a wider, open space.

The Ghost Station.

He heard Ostertag cross the rails and scramble up onto the platform; just like Moritzplatz, this station had a single platform in the center, with a track on either side. Reed started to follow, but stopped. Ostertag was already up, and probably listening; he'd be able to hear Reed climbing, and rush to attack him.

Instead, Reed waited on the tracks, catching his breath, and spoke:

"Why did you do it?"

"Because it was the right thing to do."

"To betray your friends?"

"To save them from Nazis," said Ostertag. "The BND is full of them—it was founded by them. That makes the entire organization corrupt, and every American who saw fit to work with them."

"The man who started the BND was a Nazi in name only," said Reed. "He tried to kill Hitler, for crying out loud."

"And I suppose that's enough for some people," said Ostertag. "My ideology is less forgiving than yours." Reed heard footsteps; Ostertag was moving on the platform. "We had hoped to convince Frank Schwartz of the same; our agents were making good progress on that, though I suppose that's all ruined now."

"It was all a ruse anyway," said Reed. "We found Anselm, and we knew what Talon really was, and Frank was being groomed as a triple agent."

"Ahhhh," said Ostertag, slowly. "Then it appears I am not the only one lying to his friends."

Reed shook his head. "We didn't know it was you we were lying to."

"It is funny," said Ostertag, "that we pretend that makes it better."

Reed heard a lock click, and a chain clank against a metal door. Someone was coming; Reed had to act now. He moved to

the platform, started to climb, then immediately dropped backward, hoping the noise would prompt a counterattack.

It worked.

He heard Ostertag rush toward him, footsteps clattering in
the dark, and felt the whoosh of air as his former friend kicked
the space he'd expected Reed to be in. Reed reached in under
the blow and grabbed blindly, catching Ostertag's leg and
yanking as hard as he could. The man fell with a thud and a
grunt, and Reed used the opportunity to scramble up next to
him, onto the platform.

The rise in height was barely four feet, but Reed was so
woozy from the drugs that the sudden change made him dizzy.
Ostertag rolled into him, knocking him down, and then with a
harsh screech of metal a makeshift door opened. The stairs that
led down from the train station above were opening, and light
flooded the platform. Reed blinked at the sudden pain in his
eyes, looking away. As his eyes adjusted he saw the shaft of
light from the doorway stretching out across the floor, revealing
dust and debris and the droppings of rats. A line of pillars
reached off into the darkness, just like in Moritzplatz. A man's
shadow stretched with them, reaching out of the doorway like a
long, thin, stiletto. Reed turned toward the door, struggling to
stand, squinting at the silhouette.

"You're here," said Ostertag, walking toward the open door.
"Thank you for the—" There was a single, suppressed pistol
shot, and Ostertag slumped to the floor.

Reed stared in shock, then looked again at the silhouette.
"You killed him. You ... brought him here just to kill him."

"An exposed informant is of no use to us," said the man.
His accent was Russian. "Now he is of no use to you."

Reed heard the distant roar of a train: the southbound D
train, right on schedule. He looked at the man in the doorway,
and knew there were only two ways this could end. He started
circling to the side of Ostertag's body, moving in short, shuffling

steps, looking down as his former friend struggled feebly for air. Blood bubbled up from his mouth; he had been shot in the lung, and probably the heart. Reed stopped his shuffle, bracing his arms against his knees in a pained, exhausted crouch, and looked at the silhouette in the doorway.

"What about me?"

"An officer of the CIA is of great use to us indeed," said the Russian man. "The one thing your friend was never able to give us was the identity of agent Longshore, but you are Wallace Reed, are you not? You can give us everything."

"And you're Tsyganov," said Reed. "Sergei, I think? That's our best guess, but we've never actually confirmed it."

"You never will," said the Russian. "Well, I suppose *you* will, but you will be in no position to relay that information to the rest of the CIA." He stepped out of the doorway, and gestured with his gun. "Now. Come along."

Reed began shuffling again, each step an agony. "Maybe I won't talk to anyone, but what about the train?" The tunnel was growing lighter; the southbound D train's headlights were getting closer, turning the stark light from the doorway into a gentler, multidirectional glow. Turning the Russian man's silhouette into an ever lighter image of the man's full face. "You can come and get me," said Reed, "but every passenger here is going to see you, and I can guarantee my friends in the CIA are going to interview every last one of them." He kept shuffling, kept circling, and now he reached the pillars in the center of the platform. "Which do you want more? Me, or anonymity?"

In that instant Reed ducked behind the nearest pillar. The Russian fired his gun, and then the loud, bright train rattled through the tunnel. The same train Reed had ridden a hundred times, looking out through the windows at the empty, lifeless platforms. Now he looked back, a ghost in the station, and wondered if any of the passengers had seen him. What they would think of him if they had. A nameless face, haunting the underworld.

The train hurried on, and the light disappeared—not just the train's light, but the door's light as well. The Russian man had closed it. Reed peeked cautiously around the pillar, but all he could see were the bobbing dots of flashlights in the northbound tunnel; all he could hear were the shouts of rescuers coming toward him in the darkness.

The platform was empty, and the Russian man was gone.

Reed limped toward the closed door leading up from the ghost station, but stopped, too wary to approach. He stared for a moment, then lowered himself to the ground, and crawled to Johannes Ostertag's body. He found him in the dark, listened for breathing, and checked his pulse. Too late; the man was already dead.

Reed found his old friend's hand, and sat in the dark and held it.

West Berlin

"ERICH GUNTER ANSELM GOT AWAY," said Davis. He was sitting in Reed's hospital room, watching him intently. Reed watched him back, though he was still a little hazy from the drugs—authorized this time, and administered by the hospital, but powerful enough to have kept him unconscious for hours.

His foot had been cleaned and wrapped in bright, sterile bandages. It hung in a small sling, raised slightly off the mattress. Reed tried to move it, and found that it was still numb. He struggled to wake up more fully.

"Anselm got away?"

"Rolling him into the corner like you did saved him—the train didn't hit him, and the people on the platform were able to pull him up when it left. But they didn't think to hold him, and when he woke up he slipped away. We didn't realize who we'd missed until Frank woke up a few hours later."

"So Frank's okay."

"Better off than you were," said Davis. "Twice as many gunshots, but then he didn't walk around on them all day like a fool."

"I didn't have a lot of options."

"I suppose that's true," said Davis, and sighed. He sat for a long moment, staring at Reed, before turning his head and looking out the window. "Options are in short supply for everyone these days, I suppose."

Reed didn't like the sound of that at all.

"We live in the heart of a massive machine," said Davis. "The USA, the USSR; the superpowers make big decisions, and take big actions, and seen from the outside I'm sure it looks like the machine is moving freely, going wherever it wants to go, but we're not the machine, Wallace, we're the gears that move it. The Cold War twitches, and that moves one gear, and that moves another gear, and all we can do is move with them. Or be crushed."

His words were defeated, his voice resigned to a course of action he obviously didn't want to take.

"I'm on your side," Reed insisted. "I'm one of the good guys."

"Good guys don't go behind their boss's back," said Davis. "Not in this business. Secrets, yes; we're drowning in them. We have a million or more. But acting on those secrets in unsanctioned operations, risking the lives and livelihood of everyone in your office ... That we don't do. And cannot allow."

"I may have stopped a war."

"You may have," said Davis. "And I thank you for it." He shook his head. "You know what burns me the most? The fat, glossy turd on the top of this whole disgusting mess? Losing Longshore."

Reed looked up sharply. "He's dead?"

"He's alive," said Davis, "but what good does that do me? You understand the position you've placed me in, right? You told me last night—half-delirious from pain and meds, but you told me, and it makes sense. Tsyganov gave three suspected moles three different sets of false information, so they could watch us and see which lie floated down through the other end of the pipe. Longshore was told that you were a mole, and now if anything happens to you the suspicion falls on him. I can't trust you, but I can't fire you either. I certainly can't kill you. Options, as I said, are in very short supply."

Reed allowed himself a sliver of hope. "You're pulling him out?"

Davis frowned at Reed's obvious cheer. "That is not a good thing."

"You're done with me anyway," said Reed, allowing some of his anger to show through. "I'll take my pleasure where I can."

"Fair enough," said Davis.

Reed probed for more information. "With him safe, your options open up. Will I be fired, or ... fired *at*?"

"Fired," said Davis. "Lise, too. Just because she was smarter about her betrayal of trust, doesn't make it any less of a betrayal. And you'll be debriefed to hell and back before you go, too, but that can wait." He stood up. "Officially, you're hospitalized until Longshore is safe, at which point you will be unceremoniously fired. Unofficially ..." He held out his hand, and after a moment of confusion Reed took it. "Thank you for your service. Thank you for finding our mole. And thank you for keeping us safe from the shadows."

Reed stammered. "It's—it's my job, sir."

"It was. And you were better at it than anyone realized." He squeezed Reed's hand firmly, then let go. "I hope you get to do it again, wherever you end up."

"I think I'm still happiest behind a desk, sir. Field work is too much. I'll stick with cryptography."

"Not a lot of call for that in the civilian sector."

"Computers, then," said Reed. "Same basic principles, I hear."

"Good luck." Davis looked at the door, then back at Reed. "I'll leave you two alone, then."

"Two?" asked Reed, but Davis left without a word.

A moment later, Lise peeked in around the door.

"Hi," she said.

"Hi," said Reed.

She stepped in slowly, awkwardly, as if she was intruding in a sanctum where she knew she didn't belong. She stood for a moment, hesitated, and then pointed at Reed's foot. "Sorry about that."

"You did what you had to do."

She nodded. "You would have done the same."

"No, I wouldn't have," said Reed. "All the more reason to be glad I'm getting out of this, isn't it?"

"I suppose." Lise stood silently for another long pause—long enough to fill Reed's head with a hundred uncomfortable theories.

"Lise," he said, but she cut him off.

"I never answered your question."

He wanted to ask which question, but there was only one it could possibly be.

"I do not love you," she said, and his heart shattered.

"I do not think I ever could have," she continued. "Not before. Not lying, not ... suspecting everyone, and everything. I was too paranoid, and too guarded, and too ... Well. Too good at my job." She shifted her feet, and looked at him with a faint smile. "But now I do not have that job anymore, do I?"

Reed frowned, not sure where she was going.

"I have been in intelligence since I was a girl. It is the only thing I have ever known. And now I am kind of looking forward to being free." She shrugged. "Starting a real life."

"I hope you have a good one," he said.

"You will be sent home," she told him. "You are here on a

government visa, for a government job, and without that job they will not let you stay in West Germany. You will go home to the US, and you will find a good job, and I hope a good life. But if you ever ... come back. If you ever see me again, or I see you. If I travel to the States, looking for a job, or to go to school. If we ever run into each other, in a street or a park or an office ... Maybe we can start over, as real people this time. Not agents, not lies. Not ghosts. We can tell each other the truth, and we can see where that takes us."

"I'd ..." Reed swallowed. "I'd like that."

"I would too." Lise smiled again, just a tiny flash, then composed herself and stepped forward and offered her hand. "You were a good officer, Wallace Reed. And a good man."

"You were a good officer, too," said Reed. He shook her hand firmly. "And a good woman."

"Stay safe," she told him, and let go of his hand, and walked out the door.

Reed listened to her footsteps on the hard tile floor, counting every one until they were gone.

ABOUT THE AUTHOR

New York Times bestselling author Dan Wells is best known for his horror series *I Am Not a Serial Killer*, of which the first book is now an award-winning movie through IFC Midnight. His other novels include *The Hollow City*, a supernatural thriller about schizophrenia, *Extreme Makeover*, in which a beauty company destroys the world, and two young adult science fiction series: the post-apocalypse Partials Sequence and the cyberpunk Mirador. He has written for television on the science fiction series *Extinct*, and wrote and produced the horror comedy stage play *A Night of Blacker Darkness*. He cohosts the Hugo-winning podcast for aspiring writers called *Writing Excuses*, which has expanded to include its own writing conference. He is also a co-host of the YouTube series *Intentionally Blank*, with Brandon Sanderson. He occasionally writes short fiction and game fiction, and edited the anthology *Altered Perceptions* to help raise funds for and awareness of mental illness. Dan lives in northern Utah with his wife, 6 children, and more than 400 boardgames.

OTHER PRINCE OF CATS LITERARY PRODUCTIONS TITLES BY DAN WELLS

Zero G

Dragon Planet